Books by B.K. Stevens

Interpretation of Murder
Fighting Chance

Fighting Chance

B.K. Stevens

The Poisoned Pencil
An imprint of Poisoned Pen Press

the
poisoned
pencil

The Poisoned Pencil
An imprint of Poisoned Pen Press
6962 E. First Ave., Ste. 103
Scottsdale, AZ 85251
www.thepoisonedpencil.com
info@thepoisonedpencil.com

Printed in the United States of America

In memory of
Eloise Gershone
a woman of valor

One

From the minute he walked out to the center of the gym, something about him felt wrong.

Not that he looked all that intimidating. He was Bobby Davis, the announcer said, from Kelly's Dojo in Richmond. He seemed about the same age as Coach Colson—midtwenties—but was several inches shorter, with sort of a baby face and hair this weird dark orange, slicked back hard from his forehead and combed to a precise point at the back of his neck. He dyes his hair, I thought, and every morning he must work in a ton of mousse and comb for ten minutes straight. And his black belt wasn't tied right—just a bulky double knot, instead of the tight, neat square Coach always insisted on.

So it wasn't the way he looked that bothered me. The thing was, he didn't stretch out at all. He just planted his feet shoulder-width apart, folded his arms over his chest, and stood there watching Coach, his mouth twisting in a half-smile, half-smirk. That's dumb, I thought. Everybody should warm up before a sparring match. This guy definitely should. He'd barely won his first two fights, and Coach had aced both of his. So why was Davis taking it easy, looking smug?

Coach wasn't taking it easy. He was swinging his arms, rolling his shoulders, shaking his legs. He can't wait to get started, I thought. Well, that's typical Coach. On either side of them, in the other two masking-tape circles we'd marked on the floor last night, little kids and middle-school students traded kicks and punches while referees tried to keep them from hurting each other. Floor judges watched from their folding chairs, and parents crowded in with video cameras, shouting encouragement. Coach paused to catch his breath, turned to us with a grin, and started bouncing in place.

I sat on the home-team bench with the other five members of the Ridgecrest High martial arts club, waiting for the match to begin. Derrick turned to me and frowned.

"Damn, Matt," he said. "Why is he even out there? The other coaches aren't competing. And the way he's jumping up and down—he's acting like a kid."

I lifted a shoulder. "It's his first chance to compete as a black belt, and it's the first tournament the school's ever hosted. Naturally he's excited. Me, too. I never thought we'd draw this many people."

I glanced around the gym—over a hundred competitors, most in white uniforms, some in black, a few in red or dark blue. At least twice that many spectators crowded the bleachers, cheering while they shoveled down popcorn and nachos from the concession stands. We'd drawn people from as far away as Lynchburg, Coach had said, even a guy from Roanoke.

Berk sat forward on the bench, his fingers tapping against his knees, his whole body bristling with excitement, like an electrical current was running clear through him, and his skull might light up any minute. "Coach shouldn't have any problem winning this one. It's almost too bad. I wanted him to get at least one real fight, so we could see what he's like when he's up against someone good. This guy can't do anything but block."

"And kick," Joseph said. "His front kicks—those are very fast."

"But they don't have much power," I said. "They seem to be his only kicks, too, and he doesn't use his hands enough. He didn't try a single combination. Plus he always seems a little off balance, and he shies away from close contact. Black belts should be more aggressive. They should have more moves they can draw on."

"Like you'd know," Derrick said, and snorted. "So you're top belt now. So what? You think that makes you an expert?"

Derrick still hadn't gotten over it that I'd been promoted to green belt at our last testing. "Top belt in a six-person club is no big deal," I said, "and obviously I'm no expert. All I'm saying is, Davis scored all his points with last-minute front kicks. For a black belt, that seems pretty limited."

"He's scared," Derrick said. "*That's* why he only kicks. He's afraid to get close enough to get punched. And okay, so he looks built, but he's short. *I* could take him out."

No, you couldn't, I thought. Skill matters most—Coach had told us that, lots of times. Size doesn't matter half as much, he'd said. But Derrick's a football player, the best tackle our school has. To him, everything comes down to size. You'd think he might've changed his mind when a skinny fifteen-year-old girl from Appomattox beat him in his first match. Naturally, though, Derrick said he'd lost because the referee did a lousy job, because floor judges always let girls win. He couldn't have lost because he's a sloppy fighter who's never practiced hard enough to get better.

I glanced down at the yellow pad Coach had left on the bench, at the notes he'd jotted during our matches. The words stood out on a page bordered with doodles of ducks, of two flowering trees, of a lopsided house with a chimney. "Derrick," Coach had written. "Needs to work on speed—shouldn't count on strength. Forgets to protect midsection. Weak techniques." That summed Derrick up, all right.

The match got started. Coach Colson and Bobby Davis faced each other as the referee gave instructions: light contact only, no uncontrolled moves endangering either fighter, no hand contact to head, face, or neck. Coach looked intense but smiling. Davis stared straight at him, eyes narrowed to thin slits. They wore similar protective gear—helmets, blue chest pads, gloves, leg pads, foot pads. The referee nodded, they touched gloves and backed away from each other, and the referee raised his hand and brought it down.

"*Shee jahk!*" he yelled.

Berk held out his cell phone to film the match. For the first minute, not much happened. They both seemed cautious, sizing each other up. Coach used his sharply focused side kicks, Davis used his limp front kicks, but they both blocked effectively. Nobody connected. Nobody scored. Then, his eyes still fixed on Coach, Davis let his arms droop, exposing his midsection. There's an opening for you, Coach, I thought.

Sure enough, Coach moved in, aiming a side kick at Davis' stomach. But at the last possible second, Davis brought his right arm up fast, knocking the kick aside so hard he threw Coach off balance, making him hop backward to keep from falling over. I saw Davis' mouth twitch, like he was trying not to smile.

"Coach nearly got him that time," Berk said. "Davis really let his guard down."

"Yeah, he did," I said, but felt puzzled, almost uneasy. The way Davis had been watching Coach, the way he'd brought his arm up at exactly the right moment, the way he'd fought a smile afterward—it was almost like he'd let his guard down on purpose, like he'd been testing Coach to see how he'd react. But why would he do that? No reason, I decided, and focused on the match again.

They'd gone back to circling each other, to kicking without connecting, to taking turns blocking each other's moves. Right before the first two-minute period ended, Coach took advantage of Davis' post-kick wobble to use the combination he'd drilled us on—roundhouse kick, right jab, left punch. Stepping in close after the kick, he landed a solid punch to Davis' chest. For a moment, Davis looked a little surprised, a little mad. Then he shrugged.

Coach bounced back, turned to us, grinned, and bowed, bending deeply at the waist, sweeping his right arm high into the air. All six of us shot up from the bench.

"Way to go, Coach!" Berk shouted. Next to him, Suzette jumped up and down, clapping, and Berk started forward like he was going to hug her. Then he pulled back, settling for giving her a thumbs-up.

"Point!" Graciana cried, her long black ponytail flipping back over her shoulder. "Point!"

"About time," Derrick said, and sat down.

It was pretty cool—like Coach had been holding back, passing up chances for easy points, waiting to score with that particular combination so he could show us how effective it is. Now, that's a teacher, I thought. "Great combination, Coach," I called.

Joseph seemed to be having the same thoughts I was. "Most instructive," he said. "Mr. Colson said we should try to score such way—roundhouse kick, right jab, left punch. Now he has performed one, to demonstrate us how to aspire."

Derrick drew his head back. "To demonstrate us how to aspire? What's that—Latin? What the hell are you saying?"

"You know exactly what he's saying," I said. "Don't be a jerk, Derrick." Joseph's from Kenya. His family left five or six years ago, after his father got killed, and moved around until the Episcopal Church found his mother a job in Ridgecrest. In some ways, Joseph's English is probably better than mine. It's definitely better than Derrick's. He's got a formal way of putting things, though, and sometimes his vocabulary's off—natural enough, I guess, if you learn English in a classroom instead of at home. There's no point making a big deal whenever something comes out strange.

Coach Colson didn't bother to sit down during the one-minute break between rounds, just stretched and smiled. Bobby Davis didn't sit down, either. He stood still with his arms folded, watching Coach like he was measuring him. On the wall behind them hung a huge yellow banner with glossy black letters: "Ridgecrest High School—Twenty-Five Years of Serving Our Community." It'd been there since September and looked limp, almost tired, as if after so many months of hearing people shout and smelling people sweat, it wanted to roll up in a closet and rest.

I glanced up at the bleachers, at the Ridgecrest High cheering section. Of course, Dr. Lombardo had come. She'd been principal for ten years, and I don't think she'd ever missed a school event—not a junior varsity volleyball game, not a chess club ice-cream social. She'd announced a few weeks ago that she was resigning to become superintendent for the whole district, but she still came to everything at the school. Mr. Quinn, our guidance counselor, sat next to her, talking to some coaches. Four or five teachers had shown up, too. And most guys from the basketball team had come, including our captain, Paul Ericson. I was especially happy to see Paul, especially since I'd done well. Even with basketball season over, even though he'd be graduating soon, it still felt good to impress him.

Then there were families—Berk's mother, Joseph's mother and sisters, Derrick's father, Suzette's parents, Graciana's parents. My own parents had said they'd come, but I'd told them not to bother. There won't be much to see, I'd said—I'll probably be eliminated after one four-minute match. They'd glanced at each other, and said, "If you're sure, Matt," and looked relieved.

No big surprise. When they come to my basketball games, they try to act interested but check their watches every two minutes, and afterward they talk about how it's sad people boo and stamp their feet when players from the other team take foul shots, about how much more respectful people were when they went to school. I could imagine how they'd react at a martial arts tournament—my mother covering her eyes whenever someone connected with a kick, my father frowning about how violent it seemed. So when they'd stayed home, I'd been glad.

As things turned out, though, I'd lasted through three matches, getting a second-place trophy. And now, especially since everyone else in the club had family here, I felt almost sorry my parents hadn't seen me win.

I shrugged it off, glanced at the other side of the bleachers, and spotted Marie Ramsey, this goth-type girl who'd haunted my social studies class last year, sitting hunched up and silent in the back row, staring at the floor. I wouldn't have expected to see her at anything related to sports—especially now. Her sister had committed suicide barely two weeks ago, and everybody said her whole family's messed up—her father was in prison, her mother was a drunk, and her brother had a long record of minor-league crimes. Maybe Marie just needed to get out of her house, and she hadn't much cared where she went.

The break ended. Coach Colson and Bobby Davis came to the center of the ring again, touched gloves again, squared off again. This time, Coach didn't hold back. He moved in close, scoring two quick points with his side kick, knocking Davis' blocks aside easily. Davis changed his approach, too.

"Look," I said to Berk. "Davis is bouncing around more, and his stance seems better."

"It's the competition," Berk said. "He's down three points and wants to fight back. He still hasn't scored, though."

Coach tried a front kick without connecting. He's getting tired, I thought. I saw sweat working down his cheeks, saw his face growing redder.

Davis still hadn't broken a sweat, and losing all those points didn't seem to bother him. His mouth curled into a mocking grin. Suddenly, almost casually, he landed a gentle front kick, roundhouse kick combination, catching Coach first in the stomach, then in the ribs.

"That was *good*," Graciana said. "That was *hard! Right* past Coach's block! And he didn't even put his leg down between kicks!"

"It's only one point," I said. But Davis hadn't tried anything but a simple front kick before. Where had that combination come from, and why had his stance improved so much? I sat forward, pressing an elbow against my leg, resting my chin on my fist, straining for a closer look.

At least, finally, Davis seemed to be getting tired. I saw his hands drop to his sides. Coach obviously saw it, too, and saw his chance. He moved in. He's going to use that combination again, I thought—roundhouse kick, right jab, left punch.

8

This time, before Coach could connect with the kick, Davis stepped lightly to the side. When Coach came in for the jab, Davis stopped him with a soft, sweeping block. He deflected the punch with his right hand, pushed it aside with his left, and followed up with a quick back-handed slap to Coach's face.

It wasn't a point, but it bothered me. This wasn't like the hard blocks Coach had taught us. This was faster, more flowing, much more effective. And the slap looked too soft to hurt but seemed almost like an insult, almost like a dare. I didn't like it.

Derrick didn't, either. He stood up. "What was that? A slap? Don't you know how to punch? You wimp. Fight like a man!"

The referee cautioned Davis about contact to the face. Davis nodded, one corner of his mouth nudging upward. Something's wrong, I thought. Coach grinned at Davis, turned to us, and shrugged. "No big deal," he seemed to be saying. But it *was* a big deal. I knew it, though I couldn't have said why.

They started up, and Coach moved in again, still with the same combination. This time, when Coach lifted his hand for the jab, Davis exploded with a precise, powerful side kick, catching Coach squarely in the armpit. That's a pressure point. I winced, imagining the pain. Gasping, Coach staggered backward, shaking his head numbly, exposing his throat.

And Bobby Davis stepped forward deliberately and spun around. There was a second when I saw him clearly, saw his eyes careful and businesslike as he marked his target. Then a spinning hook kick, then the impact between heel and throat, and then Davis stood squarely on the floor again, kick complete and perfect, stance solid, fists still lifted, practiced and ready.

I couldn't actually have heard Coach Colson's last gasp for air, not with the gym so noisy. I know that. But I remember the sound anyway. I know I heard Graciana's single, agonized scream, and saw Coach collapse to the floor, and felt Berk's fingers dig into my arm as he called out, already hopeless. Then, somehow, I was in the center circle, kneeling next to Coach, cradling his head in my arms.

"Where's the doctor?" I shouted. I looked up at the people in the bleachers, most still not realizing what had happened, many still hopping down the steps to get Cokes or chips. "Damn it, Coach *said* there'd be a doctor!"

The doctor got there in seconds, and he did his best. He sent someone running to call 911, prodded Coach Colson's throat with expert fingers, crouched on the floor to try to force air into his body. It was no good.

"I'm sorry," he said, voice heavy with regret. "His larynx is crushed. He's dead."

Two

I wish I could say the next few hours rushed by in a blur. They didn't. Every moment was distinct—every image, every sound, every feeling.

People came running—referees and judges from other circles, everyone on our team, the security guard Coach had hired. In the bleachers, coaches and teachers jumped from their seats, and Mr. Quinn helped Dr. Lombardo down the steps. I saw the guys on the basketball team pointing down at us and talking, saw Paul Ericson sitting rigid and silent. As people started to realize what had happened, gasps and whispers spread through the gym. Children raced to their parents—maybe they felt like they needed protection now. Their parents clutched at them, faces stunned by new fears.

Nobody left. After the first few minutes, almost nobody spoke. I heard someone crying, though, loud and broken. I glanced at the other side of the bleachers and saw Marie Ramsey sitting with both fists clenched in her lap, her chest heaving forward as sobs ripped through her, lines of black makeup streaming down her face. It didn't seem like she was even trying to get control of herself—it seemed like she'd given up on staying in control.

The paramedics arrived, then two uniformed police officers. The paramedics hovered by Coach Colson, checking things, shaking their heads the same way the doctor had. They'd take him to the hospital, they said. I guess they have to do that. The head basketball coach went along, and so did my English teacher, Ms. Nguyen.

I looked around for Bobby Davis and spotted him standing near the door to the boys' locker room, arms at his sides. I couldn't read his face. He had to be feeling something, but I couldn't see it. An officer stood nearby, keeping an eye on him but not saying anything.

Referees and floor judges crowded around the other police officer, talking fast. Hoping nobody would notice, I moved closer.

"It was a tragedy," one judge said. "A fluke."

"A fluke." The referee from Coach's match seized the word. "Exactly right. A fluke. Everything was going fine. Colson was ahead by three points. Then Davis kicked him in the arm, Colson slipped, and Davis came up with this wild kick."

"Right at the worst possible moment," a woman judge put in, "when Colson had his neck stretched back. So when Davis aimed a kick at his chest, he caught him in the throat. If Colson had been standing up straight, it would've just been a hard kick to the chest."

The referee rubbed his forehead. "I keep wishing I'd stopped the fight. But I had no reason to. Both men were on their feet, neither was hurt, and I didn't see that kick coming."

"Nobody could've seen it." The first judge patted his back. "I mean, that kick came out of nowhere. You can't blame yourself."

The officer glanced up from her notes. "So you're convinced this was an accident?"

They stared at her. "Absolutely," the first judge said. "What else could it be?"

"Just checking. The detective should arrive soon. I'd like you all to wait here until—"

"Excuse me." Berk pushed through the judges, his face red and puffy. "It *wasn't* an accident. He meant to do it. He kicked Coach in the armpit to stun him, and then he aimed straight for his throat and kicked hard."

"Ridiculous," the referee said. "He aimed for his chest, and he didn't kick him in the armpit, just the arm. If it'd been the armpit, I would've stopped the fight."

It didn't feel like the right time to start all this, but I had to back Berk up. "No, the kick was to his armpit. It happened fast—it'd be easy to miss—but that's why Coach staggered back. He didn't slip. He staggered back because Davis kicked him in a pressure point."

The first judge's voice turned angry. "Listen, son, you look like a nice kid, and we're all sorry about what happened. But you're a green belt. Your friend's an orange belt. You're not experts. *We're* experts, and we all agree. When nine black belts tell you the kick was to the arm, you oughtta listen."

A judge who hadn't spoken yet half-raised his hand. He was middle-aged and medium height, with dark brown hair and a close-trimmed beard. "I thought the kick was to the armpit. I was judging in an outer ring, my fighters were taking a break, and I glanced at the center. It looked like a hard side kick to the armpit. And that last spinning hook kick—"

"It wasn't a spinning hook," the referee said. "It looked like one, yeah, but it wasn't really any particular kind of kick. It was just wild. You weren't close enough to see clearly."

The other judge held his hands chest high, spreading his fingers, like he was backing off. "Maybe not. But from where

I stood, it looked like a deliberate side kick to the armpit, followed by a deliberate spinning hook to the throat."

"It didn't look that way to me, Aaron," the first judge said, "and I was much closer. It was an accident. In sports, accidents happen, despite all the precautions we take: the helmets, the chest shields, the leg pads—"

"But we don't pad the throat," the judge he'd called Aaron said. "It's the one vital spot left unprotected. And the gloves keep almost any punch from being lethal, but the foot pads don't cover the heel. So a well-aimed spinning hook kick would land with full impact. If I wanted to kill someone during a tournament, I'd use a spinning hook to the throat. Wouldn't you?"

The first judge sighed impatiently. "If I wanted to kill someone," he said, "I wouldn't do it during a tournament. The whole idea is crazy."

The officer tapped her pen against her notepad. "I'd like you all to wait for the detective. In the meantime, please don't compare notes or try to convince each other. Keep your own memories clear."

She walked over to join her partner. Berk turned to me, face twitching with rage. "Those guys must be blind. Why didn't—"

"We're not supposed to talk about it. Let's join the others."

It wasn't only because the officer said not to discuss what happened. I didn't want to. I knew what I'd seen, but nothing made sense. I wasn't up to trying to figure things out. I didn't have room in my head for anything but feeling miserable.

The other kids still stood around the team bench, their parents clustered nearby. Berk's mother gestured us over.

"I saw you talking to the police," she said. "What's going on?"

"She wants us to wait until the detective arrives," he said, "but she doesn't want us to say anything yet."

Suzette's father frowned. "Bad idea. We need to get you kids home. You shouldn't have to wait around after witnessing such a terrible accident."

"I'll straighten things out so we can leave," Berk's mother said. "You kids are still coming for dinner, right? I've made *so* much lasagna."

The lasagna dinner—it was supposed to be a party, to celebrate Ridgecrest High's first tournament. Coach had said he'd come. We'd planned to brag about our wins, analyze our mistakes, start planning for next year. Now, all that felt like a bad joke. "I don't know, Mrs. Widrig. Considering what happened—"

"Obviously it won't be a *party* anymore," she said, "but you can share your feelings, comfort each other, all that. And if you want to keep your club going, you should talk about finding another teacher to replace Mr. Colson."

To replace Mr. Colson. How could she say those words? Mrs. Widrig and Berk have lived down the street from us for over ten years, and she's one of the nicest people I know. Last year, when I didn't want to be at home much, I practically lived at their house, and she never seemed to mind. But sometimes, compared to her, even *my* parents seem sensitive.

"The kids need time to think," Suzette's mother said. "We could go home and talk things over, and later—"

"God, Mom." Suzette rolled her eyes. "I'm not a *baby*. I don't need *you* to tell me what to do. I don't need *instructions*. Back off."

Mrs. Widrig gave her a sharp look. "Well, if you kids decide to come, great. If not, I'll park the lasagna in the freezer. I'll go talk to the policewoman."

"I'll come with you," Mr. Link said. "Let's get this settled."

Minutes later, Dr. Lombardo came over. She's around fifty, tall and lean, and you can tell she always makes a point of looking professional. Most people had worn jeans and sweatshirts to the tournament; she'd worn a pantsuit and a pearl necklace. But she looked shaken. This must be hard on her, I realized. For ten years, she'd worked hard for Ridgecrest High—people said the school was her whole life. Now, this would be one of the last memories she'd take with her. I felt so awful about Coach, I wouldn't have thought I could feel bad for anybody else. But looking at her tense shoulders, listening to how tired her voice sounded, I felt bad for her, too.

She walked from student to student, from parent to parent, talking softly. When she got to me, she put a hand on my shoulder. "Mr. Colson was your social studies teacher last year, wasn't he? And assistant basketball coach, advisor for your martial arts club. This must be hard on you."

"Thanks," I said. "Dr. Lombardo, Coach once said his parents live in Vermont. Should someone let them know?"

"I've called them. They're flying down tomorrow to take him home. It's good of you to think of them. Have you called your own parents?"

"No. I guess I should. Thanks."

She moved on. Calling my parents—God. I hated the thought of answering their questions and listening to their sympathetic little comments. They wouldn't understand how I felt, couldn't say anything that'd help, so what was the point?

I didn't have to call yet, I decided. Telling them in person might be easier.

Mr. Link and Mrs. Widrig joined us again, looking satisfied. The policewoman had said only those who thought they had information for the detective needed to stay. Derrick and Suzette gathered their stuff, but the rest of us decided to wait.

On her way out, Suzette paused. "Are you coming to Berk's tonight, Matt?"

"I haven't decided." I noticed Coach's yellow pad still sitting on the bench. Somebody, probably the paramedics, had taken his gym bag, but they'd missed the pad. Without thinking, I shoved it into my own bag. "I'm pretty confused."

"Me too." She tilted her head, letting her long blonde hair fall over her shoulder. "I mean, it's so *sad*. Maybe it'd help to get together. To talk, you know?"

"Maybe." I looked past her. A gray-haired man in a suit— the detective?—was talking to the policewoman. Farther back, Bobby Davis said something to the officer standing next to him. The officer shrugged, and Davis walked into the boys' locker room. I stood up. "I should call my parents."

"Okay." Suzette smiled this quick little smile. "I hope you come tonight, Matt."

I nodded and walked on. I'd left my phone in my locker, so that gave me an excuse. This is dumb, I thought. Davis won't do anything worth seeing. But I couldn't stop.

I reached the door to the locker room. "Okay if I get my phone from my locker?" I asked, and the officer nodded. I pushed the door open.

At first, I didn't hear anything, didn't see anyone—just long rows of dull green lockers, narrow wooden benches bolted to the floor, the scale, the first-aid cabinet on the wall, trash cans and towel hampers. He's here, though, I thought. The man who killed Coach is back here somewhere, and nobody else seems to be around. I didn't feel scared, exactly, but my body went tense. I couldn't have said why I was there. Maybe, I thought, I want him to try something, to give me a reason to hit him back. That's crazy, I know. He's way out of my league. Right then, though, I felt like I could've ripped him apart.

I went to my locker and turned the combination, straining to hear something. No luck. Slowly, I walked between rows of lockers, toward the office at the back. Then I did hear something—a voice, low and angry. I froze.

"Damn it, you've gotta find me one," a man said. "A good one. I don't like the way these cops have been looking at me." He paused. "No, *now*. I don't care how 'awkward' it is. The detective's here. I need someone to take charge." Another pause. "Okay. But make it fast."

Before I could turn around, Bobby Davis came out of the office and stood facing me, not ten feet away. "Who the hell are you?" he demanded. "What're you doing here?"

Now I *was* scared. The first time I'd seen Davis, I'd thought he looked silly—the baby face, the slicked-back orange hair. Standing this close, I could see how built he was, see the snake tattoo covering most of his chest, see how hard and little his eyes were. He seemed to be sizing me up, and I could tell he wasn't impressed—just a tall, medium-build kid with legs that always feel too long for the rest of me.

I held up my phone. "I'm Matt Foley. I came to get my phone from my locker."

"Yeah? So why are you still hanging around?"

"I'm not. I was told to wait."

He stepped closer. "You're on his team, aren't you? And afterwards, you talked to the lady cop—you, and your little friend. What'd you say to her?"

He won't do anything, I thought. He's in enough trouble. He won't make things worse by picking a fight in the locker room. "We told her what we saw," I said, looking at him straight. "What we *both* saw."

"You weren't close enough to see anything." He glanced at

my belt and sneered. "And nobody cares what some kid with a green belt *thinks* he saw. You'll only make yourself look stupid."

"I'll risk it," I said, and turned away.

He grabbed my shoulder, yanking me back to face him. "Listen to me carefully, and make sure you get this straight. It was an accident, it's over, and you can't do anything about it. All you can do is get yourself in trouble. Trust me—you don't wanna do that. Not with me."

He shoved me aside, just enough to make me bump against a locker, and walked out. I leaned my back against the wall, catching my breath. It'd been dumb to follow him, dumber to mouth off. But I'd got what I'd wanted, what I hadn't even realized I'd wanted. The cool edge to his voice, the calm in his eyes—I knew now. He'd killed Coach on purpose.

Three

When I got home, they were all in the living room—Mom at the piano, Dad with his clarinet, Cassie with her viola. They were laughing. Naturally, they were laughing.

I hadn't called home. Too many decisions about what to tell them and what not to tell them, too many other things to think about. My talk with the detective had been brief. When I closed the front door, Mom looked up, blinked, and smiled.

"Hello, dear," she said. "We're at our wits' ends here. We're working out an arrangement for a Scarlatti sonata, and our first efforts, I'm sorry to say, have *not* gone well."

Apparently, that was a hilarious statement, because they all burst out laughing again. I didn't catch the humor, personally, but tried to smile. "Too bad."

"Oh, we'll manage," Dad said. "How was the tournament? Say—is that a trophy?"

"Second place." The trophy's pretty ridiculous—red and blue stars winding shakily around the base, some winged gilt lady perched on top, stretching her arms high for no reason I could see. I stuck it in the coat closet. "And the tournament turned out awful. This guy from Richmond kicked Coach Colson in the throat and killed him."

That stopped the laughter. They all glanced at each other, and Dad put down his clarinet. "That wouldn't be a good thing to joke about, Matt."

"I'm not joking. He's dead. That's why I'm late. We had to talk to the police. Look, I'm tired. I'm going upstairs."

Mom walked over. She reached out to touch my face, but I drew back. "Matt, I'm sorry. He meant so much to you. Would you like to talk? Why don't we—?"

"Maybe later. Right now, I want to rest. Is that okay?"

"Of course," Dad said. "But Matt—this happened during a sparring match, right? It was an accident?"

"That's the theory." I trudged upstairs.

I knew I was being a jerk. I was making them feel like lousy parents, and they'd probably spend the next ten weeks talking about how it's sad their son didn't want to communicate with them after a traumatic experience. I don't enjoy making them feel that way. Basically, they're decent parents, at least compared to other people's parents.

But the fact is I *don't* want to talk to them about things. They're nice, but it's like they live on a different planet, their own happy, perky parent planet, where the biggest problem they ever have is that not enough classical musicians composed pieces for piano, clarinet, and viola. My sister's the same way—Little Miss A-in-Everything, a genius seventh grader who likes all her teachers, walks around the house reciting Emily Dickinson poems, and thinks nothing's more fun than spending Saturday night playing charades with her parents. I know Cassie's a good kid. I just can't stand being around her for more than thirty seconds.

So this is my life right now. Living in the same house with the happy threesome, feeling like an alien life-form, feeling guilty because I don't appreciate them more, feeling like I'd go shoot-through-the-roof crazy if I tried to really talk to them. It could be worse. Lots of my friends have it much worse. But it makes me nuts.

I threw myself on my bed, grabbed my iPod, and tried to go blank. It didn't work. I paced around the room, spotted my gym bag, and took out Coach's yellow pad. I'd meant to give it to the detective, but he had shown so little interest. Pages filled with scribbled notes and with doodles of dogs, of two flowering trees, of cars and bikes and pizzas. I smiled a tight, sad smile. In some ways, Coach was like Berk. He'd had so much energy he couldn't ever just sit, always had to be doing something with his hands. I flipped pages, reading his comments about our matches. "Suzette—have a strategy, don't just block, don't argue with judges." "Joseph—nice, high round-house kick. Work on flow." "Graciana—good at anticipating opponents' moves. Work on power." "Berk—quick techniques, but keep control. Don't let emotions choose your moves." "Matt—work on jump-front kick. Great balance. Ready for spin kicks. Really quick back fist—wow."

I stared at the pad before putting it in a desk drawer. "Really quick back fist—wow." So he'd thought I had a good back fist. So what? But it made me miserable all over again.

Fifteen minutes later, someone knocked on my door. Mom, I thought, and gritted my teeth. "Come in," I said.

She walked in holding a plate and a glass of milk, looking nervous. I hate it that I make her nervous about bringing me food. "I'm sorry to disturb you, Matt. I wasn't sure if you'd had a real lunch, so I made a tomato-and-mozzarella sandwich. You used to like those."

"I still like them, Mom." I took a bite. No, I hadn't had lunch, and it embarrassed me to realize how hungry I was.

On a day like this, I shouldn't care about anything but Coach. "It's good. Thanks."

"You're welcome." She hesitated. "If you don't want to talk about it, we understand. But if you change your mind—"

"I know. I can come to you any time, and you're always ready to listen. I appreciate it. And I realize you must be curious about what happened."

"That's all right. I called Berk's mother. It sounds horrible. It sounds—heart breaking." She hesitated again. "And Mrs. Widrig said you and Berk don't think it was really an accident."

"We don't. Joseph and Graciana don't think so, either. But when we talked to Lieutenant Hill, he didn't even take notes. He probably thought we're dumb kids too upset to think straight. I guess I understand. Almost all the judges said it was an accident. They said the guy kicked Coach in the arm, which would be okay, and they said the last kick was aimed at his chest. But that's not true. He kicked Coach in the armpit, and he aimed the last kick straight at his throat. If I could see that, if Berk and Joseph and Graciana could, why couldn't the judges?"

Mom took my plate. "Maybe they *could* see it, but they didn't want to say so. If that man broke some rules, the judges might be afraid they'll get sued for not stopping the match. And I'm sure they feel bad about Mr. Colson and don't want to believe it's partly their fault. They might be rationalizing, to keep themselves from feeling guilty. Would you like more milk?"

"No, I'm good," I said, stunned. That'd explain it, all right.

"Fine. Oh, Mrs. Widrig asked if you're coming to the lasagna dinner. Should I call her with an answer?"

"I haven't decided. I'll call Berk when I do. I'm not sure I'm up to seeing people."

Mom beamed. "Perhaps it *would* be better if you stay home with us. And I found a new recipe for tofu stir-fry. It sounds like fun!"

She scurried off. Another new recipe for tofu stir-fry. What made Mom think it'd turn out better than the last eighteen recipes for tofu stir-fry? I pictured Mrs. Widrig's lasagna—layers of noodles, spicy ground beef, chunks of sausage, thick tomato sauce, four cheeses oozing through everything. And I pictured me sitting with Mom and Dad after dinner, trying to act interested while Cassie hopped around, miming gestures to help us guess that a journey of a thousand miles starts with a single step.

I grabbed my phone. "Berk?" I said. "I'm coming."

All six of us showed up. Graciana brought salad, Joseph brought this flat bread that tasted better than it looked, and Mom made me bring tiramisu. She'd never made tiramisu before, she'd said, but it sounded like fun. Mom thinks all weird food sounds like fun. It looked jiggly and smelled like coffee. Just once, I wish she'd let me bring cookies or some other normal dessert to a party.

"You don't have to eat that," I said as people cut pieces. "It's slimy."

Graciana took a bite. "It's creamy. That's how it's supposed to be. It's delicious. You should try some."

"I'm not that brave," I said, and Derrick laughed and gave me a fist bump.

"Speaking of brave," Suzette said, "I can't *believe* you followed Bobby Davis into the locker room." I hadn't told my parents about that, but I'd told Berk, and he'd told everyone else. "Weren't you scared?"

"A little. But it felt like something I should do."

"It was dumb," Derrick said, not in an unfriendly way. "And you didn't prove anything. So he called somebody to help him find a lawyer. He's from Richmond—naturally he wouldn't know lawyers in Ridgecrest. And naturally he'd want one. He must've been afraid he'd get charged with manslaughter or something."

"I don't think he *did* get charged," Graciana said. "My parents saw him in the parking lot with some cops and a tall, thin bald man—my parents think it was Michael Burns, this big-shot lawyer. He shook hands with Davis and got into a car, Davis got into a police car with the cops, and everyone drove away. Probably, they just took him to the station for more questioning."

"He should be charged with murder." Berk put down his plate. "When he kicked Coach in the armpit—"

"Can we *please* not get into that again?" Suzette said. "It was probably his arm. Even in the video you took, you can't tell for sure."

"And injuries are part of sports," Derrick said. "You guys might not understand, because you play basketball, but in *real* sports—"

"Basketball is real sports," Joseph said. "It has injuries. What happened today—most strange. For so long, Davis was only front kick, front kick, front kick, once by once. Then, too sudden, he has many kicks, and that block. Such abruptness seems unaccountable."

Derrick sighed. "So, what're you saying? He pretended to be lousy for three minutes, so Coach would let his guard down so he could kill him? Why? He didn't even *know* Coach."

"He might be a psycho," Berk said. "Somebody who likes to toy with people before killing them."

But Davis didn't act like a psycho, I thought. He acted like someone who'd come to do a job, like someone who had his emotions completely under control—sizing Coach up, testing his reactions, trying to throw him off. I'd been brooding about all that for hours, going over all the possible explanations I could imagine. I knew there wasn't much basis for any of them—I should probably just keep quiet—but I couldn't hold back. "Or someone might've hired Davis to kill Coach," I said.

Derrick half-laughed, half-snorted. "So now you think this guy's a Mafia hit man. Get serious. Why would the Mafia want to kill Coach Colson?"

"It wouldn't have to be the Mafia," I said. "Regular people hire killers sometimes. Davis wouldn't have to be a professional hit man, either. He might just be a tough guy who's willing to kill for money."

"Something like that happened in Roanoke last year," Graciana said. She's the editor of our school paper, and she's going to major in journalism at University of Virginia—she got this monster scholarship—so she keeps up on news more than most of us. "A man didn't like his mother-in-law, so he hired a guy he met in a bar to shoot her. He paid him a few thousand, I think. The guy got caught, and now they're both in prison. Those things *do* happen."

"That doesn't explain why someone would want Coach Colson killed," Derrick said. "*He* wasn't married."

You'd need to understand how Derrick's mind works to see why that almost made sense. "I can't hand you an explanation," I said, "but Coach came to Ridgecrest just two years ago. How much do we actually know about him?"

"He enjoyed to bicycle," Joseph said, treating it like a real question. "Once, he mentioned how, on weekends, for many hours he'd bicycle, exploring outside town."

"And he hated turnips," Derrick said solemnly. "Totally hated them."

"My point is, we don't know much," I said, getting impatient. "Someone might've had a grudge against him."

"That's true," Graciana said, "but it doesn't mean we should leap to conclusions about hired killers. The likeliest explanation is that *Davis* had a grudge against him. Even if they'd never met before, even if Coach Colson had never heard of Davis, Davis might've heard of Coach. He might've had a reason to hate him."

"I don't get it," Derrick said, squinting. "Why would he hate someone he'd never met?"

Graciana shrugged. "Lots of possibilities. Let's say there was a car accident. Coach Colson was driving, and someone Davis loved was killed. Maybe it wasn't Coach's fault, so he never got charged with anything. Davis was out of town when it happened, but when he came home, he heard about it and decided Coach was responsible and had to die."

"Yeah, something like that could happen," I agreed. "And it's probably more likely than the hired killer idea."

Joseph frowned. "All this is much speculation with few facts. Besides, killing with many watching produces danger. If Davis wished Mr. Colson to die, why not shoot him in a dark place, where there is nobody?"

"Because then it would obviously be murder," Graciana said. "This way, it looked like an accident."

"It probably *was* an accident," Derrick said. "If not, the cops will find out."

"Not if they're not trying," Berk said. "Lieutenant Hill acted like he's already written it off. We can't count on him to find the truth." He stared down at his plate for a few seconds, pushing the last crumbs around with his fork, then looked up. "Look, I've been going nuts thinking about this thing, and I don't want to accuse anyone, but one thing seems really suspicious to me. Someone who was at the tournament didn't belong there and acted strange. And she's weird in general and has probably done illegal things. I can't help thinking she's connected to this somehow."

"Who do you mean?" Derrick asked.

Berk hesitated again, then let loose. "That girl who always wears black. Marie Somebody. Remember, Matt? She was in our social studies class with Coach Colson last year."

"Marie Ramsey," I said. "I noticed her at the tournament, too."

"Yeah, what the hell was she doing there?" Berk said. "After Coach got killed, she was crying really loud—practically *howling*. Why would *she* care about martial arts? She's not exactly the athletic type. And everybody says she's into drugs and Satanism and other twisted stuff, like her sister was."

"Hold on," Graciana cut in. "I don't know Marie, but I knew her sister a little, and I never saw any signs she was involved with drugs or Satanism. Sometimes, the things people say about people aren't based on anything. And lots of people who aren't athletes like to watch martial arts. I have an uncle who's the least athletic person you could imagine, and he owns dozens of martial arts movies."

"Maybe Marie just wanted to get away from her house and be around people today," I said, remembering the thoughts I'd had earlier. "Maybe she felt sad about her sister and wanted any distraction she could find."

"Good point." Graciana shot me a smile so big it knocked me back six inches.

"So where does that leave us?" Berk asked. "Coach Colson was killed, most of us think Davis did it on purpose, and it looks like the police won't even bother to investigate." He breathed in deep, like he knew the next thing he said would sound crazy. "*We* should investigate, and then tell Hill what we've learned."

That *did* sound crazy. "I don't want Davis to get away with this, either," I said. "But we don't know how to investigate anything. We could tell Hill about our ideas."

"He won't listen," Graciana said, "Berk's right. If we want Hill to change his mind, we need to bring him evidence."

Suzette rolled her eyes, the same way she had this afternoon. "Ooh, 'evidence.' Sounds fancy. How are *we* supposed to find 'evidence'?"

"We start by finding out more about Bobby Davis," Graciana said, not missing a beat.

"I tried," Berk said. "I Googled him—'Bobby Davis,' 'Richmond.' Wanna guess how many thousands of hits I got?"

"So this time we don't rely on Google." Graciana sat forward. "I say we drive to Richmond tomorrow. We know he goes to Kelly's Dojo. Let's start there. I checked the website and found the address. We can use my brother's car."

The words shot through me. Ever since I'd watched Coach die, I'd been burning up with the feeling I should *do* something. But I couldn't think of anything. Already, I'd almost gotten used to the idea his death would be one more thing to feel frustrated and angry about. Now here was Graciana with a specific plan. I didn't know if it'd do any good, and I wasn't crazy about possibly facing Davis again. Still, it was something.

Derrick laughed. "Hold on, Gracie. You can't—"

"Graciana," she said. "Please. I don't like Gracie."

"Excuse me, Your Highness. I didn't realize you were so special."

"It's my name," she said. "I've got a right to be called by my name."

"Yes, Your Highness." He seemed to think that was hilarious. "Listen, you don't wanna mess with Davis. He almost clobbered Matt, just for getting his phone. What'll he do if he finds out you're 'investigating' him? Anyhow, what can you learn by going to some gym? It's stupid. I'm not going."

"Me neither," Suzette said. "I think it's stupid, too. Plus my father would go ballistic."

"So don't tell him," Berk said. "Say we're going for a drive. That's what I'll tell my mom."

"He'd find out anyhow. *You're* not going, are you, Matt?"

I nodded slowly. "Yeah. I'll go. I'll tell my parents we're going for a drive."

"I would like to go," Joseph said. "However, I have church. My mother is adamant."

"So are my parents," Graciana said, "but I can go to early mass. Berk, Matt, I'll pick you up around eleven. Kelly's has a beginners' class at one. We'll say we're thinking of signing up and want to observe, and then we'll mingle and get people talking about Davis." She checked her watch. "I should go. I told my brother I'd babysit. Berk, will you thank your mom for me, say I loved the lasagna? Thanks."

Derrick waited till she'd gone. "Wow. Gracie's a take-charge girl, isn't she?"

"She's *so* stuck up," Suzette said. "She thinks she's a big-shot reporter, and she'll solve a murder and write articles about it and win a Nobel Prize. Plus she had a huge crush on Coach Colson. I don't know if it went anywhere, but my friends heard that's why she joined the club."

"You're kidding," Derrick said. "He was like twenty-five, twenty-six."

Suzette shrugged. "Some girls like older men. You've heard about her and Mr. Bixby, haven't you? Everybody says they've been sleeping together since last spring."

"Mr. Bixby is married," Joseph said. "He has children."

She shrugged again. "Some girls don't care. Now, I don't know for sure, but they stay late in his classroom, just the two of them, with the door closed, supposedly working on the newspaper. Last month, when I was at school one night for a dance team rehearsal, I walked past his room, and I heard them talking and laughing. They sounded drunk." She sighed. "I mean, *I* think it's disgusting, but I guess that's how you get to be editor."

"Wow," Derrick said. "Maybe that's why none of the guys can get anywhere with Gracie. She only goes for teachers."

"I doubt this," Joseph said. "Though the door was closed, I hope for valid explanations. Graciana appears a proper girl."

Suzette smiled. "You're a proper boy, Joseph. Naturally you think everybody else is proper, too. But not everybody is." She flexed her shoulders, as if letting bad thoughts roll off. "Enough about that. Anybody want to do something fun?"

They started trading ideas. I let it pass by, thinking about what Suzette had said. There couldn't have been anything between Graciana and Coach Colson, could there? He wasn't the type to go after students. I didn't know Mr. Bixby, though. And Graciana's awfully pretty. Suzette's pretty, too, one of the prettiest girls in school—nice body, nice hair, face all sweet and soft and smiley. Graciana's different. She's got a nice body, too, and great hair, but she's—well, not as soft and smiley. I don't know how to put it, but when you look into her eyes, you can tell a lot's going on inside her head, all sorts of thoughts and stuff. Sometimes, I've caught myself staring at her eyes, wondering what she's thinking.

I've never tried to get close to her, though. She's a senior, I'm a junior, and like Suzette said, she seems stuck-up. But tonight, when she sounded so strong and sure, I'd felt a bond, almost. Now, thinking about her and Mr. Bixby—God. Suzette didn't know for sure, but it sounded bad. And Mr. Bixby's wife had another baby last year. Much as my parents get on my nerves, at least they're together. Berk sees his father two or three times a year. He acts like it's no big deal, but I can tell it hurts him. Nobody should mess with a family.

"So, miniature golf," Suzette said. "How does that sound, Matt?"

She gave me a sweet, open smile. And her eyes were so blue, so clear, so friendly. She really *is* pretty, I thought, and smiled back. "Sounds fine," I said.

Four

We didn't fool Mr. Kelly for one minute. While Graciana told him our story, he stood with hands on hips, lips pursed tight. A tall, skinny guy who looked around thirty stretched out nearby, listening and grinning.

"So, you might take classes," Mr. Kelly said. "You kids live in Richmond?"

"In the area," Graciana said. Pretty quick, I thought, and not quite a lie, not if you consider about a third of Virginia an "area."

"I see," he said. "Why'd you decide to start now?"

Graciana must've sensed the hostility in his voice, but she didn't back down. "Today seemed like a good time."

"This wouldn't have anything to do with the tournament in Ridgecrest, would it? With the stories on the news?"

Graciana sighed. "Why do you ask?"

"Because ever since yesterday afternoon, my phone's rung every five minutes—cops, reporters, parents, total strangers. And you're the third group that's dropped by today, saying you wanna observe a class, when obviously you've really come to gawk at the Killer Dojo, hoping Bobby Davis will stroll in and give you a thrill."

"You're partly right, Mr. Kelly," I said, "but partly wrong. We're from Ridgecrest. The man who got killed, Randy Colson, was our martial arts teacher. He meant a lot to us, and we're trying to understand what happened. We thought learning more about Davis might help. That might not make sense, but it's how we feel."

His face softened. "No, it *doesn't* make sense, but I understand. Well, I'll tell you what I told everyone else. I've never met Bobby Davis. I never heard his name until yesterday. He's never been a student here. I checked my records. Never."

"Why would he say he's from your school?" Berk asked.

"Everyone in your tournament had to be from a martial arts school in Virginia, right? That's what the cops said. Probably, Davis wanted to compete but wasn't taking classes, so he picked my place out of the phone book. Did you ask for proof people went to the schools on their registration forms?"

"No," Graciana said. "We never thought people might lie about their schools."

"People lie about everything." He smiled grimly. "You seem like nice kids. Forget this guy. From what I hear, he got mad because your coach was winning, and he lost control. People with nasty tempers got no place in martial arts—I tell my students that, all the time. Don't mess with him. You wanna do something for your coach, have a bake sale, raise money for his favorite charity."

"Good suggestion." Graciana shook his hand. "Thanks, Mr. Kelly."

We went outside and stood around, not knowing what to do.

"Now what?" Berk asked. "We go home and bake cookies?"

"A bake sale's actually not a bad idea," Graciana said. "But I want to find out more about Davis, too."

The skinny guy who'd been listening in on us came outside. "Hey," he said. "This Bobby Davis at the tournament—sorta short? Orange hair, snake tattoo?"

"Right." I turned to face him. "You know him? Mr. Kelly said he doesn't take classes here."

The guy grinned. "The Bobby Davis I know wouldn't take classes anywhere. I just wondered if it's the same guy. Guess so."

"Do you know where he lives," Graciana asked, "or where he works?"

"Where he lives? No. Where he works—lots of places. I see him around sometimes."

"Where?" Berk asked.

His grin got bigger. "No place you kids should go. Your coach—black belt, right? What degree?"

"First." My stomach tightened. "Does Davis have a higher degree belt?" If he did, he must've lied on his registration form. The judges made sure fighters were evenly matched.

"I don't know what degree belt Bobby has. I don't think belts go that high. Did anybody tape the fight? Can I get a copy?"

This guy was seriously sick. "I taped it on my phone," Berk said. "If you tell us how to find Davis, you can watch."

"A cell-phone video?" His lower lip curled up. "Can you really see anything?"

"Yeah," Berk said. "Where can we find Davis?"

"Video first." He held out his hand.

Berk gave him the phone, and the guy watched the video, complaining about how blurry it was. He watched it twice, though. "Not worth copying," he said, handing the phone back. "You can barely see the best parts."

The best parts. "So tell us how to find Davis," I said.

"He hangs out at this bar downtown. The Range, on Ere-whon. But you shouldn't go there." He started to walk away, then turned back. "If you find someone with a better video, let me know. There might be money in it for you. If I'm not around, tell Kelly you wanna see Craig. He'll know how to find me."

"My God," Graciana said when he'd gone inside. "Why would anyone want to watch someone get killed?"

"I hated to give him my phone," Berk said, "to let him get a thrill that way. But now we know where to get started. Not that it does us much good. We can't go in a bar."

"We can park across the street," I said. "We might spot Davis coming out, and then we can follow him. We drove all this way. I don't feel like giving up yet."

"Neither do I," Graciana said, and got in the car.

We weren't surprised when The Range turned out to be a crummy-looking bar in a crummy part of town. Graciana parked down the street, and we settled in to watch. She'd stowed a cooler in the backseat, with Cokes and chicken sandwiches, so we had those while we talked about what Craig said, about whether he'd been telling the truth or making stuff up to scare us.

A girl who didn't look much older than us strolled down the street, swinging this small, glittery purse, stopping outside the door to The Range and leaning her back against the wall. She lit a cigarette and stood watching cars drive down the street. Maybe she was waiting for someone, or maybe she was killing time. She was real thin and sort of pretty, with long, straight blonde hair, wearing a short black silk dress and a shiny blue jacket.

"You should talk to her, Matt," Graciana said. "Ask her if she knows Bobby Davis. If she does, ask her to go inside, see if he's there, and come back and tell you."

I hope I didn't actually jolt back in my seat. "Why would she even talk to me?"

"Because you're a good-looking guy," Graciana said, "and she looks lonely. Flirt with her."

"It won't work," I said. "She's gotta be five, ten years older than me. And I'm not much for flirting."

"I've noticed." Graciana smiled. "Give it a try, okay?"

"*I'll* talk to her," Berk offered.

Graciana hesitated. "No, let Matt try. He's taller, and he looks older."

She thinks I'm better looking than Berk, I thought, and felt myself start to blush. All of a sudden, getting out of the car seemed like a good idea. "Okay. I'll try."

As I opened the car door, Graciana lowered her voice. "Say you're a friend of Bobby Davis. Say you owe him money and want to pay him back. Don't use your real name."

I walked toward the bar, feeling like an idiot. I stopped five feet short of the girl and shoved my hands in my pockets. "Hi," I said.

She turned to face me and broke into a big smile. Close up, she looked older, not as pretty. "Hi," she said. "I haven't seen *you* here before. What's your name, honey?"

"David Foley," I said, and instantly wished I could call it back. Why had I used my father's name? But I was nervous, and it came out before I could stop it. I'd spoken three words to this girl, and already I'd messed up. "What's *your* name?"

She moved closer. "Valerie. I hope you think that's a pretty name."

"Sure." I wished I was back in the car. "I'm trying to find a friend of mine. Bobby Davis. I heard he hangs out here. Do you know him?"

She backed off a step. "Yeah, I know Bobby. I'm surprised *you* know Bobby. You don't look like one of his friends."

"I owe him money," I said. "I need to pay him back."

"Oh." Her face relaxed. "*That* kind of friend of Bobby's. Bobby has lots of friends like that. Yeah, he hangs out here. Why don't we go in, have a drink, see if he's around?"

"I can't. I'm nineteen." Actually, I'd turned seventeen last month. "Could you step inside and let me know if he's here? If he is, I'll wait and pay him back when he leaves."

She frowned. "That might take *hours*. I'll tell you what. Give me the money, and if Bobby's inside, I'll give it to him, say it's from David Foley, and come right back out."

Damn. She'd remembered the name. And I only had about five bucks on me, and if I *did* have money and gave it to her, it was a good bet she'd slip out a back door, and I'd never see her or the money again. "I'd better pay him in person. Would you see if he's here?"

She shrugged and went inside.

That's when I realized what a bad plan this was. What if Davis came out, expecting money, and saw me? Even if Berk and Graciana tried to help, it wouldn't do much good against a guy who's apparently an nth-degree black belt. Should I make a run for the car?

Before I could decide, Valerie stepped back out, alone. Thank God. "He's not here." She walked up close, stopping just short of pressing against me. "I bet we can find something else to do with your money. Wanna come to my place? I'll give you a drink. It's okay you're nineteen. I don't card."

Now she *did* press against me, hooking her right hand around my neck, resting her left hand on my hip. I could smell perfume in her hair, feel her body beneath the flimsy silk. Too much. Way, way too much. "I don't drink. Anyway, I'd better get home. My mother—"

"Your mother's fine," she said, her grip on my neck tightening, her breath warm on my face. "I know you're young. I don't mind. I like young boys. Come home with me, David."

That did it. Hearing my father's name totally freaked me out. Out of nowhere, the choke-hold release Coach taught us came to me. I lifted both fists in the air and brought them down hard against the insides of her elbows, sweeping her arms aside. She jerked her head back, eyes wide. I stepped back. "Thanks, Valerie. You've been a big help. I gotta go."

I ran like hell for the car. Berk and Graciana were almost spitting with laughter. "Drive," I said. "Get me out of here."

Graciana drove, still laughing. In one minute, I started laughing, too.

"You used a choke-hold release on a girl trying to kiss you," Berk said. "I don't believe it."

"She's a hooker," I said. "Graciana *knew* she's a hooker. Didn't you?"

"I didn't. I swear. I just thought she looked lonely. When she got so friendly so fast, though—yeah, I started to wonder."

It took us fifteen minutes to calm down enough to really talk. The trip to Richmond hadn't been a total waste. I told them what Valerie said, and we decided Davis might be a drug dealer or a collector for a loan shark. Sort of cautiously, Graciana suggested Coach might've owed Davis money, and maybe that's why Davis killed him.

Berk and I shot that idea down fast. No way would Coach have gotten mixed up with drugs or loan sharks. Besides, if Davis had been squeezing him for money, Coach would've recognized him at the tournament, and he obviously hadn't. And if Davis wanted money from Coach, killing him wasn't exactly the best way to get it. Graciana backed off, saying she hadn't really thought that could be the explanation, either.

"One thing's for sure," I said. "From now on, we don't do anything without thinking it through. If Davis had come out and seen me, it could've been bad. We've gotta be more careful."

"I agree." Graciana took the exit leading back to Ridgecrest. "And I already know what we should do next."

Five

Coach had told us stories about Mrs. Dolby. He'd rented a three-room apartment at the back of her house, and they'd gotten friendly. Most days, he'd said, he didn't have to cook, because she'd ambush him before he got to his door and force meatloaf or tuna casserole on him. When we got back from Richmond, we bought some daisies and rang her bell.

She's sort of heavy, with short, sparse reddish-brown hair. The loose purple-and-yellow thing she wore looked like a cross between a dress and a bathrobe, with big yellow buttons down the front.

"Mrs. Dolby?" Graciana said. "I'm Graciana Cortez, and these are my friends, Matthew Foley and Berkeley Widrig. We belong to the martial arts club at Ridgecrest High. We know you were special to Coach Colson, and we're sure he was special to you. So we got you these flowers."

"Goodness!" Tears pooled in Mrs. Dolby's eyes. "Isn't that the *nicest* thing! Come in, come in. I'll get you some cookies."

I'd figured there'd be cookies. Mrs. Dolby's living room is cluttered but friendly, with sagging red-flowered couches, different shapes and sizes of end tables, and lots of little statues—glass dolphins, brass owls, ceramic squirrels. She lowered herself into an armchair and sighed.

"Randy *was* special to me," she said. "It felt like having one of my sons home again. Old ladies need someone to fuss over, you know. When I got the call yesterday—goodness!"

"We're broken up about it, too," Graciana said. "And we want to do something. We thought we'd have a bake sale and donate the money to his favorite charity."

"Goodness!" Mrs. Dolby looked ready to cry again. "I'll *definitely* bake something for your sale. *Lots* of things."

"That's great," I said. "The problem is, we don't know what his favorite charity was. Do you?"

Her forehead scrunched up. "He never mentioned one. But he *loved* Ridgecrest High. He talked about it all the time, and he loved hearing me tell stories about the school's early days. I had lots to tell, since all my children went there—my oldest graduated two years after the school opened, and my youngest graduated the year Dr. Lombardo became principal. Maybe you could donate the money to Ridgecrest High, and start a scholarship in Randy's memory."

"Good idea," I said, disappointed. We hadn't learned much about Davis, so we'd decided to try learning more about Coach by asking Mrs. Dolby about his favorite charity. We'd do the bake sale, too—we wouldn't lie about something like that—but mainly we wanted to learn about his interests, stuff like that. Hearing he'd loved Ridgecrest High wasn't exactly news.

"Perfect," Graciana said, and paused. I could practically feel her thinking, searching for ways to get more information. "Also, I'm the editor of the school newspaper, and I'd like to put out a memorial issue in honor of Coach Colson. We'd interview people he knew well and talk about what made him special. Could we start by interviewing you? Then maybe you could point us to other people he was close to."

"A memorial issue! How lovely!" Mrs. Dolby smiled at us. "Are you boys on the newspaper staff, too?"

"Not usually," Graciana said, jumping in so we wouldn't have to make something up. "But Coach Colson was their social studies teacher, and they're on the basketball team, so they knew him well. And Berk's interested in film and photography, and Matt won a prize for this amazing essay he wrote last year. So they've both got skills we can use. Right, Matt?"

I nodded but felt too stunned to speak. I couldn't believe Graciana had come up with such a great idea off the top of her head. I couldn't believe she'd managed to weave in practically everything she knew about Berk and me and not tell any flat-out lies. Mostly, I couldn't believe she'd remembered that dumb essay.

I hadn't wanted to enter the contest. Some college sponsored it, asking for essays about citizenship, and my English teacher made us all write on the topic. For some reason, she submitted mine. When I won, my parents went nuts, sending copies to everyone we've ever met in our lives, and the guys on the basketball team called me Shakespeare until I threatened to flatten them. The savings bond I got as a prize was good, but otherwise the whole experience was pretty much a nightmare. Now this. I wouldn't have guessed Graciana had even read the essay, and for her to remember it a year later—that didn't make sense.

Mrs. Dolby wiped her eyes. "You're simply the *nicest* young people. I'll be happy to talk to you about Randy. Let's see. Where should I start?"

She started with the day Coach called to ask about the apartment, and she went on for over an hour. Graciana whipped out a notebook—I bet she always carries one in her purse—and asked lots of questions. Berk and I mostly listened, nodded, and ate cookies.

"Randy did lots of favors for me," Mrs. Dolby was saying. "If a window got stuck, for example, or I needed to change a light bulb I couldn't reach. And whenever I ran errands, I always asked if I could pick anything up for him." She sighed. "Just yesterday morning, I told him I was going to the public library, and he asked me to check a book out for him."

She pointed to the coffee table. Graciana picked up the black-and-red book and raised her eyebrows. "*The Bell Jar?* Coach Colson asked you to get him *The Bell Jar?*"

"Yes, he was quite a reader. Not novels so much—that *is* a novel, isn't it?—but he'd gotten very interested in Virginia history since moving here, especially Ridgecrest history. He'd bicycle all around the area, taking notes and pictures."

"Was he writing an article?" Graciana asked.

Mrs. Dolby nodded. "He wrote a draft of one for the local paper and showed it to Heather Quinn. That's right—you asked for suggestions about other people you should talk to. You should *definitely* talk to Heather—but I should call her Ms. Quinn."

"That's okay," I said. Ms. Quinn's the head of the social studies department, and she's married to our guidance counselor. "She was close with Coach Colson?"

"Oh, yes. During Randy's first year, she was his mentor, since she's been at the school so long, and they became good friends—lots of times, he mentioned having lunch with her." Mrs. Dolby's face crinkled around a soft, wistful smile. "Randy had other friends at Ridgecrest High, too, like that pretty young Asian teacher, Katie Somebody."

"Ms. Nguyen?" I said. "She's my English teacher."

"That's right—Nguyen. I met her four or five times—so friendly, so sweet. Let's see. Who else should you talk to?"

After Mrs. Dolby rattled off more names, Graciana closed her notebook. "Thank you. You gave us some wonderful stories. Would you mind if Berk takes a picture of you? He'll use his cell phone camera."

Mrs. Dolby shifted around in her chair, patting her hair into place. "Pictures—I don't know. I'm sure my eyes are still puffy from crying. But Randy had a really nice snapshot of the two of us—he kept it in his kitchen. We can go get it." She rummaged in a shiny red box until she found the right key. "I haven't opened his door since it happened. His parents called, and I said I'd pack up his things for them, but I haven't had the heart to begin. It'll be easier to go in there for the first time with all of you with me."

It wasn't so easy. Coach's living room was a mess—drawers pulled out of his desk and dumped on the floor, books everywhere, cushions stripped off the couch. Bureau drawers in the bedroom had been dumped out, too, and storage boxes emptied. As we walked through the apartment, Mrs. Dolby kept saying, "Goodness!" and pressing her hands against her cheeks. Finally, she wandered back to the living room and sank onto the couch.

"A burglar!" she said. "And I didn't even know! I didn't hear a thing!"

Berk pulled back the curtain in a large window. "The glass is broken, and the screen's sliced from the frame. That's how he got in. You'd better call the police."

Mrs. Dolby nodded, looking numb. "Will you stay until they come? It's silly—the burglar's obviously gone—but I don't want to be alone."

"Of course we'll stay," Graciana said. "This must be so upsetting, Mrs. Dolby."

"It is. And why would someone burglarize Randy's apartment but not take anything from my house? I have *so* many pretty things!"

Maybe. I don't know how many burglars would steal a clock with a mermaid curled around it. But Coach wasn't rich, either. What did *he* have that'd attract a burglar? "Can you tell what's missing?" I asked.

She looked around. "Well, Randy had a laptop computer. I don't see that. Or his briefcase. But Randy just kept books in that, and notes and things—why would anybody take *that*? And his television's still here, his espresso maker—why didn't the burglar take *those*?"

Good questions. I picked up a notepad from the floor. No, not a clue, just a grocery list, decorated with doodles of fish and two flowering trees and dinosaurs.

Before long, two uniformed officers arrived; five minutes later, Lieutenant Hill, the detective we'd talked to yesterday, showed up too. He didn't look happy to see us.

"We shouldn't have this many people at a crime scene," he said. "You kids—come outside with me."

Graciana gave Mrs. Dolby an index card. "Thank you for the delicious cookies, Mrs. Dolby, and for giving us so much information. Here's my phone number in case you'd like to get in touch about the bake sale, or about anything else."

Mrs. Dolby nodded, hugging each of us. We followed Lieutenant Hill to the front porch, and he stood facing us, leaning his back against the railing. "What's this about a bake sale?"

"We want to start a scholarship named after Coach Colson," Berk said. "We're having a bake sale to raise money."

Hill nodded. "Fine. Have all the bake sales you want." He pointed at Graciana. "You said she gave you information. About what?"

"About Coach Colson," Graciana said. "I'm the editor of the school newspaper, and we're putting together a memorial issue about him."

He thought that over for a minute. "If it's just stories about how nice he was, okay. But don't start digging for dirt, getting people stirred up over nothing. Did you scare Mrs. Dolby with that garbage you tried to sell me yesterday? All that crazy talk about murder?"

"We didn't say anything about the tournament," I said. "But what we told you wasn't garbage, Lieutenant. We wish you'd take it more seriously."

He stepped closer to me and folded his arms across his chest—not a threatening move, but it felt like he was crowding me. "And I wish you'd stop telling me how to do my job. Who the hell do you three think you are, Nancy Drew and the Hardy Boys? This isn't some game. You're messing with people's lives. I spent a long time talking to Davis yesterday. Nobody's sorrier about the accident than he is. And you tried to get the poor guy charged with murder."

Graciana folded her arms, too, and took a step toward Hill. "If 'that poor guy' killed Coach Colson on purpose, he *committed* murder. And now we know Coach's apartment got burglarized on the same day he was killed. You really think that's a coincidence?"

"Yeah, I do. Life's full of coincidences. Usually, they don't add up to a damn thing. Maybe you'll figure that out when you grow up. This was an ordinary, everyday burglary. So go organize your bake sales and have fun with your little club. But don't scare old ladies with crazy talk, and don't start thinking you're Woodward and Bernstein." He turned his back on us and walked into the house.

We got into the car and drove in silence for several minutes. Then Berk spoke up. "Woodward and Bernstein?"

"*Washington Post* reporters," Graciana said. "They helped uncover the truth about Watergate, back in the seventies. God! I couldn't *stand* how sarcastic Hill was. And where does some cop get the right to tell me what I should and shouldn't do with my newspaper?"

Her newspaper. Some people might think it's the school's newspaper. But like Derrick said, Graciana's the take-charge type. "Maybe you should check with Mr. Bixby, though," I said, "and ask if it's okay to do a memorial issue."

She shrugged. "I'll call him tonight, but I'm sure he'll be fine with it. Honoring a teacher who died at a school event—how could he object?"

"So we're really doing this memorial issue?" Berk asked. "Okay. I liked listening to Mrs. Dolby's stories about Coach. But she didn't say anything that could help us figure out what happened."

"It's too soon to know what information might be relevant, or how facts might fit together," Graciana said. "It certainly could be relevant that somebody burglarized Coach's apartment, left behind things that could be fenced, but took his papers. And we learned interesting things about him. For example, I wouldn't have expected him to read *The Bell Jar*."

"Yeah, you seemed surprised by that," I said. "You've read that book? What's it about?"

"It's hard to sum it up in a sentence or two, but I'd say, among other things, it's a portrait of depression, and of the search for identity. The protagonist's very intelligent, but she has trouble finding a direction for her life, and she feels stifled by the limited choices available to women at the time."

Definitely a chick book, I thought. I wouldn't have expected Coach to read it, either. "Maybe it's because of Ms. Nguyen," I said. "Mrs. Dolby hinted she and Coach might've been involved. And Ms. Nguyen teaches English. I can see her liking that book. Maybe Coach wanted to read it so they could discuss it."

"So we should talk to Ms. Nguyen," Berk said. "If Coach had a problem, he might've told her. What about the other people Mrs. Dolby mentioned?"

We spent the rest of the drive talking about that. All the time, I kept thinking about what we were up against. Bobby Davis had warned me to back off, and he could kill with nothing but his hands and feet. Lieutenant Hill saw us as a bunch of stupid kids who would just get in his way, and our parents didn't know what we were doing and wouldn't be happy if they did.

Too many people against us—trying to find the truth about what happened to Coach was probably a really, really bad idea, especially since we didn't seem to be making much progress. But I couldn't give up. Not yet.

Six

On Monday morning, Cassie bounced into the kitchen. *"Bonjour, mon frère!"* she said. *"Comment allez-vous?"*

I looked up from my cornflakes. "What?"

Cassie opened the refrigerator and stood hand on hip, scouting out possibilities. She's borderline gawky, with long, wispy light orange hair and too many freckles. "It means, 'Hello, my brother! How are you?' Yesterday, Mom and Dad and I decided we should all learn French."

Naturally that's something they'd decide we should do. I bet they all thought it sounded like the most fun ever. "Why? Are we moving to Paris?"

"No, silly. But we realized I'm taking Latin, you're taking Spanish, Mom took Italian, and Dad took German, but not one of us has taken French! Isn't that amazing?"

"Yeah," I said. "I'm stunned."

"Us, too!" The sarcasm had zipped past her. She squinted into the refrigerator. "Cottage cheese! I can have cottage cheese! With peaches! Want some cottage cheese with peaches?"

"No, thanks." In the morning, I don't even like to think about cottage cheese.

She eased a knife into a peach, carving out one cautious slice. "So I found an online list of Fun French Phrases." She looked up shyly. "I made you a copy. Want to practice at breakfast?"

Little Miss Take-Charge, I thought. "I'm not really up for learning French."

"Oh, come on. It'd be *fun*, and it's something we could do together."

"I've got too much other stuff going on. Should I pick you up after school, or do you have Special Chorus?"

Now she really lit into the peach, bringing the knife down hard and fast against the pit. "I'm not in Special Chorus anymore. Yeah, I'd like a ride."

"You dropped Special Chorus?" The music teacher had started it this spring, and Cassie had gone nuts about being one of the twelve girls picked. They were learning madrigals and other extra-fancy songs to perform at nursing homes and stuff, and there's nothing Cassie likes better than getting up in front of people and showing off. "How come?"

"Because it's dumb." She dumped cottage cheese on her plate. "And *I've* got other stuff going on, too."

"Okay, okay. Sorry I asked. We leave in twenty minutes. All right?"

She bit her lip, then turned to me with a big smile. *"C'est bien!"*

I guess that meant yes.

In homeroom, the teacher handed me a note: Go to the Guidance Center. So the school had decided to help us cope.

The Guidance Center's got a room set up for small groups: whiteboard, round table, posters with inspirational sayings and pictures of people climbing mountains and crossing finish lines. Mr. Quinn had written five words on the whiteboard in big red letters: DENIAL, ANGER, BARGAINING, DEPRESSION, ACCEPTANCE. I was the last martial arts club member to slump into a chair.

Mr. Quinn graduated with Ridgecrest High's first senior class, twenty-five years ago, so he must be about forty-three. He's in great shape, though. Every year, at the student-faculty basketball fundraiser, he makes us sweat for every point. Right after college, he came straight back to Ridgecrest to be guidance counselor—it's the only job he's ever had. A few years after that, he married Ms. Quinn, and they've both worked here ever since. Sometimes, he jokes about feeling like he never graduated, like he can never escape. But you can tell he thinks going to Ridgecrest High was the best thing that ever happened to him, and it's the best thing that'll ever happen to us, too.

He walked up to the whiteboard, doing a big sigh, jerking his shoulders back on the inhale, drooping them forward on the exhale. "This is a sad day for Ridgecrest High," he said. "Mr. Colson was a dedicated teacher, a great coach. I was proud to call him my friend. So I thought we should get together to help you understand your feelings."

He picked up his note cards and pointed to the big red words. "When you lose somebody, you go through stages of grief. There's nothing wrong with these feelings. They're part of the process. The goal? Moving from denial to acceptance. What do you think denial means?"

Damn, I thought. Will we have to talk about all five of these? This didn't have anything to do with the feelings I was having. It felt like some gimmick guidance counselors use to make kids open up. If he'd just given us a chance to talk, fine. But Mr. Quinn always complicates things. He has to break feelings down into steps, and he can't talk to us without a stack of note cards in his hands.

I hunched forward, staring at my folded hands. If I looked up, he might call on me. Finally, Joseph raised his hand. He's an awful nice guy. He always cooperates with teachers, even when they want us to do something dumb.

"Does it mean," he said, "when sad things happen, people try to not believe, because believing makes too much hurt?"

"Nailed it! My man!" Mr. Quinn held up his hand for a high five. Wincing, Joseph gave him one. Like I said, he's an awful nice guy.

"So that's denial," Mr. Quinn said, looking all happy because we were communicating so well. "Did you feel denial after the accident? I sure did. I kept thinking, 'He can't have passed away! The paramedics will save him!' It's natural to have those feelings. But we gotta get past them. There was an accident, Mr. Colson passed away, and we've gotta accept those facts. Next comes anger. Who felt anger Saturday?"

Nobody spoke. I stared at my hands harder.

"Matt?" he said. "Did you feel anger after the accident?"

I should've come up with a sentence that'd make him leave me alone, so he'd call on somebody else to make up crap about bargaining. But I felt too fed up.

"Yeah," I said. "I'm still angry. Maybe that's partly because of this process or whatever, but it's also because I know—I *know*—it wasn't an accident. And Lieutenant Hill won't listen to us, and Davis will probably get away with murder. *That* makes me angry."

Mr. Quinn shuffled through his note cards. "I heard some of you felt it wasn't an accident. That's okay. It's natural. Now, though, I want you to look at those feelings carefully—and honestly. Aren't they a form of denial?"

"No," Berk said. "And it's not just feelings. We saw—"

Mr. Quinn held up a hand. "Berk, calm down. I'll tell you a story. Fifteen years ago, my wife had a miscarriage. How do you think I felt?"

Suzette raised her hand. "Sad?"

Mr. Quinn beamed. It was the answer he'd wanted. "Not at first. First, I felt angry. I convinced myself it must've been the doctor's fault. Now, I think I purposely made myself angry. Do you know why?"

He turned to the whiteboard and tapped the fourth red word. "Depression. I didn't want to go there. It's scary. Feeling angry is easier than feeling miserable. Once I admitted the miscarriage was nobody's fault, that's how I *did* feel. But that's the only way to get to acceptance." He smiled. "Now, my wife and I have two healthy girls. We couldn't be happier. I want *you* to be happy, too. First, though, you have to accept the truth. Bad things happen sometimes—no reason, nobody's fault. That's why life's hard."

"Sometimes that's why life's hard." Graciana was staring at her hands, just like I was. "But sometimes it's hard because people do bad things on purpose. Sometimes, it *is* somebody's fault. We want to know which kind of hard thing this is."

Mr. Quinn pulled his lower lip in over his teeth. "You know what, Graciana? I bet, deep down, you already know it was an accident. You can't face that yet, because then you'd have to face depression. It's easier to distract yourself by thinking somebody's guilty. But you'll never reach acceptance that way." He glanced at his watch. "Let's move on."

He wrote THE FUTURE on the whiteboard. "We can't change the past. Let's list constructive things you can do to help yourselves heal. Derrick?"

Derrick blinked. "Matt says we should have a bake sale and start a scholarship named after Coach."

"Fantastic!" Mr. Quinn wrote BAKE SALE on the board in huge purple letters. "Any other constructive ideas? Graciana?"

Her face looked like solid stone. "We're doing a memorial issue of the school newspaper to honor Coach Colson. Matt and Berk are helping, and I hope the rest of you will, too."

Mr. Quinn didn't write anything on the board. "With final exams six weeks away, beginning a time-consuming project might not be smart. You know what *would* be smart? Exercise! Martial arts are a great way to get exercise. I know—during college, I got a black belt in karate. Who wants to keep taking martial arts?"

I hadn't thought about that since Saturday. It's not like I've always wanted to be a ninja or something. I got interested in martial arts last year when Coach got his black belt. Now, maybe it'd feel too sad to keep going.

I glanced around the table. Derrick's hand shot up. Then Berk, Joseph, and Graciana raised their hands, too. So I raised mine. That's when Suzette raised hers.

"Great!" Mr. Quinn said. "I'd love to advise your club, but my wife thinks I do too much extra stuff for the school already. So I made a list of martial arts schools in town."

Of course he'd made a list—alphabetical, with illustrations. Like I said, he complicates everything. When I got my copy, one name jumped out. Eye of the Tiger Martial Arts—Aaron Roth, Master. I thought of the judge who'd said Davis deliberately kicked Coach in the armpit and throat. Hadn't another judge called him Aaron? "Eye of the Tiger school might be okay," I said. "I think Aaron Roth was a judge at the tournament. He seemed nice."

Berk nodded sharply. He remembered, too.

"Glad to hear you make a constructive suggestion, Matt," Mr. Quinn said. "It means you're moving toward acceptance."

At last, the bell rang. "That's it for today," Mr. Quinn said. "Remember, if you ever want to talk, I'm always there for you. Matt, could I talk to you?"

He waited until the others had gone, then gave me his official I'm-concerned-about-you look—head lowered, eyes scrunched, mouth edging toward a frown. "I checked with Mr. Pavlakis. He said your last chemistry quiz didn't go well."

Damn. I'd been afraid Quinn would find out about that. "Yeah, it was a tough one. But I passed, and it was only a weekly quiz. I should still have a solid B in the class."

He shook his head. "You said you'd work at getting that up to an A-minus. Science and math are your strengths, Matt. Those are the grades that'll get you a scholarship."

My grades won't ever get me a scholarship, I thought, and basketball won't do it, either. Mr. Quinn pushes athletes hard on getting scholarships, and he's had some big success stories. Sooner or later, he'd have to get used to the idea that I'm simply not scholarship material. "I'll study harder for the next quiz. Promise."

His mouth moved closer to a full-scale frown. "Mr. Pavlakis says you never come to his Wednesday after-school review sessions. This week, you're going. I'll check with him Thursday morning to make sure you showed up."

Damn. That meant I'd actually have to go. I nodded and headed out.

In the hall, Graciana was waiting for me. "Aaron Roth—is that the judge you told us about? The one who told the truth?"

"I think so. He might be worth talking to, whether we take classes or not. I'll check his school's website. If there's a class tonight, you want to go?"

"Absolutely. And I called Mr. Bixby. He thinks a memorial issue's fine but wants us to get Dr. Lombardo's approval. Should I make an appointment for us to see her after school?"

I nodded, and she rushed off. She was wearing a long denim skirt. I liked watching the way it swished as she walked.

Then Mr. Bixby stepped out of his classroom, and Graciana paused. He handed her some papers, and she looked at them and laughed.

I remembered what Suzette had said and thought about Mr. Bixby's family, about the baby who wasn't even a year old. I looked at Graciana again, then turned away and headed for my next class.

Seven

Dr. Lombardo loved the bake sale idea—no big surprise. She wasn't sure about the memorial issue. No big surprise there, either.

Graciana and I sat in her big, sunny office, its walls crowded with diplomas and awards, with laminated copies of newspaper articles about Dr. Lombardo's accomplishments. Within five minutes, she'd set a date for the bake sale and decided Ms. Quinn should be our advisor. She also decided we should have a meeting after school tomorrow for anyone who wanted to help and that the money should be used to start an award for an outstanding history student, not a scholarship. Kids would feel good about an award even if it wasn't much money, she said, but a fifty-dollar college scholarship would seem lame. True enough.

When we shifted to talking about the memorial issue, things slowed down. "I understand your eagerness to honor Mr. Colson," she said. "But the issue has to be limited to articles about his contributions to the school. I need your guarantee about that, Graciana. No attempts at investigative journalism. None."

I don't know if it's actually possible to see a person's jaw stiffen, but I'm positive Graciana's did. "I don't foresee the need for investigative journalism," she said, meeting Dr. Lombardo's eyes evenly.

"That's not a guarantee." Dr. Lombardo sat forward. "I'll speak frankly. I haven't been pleased with some pieces in the newspaper this year—the piece about the alleged prevalence of plagiarism, for example, or the one about perceived inconsistencies in disciplinary policies. They upset some hard-working people, and they didn't do the school's reputation any good."

Graciana didn't flinch. "Those pieces were balanced and responsible. They drew attention to important issues, and we were careful not to overstate our conclusions."

"That's debatable. In any case, we don't need more negative publicity. It's been a difficult spring—first that poor girl's suicide, then this tragic accident. And this is an important time for Ridgecrest High—the twenty-fifth anniversary, the announcement of the new principal's name at graduation. We'll attract widespread media attention, and we have to make sure it's positive. It can't focus on the sorts of random misfortunes that can strike any school. So I'll need to approve this memorial issue before it goes to press."

Graciana's eyes blazed. "The First Amendment—"

"—does not give students the right to print whatever they feel like printing," Dr. Lombardo cut in. "In several cases, the courts have ruled that a public school newspaper is part of the educational program, funded by taxpayers and under the authority of the administration. Furthermore, I've heard some students are spreading rumors about Mr. Colson's death, saying it wasn't an accident—even though the police determined it was, even though the martial arts experts at the tournament confirmed their opinion. I don't want that sort of unfounded sensationalism in the newspaper, and I don't want you stirring up negative feelings by inviting people to speculate about it. Understood?"

"Yes," Graciana said, "but I don't agree. My sister's in law school. I'll ask her what she thinks."

"Fine. I can also give you the name of a lawyer who's advised us on several occasions. He's a Ridgecrest High graduate, and he's taught Constitutional Law as an adjunct at the University of Virginia. Your sister might find his opinions illuminating."

They sat glaring at each other. In the last five minutes, I hadn't said one word. Now, I felt like I had to break the silence.

"Thanks, Dr. Lombardo," I said, feeling like an idiot. "We'll work hard and try to make this issue really good. Graciana? I guess we should go?"

She looked at Dr. Lombardo, looked at me. "I guess." She stood up.

Dr. Lombardo shook our hands. "We've had some disagreements, Graciana, but I appreciate your hard work on the newspaper. I might as well tell you that you're a top contender for Outstanding Senior. When the committee meets to make its final decision, I'd like to be one of your advocates."

"Wow," I said when we got out into the hall. "Outstanding Senior. Mr. Quinn won that, the first year Ridgecrest High opened. If you win it on the twenty-fifth anniversary, that'd be something. You could put it on every job application for the rest of your life."

Graciana was walking fast. She gave her head one quick shake. "Paul Ericson has that award sewn up. Captain of the basketball team, homecoming king, full athletic scholarship to a Big Ten school. He's a good student, too, and he's Mr. Quinn's favorite protégé, living proof Quinn's the world's greatest guidance counselor. Quinn worked night and day to get him that scholarship, and you can bet he won't let anybody else win Outstanding Senior. Dr. Lombardo said that to try to bribe me. She's *such* a hypocrite."

"I wouldn't say that. She stays late every day, comes to every event. She really cares about the school."

"She's ambitious," Graciana said. "All she cares about is her own career. Ridgecrest's a stepping stone to her—I bet she's frustrated as hell she got stuck here so long. Now she's got her chance to move ahead, and she doesn't want anything to mess it up. She wants everybody to think she made Ridgecrest High into a perfect paradise where nothing could go wrong, except 'random misfortunes.' That's how she wants everyone to see Coach Colson's death. You think she cares about finding the truth? She wants to cover it up, so her big moment won't be clouded by controversy."

I tried to take all that in. I'd always liked Dr. Lombardo. Then again, Graciana knew her better than I did. "Maybe," I said.

Graciana stopped walking and turned around to smile at me. "Sorry. Did I sound bitter? I am, but not about the stupid award. Lombardo's given us a hard time all year. At least she said we can do the special issue. Want to get a Coke and make plans?"

I pictured Graciana laughing with Mr. Bixby in the hall, thought of the things Suzette had said. Suzette didn't know for sure, but it looked like Graciana was having sex with a teacher, a man with a family.

"No," I said. "I'm picking my sister up."

Did my voice sound too sharp? Graciana gave me a strange look. "Okay. I'll see you tonight, at Eye of the Tiger School."

I could've offered to pick her up. I'd already offered rides to Berk and Joseph. But I didn't feel like it. I drove off to get Cassie.

At dinner, when I told my parents about the bake sale, Mom said she'd make truffles. I didn't know what those were, but they didn't sound promising. When I said I'd be working on a special issue of the school paper, Mom and Dad got excited. They always do, whenever I seem interested in anything that sounds academic. They couldn't have cared less when I won the game ball twice this year—I think it half embarrasses them that I'm good at sports—but they bubbled over for ten minutes about how working on the newspaper would broaden my horizons. They almost made me feel like not doing it.

"There's something else," I said. "We're going to this martial arts school tonight. If we decide to take classes there, it'll cost something. I don't know how much. Okay?"

I expected them to say "fine" right away. They always do. This time, Mom raised her eyebrows and glanced at Dad. He paused, helped himself to more bok choy, and smiled.

"Fine," he said. "Just make sure the school doesn't let things get too rough. I wouldn't want you to stay away from something you enjoy because of what happened Saturday, but safety's important."

"Maybe," Mom said, "we shouldn't decide till you find out what it costs."

"It can't be enough to make a difference, Rose," Dad said. "So, how's the new cashier doing?"

Mom's a manager at Wendy's World, this store that sells books and educational toys. She plays organ at our church, too, and gives piano lessons at night. Dad's a general contractor at Edson Construction, the biggest company in town. He takes charge of projects, everything from figuring out how much things cost to making sure people do what they're supposed to. It's an important job. Last month, he finished overseeing renovations at a building that used to be a shoe factory, turning it into an extra-classy pizza place. It looks good, and lots of my friends have said they like it.

"You know, Matt," Mom was saying, "you're welcome to invite your friends over after the class. I made a big batch of hummus today."

"Thanks," I said. "But I've got a math quiz tomorrow. I'd better study."

It's not like I'm embarrassed about having people over. Not exactly. But my parents *are* different from other people's parents. For one thing, they're older. Sometimes, people think they're my grandparents—Mom with her frizzy white hair clear down to her shoulders, Dad with his big glasses and bushy gray beard. When my friends come here, Mom keeps pushing them to try food nobody else's moms make, and Dad gets all jolly and asks them about their interests, places they've traveled, like it's a job interview. I know they're trying to be friendly, but it makes people uncomfortable. It makes me uncomfortable, too.

It felt good to get away. I picked up Berk and Joseph, and we arrived at the school right when Suzette was getting out of her father's car. She puffed out a sigh.

"You wouldn't *believe* what I had to go through to get here," she said. "My mom was totally *weeping*, going on and on about Coach Colson, saying I'd get killed if I came. I said, 'Mom, calm down. Take a pill.' Finally, she zoned out, and Dad drove me. But he's got a meeting, so he can't pick me up. Give me a ride home, Matt?"

"No problem," I said, and we went inside, where Graciana and Derrick stood waiting.

The place is bigger than it looks from outside. First comes an office, with a display of tee-shirts and water bottles, followed by locker rooms that are really just big bathrooms, with hooks for jackets and shelves for shoes. Next comes an exercise area, where people were warming up on treadmills and stationary bikes. In the gym itself, dark blue mats cover most of the floor, and big red-and-white signs hang on the walls—RESPECT, EFFORT, COURAGE, HUMILITY, INTEGRITY. At least they weren't stages of grief.

We spotted Aaron Roth and walked over to introduce ourselves. "I'm sorry about your coach," he said, shaking hands. "I met him at planning sessions for the tournament and liked him very much. What can I do for you?"

"We wanna keep learning tae kwon do," Derrick said. "So we're looking for a school. How much does yours cost?"

It sounded rude to ask about cost first, but Aaron Roth didn't seem to mind. "That's right. You don't have a teacher now. The other judges and I should've thought about that. Well, if you decide to take classes here, you can come free until the school year ends. Your club meetings would've ended then anyway, right? After that, if you want to keep coming, we'll work something out. If you want to stick with tae kwon do, though, come back tomorrow. Tae kwon do classes are Tuesdays and Thursdays. Mondays and Wednesdays are krav maga."

"I've read about that," Graciana said. "It's Israeli, right?"

"Right," he said. "You could use skills you've learned in tae kwon do, but there's a fundamental difference. Tae kwon do is essentially a sport. At least, that's how it's usually taught in the United States. Krav maga is a survival system. We emphasize countering attacks—avoiding them if possible, repelling them if necessary. It's all about learning how to protect yourself against people who don't play by the rules."

The image came back—Bobby Davis looking at Coach cold and steady, lifting his leg, slamming his foot against Coach's throat. Learning how to protect myself against someone who doesn't play by the rules didn't sound like a bad idea. "Could we keep the belts we earned in tae kwon do?"

"No belts in krav," he said. "Some schools have them, but we keep things simple. And no uniforms, no tournaments. Krav isn't about earning belts or winning trophies. It's about surviving attacks, even if the attacker is bigger and stronger and better armed."

Derrick was having a hard time taking everything in. "I never heard of 'krav mag-na.' How did some Israeli martial art end up in Ridgecrest?"

"No big mystery," Aaron Roth said. "My wife got offered a job at the veterinary clinic, this space was available, and we liked the town. Krav's spreading—it's getting more popular all over the country. There are classes in Lynchburg and Richmond, too. You could try a class tonight and then decide which art you'd rather study. Are you all sixteen or older?"

We nodded. "So you admit no children?" Joseph asked.

"Not in krav. We have kids' classes in tae kwon do, judo, karate. Those teach kids enough to protect themselves from schoolyard bullies. Adults need to learn how to protect themselves from knife attacks, gun attacks, people who want to kill them."

Again, that sounded right—at least, these days it did. I didn't feel great about putting aside the green belt, but I'd get back to it someday. "*I'd* like to try krav maga," I said.

"So would I," Graciana said, and the others nodded.

"Fine." He looked at his watch. "I'll have Linda start class while I give you a quick orientation. Let's head to the exercise area."

"What should we call you?" Berk asked. "Coach, Sensei, Mr. Roth?"

He grinned and peeled off his jacket. "Call me Aaron. First names only in krav. Now, let's get started."

Eight

Someone turned on a CD player, and "We're Not Gonna Take It" blared out. We all jumped.

Aaron grinned again. "We play loud music during class, except when we're giving instruction. It's partly to get our energy up, mostly because life's full of distractions. Focusing is easy when everything's calm and quiet. When things aren't so quiet, it's not so easy. Does anybody know what 'krav maga' means?"

"Is it 'close combat,'" Graciana asked, frowning, "or 'contact combat,' something like that?"

"Good," Aaron said. "It was developed by the Israeli army during and after the Second World War. It's a simple, practical system anyone can use—man or woman, young or old, fit or unfit. Obviously, the more fit you are, the better. Skill matters most, but endurance matters, too. If you can outlast a more skilled opponent, you improve your chances of surviving. So we begin class with twenty minutes of physical conditioning."

That sounded like the workouts the head basketball coach puts us through. He's a real gym rat—if there's anything he loves more than parading his biceps, it's making people run laps. With Coach Colson, we just limbered up for two minutes before getting started. That's one reason we all liked him.

"You can spend a lifetime improving your krav skills," Aaron said, "but you can learn the basics quickly. The system's designed to help civilians who aren't martial artists defend themselves. The goal is survival. If you go up against someone stronger, you'll probably get hurt. If you go up against someone with a knife, you'll probably get cut. That's okay. You can get a Band-Aid later. But if you keep your head and use the techniques, you might survive. I think the best way to show you is by demonstrating a weapon defense." He tossed Derrick a rubber gun. "You're Derrick, right?"

"Right." Derrick smirked, probably thinking this middle-aged guy wouldn't be a challenge.

"Point the gun at me," Aaron said, "but don't put your finger on the trigger—you might get hurt. Now, shout something scary."

"Something scary?"

"Yeah. 'Give me your wallet,' 'I'm gonna kill you,' something like that."

Derrick did a deep, bored sigh. "Give me your wallet," he said, flatly.

"Not much of a shout," Aaron said, "but okay."

He lifted his hands in the air and stepped closer, as if getting ready to hand over his wallet. Then, in about three seconds, he grabbed the gun, shouted, faked punches to Derrick's face, twisted around, wrenched the gun from his hand, and stood pointing it at him, face hard with warning. "Down on the ground!" he shouted, backing away. "Now, or I'll shoot!"

Derrick looked ready to do it. Then he caught himself. "Wow," he said.

The rest of us laughed nervously. This was more reality than we'd expected.

"Let's do that again," Aaron said, "and I'll explain what happened. If someone points a gun at you, you'll be tempted to back away. That's a natural reaction, but it's wrong. You can't back away so far a bullet won't hit you, and you can't take control unless you're close enough to grab the gun. So move in on the attacker. Since you've studied tae kwon do, you might be tempted to go into a fighting stance. That's wrong, too."

"So you stick your hands up?" Berk said. "That looks like you've given up."

"That's the point. If you take a fighting stance, you put your attacker on warning. In krav, putting your hands up is the ready position. It makes your attacker relax too much. Plus you can move more quickly. Now, the basic strategy for weapons defense is to deflect and take away. Derrick, point the gun at me and shout—*really* shout this time. We shout at each other a lot in krav, because most of us are usually around nice people who speak to us politely. When someone shouts, it can intimidate us. We've got to get used to not being scared when somebody shouts. Go ahead, Derrick."

Derrick looked nervous, but he did it. "Give me your wallet!" he yelled.

"Great." Aaron put his hands up. "Watch. I move toward him, grab the gun with my left hand, twist my body, and knock the gun to the side. Now it's deflected. Even if it goes off, the bullet won't hit me—it'll go into the ground." He did things in slow motion as he described them. "Now Derrick's off guard, and he's focused on the gun. It's time for me to get aggressive and keep him from being able to maneuver. So I'll shout to intimidate him and punch him in the face." He shouted and faked punches again, and Derrick flinched again.

"Next I reach down with my right hand," Aaron said, doing it, "and grab the gun, jerk my body to the left, and wrench the gun from him. That's the takeaway part of weapons defense." He went through the moves, and Derrick couldn't stop him. Aaron grabbed the gun and jumped back. "On the ground, or I'll shoot!"

Derrick lifted his hands and laughed. "You win."

Aaron shook his hand. "You can all learn to do that, and it won't take long. You just have to know what to do, and you have to practice until it becomes second nature and comes back to you in a crisis. Any questions? Okay. During conditioning, push hard, but don't hurt yourself. If you're reaching your limit, sit down and rejoin the class when you're rested. Don't be embarrassed—people do it all the time. If you're ready, shout 'yes, sir' and get out there."

"Yes, sir!" we shouted, and ran to the center of the gym.

Students were doing sit-ups. Some had paired off and sat facing each other, ankles hooked together. When they sat up, they slapped their hands against each other and shouted. I looked at Berk, and he nodded. It works. You can't fake it by not sitting up all the way, shouting gets your energy going, and you motivate each other. No way would I stop doing sit-ups before Berk did.

Next came jumping jacks, then laps. When conditioning ended, I felt exhausted. I've got to get back in shape, I thought. I've been too easy on myself since basketball ended.

"Form two circles," Aaron called, walking around with a big cardboard box. "Everyone take a gun or knife. One person stands in the center with no weapon, and the others attack that person one at a time. Don't go around the circle in order. Take the person by surprise. And the person in the center shouldn't use the same disarming technique every time. Mix it up. When I yell 'change,' someone else takes a turn in the center. New students, you're not ready to stand in the center, but attack all you like. Everybody ready? Go!"

A short, slender woman who looked about fifty stood in the center of our circle. People started rushing her one at a time, aiming their weapons, shouting, "Give me your money!" or "I'm gonna kill you!" She shouted back, disarming every one of them, always countering—throwing some people to the floor, forcing others to their knees, stopping others by faking punches, kicks, or elbow strikes. At first, I held back, feeling silly about charging a middle-aged woman. But what the hell.

I lifted my rubber knife. "Give me your money!" I shouted, and ran at her. Then I was on the floor, and she was holding the knife on me, yelling at me to stay down.

That's when I got into it. I charged to the center again and again, getting flipped over and forced to my knees and not-quite-hit. Nothing hurt, I liked seeing the different techniques people in the center used, and shouting felt good, like I was getting rid of feelings I'd held back since the tournament, almost like I was fighting back. It didn't matter that I always lost. Before long, if Aaron was right, I'd be ready to take a turn in the center. I was willing to bet that'd feel *really* good.

Joseph and Suzette were in my circle. Joseph took plenty of turns, breaking people up when he shouted, "I will now please have your wallet!" Suzette only watched. Maybe she felt scared. I could understand—the shouting, people rushing forward from all directions and getting thrown around, everything happening fast. She'll get used to it, I thought, and smiled, picturing dainty little Suzette charging someone with a rubber gun.

Aaron turned the music off and called us to the center. We dumped our weapons in the box and sat on the mats.

"I'll need someone to help me," Aaron said. "Maybe a new student?"

Might as well, I thought, and raised my hand.

"Matt, right?" Aaron said. "For this demonstration, to be extra safe, we'll use gloves."

He tossed me a pair. They were the same kind we'd used Saturday—smaller than regular boxing gloves, with fingers left uncovered for flexibility. Images from the tournament started coming back, but I shut them out. I wanted to focus on now.

"Let's talk about blocking punches," Aaron said. "If an attacker's a foot or more away, and you're expecting the punch, you've got plenty of options. Matt, show us something from tae kwon do."

I took a fighting stance, he threw a punch at my face, and I knocked it aside with my left arm.

"Good," he said. "But what if the attacker's very close, and the punch comes out of nowhere?"

With one quick movement, he stepped right up to me and threw another punch at my face. Even though he'd described what he was going to do, it caught me off guard. I jerked my head back and lifted an arm to protect my face.

"That won't work," he said. "I can knock your arm aside and punch you with my left hand. When you don't have enough time for a conventional block, use something else. Matt, this time you throw the punch."

I'm going to end up on the floor again, I thought. I stepped in close and threw the punch, and he brought both fists up in front of his face, keeping his elbows in. "This is like a boxing block," he said. "Don't close your eyes or turn your face away. Those are natural reactions, but if you flinch, you make yourself a victim. Keep your eyes on your attacker. Keep punching, Matt."

I punched his arms a few times. "I'm taking some hits to my arms," Aaron said. "If I get some bruises, who cares? The crucial thing is I'm watching him, waiting until he pulls his arm back slightly as he gets ready to punch again."

Right then, as I pulled my arm back, he reached underneath to trap it, so I couldn't punch anymore. Moving forward, he shouted "kadima!" again and again, faking strikes to my face with his right elbow, grabbing the back of my neck and pulling my head down. Then two fake knee strikes to my stomach, and he spun around and flipped me onto the mat.

"If those knee strikes had been full force," Aaron said, helping me up, "I would've knocked the air out of him. You okay, Matt?"

"Fine." I caught my breath. "Even without full force, you knocked out plenty of air."

People applauded, I sat down, and Aaron called two experienced students up, showing them how to use the block on each other. Then we paired up. My partner was a man in his thirties, almost as big as Derrick. He'd been taking krav for three years, but I could still block his punches and throw him when it was his turn to attack. That felt good.

Fifteen minutes later, class ended. No bowing-out ritual—instead, Aaron said, "Great job, everyone," and started applauding. We all joined in. Afterward, he stood by the door, saying goodnight as people headed out. "So," he said to us, "have you decided? Tae kwon do or krav?"

"I'd like to take krav maga," Graciana said. "I like tae kwon do, too, and I'm sure I'll study it again some day. Right now, krav seems more—practical."

The rest of us nodded, Suzette reluctantly. "It's nice of you to let us come for free until school ends," I said. "You're sure that's okay?"

Aaron shrugged. "Doesn't cost me anything to have you here. And you guys were left in a rough situation. I'm glad I can help."

"One question," Joseph said. "Many times, people shouted 'kadima.' What does this mean?"

"It's Hebrew," Aaron said. "It means 'forward.' We shout that to remind ourselves to keep moving in on our attacker. Good question, Joseph. I'll see you guys Wednesday."

When we got to the car, Suzette cried "shotgun," so Berk and Joseph got in back. The other guys and I talked maybe two hundred words a minute, reliving class. Suzette didn't say much, just agreeing with something now and then, laughing and slapping my shoulder when I made a joke.

"It *was* fun," she said eventually. "But I like tae kwon do better. And you've got a *green* belt, Matt. Isn't it hard to stop when you've made it so far? Don't you want to go for a black belt?"

"Someday," I said. "There are tae kwon do classes everywhere."

"I guess." She settled back, looking grumpy. When we dropped Joseph off, she perked up. "So we'll take Berk home next?"

"No, he lives on my street. We'll go to your house first. How do I find it?"

After she left, Berk moved to the front seat. "She likes you," he said.

"Who, Suzette?" I looked at him in surprise. "No. Of course not."

"Sure she does. Remember Saturday night, when she gushed about how brave you were for following Davis into the locker room? Tonight, she tried to talk you into sticking to tae kwon do, so you two could go to classes together while the rest of us take krav. And she wanted you to drop me off first, so she'd be alone in the car with you."

"No way," I said, but thought it over. Suzette Link. She's really pretty, really popular. I'd always figured she was out of my league. "You think so?"

"Yeah." He stared moodily into the darkness. "And it's okay with me. If you want to date her, go ahead."

It took a minute for that to sink in. "Damn. You mean *you* like Suzette?"

He sighed. "I thought it was obvious. I've been trying to catch her attention for months. But she barely looks me. I've given up. So it's fine for you to ask her out."

The idea of dating Suzette hadn't occurred to me until one minute ago. It hadn't seemed possible. Now, it definitely wasn't possible. "I'd never ask out a girl you like. Not in a million years."

"I told you, it's fine." I'd pulled into his driveway, and he opened his door right away, not looking at me. "She'll never notice me anyway. You *should* ask her out. I *want* you to."

He slammed the car door and practically ran to his porch. Not in a million years, I thought again. No matter what Berk said, he wouldn't like it. And I'd never risk our friendship for some girl.

But if Suzette actually liked me—damn.

I put it out of my head. When I got home, I gave my parents a two-sentence description of class, ate hummus to make Mom happy, and told Cassie sorry, I couldn't watch the cat video she'd found on YouTube—I had to study. In my room, I stared at one page for ten minutes before slapping my trig book shut. Basically, I knew this stuff, and Ms. Powell's quizzes are super easy.

Thoughts about Suzette crept back, and I shook my head to keep them out. Too much possibility for disaster. Besides, I had more important things to think about—the special issue of the newspaper, the burglary at Coach's apartment. And Bobby Davis.

I stood up. A quick, unexpected punch at close range, I thought. I put both fists up in front of my face. Don't close your eyes, I told myself. Don't flinch. I watched and waited. When the imaginary attacker pulled his arm back for another punch, I reached underneath, trapped his arm, moved forward, grabbed his neck, forced his head down, kneed him in the stomach, spun around, and threw him down.

I went through the moves twenty times, maybe more. Every time, the imaginary attacker had Bobby Davis' face.

Nine

On Tuesday, I got up early. Jumping jacks, sit-ups, push-ups, and a quick run—four blocks to the Methodist church, two laps around the parking lot, home again to shower and dress. When I came to the kitchen, Mom stood at the stove.

"Cassie's not going to school," she said. "She has a terrible headache. At least she's got an appetite. She asked for *pain perdu*, so I'm fixing you some, too."

Great, I thought. More weird food. But it's basically French toast, only lemony, with powdered sugar instead of syrup. "That was good, Mom," I said. "Tell Cassie I hope she feels better." I grabbed my books and headed out.

During homeroom, Dr. Lombardo made a public address announcement about the bake sale meeting. So after school, about forty people squeezed into Ms. Quinn's classroom—mostly girls, but a few guys from the basketball team. Not Paul Ericson, though. Too bad. Several teachers came, too, including Ms. Nguyen.

The person I was most surprised to see was Marie Ramsey, the goth-type girl who'd cried at the tournament. Naturally, she sat in the back row, hunched over her sketch book and drawing like crazy, her long black hair almost hiding her face.

She didn't speak to anyone; the few times she glanced up, she looked almost scared. She hates being here, I thought. She isn't comfortable around this many people. She must've really liked Coach, or she wouldn't have come. That must be why she'd come to the tournament, too, and why she'd cried so hard.

Ms. Quinn asked Graciana and me to lead the meeting. I talked for maybe a minute about why we were doing the bake sale. Then Graciana took over. She'd typed up sign-up sheets for committees, she'd made copies of a timeline about what we needed to accomplish by certain dates, and she led the discussion and answered questions. In half an hour, everything was settled.

While most people filed out, the martial arts club members moved up to the front row. Ms. Quinn sat down with us. She's relaxed-looking, not fat but definitely not thin, and she has short, curly hair, dark brown with lots of gray mixed in. As usual, her clothes looked rumpled and beige and loose, as if she doesn't feel like bothering to get the size exactly right and only cares about being comfortable. She congratulated us on a well-organized meeting, we settled some final details, and then Graciana said she, Berk, and I were planning a memorial issue. Joseph immediately offered to help; Derrick begged off, probably figuring he'd have to write something eventually.

Suzette sat turning a bright pink pen over and over in her hands, pursing her lips. "Would Graciana be in charge of the special issue?"

Graciana shrugged. "I'm the editor. But if you have suggestions, I—"

"Then I'll stick to helping with the bake sale," Suzette cut in.

Not subtle. Ms. Quinn cleared her throat. "Maybe Derrick and Suzette should be co-chairs for the bake sale, so the rest of you can concentrate on the special issue. My husband mentioned it last night, and I think it's a fine idea. When you interview people, be sure to include me."

"Thanks," Graciana said. "The four of us could meet tomorrow to make other plans. In the library, after school?"

"I'll probably be a little late," I said, "but I'll be there." If I didn't show my face at the chemistry review session, Mr. Quinn would give me a hard time. But I wanted to help tell Joseph about our real reasons for doing the memorial issue.

The meeting broke up. When I walked out to the parking lot with Graciana and Berk, there was Marie Ramsey standing right outside the door, pressing her back against the wall like she was trying to blend into it. She spotted us and walked over to Graciana.

"Here." She thrust out her hand, showing us a rumpled ten-dollar bill. "For the bake sale."

"We haven't talked about taking cash donations," Graciana said. "Maybe you could use the money to buy baking supplies. Did you sign up for a committee?"

Marie shook her head. "I can't be on a committee. And I don't know how to bake."

"You could ask your mom to bake something," Berk said. "My mom's going to."

"My mom doesn't bake. Nina did. Every year, she baked a cake for my birthday." Marie looked at Graciana. "It was nice of you to come to the funeral. Not many people from school did."

"I wanted to be there," Graciana said. "I didn't know your sister well, but we were in the same German class last year. I liked her sense of humor."

"So did I." Marie held out the money again. "Will you take it?"

"Sure," Graciana said. "Thanks. I bet other people will want to make donations, too. I'll start a list of names and—"

"Don't put my name on a list," Marie said. "Don't tell anyone." She practically ran to the other end of the lot, hugging her books, keeping her head down. A guy was waiting for her there, just over six feet, broad shoulders, standing next to a battered red Mustang, his hands on his hips. He said something to her, she said something back, he lifted a hand in the air, and she flinched and got in the car. He stood there another minute, staring at us. Then he got in the car, too, and they drove away.

"Wow," Berk said. "She *must* be on drugs."

"I don't think that's how people on drugs act," Graciana said. "She's in mourning. Nina was barely a year older than she is, and I think they were very close."

"Yeah, having your sister jump off a bridge—that'd be hard to take." Berk lowered his voice. "The whole family's messed up. People say her mom's a drunk, her dad's always in and out of prison, and her brother—"

"People say lots of things," Graciana cut in, then paused. "It's hard to tell what's true, and normally I'd say it's none of our business. But Marie's father *is* in prison, for stealing a truck and some tools. It's not his first conviction, so he'll probably be there a while. He had to come to his daughter's funeral in handcuffs and leg irons. I'm sure that was hard on Marie— I'm sure lots of things are hard on her right now. Maybe we should all look for ways to be friendlier to her."

Berk looked like he wasn't crazy about the idea. To tell the truth, neither was I. But I knew Graciana was right.

"Sure," I said, and Berk nodded.

On the drive home, Berk and I talked about the memorial issue, about krav, about the chemistry quiz. We didn't say one word about Suzette. But it was like we both knew we weren't talking about her. Someone listening in might've thought it was a normal conversation, but it wasn't, not for Berk and me. I hadn't even asked her out, and already things between us had changed.

At dinner, Cassie seemed fine, asking for seconds on frittata and saying the *haricot verts* tasted *très bon*. When Dad asked how she felt, though, she said she still had an awful headache and probably shouldn't go to school tomorrow. Cassie's the last person on Earth who'd ditch school. She loves school. And she'd never had a headache that lasted two days. She almost never has headaches at all. I hoped she didn't have something serious.

"You should work at getting rid of this headache, Cassie," Mom said. "Don't stay up late tonight, and don't spend the whole evening reading. Do something that'll let you rest your eyes."

Cassie looked around the table hopefully. "Maybe we could all play charades."

Yeah, or maybe we could take turns jamming toothpicks under our fingernails. I didn't know which I'd hate more. "I have to study," I said. "I've got a chemistry quiz Friday."

"I could help," Cassie said. "I could make flash cards or drill you on vocab or—"

"Thanks, but Mom says you should rest your eyes." I smiled at her and stood up. "I'd better go hit the books."

That was close, I thought as I headed upstairs. True, escaping from charades and Cassie-Plays-Teacher meant missing dessert, but I didn't mind. Mom had said she'd made something called *flan*, and I didn't like the sound of that.

Ten

"I was afraid you wouldn't make it," Graciana said.

I slid into a chair at the library table, between Berk and Joseph. "Sorry. I'd planned to sneak out sooner, but whenever I tried, Mr. Pavlakis spotted me and asked me a question I couldn't answer. Have you told Joseph about Richmond, and about Mrs. Dolby?"

"Yes," Joseph said. "And I agree the special newspaper is suitable to do for Mr. Colson. But will it lead to an explanation of his death?"

"We're just gathering all the information we can," I said, "hoping something will click into place. And we're hoping if something was bothering Coach, he told someone he liked, and that person will tell us."

Berk sighed. He made a big deal of it—breathing in loud and yanking his shoulders up to his ears, huffing out hard, plunging his shoulders deep. "That's a hell of a lot to hope for. We'll just waste time talking to people who don't know anything."

"Not necessarily." Graciana hesitated, then went ahead. "The fact is, when there's a murder, unless it's a drive-by shooting or something, it usually turns out someone close to the victim was involved."

"We'll be talking to students and teachers at Ridgecrest High," Berk said. "You think someone at Ridgecrest High could be involved in a *murder*?"

"I know it sounds unlikely," Graciana said. "But think about the news reports you see when someone's arrested for murder. The neighbors always say, 'He seemed so nice. She seemed so friendly.' Probably, the person *was* nice and friendly, most of the time. But even nice, friendly people can get drawn into a murder if they're greedy enough, or scared enough, or angry enough."

Berk laughed, but it didn't sound natural. It sounded like he was forcing it, because he wanted to prove how dumb we were being. "Ms. Nguyen!" he said. "I knew it! Bobby Davis is her secret lover. She pretended to like Coach and got him to write a will leaving her all his millions. Then she got Davis to kill him so that she'll inherit everything, and she and her sweetie will spend the rest of their lives living in a mansion on an island somewhere."

Berk's my best friend, but sometimes he does a pretty good impression of a five-year-old. "Cut it out," I said. "Graciana's making good points. And maybe interviewing Coach's friends isn't a perfect plan, but what else can we do?"

"Perhaps," Joseph said, "we could find the lawyer."

"What lawyer?" I asked, and immediately felt like an idiot. Oh, yeah—*that* lawyer.

"Do you not remember, Matt?" Joseph said. "After the tournament, you heard Bobby Davis talking on the phone, asking someone to get him a lawyer. Later, Graciana's parents saw Davis in the parking lot with someone they thought was a lawyer. Michael Burns—was that not the name, Graciana? Very probably, if someone else was involved in the murder, this was the person Davis called, and this person then called the lawyer. So if we ask Mr. Burns who called him, we will know who else might have been involved."

I smacked my forehead and slid my hand down to cover my eyes. Could it really be that simple? I spread my fingers apart and looked at Graciana. "Would that work?"

She shook her head. "Burns won't tell us anything. Lawyers have to be careful about confidentiality. And asking him could be dangerous. When we talked to Dr. Lombardo Monday, she mentioned a lawyer who's advised the school. I bet you anything she meant Burns. During my sophomore year, he helped the school avoid a lawsuit when a rookie football player was injured during a hazing incident. If we call him, he might tell Lombardo, and then we'd be in real trouble. She warned us not to do any investigative reporting about Coach's death."

"So where does that leave us?" I asked.

Graciana sighed. "I don't know. And the library's closing soon, and we've got krav tonight. Should I ask my parents if we could meet at my house tomorrow at seven and talk more? Would that work for you guys? Great." She grabbed her books and left.

"Graciana proceeds with efficiency," Joseph said.

"That's one way to put it," I said. "Want a ride home?"

Joseph accepted, but Berk said he felt like walking. It's over a mile—he doesn't usually feel like walking that much. Then, right before dinner, he called. I didn't need to give him a ride to krav tonight, he said, because he had to work on the English essay due next week. I know Berk. He never works on essays until the night before they're due.

"Are you sure?" I said, and paused. "Is this about Suzette?"

"No," he said, but the starch in his voice told me it was. "I couldn't care less about her."

"Okay. But if it *is* about Suzette, I told you, I won't ask her out. I'm not even sure she likes me. If she does, it's not my fault. I've never done anything to encourage her."

"*Sure* you haven't," he said, and hung up.

That's not fair, I thought. I know he's hurting, but he's got no reason to act like I've betrayed him or something.

Seconds later, Suzette texted me, asking if I could drive her to krav. That means I'll drive her home, too, I thought. And since Berk's skipping class, I'll be alone with her after we drop Joseph off. Maybe I should avoid that. Then I remembered how unfair Berk was being. I texted her back: No problem.

At dinner, I found out Mom had taken Cassie to the doctor, and he said she seemed fine and could go to school tomorrow. Good. I smiled at her, but she didn't smile back, just kept picking at her broccolini couscous. Well, I'm no fan of broccolini couscous, either. She'd feel better once she got back to school and spent time with her friends.

I picked Suzette up and immediately launched into talking about the bake sale, not letting her steer the conversation toward anything personal. I tried not to notice how nice she looked in a black tank top and jeans that were probably too tight for sit-ups.

Class was intense. Twenty minutes of jumping jacks, push-ups, and running laps felt like forty. Aaron turned the music off.

"Let's talk about hostage situations," he said. "A killer's trying to get away and grabs you, using you as a human shield to keep the police from shooting. He's got a gun. If he escapes, he'll kill again, starting with you. What do you do? Joseph, grab a rubber gun, get behind me, and hook your left arm around my neck. Move in close, so I can't get away. With your right hand, point the gun at all those imaginary police officers out there."

Joseph did it, and Aaron raised his hands. "Now my hands are in the ready position. Joseph thinks I won't resist. And he thinks he's safe, because the police can't shoot him without hitting me. He seems to have an insurmountable advantage. But there's always a defense. Watch."

With his left hand, Aaron grabbed the barrel of the gun, forcing it down. "See? That's the deflecting part. Even if the gun goes off, the bullet will go into the ground. The takeaway comes next. Notice that when I grabbed the gun with my left hand, my right hand went down. Now I swing my right fist up to strike Joseph's wrist—his gun hand's being twisted from two directions, so I can wrench the gun away. Next I turn my body to break away from his arm, and I shove him with my shoulder. That's it. I'm free, and I've got the gun. I back away at a forty-five-degree angle, keeping the gun pointed at Joseph. I'm out of the line of fire, so the police can shoot him if necessary. But he'll probably give up, and they'll move in and arrest him."

"Should you not yell?" Joseph asked. "Should you not threaten to shoot?"

"I'll let the police handle that. I'm only the hostage. I've got your gun, so I can provide backup if necessary. But chances are, once you're handcuffed, I'll simply give the police your gun, go home, and wait for my Good Citizen commendation to come in the mail. Let's go through that again."

When Aaron told us to pair up, I saw Graciana sitting nearby. "Want to try it?" I asked. She nodded, and I ran to get a gun.

It wasn't until I'd stood behind her and hooked my arm around her neck that I realized how awkward this could get. Aaron walked around the room, calling out instructions.

"Attackers, get a good grip on your hostages," he said. "Don't make things easy for them. Matt, move in closer to Graciana."

I moved in, my body pressing against hers. She looked great tonight, even in sweat pants and a baggy orange tee-shirt. She'd had her hair tucked into a loose knot, but it'd come undone while we ran laps. It fell over her shoulders now, brushing against my face. Its soft, warm smell reminded me of honey.

Damn. I felt like a pervert, getting turned on by my partner during a martial arts lesson. Focus, I told myself. I imagined a line of cops facing me and lifted my arm.

Graciana glanced at my hand. "Take your finger off the trigger, Matt. I don't want to hurt you when I grab the gun."

What a dumb mistake. At least I was standing behind her, so she couldn't see me blush.

She didn't have any trouble forcing the gun down, knocking my arm away, twisting the gun from two directions and pointing it at me as she backed off at an angle. She smiled.

"You're going to jail, mister. Better call a lawyer. I can recommend a tall, thin, bald one."

"You'll never take me alive!" I clutched my chest like I'd been shot and flopped down on the mat—dumb, but if she noticed I was out of breath, she'd think it was because I'd hit the floor too hard.

We kept practicing for ten minutes. It was easier when I played the hostage and could focus on the technique, not on how good her hair smelled. Then Aaron called us together again and demonstrated a grappling technique to use if an attacker pinned us to the floor. When we practiced that one, I made sure to pair up with Joseph.

Afterward, back in the car, Joseph said something about looking forward to working on the memorial issue, and Suzette let out a snort. She's the kind of girl who can make even a snort sound cute.

"I bet Graciana's looking forward to it, too," she said. "A special issue of the paper—she'll have to put in lots of late-night sessions with Mr. Bixby. You know, one of my friends goes to the same church as Mr. Bixby's family, and she says he's stopped coming to services with his wife and kids. People are wondering if they've split up."

"That has no necessary basis," Joseph said. "Perhaps he is simply not religious."

Suzette smiled wisely. "You always want to explain things away. Now, I don't know if he's actually moved out, or if they're still thinking about it. And I don't know for sure it's because of Graciana. But if Mrs. Bixby *does* know about her, that can't be helping." She sighed. "Those poor kids!"

I couldn't let that go. "Look, we don't know what's going on. Graciana and Mr. Bixby are both interested in newspapers, and they probably like each other, but maybe they haven't—done anything."

Suzette gave me a sad little smile. "You're sweet. And I hope you're right. Maybe it's a coincidence Mr. Bixby's marriage is in trouble. I like Graciana. I'd hate to think—let's not talk about it anymore. Did you guys hear we might finally get a lacrosse team? My dad's pushing for one."

After we dropped Joseph off, Suzette started talking about this movie she wanted to see, about how her friends said it was funny but also had good action scenes. She was *dying* to see it, she said. But she hated going to movies alone.

After that, it'd be almost rude not to suggest going together. Besides, I wanted to see the movie, too, and if we went with a group, it wouldn't be a date. Maybe I could talk Berk into coming. "If you want, we could go this weekend. Maybe some of the other guys—"

"I think everybody's already seen it. But I'd *love* to go with you, Matt. And my grandparents gave me an Olive Garden gift card for my birthday, and it's enough for two. So we can have dinner before the movie. Saturday night?"

Just the two of us, dinner and a movie, Saturday night. I guess you'd have to call that a date. Berk must be right. She *did* like me. And an Olive Garden gift card sounded like a strange present for her grandparents to give her. I half-suspected she'd buy the card herself tomorrow, to make it official we were dating now.

A few hours ago, I'd told Berk I wouldn't ask her out. I hadn't, not exactly. But good luck getting Berk to believe that.

I glanced at Suzette. She practically glowed, her big blue eyes dancing with light, her hair a soft gold cloud around her face. God, she was pretty. And she was happy, just because she was going out with me.

It made me feel good to think a girl like Suzette could get so excited about that. Yes, she'd almost tricked me into it, and she'd probably lied about the gift card. Probably, that should irritate me. It didn't. I felt flattered, and I thought it was cute.

And suddenly I didn't much care if Berk believed me when I tried to explain. If he wanted to keep being a jerk, if he wanted to throw our friendship away for no reason, I couldn't stop him. If he got over it and started being reasonable again, good. If not, I'd survive. I was glad I'd asked Suzette out.

Eleven

We sat in Graciana's basement family room, demolishing the cinnamon-sugar butter cookies her mom had made, talking.

"So now we do what?" Joseph asked. "You said Burns will not speak of who called him, because it breaks confidence. Is all hopeless?"

Graciana lifted a shoulder. "Probably. We could find an excuse to see him—we could say we're writing profiles of Ridgecrest High graduates, for the anniversary. But I don't see how we could weave in questions about Davis and trick Burns into telling us anything."

"So we'll be straight with him." Berk sat forward, face hard with determination, knees bouncing. "We'll explain why we think Davis killed Coach on purpose, and why the person who called him might be involved."

I shook my head. "We couldn't even get Mr. Quinn to take us seriously—why would a lawyer who's never seen us before? And if Burns thinks we're stirring up rumors that'd hurt the school, he'll call Dr. Lombardo."

"So you're saying we shouldn't even try?" Berk said. "That's stupid."

"No, Matt's right," Graciana said. "Lawyers aren't exactly eager to hand out information that might implicate their clients. Talking to Burns would be taking a big risk with practically no chance of success. So let's push ahead with the memorial issue."

Joseph nodded slowly. "I agree. Cautiousness can frustrate, but often is wise."

He shot a smile at Berk, but Berk didn't even look at him. He threw himself back on the couch, folded his arms across his chest, and stared at the wall.

Graciana picked up a yellow pad. "I made a list of people to interview. I think we should work in pairs, so both people can compare their impressions. Matt and Berk can be one pair, and Joseph and I—"

"I'll work with Joseph," Berk cut in. "*You* take Matt."

She looked surprised, then erased what she'd written. "Okay. Berk and Joseph, Matt and me. Let's split up interviews. The head basketball coach—that's an important interview, and both Berk and Joseph are on the basketball team and know him well. Matt and I can take Ms. Quinn. Dr. Lombardo— another important interview. Berk, can you and Joseph handle that? Matt and I will take Ms. Nguyen. Next, Paul Ericson, captain of the basketball team. A *very* important interview. Berk, you and Joseph—"

"No," Berk said. "You take that one."

I rubbed my hand across my mouth to hide a smile. Months ago, Berk had been late to practice twice, Paul had chewed him out in front of the whole team, and Berk had never forgiven him. I understood how Berk felt. Paul should've taken Berk aside—that's what I would've done. On the other hand, Berk had never been late again. Things like that are hard to call.

Graciana sped through the list, assigning one person to Berk and Joseph, one to her and me, not seeming to follow any pattern. "We can talk to them at school or at their homes," she said, "or wherever they feel most comfortable. I can usually borrow a car when I need to, and it seems like Matt can, too. What about you, Joseph? Berk?"

Joseph's head slumped. "I do not yet have a license. My mother says before I attempt the test, I must increase practice. She has reasons. Often, when it reverses, the car does not go where I wish."

"And my mom's stingy with her car," Berk says. "So no, I can't always get it."

In fact, he wasn't getting it at all these days, not since he'd flattened a mailbox two weeks ago. His mom had taken his driving privileges away for a month. I didn't blame him for not wanting to mention that.

"Well, interview people at school, then," Graciana said. "Next, let's draw up a list of questions."

We all nodded. There's no stopping Graciana once she gets going. I didn't disagree with anything she'd said, but sometimes she makes me feel like I'm on a bike, trying to keep up with a train.

"We'll start with softball questions," she said. "That's standard interview procedure. We'll ask about Coach Colson's contributions to the school, why he was special, what their favorite memories of him are. Then, when they're relaxed, we slide in tougher questions."

"These tougher questions," Joseph asked, "what are they?"

Graciana sat back. "*That's* a tough question. We want to find out if Coach mentioned a conflict with anyone or said someone threatened him, but we can't ask about that straight out. If we do, people will think it's strange. We need questions that will get at the information in a less obvious way."

I shrugged. "We could lie a little. We could talk about how upbeat Coach always was and then say, 'Lately, though, he seemed down, like something was troubling him. Did you notice that?' Maybe that'd get people talking."

Berk half-snorted. "How would it get people talking? It isn't even true. Did Coach ever tell *you* he was feeling down?"

God, Berk can be annoying. I strained to keep my voice calm. "I *said* it was a lie. I'm hoping Coach told other people more than he told us. Maybe telling this lie will make people open up about the truth."

"An oxymoronic approach," Joseph said, "yet it might work."

I didn't have anything to say to that. Neither did Berk. He probably didn't know what "oxymoronic" means, either.

Graciana nodded. "I agree. We'll try that. Any other ideas?"

Berk's turn to shrug. "We could say, 'Most people thought Coach Colson was a great guy. Do you know any trouble he ever got into?'"

That wouldn't work, I thought, but didn't say it. I didn't want Berk to think I was criticizing his idea because he'd criticized mine.

"That wouldn't work," Graciana said. "People aren't going to give us negative information to put in the newspaper. They'd be afraid of making people mad."

"Maybe," I said, "we could say, 'Tell us one thing about Coach Colson that most people would be surprised to hear.'"

Berk did his half-snort again. "*That's* brilliant. You think someone's gonna say, 'Well, most people would be surprised to hear he once did something that made Bobby Davis hate him? That Bobby Davis had an obvious reason to kill him'? Give me a break!"

I was too mad to say anything. Graciana and Joseph stared at him. Then Graciana spoke, quietly. "Obviously Matt doesn't think anyone would say that. But most people will naturally start by saying how friendly and helpful Coach was. This question might make them move beyond that. We might learn things we don't know yet, and that's the point of doing interviews."

"Fine." Berk looked off to the side. "I guess everybody has good ideas except me."

Joseph's cell phone rang, and he glanced down. "Apologies. My mother."

He spoke to her in another language—Swahili, he'd told me once—and closed his phone. "Additional apologies. She must attend a meeting and wishes me to stay with my sisters. She is coming to drive me home." He stood up.

Berk stood, too. "Can she drop me off? Then I won't have to call my mom for a ride."

"Come off it, Berk," I said. "You don't have to call her anyway. I'll give you a ride."

"I'd rather leave now. Thank your mom for the cookies, Graciana."

He shot upstairs without looking at any of us. Joseph paused awkwardly, lifted both hands to face level, praised the cookies, and left.

Now it was just Graciana and me. After we came up with several more questions, she said she'd type them up, make copies, and schedule interviews. She paused.

"I don't know Paul Ericson well, and you probably see him all the time. Could you set that interview up?"

I didn't see Paul often, actually, now that basketball season was over, but I didn't mind. "Sure." I stood up. "Those were great cookies. Thank your mom for me?"

"Sure." She picked up the empty plate. "Did you and Berk have a fight?"

"Not exactly. He's mad at me about something, but he'll get over it."

"I hope so." She paused. "Matt, do you think the interview teams are okay? Maybe you should work with Joseph, and I should work with Berk."

I laughed. "So you don't want to work with me, either. Mr. Popularity—that's me."

"It's not that. But I'd been thinking you should be on one team, and I should be on the other, to make sure all the interviews get done right. God, that sounds conceited. But Berk's resisting the whole idea of doing interviews, and Joseph has language issues. He might miss some nuances."

I laughed again. "Maybe I'm the one with language issues. Joseph probably knows what 'nuances' are. I don't."

She laughed, too. "Okay. I'm sure they'll do fine. Anyway, you and I probably have all the important interviews."

"Sorry," I said. "I must've missed a nuance. Why are ours more important?"

She blushed. "Because I manipulated the lists. I gave us the people Coach Colson was closest to, and I assigned the people who aren't likely to say anything helpful to Berk and Joseph. I tried not to be obvious about it."

"You weren't. It slid right past me. You kept talking about how important their interviews are."

Graciana grimaced. "They're interviewing important *people*. But Lombardo won't reveal anything—she's too slick, too focused on protecting her image. And I never got the impression Coach Colson and Coach Tomlinson were close. Is that right?"

"It's right," I said, amazed she'd noticed. "Tomlinson never showed Coach Colson much respect, never let him make decisions—he treated him like an amateur, maybe because he taught social studies instead of phys ed. I don't think Coach Colson liked him much."

"That's what I thought." She looked pleased with herself. "Tomlinson will just spout clichés about teamwork. I figured that was a throwaway interview. *We've* got the ones that count."

As I drove home, I felt bowled over by how sharp Graciana is about picking up on things, how subtle she is about managing things. I'd known she was smart, but this was—well, sneaky. I had to admit it was probably better she and I had the more important interviews. But she'd manipulated all three of us, and we'd never realized she was doing it. Sometimes, I felt close to Graciana. Other times, I felt like I never knew what was going on in her head. It threw me off.

I drove past Berk's house. There's something else that's throwing me off, I thought. For years, Berk and I had hung out together, stood up for each other, talked about stuff we didn't talk about with anybody else. Having him treat me like an enemy was messing me up.

Hell, I decided. I hate this. I drove back to his house and rang the doorbell. Mrs. Widrig seemed surprised to see me.

"Sorry it's so late," I said. "Can I talk to Berk for a minute?"

"Of course. But weren't you with him at Graciana's house?"

Berk must not have told her we weren't getting along. Well, I hadn't told my parents, either. "This is about something that happened after he left. Okay if I go to his room?"

She said fine, and I raced up the stairs I'd raced up probably thousands of times before. Berk's door was open, so I walked in. He was at his desk, playing some online game.

"Berk, this is stupid," I said. "We've gotta talk it out."

He didn't look away from the screen. "Yeah? You wanna talk about your big date with Suzette Saturday night?"

Damn. "How'd you hear about it so fast?"

"It's all over school. Plus Suzette posted it on Facebook. Dinner and a movie. Sounds nice. I thought you weren't going to ask her out."

I sat on his bed. "I wasn't, but I got mad at you, for being so mad at me. And if you want the truth, *she* pretty much asked *me* out. So you must've been right—she must like me. I'm sorry that hurts your feelings, but we've gotta find a way to deal with it."

He turned in his chair to face me. "Do you like her?"

I lifted my shoulders. "I'd never thought about her that way before. I mean, she's pretty, she's friendly, but I've never had special feelings for her."

He winced. "Maybe you'll get 'special feelings' Saturday night."

"I might. I might not. Either way, we can't let this ruin everything. We've been friends too long."

"I know." He let out a sigh. "I've felt lousy, too. I know I'm being a jerk. I know you can't help it if she likes you. But I can't stop feeling mad. It's stupid."

"It's not. If it'd happened the other way around, I'd feel mad, too. But let's try to get past that. Why don't we do something tomorrow night?"

He winced again. "Dinner and a movie?"

Not much of a joke, but it was the first friendly thing he'd said since Monday. "Maybe not. We can hang out, watch TV, whatever. If you feel like yelling at me, go ahead. If you wanna take a swing at me—"

"No way. You know too many defenses."

I grinned. "You should've come to krav last night. We learned some good ones. How about it? Want to do something tomorrow night?"

He thought it over. "Yeah. And I know what I wanna do.

97

I wanna go back to Richmond, to the bar where Davis hangs out. I wanna park across the street, watch for him, follow him, see where he goes. These interviews—maybe none of these people knows anything that'll help. Davis does. I wanna get things moving. How does that sound?"

Going to that neighborhood on a Friday night, hanging around that bar, following a killer—it sounded like the dumbest idea I'd heard in a long time. But I hated to say no right when Berk was starting to act normal again. "It sounds risky. We could ask Graciana if—"

"No. She'll try to talk us out of it, or she'll take over, like she does with everything. If we do this, it's gotta be just you and me. We don't tell Graciana, or Joseph, or anybody. Okay?"

I didn't like it. But if we didn't get out of the car, how dangerous could it be? And I needed to make things right with Berk. "Okay," I said.

Twelve

Graciana works fast. She caught up with me before lunch on Friday and said she'd arranged for us to interview Ms. Quinn after school.

"That's the list of questions," Graciana said, handing me a typed sheet. "Let's take turns asking them. You want odd-numbered questions or even-numbered ones?"

I didn't have time to figure out which questions felt more comfortable, but if I picked even, she'd have to go first. "Even," I said.

"Fine," she said, and was gone.

In the cafeteria, I spotted Paul Ericson sitting with his girlfriend, Carolyn Olson, and a couple of her friends. Paul and Carolyn had been homecoming king and queen, and they were a sure bet to be king and queen at prom, too. Girls gush about how handsome Paul is, and as for Carolyn, "pretty" doesn't cover it. She's the same type as Suzette—great hair, great body, really sweet face with big, sparkly blue eyes—only more so. The few times I'd talked to her, I hadn't even tried to make eye contact. I'd just concentrated on not drooling.

I walked over to their table and did the what's-going-on, nothing-much routine. Carolyn gave me a full-wattage smile.

"Looking for advice on how to be a good team captain?" she said. "I've heard lots of talk about you."

I blushed. I couldn't help it. Probably, almost anything she said to me would make me blush. "I don't take that seriously. I wanted to ask Paul about something else. Some members of the martial arts club are helping Graciana Cortez with a special issue of the school newspaper, a tribute to Coach Colson. We'd like to interview you, since you're captain."

Paul frowned. "An interview? What kinds of questions?"

"About what made him special, favorite memories, like that. Would some time this weekend work, or after school next week? It'll take about fifteen minutes."

Paul ran a hand through his hair. "I don't know. I wouldn't have much to say. I wasn't all that close with him. Ryan Croft probably knew him better, or Sean—"

Carolyn gave him a playful little slap on the arm. "What are you *talking* about? Those guys didn't know him *half* as well as you did. You're the *captain*. You *should* do an interview. You'll have *lots* to say. Will there be a picture?"

"There could be," I said. "I guess."

"There should *definitely* be a picture." Now Carolyn was rubbing Paul's arm, tilting her head, smiling up at him, trying to get him to look at her. "A *big* picture, on the front page."

"I've had my picture in the school paper before. It's no big deal." He stared down at the table. "Look, I'm gonna pass. I'm awful busy. My folks dumped a bunch of extra chores on me, and—"

"That's *perfect*." Carolyn gave me another one of those smiles. "Paul's parents told him he has to work on the lawn at the lake house on Sunday, to get it ready for summer. It'll take him the whole afternoon, and he'll *have* to take breaks. You can interview him there. You know where it is, don't you?"

"Sure." It's a great place. Paul's parents have the team over for a cookout every fall.

Paul shook his head. "I shouldn't make Matt drive all that way."

"All that way!" Carolyn slapped his arm again. "It's twenty minutes, silly. It's *nothing*. Matt doesn't mind—do you, Matt?"

"No," I said. It's closer to forty minutes, but I didn't feel like disagreeing with Carolyn about anything. "We don't mind."

"We?" Paul looked up. "Who else would come? Berk?"

"No, Graciana," I said.

One of Carolyn's friends perked up. "Ooh, Graciana. Maybe Carolyn doesn't like *that* so much."

Carolyn gave her a sour look. "I'm not worried. Let Mrs. Bixby worry. *My* man doesn't go for that type. Paul, if you don't do the interview, people will think it's strange."

He gave up. "Fine. Whatever. Sunday afternoon at the lake house, fifteen minutes."

"Great. Thanks." I took off. It was weird Paul hadn't wanted to do the interview. Coach had treated him almost like an equal, more than a kid, and Paul always talked how great he was. But maybe Paul was worried he'd get too emotional.

Anyway, Carolyn sure had him wrapped around her little finger. As I got my food, I grinned, thinking about it. It must be great having someone that gorgeous as a girlfriend—but since it was Carolyn, it must be rough, too. Carolyn's father is a pastor, and she's signed some pledge about saving her first kiss for the altar. She definitely wasn't saving flirting for the altar, though. I thought of all the arm-rubbing and smiles and playful little slaps. And they'd been going with each other for about two years, and I'd heard she didn't think they should get married till they graduated from college. Over four more years of having her paw at him without even giving him a kiss—man. Paul must be a strong guy.

Then I thought about what Carolyn and her friend had said about Graciana, and I stopped grinning. So Suzette wasn't the only one who thought something was going on between Graciana and Mr. Bixby. Seniors were talking about it, too, and they were the ones who'd know Graciana best. I'd been hoping maybe Suzette was wrong, but chances didn't look good.

After school, I headed for our first interview. Ms. Quinn's classroom is like her—nice, but basic. Some teachers must spend hours on their bulletin boards, hunting for pictures and tacking up borders and figuring out the best way to arrange everything. Then, every month or so, they take all their bulletin boards down and put up new ones. Ms. Nguyen is like that, and so was Coach Colson. I had Ms. Quinn for social studies freshman year, and her bulletin boards never change: a map of the United States, a map of Virginia, and laminated posters about the Declaration of Independence and how a bill becomes a law. She's a great teacher, but you can tell there are things she doesn't feel like fussing about.

Including how she looks. When she sat down with Graciana and me, her clothes were baggy and rumpled, as usual, and her hair looked like she'd lost her comb a week ago. "So," she said, "what can I tell you about Mr. Colson?"

We went through the first few questions, the ones Graciana had described as "softball," and Ms. Quinn told some great stories. Several times, her eyes misted up, and her voice quivered, but then she'd give her shoulders a shake and say something funny or sarcastic. When Graciana asked her to name one thing that made Coach Colson special, she got misty again.

"He cared about every single student." She paused, pushed her lips together, and did the shoulder-shake thing. "I know.

That's a cliché. Whenever you praise teachers, you say they care about students. Most do—some of us more than others, and some of us get bitter, but most really do care. Randy—Mr. Colson—took things to a different level. He was determined to reach every student, and he never gave up. That was partly because he was new, of course. It was partly naïveté. But it was also something deeper. Sometimes, he'd get frustrated because a student wasn't doing well, and he'd ask for advice. And sometimes I'd say that it was hopeless, that I knew the student and knew no one could help. He never accepted that. He always kept trying, and sometimes he succeeded more than I'd thought anyone could, because he kept trying when any sensible teacher would've given up."

"That's wonderful," Graciana said. "Could you give us an example?"

Ms. Quinn laughed. "Could I give you a name you can put in the newspaper? No. I don't think anyone would enjoy being singled out as a student most teachers consider hopeless. Let's leave it vague."

I thought of Marie Ramsey. She's the kind of student most teachers might think of as a loser. That's how I'd always thought of her. But I remembered how Marie would be sitting in the back row, silent, staring at the floor, and sometimes Coach would ask her a question. She always knew the answer. She'd mumble so low you could hardly hear, but she always knew. Then he'd compliment her and try to draw her out some more, and sometimes she'd whisper a comment that was actually pretty sharp. Maybe that's why she'd liked him, I thought, because most people, including me, wrote her off as weird, but Coach never gave up on her. And after he was killed, maybe she'd cried because the only person who'd believed in her was gone.

"So," Graciana said, "Mr. Colson was exceptional because he was so dedicated to his students."

"Yes," Ms. Quinn said, and paused. "Of course, it's possible to be *too* dedicated. I had to caution him about that, remind him about the dangers of the Anne Sullivan Syndrome."

"The Anne Sullivan Syndrome?" Graciana frowned. "Helen Keller's teacher? *The Miracle Worker?*"

"A-plus," Ms. Quinn said. "Lots of teachers start out thinking they'll be like Anne Sullivan—utterly devoting themselves to their students, spending every moment thinking about ways to help them, working miracles. Helen Keller probably needed that sort of devotion. But most students aren't blind and deaf. They need us to care about them, yes, but they also need space. If we try to protect them from every mistake, we smother them. And Anne Sullivan paid a heavy price for the miracles she worked. Living with Helen Keller, with no time or energy for a life of her own, a family of her own—that's too much to ask of any teacher."

Ms. Quinn stopped talking. For two solid minutes, words had poured out, and then they just ended. I could see her lower lip curl up, her jaw stiffen, her eyes harden as she stared at a poster about the Bill of Rights. It felt strange. I cleared my throat.

"You think Coach Colson—Mr. Colson—had this Anne Sullivan Syndrome?" I said.

Ms. Quinn's eyebrows shot up, and she took a deep breath in, a deep breath out. "No. He was just new. And this place will eat you alive if you let it. There's always one more thing you can do, one more student you can help. You've got to find a balance. And Randy—Mr. Colson—*was* finding his balance this year. If he'd had more time, he—oh, God. I'm sorry."

She started crying, but not for long—a jagged sob, a few tears, and then she dug a tissue out of her pocket, wiped her eyes, blew her nose, waved her hand. "Sorry. Sorry, sorry, sorry. But it hasn't even been a week yet. Do you have more questions?"

I looked down at the list. An even-numbered question—my turn. And this was a sensitive one. Damn. "Mr. Colson was always such an upbeat person. Lately, though, he seemed down, like something was troubling him. Did you notice that, too?"

Ms. Quinn stared at me. "No. He never seemed down. The last time I saw him, all he could talk about was how excited he was about the tournament. You thought something was troubling him?"

"Just an impression," Graciana said quickly. "One last question. Could you tell us something about him most people would be surprised to hear?"

Ms. Quinn laughed. "He was a good actor. He could recite blank verse with the best of them. How's that?"

"That sure surprises *me*," I said. "You saw him act?"

"Only in a *Scenes from Shakespeare* rehearsal. Some students wanted to do a scene from *Macbeth* but didn't have anyone to play Banquo, so Ms. Nguyen recruited Mr. Colson."

"Ms. Nguyen?" Graciana said. "Doesn't Mr. Van Zant always direct *Scenes from Shakespeare*?"

Ms. Quinn nodded. "For twenty-five years. But he's retiring, so he's grooming Ms. Nguyen to take over. She sweet-talked Mr. Colson into playing Banquo—she could probably sweet-talk him into anything. He didn't have many lines, but he practically stole the scene. Well, Mr. Van Zant says acting's a gift. Some people have it, he says, and some don't."

Someone cleared his throat, and we all looked around to see Mr. Quinn standing in the doorway. "I saw your car in the parking lot," he said, looking at Ms. Quinn. "I'm surprised you're still here. Where are the girls?"

She sighed. "At home. They're old enough to manage for an hour or so without adult supervision. And I'm about to head home. How about you?"

"I'll be a while. The Jessups aren't happy with the financial aid package Randolph-Macon offered Nick, so I found a college in Pennsylvania that's still looking for wrestlers. It could be a good opportunity, but we have to act fast. Better have dinner without me."

She bit her lip. "Fine."

Mr. Quinn looked at us. "So you're going ahead with the memorial issue."

"Dr. Lombardo approved it," Graciana said.

"I know. But she doesn't want you spending too much time on it, and you need to keep it in good taste. Don't forget that. Did that martial arts school work out?"

"Yeah," I said. "We're all taking classes Mondays and Wednesdays."

"Good. That's positive and forward-looking." He scraped up a smile. "Matt, I asked Mr. Pavlakis about this week's quiz. Eighty-five—significant improvement, but it won't get you to A-minus. Keep going to those review sessions. And next time, don't leave early. If you do, I'll know."

He wagged a finger at me, wiggled his eyebrows, and grinned. I guess it was supposed to be friendly, maybe funny. But as Mr. Van Zant said, some people have it, and some don't.

After he left, we all sat silently, feeling awkward. Then Ms. Quinn lowered her voice. "The Anne Sullivan Syndrome. I rest my case."

Probably, she shouldn't have said it—he's her husband, after all, and our guidance counselor—but I couldn't help laughing. We finished the interview, thanked her, and walked outside. My thoughts were racing.

"That was interesting," I said. "But we didn't learn anything that can help us figure things out." I paused. "Or did we?"

Graciana kept walking. "If you've got something on your mind, say it."

"Okay." I stretched both arms out in front of me. "It's elementary, Watson. Ms. Quinn's fed up with her husband. She and Bobby Davis were having a hot love affair—until she met Coach Colson. She dumped Davis and started an even hotter affair with Coach. Davis found out, got mad, and killed Coach in hopes of winning back his one true love."

"Makes sense to me." Graciana kept her voice deadpan. "Of course, Ms. Quinn's about fifteen years older than either Davis or Coach, but they wouldn't mind that. After all, she dresses in a way that's sure to attract younger men. Or try this one. She was having an affair with Coach Colson, Mr. Quinn found out, and he hired Davis to kill the man breaking up their happy home."

"Even better," I said, "especially since Mr. Quinn's obviously so passionately devoted to his wife that he'd kill to keep her."

We'd reached Graciana's car. Finally, we looked each other in the eyes and laughed—not much, because nothing we'd said had been funny, but enough to show we felt embarrassed.

"God," I said. "We're awful. Why are we making jokes about something so serious?"

"Maybe," Graciana said, "because we're afraid it's true."

"Oh, come on. We were making stuff up. Ridiculous stuff."

Graciana nodded. "Yes. Nothing we said could be *exactly* true. But maybe we're afraid we might not be far off."

I'd been thinking the same thing. "Like you said the other day, in most murders, the killer's someone who was close to the victim. In Ridgecrest, was Coach Colson close to many people outside of school?"

"Mrs. Dolby didn't mention any," Graciana said. "And Ms. Quinn certainly saw him as very caught up in the school—*too* caught up, in her opinion. And we're interviewing the people he was closest to, so, well…"

She didn't have to finish the sentence. I looked down and started nudging a pebble around with my foot. "But we don't *know* anyone from school was involved, right?"

"Absolutely not. We don't know much of anything yet. There could be lots of possibilities we haven't thought of. Oh, that's right. I set up an appointment with Ms. Nguyen for after school Monday. Does that work?"

"Sure. And I talked to Paul Ericson. He wants us to come out to his lake house Sunday afternoon. Okay?"

She hesitated. "Will that girlfriend of his be there? Carolyn Olson?"

I'd never heard anyone refer to Carolyn Olson as "that girlfriend of his." "I don't think so. He'll be cleaning up the yard."

"Okay. I should get home." She gave me this odd little smile, almost a sad little smile. "Have fun tomorrow night. I hear the movie's good."

So Berk had been right again—talk about Suzette and me *was* all over school. Probably, people were trading theories about how far things would go, how long it'd last. When you live in a small town, people always talk. But knowing people were talking about Suzette and me made me squirm.

Put it out of your mind, I told myself. You've got bigger things to worry about, like going to Richmond tonight and maybe having another run-in with Bobby Davis. And maybe, with luck, surviving.

Thirteen

We got lucky. Around nine o'clock, Berk and I got to the Range. The street was much more crowded than it'd been on Sunday, but as we drove up, someone pulled out of a parking space right across from the bar. We grabbed it.

I'd insisted we both wear jackets with hoods. Berk thought it was dumb, but Bobby Davis had seen me close up, and he knew my name. I didn't want to risk having him recognize me. So we pulled up our hoods and settled in for what we figured would be a long wait. Chances are, I thought, we'll never see him. Fine. We'll sit in the car a few hours, talking and joking. Then we'll head home, say how disappointed we are, and be friends again. That's all I wanted to accomplish tonight.

But fifteen minutes later, Davis walked out of the bar with two other guys. Even in the dim light of the streetlamps, there was no mistaking him—compact build, confident strut, slicked-back dark orange hair, smirk. Damn, I thought. The three of them got into a white Chevy.

"I never thought we'd spot him so soon!" Berk said. "Now we follow him."

No way to avoid it—that's why we'd come. I pulled onto the street, hanging back as they turned down a side street and drove through a run-down part of town—old apartment buildings that seemed mostly dark, cruddy-looking shops with iron grates covering windows and doors. Then they parked across from a grocery store that'd probably gone out of business years ago. I kept driving.

"Don't leave," Berk said. "We've gotta find out what they're up to."

"I don't want them to spot us. I'll go around the block."

By the time we got back, the three men were walking through the grocery store's parking lot. A silver Mitsubishi had parked nearby, and two men got out.

"Maybe it's a drug deal." Berk's voice had the bristly sound it gets when he's excited. "Maybe we should call the cops."

"And tell them what? That some guys parked on a quiet street?" Slowing down, I saw a tall wooden fence at the far end of the lot. Davis and his friends seemed to be heading for that. I circled the block again.

This time, when we got back, we saw more cars, more people walking across the parking lot—all men, at least a dozen now, most in their twenties or thirties, several carrying six-packs.

"You should park," Berk said. "We could blend in, see what's going on."

"Not yet. Too risky. If more people come, we'll think about it."

Even thinking about it was dumb. But I was curious, too, and the whole thing felt—I don't know, like it was a movie and we could watch for a while and walk away, no problem.

I kept circling the block. Each time we came back, more cars were parked along the street, more men were walking across the parking lot, carrying six-packs or drinking from paper bags. They all walked to the wooden fence and slipped out of view.

"If you keep driving by," Berk said, "somebody's gonna notice *that*. Might as well park."

He was right. With all these cars parked along the street, who'd pay attention to one more? We could slump down in our seats and watch people arrive. I parked. We waited until thirty or forty men had walked across the lot, until cars stopped coming.

"Not a drug deal," Berk said. "Too many people. Wanna check it out?"

It was a really bad idea. But yeah, I wanted to check it out. "Keep your hood up. One quick look, then straight back to the car." I shoved the flashlight from the glove compartment into my pocket. Not that Mom's plastic flashlight would make much of a weapon, but I felt better having it.

We walked across the parking lot, walked behind the wooden fence. Big surprise—another parking lot, this one behind a row of small stores, all dark, probably half of them out of business. A loose circle of men, drinking, laughing, cursing, sometimes cheering. A broad-shouldered man with a short black beard walked around the circle, taking money other men held out. Davis stood with the two men from the bar, laughing quietly at some joke. In the center of the circle, two shirtless guys pounded on each other, kicking and punching and grabbing, faces bloody.

It was a fight club. I'd heard about those, but I hadn't thought they really existed. And I'd seen the movie, but this wasn't like the fight club in the movie. This one was all about gambling and drinking, and getting thrills from watching other people bleed.

We should've left right then. But we stayed, because there was something else we needed to see. We needed to see Bobby Davis fight.

One of the guys in the center, the shorter one, was getting tired. He started stumbling, his punches got weaker, and he couldn't keep his balance after he kicked. The taller guy backed off and then came in hard, slamming a full-force front kick into his chest. The shorter guy fell on his back, and the taller guy kneeled on top of him, punching his face. When the shorter guy's head fell to the side, the taller guy jumped up, raising his fists in the air. People cheered and had another drink. The man with the short black beard walked around the circle again, giving money to some people, taking more money from others.

Someone tapped me on the shoulder. "I know you," a tall, skinny guy said. "Ridgecrest High, right?"

It was Craig, the weird guy from Kelly's Gym. "No," I said, making my voice gruff.

"Sure you are." Craig squinted at Berk. "And you took that lousy cell-phone video, and you both asked about Bobby. So you decided you wanted to see him in action again?"

Berk gave me a terrified look. If this guy told Davis two kids from Ridgecrest High came to Kelly's asking questions about him and then showed up at the fight club—damn.

"We gotta go," I said.

Craig clutched my arm. "Not yet. It's just getting good. See, after every match, Bobby fights the winner. And you don't ever wanna bet against Bobby."

Davis peeled off his jacket, peeled off his shirt, and headed for the center of the circle. I knew moves I could use to make Craig let go of my arm, but part of me wanted to see.

The tall man watched Davis warily. Davis took a loose stance and stood grinning, waiting. The tall man hesitated and then charged forward, bellowing, throwing a right punch.

Davis let him come, then stepped to the side, reaching up with his left hand to grab the man's outstretched arm. He stopped the man's right leg with his left foot, used the man's own weight to knock him off balance, and pulled him forward, grabbing him behind the head, still holding his leg solid, dropping him to the pavement. When the man fell, groaning, Davis held him down and punched him in the face, quick and hard. The man gasped, rolling into a ball, holding his face in his hands. I saw blood flowing between his fingers. Davis jumped up and went into a lazy stance again, waiting to see if the man wanted more.

Craig let go of my arm, thrusting his fist into the air and cheering. We can go, I thought. But the man with the short black beard stood in front of me.

"Hey," he said. "Where's your money? You two haven't placed a bet."

Damn. "We don't want to bet. We're leaving right now. We—"

He moved in close. "You can't watch and not bet. Where's your money?"

"We don't have any. I'm sorry, but—"

Out of nowhere, his right fist headed straight at me. I put both fists in front of my face, kept my elbows in, didn't close my eyes, didn't pull my head back, watched him, took a few punches to my arms. When he pulled his arm back for another punch, I reached underneath, trapping his fist with my left arm. Then I moved forward, striking him twice in the face with my elbow, grabbing the back of his neck, pulling his head down, kneeing him in the stomach. I spun around and threw him to the ground.

I grabbed Berk's arm. "Run like hell," I said, and we ran back across the parking lot. Behind us, I heard people clapping and cheering, maybe for Bobby Davis, maybe for me. The flashlight fell out of my pocket, but no way was I stopping to pick it up.

We reached the car. Nobody seemed to be chasing us, but I didn't wait to make sure. I jammed the key into the ignition and didn't slow down to the speed limit until we were a mile away.

Berk collapsed against the seat. "Oh, man. That was the block Aaron taught us. And you did it like it was nothing!"

"It just came to me," I said, still trying to catch my breath. "I've been practicing—every morning, every night."

"Oh, man," Berk said again, and burst out laughing. He raised a fist. "Kadima!"

I started laughing, too, and we both shouted "kadima!" until we were almost hoarse, until the tension lifted and we felt normal again. My arms felt sore, but I didn't care. All I could think about was that I'd done the block exactly right, I'd done it for real, and I'd thrown that guy. For the first time in my life, someone had actually attacked me, and I'd won. I felt almost high.

And I felt hungry—we both felt really, really hungry. I pulled into the drive-through at a Wendy's, we got cheeseburgers and Cokes, and we hit the interstate.

"That was stupid," I said. "That was seriously stupid. We could've got killed."

"But we didn't." Berk's voice bristled with excitement again. "And we found out Davis is practically a professional fighter. He must make money by fighting in this club. It looks like it's a regular thing, with rules and everything, and Davis is the star. No way he should've competed as a first-degree black belt. We should tell Lieutenant Hill all this tomorrow."

"Maybe we should wait. We don't have any ideas about what the motive might've been. The interviews might help us figure that out. Let's get those done, pull all our information together, and then think about going to the police."

"I guess." Berk hesitated. "Matt, do you think that guy from Kelly's will tell Davis about us? Do you think somebody came after us and wrote down your license plate number?"

The last part hadn't occurred to me. Damn, I thought. My mother's license plate number. What if someone *had* written it down? What if fight clubs have people who write down numbers for all cars parked nearby, in case somebody doesn't make good on a bet? Tonight might've been even dumber than I'd thought.

"I don't know," I said, "but we can't be sure the danger's over just because we got away. We've gotta watch for signs of trouble. And from now on, we've gotta be more careful."

Berk nodded. "Absolutely."

"Good," I said, but felt uneasy. On Sunday, the last time we drove home from Richmond, we'd all promised to be really, really careful from then on. And tonight, Berk and I had rushed ahead and done something really, really stupid.

Maybe this time we'd learned our lesson. Maybe, this time, we'd stick to our promise, and we'd stop taking stupid chances. Or maybe not.

But I wasn't really focused on that now. Instead, I was focused on a possible explanation for why Davis killed Coach. Just hours ago, that explanation had seemed like a joke. Now, it didn't seem so funny.

Fourteen

The minute I saw Suzette, I knew I should've worn a tie.

Mom had wanted me to, but I'd said no, Suzette would probably wear jeans, and that's what I'd wear, too. Mom ruled out jeans, I ruled out the tie, and we finally compromised on dress slacks and a long-sleeved shirt. No tie.

Mom seemed more excited than I was, maybe because I'd never gone on an official date before and she saw this as some kind of step in growing up. I'd gone out with a girl last fall, but mostly we'd just hung out, without deciding in advance what we'd do. That ended—no major trauma on either side. Since then, sometimes I'd get talking to a girl at a party or whatever, and we'd spend the evening together, maybe get something to eat. It never got intense or long-term, and that was okay with me.

Tonight definitely counted as an official date. I'd hoped Suzette would watch for me and come out when I pulled into the driveway, but no, I had to go to the front door and ring the bell. Mr. Link answered, saying Suzette was upstairs and asking if I'd like to wait in the living room.

No, actually, I wouldn't like that. I'd rather wait in the car. But Mom had said if he asked, I had to say yes. The date hadn't even started, and already it was awkward. I followed him into the living room feeling like I'd gotten caught in a time warp and it was 1950 again.

I sat in this spindly wooden chair, wondering if it was an antique, while Mr. Link fired out questions about basketball. Like Mr. Quinn, Mr. Link was in Ridgecrest High's first graduating class, and they still come to every game together, sitting in the front row, second-guessing every play we make. It felt uncomfortable to sit in his living room while he grilled me about what I thought of this player or that player, or of our chances against this team or that team next year. When he asked what I thought of my chances of becoming captain next year, things moved from uncomfortable to weird. Finally, we heard someone on the stairs, and he glanced up. "Guess who's ready. You look beautiful, sweetheart."

He was right. Suzette walked down the stairs slowly, like she was a queen on her way to get crowned. She wore a sleeveless dark blue dress, really low cut, and silver shoes with heels so high you wouldn't have thought anyone could walk in them. Over her arm, she carried a sparkly blue-and-silver shawl. Her hair looked like soft gold. Damn, I thought. And I almost wore jeans.

"Hello, Matt." She handed her phone to her father. "Take a picture of us, Daddy? Take a few, so I can post the best one on Facebook." She latched onto my arm and broke out a smile too big for me to match.

He must've taken a dozen pictures, with Suzette adjusting her pose each time. Finally, he gave her phone back and shook my hand. "Take good care of my little girl. Did you say goodbye to your mother, sweetheart?"

Suzette grimaced. "She's in her room. I figured she's asleep. Again. Goodbye, Daddy." She handed me her shawl.

At first I thought she wanted me to carry it for her, not that it was heavy. At the last possible second, just before I would've made a total idiot of myself, it hit me: She wants me to help her put it on. That's one of those things guys do on real dates.

I tried to find the middle, then held it up so she could back into it. She shrugged it down so the tops of her arms still showed, and we finally, finally left the house.

As I was backing out of the driveway, I sneaked another glance at her. She hardly even looked like Suzette. She looked like a model or an actress, so perfect and delicate she might shatter. I didn't know how to talk to her. "You look amazing," I said.

"Thank you." She turned to me with another melt-your-shoes smile before settling back. "Oh, my God. My mom was *such* a pain. She *totally* didn't want me to wear this dress. All day, she was like, 'Won't you be cold?' and, 'Shouldn't you save that for Aunt Amy's wedding?' Finally Dad told her to give it a rest, and she started crying, saying she had a headache and thought she was getting sick. So he got her to take a pill. I mean, God! All that drama over *nothing!*"

I thought about Cassie's headache. "Does she get sick a lot?"

"She *thinks* she does. It's mostly to get attention. Plus she'd been drinking, as usual. But let's not talk about her." Suzette sighed. "Isn't it a beautiful night?"

"I guess." I looked around, trying to see if there was anything special about the night. Our weather's generally okay, except if it gets really hot or rains really hard. But it never gets too hot this early in April, and it wasn't raining. The night was pretty much what you'd expect.

When we got to Olive Garden, I walked around to open Suzette's door, since I figured she'd expect me to. Inside, while we talked about the menu, I liked looking across the table at her and then glancing around the room, thinking about how she looked prettier than the other girls there. Sometimes, when she focused on the menu, I let my glance slide down and rest on the pale crescents of breast showing against the dark blue of her dress. I didn't stare, but it was hard not to look. It made me uncomfortable, but in a way I enjoyed it.

I didn't have to work at keeping conversation going, because Suzette always had something she wanted to say. She told stories about how her friend Ashley had a huge crush on Derrick, about how her mother tried to make a soufflé and got hysterical when it collapsed.

By the time our dinners arrived, Suzette slowed down, and I figured I should take a turn. It'd be fun to tell her about the fight club, especially about how I'd thrown that guy, but Berk and I had agreed not to tell anyone except Graciana and Joseph. We didn't want talk getting around. And Suzette told me about Ashley's crush on Derrick, even though Ashley probably wouldn't want me to know. I'd better not trust her to keep quiet about last night.

Instead, I said something about basketball. Suzette said she was sure I'd be captain next year, and I said some people thought Tyler Mitchell would be better. That got her going. She said her dad doesn't think Tyler's much of a player, and Megan sits behind him in math and says he smells, and Ashley saw him at a party and thought he was drunk because he acted so weird. I stuck up for Tyler, even though he *does* hog the ball, but the stories about the things he did at the party were pretty funny. We were both laughing when the waitress brought the check. Suzette hesitated, then reached for her purse.

Before I'd left the house, my father slipped me fifty dollars. "Let's not mention this to Mom," he'd said, "but if you don't want Suzette to use her gift card, if you'd rather pay for dinner, go ahead."

I hesitated, too, then made up my mind. "I'll get this," I said, picking up the check. It sounded cool, like a line from a movie.

Suzette's face lit up. "If you *insist*."

I wondered if that'd make Facebook: "Matt *insisted* on paying for dinner." Fine. I'd been half-embarrassed about the gift card—Dad was right about that. And Mom still doesn't understand how Facebook works, so it shouldn't be a problem.

We got to the theater late, had to park near the back of the lot, and hurried in, Suzette tottering on those narrow heels. The movie had some funny lines, but when someone pointed a gun at the hero, he just gave up, even though he was close enough to take it away. Suzette covered her face with her hands and huddled against my chest. She couldn't really have been scared—it was only twenty minutes into the movie, the actor playing the hero had top billing, no way would he get killed so soon—so I figured it was a cue and put my arm around her. She cuddled against me for the rest of the movie. I won't pretend it didn't feel good.

After the movie ended, she wanted to comb her hair and took a long time, so we were about the last people to leave the theater. As we walked out, we were both quiet, probably both wondering what came next. Well, we hadn't had dessert, and I had some money left.

"You want ice cream?" I asked. "Barney's is still open."

"Or we could go to my house." She gave me a sly little smile. "We've got plenty of ice cream, and we've got a really nice family room in the basement."

That sounded interesting. "Okay," I said, putting my arm around her shoulder again. Then I spotted the car.

My mom's car, parked near the back of the lot, both head-lights smashed, the windshield shattered, looking like someone had pounded it with a baseball bat. And right in the middle of the hood sat my mom's plastic flashlight, the one that fell out of my pocket at the fight club in Richmond.

Fifteen

I grabbed Suzette's hand and headed back to the theater, as fast as she could move on those spindly heels. She talked the whole time, mostly "Oh, my God!" and "I'm *so* scared!" I kept looking around, expecting Bobby Davis to step out of a shadow, but he'd obviously gone. Assuming it *was* Davis. But I felt pretty sure.

When we got back to the theater, I called my dad. He didn't yell about the car or blame me for one second. He was so nice he made me feel guilty, since I *was* to blame. This happened because of something I'd done.

"I'm glad you didn't drive it in that shape," he said. "I'll come right away and get the car towed. You can call the police."

"Do we have to?" If we called the police, would I have to tell them about Richmond? "I mean, what're the chances they'll catch the guy?"

"Not good. But the insurance company will ask if we filed a police report."

Damn, I thought, but made the call. Then we stood by the popcorn machine, waiting. Suzette texted friend after friend with thrilling little hints about our adventure while I stared into the parking lot. I can't lie, I decided, but if their questions leave me room to maneuver, I don't need to tell the full truth yet.

That ended up being easy. The squad car showed up minutes after my dad did. The two young cops seemed to see it as no big deal—some kids got drunk, smashed some glass, giggled, and walked away. Not much chance of catching them, no one got hurt, and insurance would cover most of the damages, so why waste much time on questions?

They asked if I knew who did it, and I could honestly say no—I didn't *know*, not for sure. When they asked if anyone at school was bullying me, I could say no again. They asked if there was anything else I wanted to tell them—it was really easy to say "no" to that. One cop kept staring at Suzette. She noticed, smiled, and shrugged her shawl down another inch. The other cop mostly yawned. Five minutes, tops, and they took off.

"I'll wait for the tow truck," Dad said. "You can drive Suzette home and come back for me. I'm sorry your evening's been cut short."

"It's okay." Frankly, I felt relieved. Nice as Suzette looked, good as it'd felt when she nestled against me, I was ready for the date to end. In lots of ways, she'd been awful sweet tonight. In other ways, I felt like I'd been playing a role in some script she'd worked out in advance. And ever since we'd seen the car, I'd focused on figuring things out, not on her. That probably meant I didn't have special feelings for her yet, and *that* meant I didn't have any business going to her family room for ice cream and whatever. Time to take a break and get my head clear.

I walked her to her front door, and she gazed into my eyes with a wistful smile. "Can't you come in for a few minutes?"

"My dad's waiting. Thanks for tonight. I'm sorry it got messed up at the end."

"It wasn't your fault." She moved closer. "Call me?"

"Absolutely." She seemed to expect me to kiss her, so I pulled her close. I felt her slim, perfect body press against mine, felt the softness of her lips, smelled the sweetness of her hair, felt something surge through me as she went limp, not holding back at all. God, I thought. I'd wanted to kiss her ever since I'd seen her walk downstairs in that dress, and now I'd done it, and it felt overwhelming. It was hard to let her go, to feel that sweet, yielding firmness step away from my arms.

"I'll call you tomorrow," I said. "For sure."

When Dad and I got home, Mom was fine about the car, even though it's hers and she'd have to do without it until things got fixed. These days, I drive it more than she does anyhow. I should be more grateful to her for that, I thought, listening to her and Dad talk about how they'd manage with one car. They stayed cheerful and practical, not getting dramatic, not saying anything to make me feel guilty. So naturally, I felt guilty as hell.

As soon as I could, I went to my room and called Berk. At first, he sounded cautious—did he think I'd called to brag? When I told him about the car, he got excited. He'd probably been worrying about whether I was making out with Suzette. Now, he could switch to worrying about whether Davis was hunting him down. Chances are, he'd rather worry about that. We traded questions. How had Davis found my car? Would he be satisfied now? Were we in danger? We didn't come up with anything definite, except that he'd text Graciana and Joseph about getting together tomorrow. Finally, he asked how the date went.

"Okay," I said. "Dinner was good, and the movie was funny."

"Do you really like Suzette now?"

"I don't know. She was nice, but I spent half the time worrying about what to say next."

"Are you taking her out again?"

I sighed. "She asked me to call, and I said I would. I haven't really thought about whether we'll go out again. I've been too focused on this other stuff."

"Good sign." He let out a short, sharp laugh and signed off.

The next afternoon, at Berk's house, we told Graciana and Joseph about the fight club, about the broken windshield and the flashlight. I paused, bracing myself, getting ready to hear them all tell me what an idiot I was.

"This is probably going to sound stupid," I said. "The night after Coach was killed, I said someone might've hired Davis to do it. You guys didn't think much of that idea, and I agreed. For one thing, I couldn't think of how someone who wanted Coach dead would've even heard of Davis. But if Davis is sort of famous because of this fight club, if lots of people know he's a really good fighter, that could explain a lot."

Graciana nodded slowly. "I've been thinking about that, too. We haven't found any connection between Coach Colson and Davis, and Coach moved to the area just two years ago and devoted all his time to Ridgecrest High. If he had a conflict with someone, it was probably with someone at the school."

"And you think," Joseph said, "this person paid Bobby Davis to kill Mr. Colson at the tournament, and to make it look not on purpose?"

"There's no way to be sure," I said. "But right now, I think that looks like a good possibility, yeah."

"Right now, it looks like the *best* possibility," Graciana said. "I agree with Matt."

We spent the next half hour debating about whether to go to the police with what we had, finally deciding that we should finish the interviews first. Berk and Joseph had done two interviews and gotten some good stories, nothing that looked like a clue.

I glanced at my watch. "We probably won't learn anything useful from Paul Ericson, either, but if we're going to his lake house today, we should leave. Ready, Graciana?"

As soon as we got in her car, she gave me a quick sideways smile. "You and Berk seem to be getting along again. Is that why you went to Richmond, to make things all right with him? Was it a male bonding thing—you had to do something stupid and dangerous together, so you could stop being mad at each other?"

I grinned, embarrassed. "Something like that."

"I thought so." She lowered her voice to caveman level. "'Come, let us hunt the wooly mammoth, just we two, using only these pointy sticks. In the morning, if we both survive, we can again be friends.'"

That made me laugh. "When you put it like that, it *does* sound dumb."

"I don't have to make it *sound* dumb. It *was* dumb. And I'm steamed you went to Richmond without telling Joseph and me. We're working on this together, remember?"

"I know. But we thought you'd try to talk us out of it."

"Definitely. And if I couldn't, I would've wanted to come along. But that would've ruined it, wouldn't it? This had to be no girls allowed."

I hadn't thought of it that way, but she was right. "You think boys are weird. Don't you?"

"I think boys are interesting. *And* weird. I think the whole male bonding bit is weird."

"And girls *aren't* weird? Girls bond, too, right? How? Shopping?"

She made a face. "Thanks for the stereotype. But okay, some girls bond by shopping. Mostly, though, girls bond by talking. Even when shopping comes first, I think it's mostly to give ourselves a chance to talk. I think, to feel close enough to really talk, girls do all kinds of things together. With boys, it's got to be something physical, doesn't it?"

I thought that over. With most of my friends, she had a point. "It doesn't *have* to be physical. But usually, yeah. Like playing on a team together, shooting pool, going camping. Maybe that's not all that different from girls shopping together. Maybe, basically, we do stuff so we can trust each other enough to talk."

"Boys actually talk to each other? About what?"

"All kinds of things," I said, not wanting to get into details. "What do *girls* talk about? Shoes?"

"Sometimes," she admitted. "And school, music, movies. But that's probably a way to get down to talking about other things—relationships, parents, hopes, insecurities." She laughed. "And boys. We spend *lots* of time talking about boys. Do boys talk about things like that?"

"Not in front of girls. Not even in front of most other guys. I can't see a bunch of guys having a slumber party, staying up all night talking about relationships. But one-on-one, with someone you trust, yeah. Except, of course, we talk about girls, not boys."

"Interesting," Graciana said. "I hadn't known boys talk about those things."

I hadn't, either. At least, I hadn't really thought about it, not until talking to her made me put it into words. I looked out the window and saw a sign: Lake Charlotte—15 Miles.

"We're getting close," I said. "There used to be a big hotel on the far side of Lake Charlotte. Twin Dogwoods Manor. My dad says it was a resort, with a band on weekends, dancing, all that. He says people from nearby towns came on weekends for the dancing, and people from all over stayed for whole weeks for boating and fishing, and for hiking at the nature preserve."

"That's right—the nature preserve isn't far from here. And Ellis Creek." Graciana turned her face to the right, in the direction of Ellis Creek Bridge, and the corners of her mouth got tight. "Poor Nina," she said.

Nina Ramsey had committed suicide not far from here, jumping off the old stone bridge over Ellis Creek, hitting her head on the rocks beneath it and drowning in the cool, clear water. I've been to that bridge, lots of times. It's in an isolated spot, sort of pretty, that somehow feels shady and sunny at the same time. I knew guys who've taken girls there when they want to get romantic, and people who've gone there to have wedding pictures taken. I didn't know if people would still do those things at the bridge, now that a girl had ended her life there.

Graciana let out a sharp sigh. "So what happened to the resort?"

"It caught fire," I said, "when my dad was in high school. No one was killed, and the building didn't burn down, but there was lots of damage. The owners couldn't afford the repairs, so it's been empty ever since."

"It's still standing?"

"It was last year. My father worked on a project in this area and drove by the hotel every day. He talked about how he'd love to renovate the place."

"That's right. Your father's a contractor. Does he like his job?"

"Loves it," I said. She had lots of questions about what contractors do. Then she asked about my career plans, and I said maybe engineering. After she'd asked a bunch of questions, I admitted I don't know much about engineering, and I mention it when people ask me what I want to do mostly because it's embarrassing to admit I haven't figured that out yet.

"*You've* got it all figured out," I said. "You want to be a reporter. On television?"

"For a newspaper. I want to write, not stand in front of a camera and read stories other people wrote. I want to investigate stories myself, too. I like gathering facts, talking to people, figuring out what's true and what isn't."

"Then you must be loving *this* whole business."

She gave me another quick little smile. "So are you."

"Look," I said, pointing. "That's the Ericson lake house."

It's a big, spread-out, angular building with two decks and lots of oversized windows. The walls are rough and stained reddish-brown, so they look like planks nailed together. But you can tell it's expensive, and the builder made it seem rustic on purpose.

Paul stood out front, stuffing broken branches and other yard trash into a garbage bag. When Graciana pulled into the driveway, he walked over.

"Good to see you, Matt," he said, pulling off his work gloves to shake my hand. He hesitated, then held his hand out to Graciana. "Hi."

She shook it. "Hello, Paul," she said, her voice crisp and formal. "We're sorry to interrupt your work."

"I can use a break. Let's sit on the porch. Fifteen minutes, okay?"

We started with the general questions, and Paul said nice things about Coach Colson—how hard he worked, how fair he treated everybody. It sounded flat, though, and when we asked him for stories, he kept them general—"After we beat

Appomattox, he bought everyone ice cream, with his own money." I'd expected him to be more enthusiastic, more personal. I noticed, too, that when Graciana asked him a question, he never made eye contact with her—he kept his head turned slightly to the side. When she wasn't looking at him, though, he'd sneak glances at her, scanning her up and down.

She looked up from her notes, and he looked aside again. "If you had to name one thing that made him really special," she said, "what would it be?"

Paul half-shrugged. "Like I said, he was nice."

Graciana stared at him, silent, waiting for more. After a few seconds, he half-shrugged again.

"He wasn't fake," he said. "Not at all. Once, when he gave me lousy advice during a game, he apologized afterward and said it was his fault I hadn't done better." Paul gave me a look. "Not exactly like Tomlinson."

"Nothing like Tomlinson," I agreed. "If he ever admitted to being wrong about anything, I'd pass out from shock."

"We all would," Paul said, and then his eyelids popped up. "Damn. Are you gonna put the stuff about Tomlinson in the newspaper?"

"Of course not," Graciana said. "You clearly intended that to be off the record. Though for future reference, the next time you want to keep something off the record—"

Paul winced. "I should ask *before* I open my big mouth. Good tip."

We all laughed, enough to break the tension. I looked at my list of questions.

"Coach Colson was always such an upbeat, enthusiastic person," I said. "Lately, though, he seemed down, like something was troubling him. Did you notice that, too?"

The tension snapped back so fast you could practically hear it whiz by. Paul's head jerked back, and his eyes narrowed. "What do you mean?"

Damn. I should've been ready for that question. "Nothing much. He just seemed to have something on his mind, something that was worrying him."

His hands clenched into fists. "Did he say anything to you? What did he tell you?"

"Nothing. Did he say anything to *you*?"

"No. Nothing. And he didn't have anything on his mind. He was fine. I talked to him the day before it happened, and he was in a great mood."

Graciana pounced. "What did you and he talk about?"

"None of your business." Paul stood up. "What the hell are you implying, anyhow?"

"Nothing," I said, totally confused now. "I just thought—"

"You were wrong. I've gotta get back to work."

"We have one more question," Graciana said. "If you wouldn't mind—"

"I *would* mind. We're done." He started to walk away. "Foley, get over here."

It was like we were back in the gym, and he was going to chew me out for missing an easy layup. I shot Graciana a glance and followed him clear across the yard.

He turned to face me. "Tell me the truth. Did Colson say anything to you? Anything about me?"

"No." I felt sweat starting on the back of my neck. "Not one word."

"So what's this crap about him having something on his mind? Where did that come from?"

I lifted my shoulders. It was hard to give him a plausible explanation when I'd made the whole thing up to see what people would say. "I just got an impression. It confused me, and I hoped you could explain it."

He looked over at Graciana. "Did *she* tell you to ask me?"

"No." At least I could tell the truth about that. This particular lie had been my idea. "She had nothing to do with it."

"Okay." He ran a hand through his hair, and some of the tension seemed to go out of his shoulders. He looked at me with something close to a smile. "I heard you took Suzette out last night. You have a nice time?"

Where did that question come from? "Sure."

"That's good. Suzette's the kind of girl you *should* date. If you wanna be captain, the guys have to respect you. Mostly, they'll respect you for the way you treat them, and the way you play the game. But the people you hang out with—that matters, too. If you hang out with someone like Graciana, they'll think you're a joke."

I should've stood up for Graciana, but I felt too stunned to find the words. "I'm not hanging out with her. We're working on this memorial issue together. That's it."

"Good. Finish it up, and then stick with your own kind of people. And stop asking people if Colson had something on his mind. He didn't." He paused. "I heard you're taking a martial arts class. That's good. It's important to stay in shape off-season, so you're ready for basketball. You working out, too?"

"Every morning before school. I exercise, and then I run laps in the parking lot of a church near my house."

"Good." He slapped my arm awkwardly, turned away, and started picking up yard trash again.

I walked back to Graciana. "Interview's over. Let's go."

She waited until we got in the car and started down the road. "So? What did he say?"

More quick, tough decisions about what to say and what to hold back. "He asked again if Coach said anything to me, if he'd said anything about him."

"He asked if Coach said anything about *him*? Really? What else?"

Damn. "He wanted to know why I was asking about Coach's mood." I paused. "He asked if *you'd* told me to ask about that. I said no."

"Did he say anything else about me?"

I hated this. "Nothing much."

I was afraid she'd press for details. Lucky for me, she let it go.

"So," she said, her eyebrows scrunching up as she focused on the road, "he's afraid Coach might've said something about him. And any reference to this thing makes Paul angry and defensive."

"But that doesn't mean this thing, whatever it is, had anything to do with—well, with what happened to Coach. Maybe Paul cheated on a test, and Coach found out and wanted Paul to admit to it, and Paul wouldn't. That'd be enough to get Coach upset. And naturally Paul wouldn't want people talking about it, because it could mess up his scholarship."

Graciana thought it over. "That's a reasonable explanation."

Obviously, she didn't buy it. "Look, you don't know Paul the way I do," I said. "He acted uncomfortable today, and it looks like he's feeling guilty about something. Basically, though, he's a good guy. The idea he had some really horrible secret, and Coach found out, and Paul hired Davis to—I can't even say it. That's how ridiculous it is."

Graciana took her eyes off the road and turned to look at me, eyes soft. "We won't jump to conclusions. We'll gather more information, and we'll make careful decisions about where the evidence seems to point."

She shifted to talking about our interview with Ms. Nguyen tomorrow. She's being nice to me, I thought. She thinks Paul's involved in Coach's death somehow, but she realizes that idea's hard on me, so she's not pushing it. Not yet.

Sixteen

"Finally!" Ms. Nguyen said. She pulled a small rubber snake out of a sagging carton and held it up. "I *knew* we had one of these. So how, I'd like to know, did it end up in the *As You Like It* box?"

"It crawled out of the Forest of Arden?" Graciana suggested.

Ms. Nguyen laughed. "Not bad." She checked something off a list, dropped the snake into a large envelope labeled *Antony and Cleopatra*, and flipped open another box.

It was Monday afternoon, and we all stood in the prop room behind the auditorium. Mr. Van Zant wanted a full-props rehearsal tonight, so Ms. Nguyen had to locate a last few things. She didn't want our help, she'd said—the prop room was too small and crowded, and things would get crazy if more than one person tried to work. So Graciana and I stood with our backs against the wall, watching as she darted from one stack of cardboard boxes to another. Ms. Nguyen's slim, pretty, and quick, every movement small and precise. I think it'd drive her nuts if she had to stand still for a full minute. I could see why she and Coach had been friends.

"Ms. Quinn said Coach Colson was going to be in *Scenes from Shakespeare* this year," I said. "In a scene from *Macbeth*?"

She smiled. "Don't ever say that title in a theater, Matt. It's bad luck. Call it 'the Scottish play.' Yes, he was playing Banquo. He nailed it, too."

"That's what Ms. Quinn said," Graciana said. "She said she saw him rehearse the scene once."

Ms. Nguyen nodded. She was still smiling, but a wistfulness crept into her eyes. "She'd helped him learn his lines. Several other people came by to watch—Dr. Lombardo, Mr. Carver, Mr. Meyer. Mr. Quinn wandered in at one point, too, and stayed a while. Plus some guys from the basketball team, but they giggled so much Mr. Van Zant made them leave. He's lenient about letting people watch rehearsals—he thinks it's a good learning experience—but these guys were causing a distraction."

"Did Paul Ericson come?" Graciana asked, in a tone I'd come to recognize as fake-casual.

"No, I don't remember seeing him. But Brian came, and Chris and Dan." Ms. Nguyen sighed. "And poor Marie Ramsey, right at the end. I think that's one reason I remember that rehearsal so vividly. Marie's very quiet, never likes speaking up in front of a group. But she ran right up front, calling out for her sister. I spoke to her, and she was frantic—she'd gotten an odd text message from Nina and texted her back again and again, but Nina wasn't responding. I told Marie I was sure everything was all right." She winced. "Damn."

"That was the afternoon Nina committed suicide?" Graciana asked.

"Yes." Ms. Nguyen rubbed her forehead. "I keep telling myself nothing we might've done could've made any difference. Nina probably did it right after sending that message. Even if we'd called the police and organized search parties right away, we couldn't have found her in time. But when I think of how frightened Marie was, and how glib I was—damn."

"Why did Marie come here to look for her sister?" I asked. "Was Nina in one of the scenes?"

"Yes, but she wasn't rehearsing that afternoon. Until the last week or so, we don't try to get through all the scenes in one day. It's better to focus on a few and go over each again and again." Ms. Nguyen shook her head slightly. "Nina's scene was spot-on from the first time. She and Angie Kovach did a scene from *Othello*. Angie played Desdemona as a ditzy teenager—really funny—and Nina's Emilia was amazing. So smart, so cynical and irreverent, so sexy! It made me want to reread the play."

"That's great," I said, not all that interested. This wasn't getting us closer to figuring out who hired Davis. I decided to skip some softball questions. "Coach Colson was always so upbeat and enthusiastic," I said. "Lately, though, he seemed a little down, like something was troubling him. Did you—"

She dropped a handful of plastic daggers into the *Julius Caesar* envelope without looking up. "You mean Marie's doubts about Nina's suicide? He mentioned those to you? Yeah, they were on his mind. I don't think that belongs in the newspaper, though. Now, I *know* I spotted the *Much Ado* box. Where did it run off to?"

I remember how that moment felt, how everything seemed to freeze, how I got a sharp sense that we'd turned a corner. I hadn't been expecting Ms. Nguyen to say anything about Nina's suicide, but as soon as she did, it felt right. It felt inevitable, like something I'd almost-thought since the day of the tournament but never faced before.

And obviously, Ms. Nguyen had misunderstood me and thought Coach told me something he hadn't, and the honest, straightforward thing to do would be to clear the confusion up right away. But then she probably wouldn't tell us anything more. I glanced at Graciana, and she nodded sharply.

So much for being honest and straightforward. "It's not for the newspaper," I said. "It's just been bothering me. I'd hate to think Coach died with unfinished business on his mind." I remembered the phrase Graciana used. "Anything you tell us would be off the record."

Ms. Nguyen stopped going through boxes and turned to face us. "*Strictly* off the record, okay? Not one word goes into the newspaper. But I don't want you feeling upset for no reason. Okay. First, Marie was reacting the way we'd all react if someone we loved committed suicide. We wouldn't want to believe it was really suicide, because then we'd have to wonder if it was partly our fault. So when Marie came to Randy—I don't think she had anyone else she felt she could turn to, poor thing—and told him her pathetic theories, he understood and said he'd look into them."

I wanted to ask what those "pathetic theories" were, but that'd be a mistake—Ms. Nguyen probably assumed we already knew. "That sounds like Coach," I said—feeble, but safe.

She nodded. "It sure does—anything to help a student. Anyway, I asked about it a few days later, and he said he'd learned some things but shouldn't talk about them yet. Then— then the damn tournament happened." She shook her head. "The damn, damn tournament. But you shouldn't worry that he died with some big unfinished business on his mind, Matt, or that he'd found real evidence of bullying, much less of anything worse. If he had, he'd have reported it to Dr. Lombardo or the police. I think he looked into Nina's death simply so he could help Marie find closure. And maybe he wanted to understand suicide in general more fully, so he could spot warning signs in the future. He asked me some questions about *The Bell Jar*."

I hadn't thought about that title in days. Hearing it gave me a jolt. "The Sylvia Plath novel?"

"Right. You keep surprising me, Matt. I wouldn't have thought that book would interest you."

"I haven't read it," I admitted. "But Coach's landlady said he'd asked her to check a copy out of the library for him."

She smiled a tight, sad smile. "That's Randy for you. So diligent. He must not have been satisfied with what I could tell him. No wonder—it's been ages since I read that book, and it was never a favorite of mine. I don't enjoy novels about suicide."

Later, as Graciana drove me home, I gave her an accusing look. "You didn't tell me that book's about suicide."

"That's not the way I see it," she said. "Some people do, but that's too narrow. Yes, the protagonist attempts suicide—so do some other characters—and yes, Plath herself committed suicide not long after the book was published. But it seems reductive to—"

"Sounds like a book about suicide to me."

She rolled her eyes. "Whatever. Anyhow, it's interesting it was on Coach Colson's mind. It shows he took Marie's concerns seriously."

"I guess." I really, really didn't want to go down this road, but I knew we had to. "Don't string things out for me, Graciana. Say what you think. You think this is a big break, don't you? You think Coach got killed because he was trying to help Marie."

She sort of dipped her head around—not quite denying it, not quite nodding. "It's possible. Two violent, awful things have happened in our town in the last few weeks. It almost makes sense to wonder if they're connected. And it could explain the way Marie's been acting. Coming to the tournament, crying when Coach got killed, making a donation to the bake sale.

If she asked him to help and thinks he got killed as a result, naturally she'd feel guilty and horrible."

All that had occurred to me, too. "You might as well say the rest of it," I said. "You think this ties in with what Paul Ericson said. You think he's responsible for Nina's death somehow. And when Coach figured that out, Paul had him murdered."

Graciana grimaced, pulled to the side of the road, and turned to face me. "I *don't* think that, Matt. Honestly, I'm miles and miles from thinking that." She paused, avoiding my eyes, looking down at the upholstery. "But yesterday, when you said Coach Colson seemed to have something on his mind, Paul got upset, and he asked you if Coach had said anything about *him*. If Coach was looking into Nina's death and spoke to Paul about it—well. There's probably no connection. But I think we should ask Marie exactly what she said to Coach Colson and why."

"You're right." None of it felt real—it was too new, too impossible. "Do you know where she lives?"

Graciana nodded. "There was a kind of wake there, after the funeral."

I hated to think of what Marie might tell us, but anything would be better than all the ugly possibilities that kept rushing into my head. "Then let's go," I said.

Seventeen

Ridgecrest's a nice place—nothing too fancy, but nothing too rough or run-down, either. One part of town's pretty sad, though, down by the train station that closed long before I was born. It used to be the center of town, according to Dad, but those days ended when the trains stopped running and most businesses that'd depended on the trains dried up. A few businesses still hang on, though, including a red-brick diner that's supposedly famous for its chili. If putting a fried egg on top of chili is a big deal, I guess it deserves to be famous. Marie Ramsey's mother worked in that diner, and her family lived right next door, in a walk-up apartment above an out-of-business beauty parlor.

Graciana parked across the street. "Let's hope Marie's home," she said, "and no one else is. She seems to trust me because I went to the funeral, so maybe I should go in alone first. I could explain things, ask if you can join us. If we both show up at the door, she might freak out."

I looked doubtfully at the boarded-up windows of the beauty parlor, at the peeling pink paint on the upper floors. "I don't know. That place doesn't look safe. I'd better go with you."

Graciana raised both eyebrows. "It doesn't look dangerous,

Matt. Just inexpensive. Besides, I'm becoming a krav maga master. Any bad guys lurking in there better watch out. I'll call as soon as I have something to tell you."

That settled it—Graciana had made up her mind. I watched her hurry across the street and disappear into the building. I'd heard plenty of stories about the Ramsey family, none of them good, most of them about Nina.

I'd never spoken to Nina, but I'd known who she was. Of course I had. At a school like ours, someone who dresses and acts like she did stands out. She was striking in a hard, defiant way, with huge dark eyes, wavy red hair, and a body so incredible I'd heard guys compare her to Angelina Jolie. That didn't seem far off. She'd never looked like she was impressed by anything, always seemed on the verge of smirking. She'd been sent home from school lots of times because her skirt was too short or her top too low cut, and she always wore tons of makeup. She'd caught me staring at her once, and she'd given me this mocking, smoky grin, like she'd known exactly what I was thinking and didn't mind at all. It'd embarrassed me so much that I'd promised myself never to risk getting caught like that again. But it was hard not to look.

Everybody always said Nina was a hard-core drinker and drug addict; some people said she'd sold drugs, too. And everybody said she'd slept around a lot, sometimes for money. None of that had been hard to believe.

When she'd killed herself, there was more talk—of course there was. Some people said they'd seen her wandering around the halls at school that day, looking ready to cry; some said she'd been so high she was bumping into walls. I don't think the coroner's office ever said if it'd found evidence of drinking or drug use, but everyone assumed she'd jumped because she'd been stoned out of her mind. I'd felt bad about her death, the way you'd feel bad about anybody who died, but I'd never thought there was any question about what had happened or why.

I looked at my phone. Graciana had been in that building for almost twenty minutes. Damn—who knew what was going on in there? Five more minutes, I decided, and then I'm coming in after her.

My phone rang. "Marie says you can come up," Graciana said, keeping her voice low. "Watch what you say, all right? She's pretty raw."

I sprinted across the street and started up the dark, narrow stairway. The higher I went, the more depressing it got—only a little light making its way through dirty windows, a dank, stale smell I didn't even want to try to identify. On the second floor, Graciana stood waiting. She gestured me into an apartment, into a long, narrow room that seemed to be part kitchen, part living room—aging appliances and a row of white metal cupboards, a sagging lime-green couch, several mismatched chairs. Everything was jammed up against walls, making the place look more like an understocked used furniture store than a home. There was no clutter, and also no pictures, no books, no plants. Everything felt tired and old and bare.

Marie sat at a linoleum kitchen table at the far end of the room, hunched over her sketchbook, drawing. Her face was mostly hidden by her long black hair. Graciana took a seat at the table, too, and I followed her lead.

"Thank for talking to me, Marie," I said.

A shrug happened somewhere beneath all that hair. "You can't stay long. It's not safe," she said. The voice sounded hollow, almost like it came from underground.

I searched for something to say—something, anything that wouldn't make her clam up. "I'm sorry about your sister. That must hurt like hell. It must hurt every minute."

Her head moved slightly—a nod, probably. She didn't stop drawing.

Graciana sat forward. "Marie and I have been talking about Mr. Colson. I told her we have doubts about whether his death was really an accident. Marie said she's wondered about that, too. She's also wondered about Nina's death. She talked to Mr. Colson about it."

Finally, Marie looked up—only part way, but enough to fix her eyes directly on mine. The intensity of it made my head jerk back. "They lied," she said. "They made things up. They said she was depressed, but she wasn't. She was happy. She couldn't wait to graduate, and she had tons of plans—*we* had tons of plans. And why would she steal *The Bell Jar*?"

She kept looking directly at me, as if she expected me to give her the answer. Me, I was trying to get over the surprise of hearing that title again. "Who said she stole it?"

"The police," she said. "They found a copy in Nina's locker—it was from the school library, but it hadn't been checked out. This police psychologist or whatever said the book proves Nina was thinking about suicide. But she had her own copy of *The Bell Jar*—I gave it to her, for her sixteenth birthday. Why would she take a library copy? Someone must've planted it there, to make it look like she killed herself."

I felt awful for Marie, but I felt relieved, too. If she didn't have more concrete reasons for thinking Nina hadn't committed suicide, maybe I didn't have to worry about hearing some horrible revelation. Maybe Marie simply couldn't face the truth, like Ms. Nguyen had said. Don't challenge her, I decided. There's no point. "That seems strange, all right," I said.

Her eyes grew harder, driving clear into me. "You don't really think it's strange. You think I'm being stupid. That's what the police thought. When I told them she owned a copy of the book, and they said, okay, show it to us. But I couldn't find it. So they said maybe she'd lost it, and that's why she took the library copy. But she'd *never* lose that book. She loved it, because I gave it to her. Why would she lose it?"

God, I thought. She's in rough shape, if she can't think straighter than that. I nodded, not letting myself look skeptical.

Graciana took over. "How could someone plant something in her locker? Didn't she keep it locked?"

"Yes, but *I* know her combination, and she knew mine. We'd leave each other notes and little gifts. She'd exchanged combinations with Angie, too. It was a sign of trust, like if Nina wanted to get close to someone, she might give him her combination."

Him, I noticed. Marie thinks Nina gave her combination to a boy. "Do you have any ideas about where her copy of *The Bell Jar* might be?" I asked.

"Nina had a special place," Marie said. "She went there when things got really bad at home, and she called it Sherwood Forest, like in *Robin Hood*. You know?"

Graciana nodded. "A sanctuary from oppressive authorities."

"Right," Marie said. "A hideout for outlaws—Nina liked that idea. Anyway, she kept some of her things there. I don't know where it is—she offered to tell me, but I said no. I was afraid Dad would beat it out of me."

I had a hard time even imagining how miserable Marie's life must be. We shouldn't make her keep torturing herself with this stuff, I thought. She doesn't have anything real to tell us. She's just ripped apart because the only person she could love is dead. "Thanks for talking to us," I said. "We—"

"Will you tell us about the text messages now, Marie?" Graciana asked. "You said you showed them to Mr. Colson. Will you show us, too?"

Marie lifted her shoulders half an inch, then let them droop. "You won't believe me. The police didn't. Not even my mother did. Nobody does."

"Maybe we'll be the people who do," Graciana said. "The police don't believe us, either. Give us a chance."

Marie's hand kept moving over her sketchpad. I glanced at her drawing. It was a sneering portrait of Lieutenant Hill, and I was shocked at how good it was. Finally, she stopped drawing. She pulled her phone out of her pocket, found a message, and handed the phone to Graciana. "Here," she said. "This is the first one. She sent it to me at 3:52 that afternoon."

I looked over Graciana's shoulder to read the message: It's official—tomorrow night, Little Becky deflowers Captain America in a doubly shady spot! Take that, Big Brother!

What had I expected? Of course it didn't make sense. Everybody said Nina was stoned stupid that day. I looked away.

Graciana frowned at the message. "I don't understand. These names—some kind of code?"

"Nicknames," Marie said. Again, she'd started drawing. "Nina and I always used nicknames when we texted."

That sounded like a convenient way of explaining away nonsense. Might as well humor her, I decided. "So who's Captain America?"

Slowly, Marie looked up, locking her eyes on mine. "Paul Ericson. Mr. Clean-Cut Superhero. Nina couldn't stand him."

So now Paul's name was out there. I'd half-expected that, but it hit me hard.

Graciana didn't show a trace of surprise. "And Little Becky?"

"That was Nina's nickname for herself," Marie said, "ever since she read *Vanity Fair* last year. She loved that book."

Graciana nodded. "Becky Sharp. I can see why Nina would identify with that character."

Naturally she'd read *Vanity Fair*. I'd never heard of it, I had no idea who Becky Sharp was, and I was getting tired of listening to Graciana show off. We'll, she wasn't the only person who'd ever read a book.

"And Big Brother's from Orwell's *1984*," I said, nodding. "Nina's obviously referring to the guy who's always spying on everyone."

Marie blushed. "Maybe. Or maybe she was referring to Ted. He's our big brother. He's from our dad's first marriage, and he gave Nina a hard time about everything she did and everyone she saw."

So much for showing off my knowledge of literature. From now on, Foley, I thought, keep your stupid mouth shut.

Graciana was still frowning at the message. "So when she talks about deflowering Captain America, what does that mean?"

"She wanted to seduce Paul Ericson," Marie said. "She'd been working on it for weeks. She thought it'd be funny. Like I said, she couldn't stand him, and she especially couldn't stand his girlfriend, that horrible Carolyn person. She talked about getting him in bed and filming it on her cell phone and posting it on the Internet. She wanted to prove what a hypocrite he is—him and Carolyn both, with all that no-kiss-until-the-altar garbage. The message proves she got together with him that afternoon and set things up for Friday night."

No, it didn't. It proved Nina had been fantasizing about it, maybe, but it didn't prove anything had actually happened. If she'd been high enough, she might've imagined the whole thing. Or maybe Marie was imagining things. How could we know "Captain America" really meant Paul, and "Little Becky" really meant Nina?

"You mentioned a second text message," Graciana said. "May we see?"

147

"I got it at 4:43," she said, and found the second message and handed her phone to Graciana. Marie—I'm sorry. I can't take any more. It's too hard. I'm too miserable. I need rest—I need peace. Never blame yourself. You did everything you could, but I'm not strong enough. Love, Nina

No wonder Marie had come running to the auditorium that afternoon. I couldn't imagine anything that would sound more like a suicide note. "I'm sorry, Marie," I said.

She grabbed a pencil and started drawing again—hard, quick strokes. "Why are you sorry? Nina didn't write that. It doesn't sound anything like her. Look at it! It starts with my name and ends with 'Love, Nina.' Nina *never* did that in a text message! And all this melodrama and self-pity—'it's too hard,' 'I'm not strong enough.' No *way* would Nina write that kind of poor-little-me crap!"

"So you think someone else wrote it?" Graciana said. "You think someone took Nina's phone and—"

"Of *course* someone took her phone!" Marie was raging now—she hardly seemed like the same girl she'd been when we came in. "They never found it, did they? So what happened to it? And the blouse she was wearing wasn't the one she'd worn to school that day—it was one I'd never seen before. Where did it come from? And here—here!"

She seized the phone again, punched buttons, and shoved the phone at Graciana, who looked at it and then handed it to me.

Paul Ericson, kneeling, holding a pink rose, his head bowed. It took me a second to figure out where he was—a long rectangle of dirt surrounded by grass, two containers of flowers set out on the ground. Then I saw a tombstone off to his right.

I handed the phone back to Marie. "Nina's grave?"

She nodded. "I went back the day after the funeral. It was almost closing time—there didn't seem to be anyone else around. Then I saw him, and I took the picture and stood behind a tree and watched. After a few minutes, he walked away. See? He left the rose for her."

"Did you show this picture to the police?" Graciana asked.

"I showed them *everything*," Marie said. "I told them *everything*. And Hill said he'd look into it and get back to me, but he didn't, and finally I called him. And he said the investigation was closed and there were no unresolved issues and I had his sincere condolences. Then he hung up on me. I tried to—"

The door to the apartment opened, and a man walked inside. I recognized him as the one we'd seen in the parking lot with Marie—twenty-five or so, just over six feet, with broad shoulders, close-cut dark brown hair, and a bushy mustache. It had to be the older brother, Ted.

He did a double-take when he saw Graciana and me. "What's going on, Marie?" he said. "Who the hell are they?"

Marie stuck her phone in her pocket and went back to drawing, faster than ever. "Nothing's going on. They're friends."

"Don't give me that. You don't have friends." He walked toward us, his eyes fixing on me. "You selling something?"

I stood up. If we had to defend ourselves, I didn't want to start from a sitting position. "We're talking to Marie. I'm Matt Foley, and this is Graciana—"

"Never mind. I'm not interested in your names, just in how fast you can leave."

He came closer, crossed his arms against his chest, and stood staring at me. I don't know if I actually smelled liquor on his breath, but it sure felt like I did.

"Marie's not allowed to have people up here," he said. "I don't want people messing with my stuff. And don't get any ideas about messing with *her*. She's feeble-minded. It wouldn't be right. Go on, now. Get out."

I hated letting this guy push me around, hated letting him talk about Marie like that. But I didn't want to make things worse for her. I glanced at her to see if she was going to stand up to him, if she might want our support. No. If anything, she was more hunched over than before, her shoulders drawn in close, her eyes focused on her sketchpad. Probably, the best thing we could do for her was to leave.

"Nice talking to you, Marie," I said, not taking my eyes off him. "We'll see you in school tomorrow."

Graciana rested her hand on Marie's shoulder. "That's right. We'll see you tomorrow. Take care of yourself."

As we started toward the door, Ted stepped into Graciana's path. "Maybe *you* could come back some time," he said, grinning, looking her up and down. "But not with him, and only when I'm here. You're sure a pretty one."

If there were a market for pure hatred, I thought, I'd find a way to bottle the look Graciana was giving him. "Thank you," she said, but it wouldn't take a genius to translate that to what she was really thinking. She stepped around him, and we left.

Before we were halfway down the stairs, Graciana exploded. "God! I *hated* leaving her with him! He could be hitting her, Matt. He could be hitting her *right now!*"

"I hate it, too," I said. "But if we'd tried to stay, we probably would've made things worse for her. We should see if there's a way of giving her real help, long term. Maybe there's some agency we could go to. Maybe Mr. Quinn would have some ideas."

"That idiot! When has *he* ever had a good idea about anything?" She yanked her car door open, then stopped and caught her breath. "No. Sorry. That's a sensible suggestion. He's a natural person to consult. We'll think about it."

We got into the car, and she pulled onto the road. I sat there numbly as streets got cleaner and buildings got newer, trying to sort out things we'd heard. "So," I said. "What do you think?"

She sighed. "Nothing's conclusive. But that picture of Paul Ericson—*something* must've been going on. Coach Colson took it seriously, even the part about *The Bell Jar*. We can't simply dismiss it."

"Probably not," I said, hating it.

"And we're getting together with Berk and Joseph after krav tonight. We should probably tell them everything we've learned and see what they think."

"I can tell you right now what Berk's going to think. We'll be lucky if he's still speaking to us tomorrow."

She grimaced. "I'm sorry. I know you worked hard to make things all right with him again. But we agreed we'd all work on this together. I don't see any way to avoid telling them. Do you?"

"No," I said, and settled back in my seat to stare blankly at the road. This was going to be one long, awful night.

Eighteen

When Graciana dropped me off at home, Mom was standing at the stove, frying chicken and making mashed potatoes. That was a shock. Mom and Dad aren't vegetarians, not quite, but we don't see much meat at our house. We don't see many potatoes, either. Why eat potatoes when you can eat polenta or pureed rutabaga or some other weird starch? Then I saw the chocolate cake on the counter. Too much comfort food, I thought. Something bad must be happening.

I was working on my first drumstick when Dad cleared his throat. "There's something you kids ought to know. This morning, I handed in my resignation at Edson Construction. I've enjoyed working there these last twenty-two years, but I can't support some company policies. I'm going into business for myself, as a contractor and handyman. The transition may be challenging, but I'm confident I'll make things work. I think this will be an exciting new phase for our family."

The chicken turned to cardboard in my mouth. Handyman, I thought. He's fifty-three, fifty-four, and he's giving up a good job to be a handyman. What about college?

"Dad and I talked about this for a long time," Mom said. "We're sure it's the right decision. It may take a little while to build the business, but in the meantime we'll have my job, church choir, piano lessons—I'll take on more students. You two don't have anything to worry about."

I made myself swallow the chicken and look at Dad. "What were the policies you couldn't support?"

"I won't bore you with details. When Frank Edson retired and his son Neil took over, things changed. I've gone along with Neil as much as I can, but I can't go any further."

"So he fired you?" Cassie asked.

"No, he wanted me to stay, but only if I'd do things his way. It was my decision to leave. I won't mislead you about that."

"I think it's great," Cassie said, excitement building in her voice. "We should move to a bigger city, so you can get more customers. We should move right away, this week. We can rent the house and move to Richmond, or—"

"Hold on," Dad said, smiling. "I love your enthusiasm, but we wouldn't take you and Matt away from your schools and your friends. I can make a good living for us right here. Matt? What do you think?"

"Fine." I put down my fork. The mashed potatoes looked like goo now. The thought of putting that slop in my mouth made my stomach turn. "It's your decision, so fine. I've gotta get ready for krav. Joseph's mom is picking me up in a few minutes."

She was picking me up in half an hour, but I couldn't stay at the table. I sat on my bed. A handyman. Fifty-three, fifty-four, and he'll be sanding doors that don't close right, prying old toilet seats off rusty hinges. I'd always been proud to say my father was a general contractor for Edson Construction, and now I'd have to say he was a handyman. And how could he fix enough toilet seats to pay for college?

Mom tapped on my door. "Matt? I'm putting some cake

and milk on the hallway table. If you don't want them, I'll get them later."

I didn't want them. After twenty minutes, I left the house without speaking to anyone and waited on the porch until Joseph's mom arrived.

For the first time, I felt sorry when physical conditioning ended. It felt good to run and do push-ups, to move and sweat and not think. The best part was when we took out punching bags and paired up, one person punching while the other held the bag. Derrick was my partner for that, and I punched so hard I knocked him down, twice.

It was hard to stop punching and sit on the floor for instruction. "Let's try a defense against what's called the tough-guy grab," Aaron said. "I'll need help. Suzette?"

She sat folded up, hugging her knees, staring at the floor. "No thanks."

"Are you sure? It's not rough, and everyone takes a turn sooner or later."

She still didn't look up. "Not tonight."

"All right." He glanced around. "Graciana?"

She joined him up front. "Let's say we're in a diner," he said. "I'm minding my own business, but you're in the mood for a fight. You grab the front of my shirt with your right hand—like this—and say something aggressive. Got it?"

Graciana nodded. She twisted her face into a sneer, lowered her voice, and grabbed his shirt, scrunching it in her fist. "Your momma," she said.

We all cracked up, including Aaron. "Very intimidating. So I take my right hand, reach over the top, and grab *your* hand, pushing down with my thumb. Then I twist my body and push your elbow down with my left hand—see? That's called an arm lock. Now I've got you bent over. If I want, I can get you in the face with some knee strikes. But you don't look dangerous, so I'll simply force you to the floor on your knees—like this. Great. Let's go through that again."

When we paired up, Suzette walked over and raised an eyebrow. "Hey, tough guy. Wanna grab my shirt?"

That embarrassed me, but I said okay. I made damn sure I never grabbed anything but her shirt. When she was the tough guy, she told me not to force her to the floor, to just fake knee strikes. Too bad—I'd wanted to try it both ways. She doesn't really like krav, I thought. Fine. Not everybody has to. But I didn't want to think she was taking krav just to be around me. Had she joined the martial arts club at school to be around me, too? In a way, that'd be flattering. But I didn't like thinking she'd planned everything out months in advance, and I'd fallen in with it.

Another instructor took over when we circled up to practice disarming techniques, so I asked Aaron if we could talk. We stood off to the side, and I lowered my voice.

"It's about the tournament," I said. "What you told that uniformed cop, about Bobby Davis deliberately kicking Coach Colson in the armpit and the throat—did you tell Lieutenant Hill that, too?"

Aaron sighed. "I told him. I don't know if he listened. As soon as I started talking, he stopped taking notes. I guess that's natural. All the other judges said I was wrong, and most were closer than I was. I probably *was* wrong."

"I don't think so. Some of us have been looking into it. It sounds crazy, but we think someone hired Davis to kill Coach. Berk and I went to Richmond and followed Davis to a fight club. Do you know about fight clubs?"

Aaron started to look concerned. "I saw the movie. I don't

know if there are any real fight clubs. I'd be surprised if there's one in Richmond."

"Trust me, there is. We saw it. Davis is at the center. Two men fight, he fights the winner, and people make bets. The point is, he's really good. We've done other investigating, too. We're trying to figure out who hired him, and—"

"Hold on, Matt. I can see how much you and your friends care about Coach Colson, and that touches me. It really does. But why would someone hire Davis to commit murder in front of hundreds of witnesses?"

"We think we can explain that. We're gathering evidence to take to the police. I want to make sure if they question you again, you'll say the same thing."

"There's nothing else I *can* say. I'll describe what I saw, and I'll say, to me, it looked deliberate. I can't say I'm positive, because I'm not."

"Good enough. Thanks, Aaron."

"Wait a minute. Frankly, this sounds farfetched to me. But if you're right, if Davis committed murder, if someone hired him to commit murder, these are dangerous people. Who knows how they'd strike back at someone who tries to expose them? Whatever investigating you've done, I hope you don't do any more. Give any evidence you've got to the police and let them handle it."

"We'll do that soon. Thanks again." I started to walk away but turned back. "I know you can't be positive, but you *think* it was deliberate, don't you? You don't really think you were probably wrong about what you saw."

Slowly, he shook his head. "No. I don't think I was wrong."

Nineteen

After class, when the four of us got together in Joseph's family room, Berk was already in a bad mood. He and Joseph had finished their interviews. Graciana must've done a good job of assigning them the least promising people, because they'd learned exactly nothing.

"Hours of interviews," Berk said. "And not one scrap of information that brings us an inch closer to understanding what happened. I *told* you this would be a huge waste of time."

Graciana pressed her lips together. "I'm sorry it's been so frustrating. At least we've got plenty of information for the memorial issue. That'll be a nice tribute to Coach, and I hope it'll comfort his parents."

Berk blushed, mumbling about how of course that was the most important thing. I felt sorry for him. He'd let frustration push him into making it sound like he didn't care about Coach, when of course he did, and now Graciana had him on the defensive.

She reached for a yellow pad. "Matt and I *did* pick up some information that could prove useful—nothing conclusive, but we should investigate it further. I'll explain."

"No, let me," I said. They wouldn't like the things we had to say—Berk, especially, would hate them. If somebody exploded, I didn't want Graciana to take all the heat.

I started with the way Paul responded to our questions on Sunday. Joseph looked intrigued; Berk looked confused. When I described what Ms. Nguyen said about Marie, both of them looked interested. Then I started talking about our conversation with Marie. Out of the corner of my eye, I watched Berk's face shift from skepticism to anger, getting so hot and red it looked ready to melt.

"Stop," he cut in. "What the hell, Matt? You're *swallowing* this garbage? You think *Paul* was messed up with *Nina Ramsey*? Why would he have anything to do with her?"

"I don't know why," I said, "but it's beginning to look like he was—well, involved with her somehow, yeah. I don't know how much, but that picture of him at her grave—"

"That's nothing. He heard she'd killed herself, he felt sorry for her, so left her a flower. That proves he was a nice guy. It doesn't prove he was *involved* with her."

"You may underestimate," Joseph said. "It is foolish to assume too much, but assuming too little is also unwise. When I heard of Nina's death, I too felt sorry, but I never thought to leave a flower. It is a thing few people would do, unless there is some special connection."

"So what kind of 'connection' was there?" Berk demanded. "You think he was having *sex* with her? Why would he? He's going with *Carolyn Olson*, for God's sake!"

Joseph nodded slowly. "She is lovely. But people speak often of her virtue, saying she guards it closely. It is possible Paul felt unsatisfied needs, and looked to another for relief."

I'd wondered about that, too. On Sunday, when Graciana wasn't looking, Paul sneaked glances at her. Then he'd told me to date nice girls like Suzette, to stay away from Graciana.

I'd gotten the feeling that, for Paul, there were two kinds of girls—popular girls people respected, like Carolyn and Suzette; and girls with bad reputations, like Nina and Graciana. You dated a popular girl publicly, and she helped you become team captain. But if she wouldn't even kiss you until your wedding day, would you feel tempted to see another kind of girl secretly? How many problems could that lead to? How many millions of problems?

Berk was shaking his head, still looking at Joseph. "What are you saying? You think Paul was sleeping with Nina? And then for some reason he—God! You think he picked her up and threw her off that damn bridge? You think he *killed* her?"

"No," I said. "I'm sure Joseph doesn't think those things. Neither do I. You know how I feel about Paul. I like him more than you do, even. But now we've found this—this *thing*. We can't ignore it. We have to look into it."

Joseph was frowning, drumming his fingers on the coffee table. "Most provocative. While nothing is yet definitive, a connection, probably romantic, seems more likely than not. Then, if she threatened or blackmailed or laughed, if he reacted with anger and fear, tragedy might ensue. And the next consequence? Marie told her suspicions to Mr. Colson, he spoke to Paul, and Paul again took alarm. He could not let this thing be found true, so he called Bobby Davis. Is that what you find most plausible, Matt?"

Thanks a bunch, Joseph, I thought. I was positive Berk hadn't thought things through that far yet. With luck, he wouldn't, not until he'd gotten over the first shock. Now Joseph had shoved the whole thing in his face all at once.

"Why would Paul call Davis?" Berk asked, staring at Joseph, his forehead one huge, tight scrunch. Then his eyes got wide. "No. I don't believe it. You are *not* saying that."

Joseph sighed. But I noticed his right foot tapping rapidly in the air, like he was excited. "I would be most sorry to think so. And we do not yet know of any connection between Paul and Davis. This must be ascertained. Do you suggest, Matt, we continue to work in teams, or—"

Berk shot to his feet. "No. I'm not listening to more of this crap. I'm sure as hell not gonna help you do anything that might hurt Paul. I didn't think he was the best captain on the planet, but he's on our *team*. That's supposed to mean something."

"It means a lot," I said. "It doesn't mean everything. If you'd found evidence that seemed to point to me, I wouldn't expect you to give me a pass just because I'm on the team. I'd expect you to check it out and try to clear my name. That's what I want to do with Paul. I'm sure he'd never kill anyone, Berk. Let's prove it."

Berk took two steps toward me. "I don't need to prove it, because I'm *really* sure. The hell with this, Matt. Paul doesn't have anything to do with anything. Let's talk to that lawyer, Michael Burns, and find out who asked him to help Bobby Davis. That's what we should've done in the first place."

"It won't work," Graciana said. "I told you. He won't say anything that might implicate a client, and he might call Dr. Lombardo. It'd be a mistake, Berk."

Berk turned on her, eyes blazing. "Like you're the big expert on everything. You said we'd learn a lot from doing the interviews, and all we came up with is garbage. I've had it with letting you tell me what to do. Matt? What do you say?"

I lifted a hand. "I'm not comfortable with this, either, but it's the only lead we have. We have to look into it."

"Fine," Berk said. "Do your best to ruin Paul's life, and make sure you whine about how uncomfortable it makes you. I'm done."

He turned his back on us and stalked out; moments later, we heard the front door slam. Graciana winced at the sound, then turned to me.

"I'm sorry," she said. "I didn't think he'd actually walk out."

I tried to shrug. "I'll talk to him tomorrow. You're basically okay with this, Joseph?"

"Oh, yes," he said. "I too hope Paul cannot be involved, but we must consider. When people grow angry and scared, they do sometimes terrible things. I saw that too often, in my own country. I saw it the night my father died."

I nodded, trying to take it in. "I can almost see the part with Nina. Not that it sounds like Paul—he gets impatient sometimes, but I've never seen him do a mean or violent thing. But if Nina really provoked him, he might've lost control for one second and hit her and hurt her, and then panicked and decided he had to cover it up. I guess lots of people could do that much if they were pushed too far, and then they'd feel guilty and horrible for the rest of their lives. The part with Coach, though—that's not losing control for a second. That's making a decision, and making plans. That's sitting in the gym and watching it happen and not trying to stop it. I *can't* see Paul doing that."

"I know," Graciana said. "But I've read articles saying that sometimes, when people do something wrong, they *don't* feel guilty and horrible. Sometimes they feel—well, empowered. Liberated, almost. They don't feel as bad about what they did as they would've expected to feel, and that makes it easier for them to do something wrong again. I'm not saying that's what happened, only that it's possible."

"I guess." I wasn't exactly in the mood for hearing about articles Graciana had read. "So, where do we go from here?"

For the next half hour, we traded ideas. It wasn't hard to think of things not to do: Don't say anything that might start rumors about Paul and Nina, don't go to the police without more evidence, don't confront Paul until we know more. We could try to learn more about Nina's death, and Graciana and I could finish our last interview, but how much would we learn from that? The only thing that really made sense right now was talking to Marie again, and I was the logical person to do it. Graciana had a newspaper staff meeting after school tomorrow, and Joseph had never spoken to Marie.

"Since she is shy," he said, "having a new person present might make it harder for her to speak. It seems, Matt, this task must fall to you alone."

"Fine," I said, but didn't feel fine. If Marie was wrong about everything—and that felt like a strong possibility—I'd be encouraging a mixed-up girl to indulge in delusions that couldn't be doing her any good. If her brother found out, I'd be putting her at risk for no reason. And if Paul found out, he might see me as a false friend, as the worst kind of traitor. I'd have a hard time blaming him.

Twenty

"In the cemetery," Marie said, and hurried away, a hunched-over black blur.

That wouldn't have been my first choice for a place to meet, but I was surprised she'd agreed to talk to me at all. And at least she seemed to be all right. I'd asked if Ted gave her a hard time after we left, and she'd said she'd told him we were working on a social studies project. I don't know if he'd believed her. As long as he hadn't hit her, that was good enough.

Some other could-be-worse things had happened, too. My mother's car was out of the shop, the windshield replaced and all other damage repaired. She hadn't hesitated about letting me have it today, hadn't lectured me about needing to take better care of it—of course she hadn't, since she didn't know the truth about why the car had been attacked. I should've probably felt guiltier about that, but mostly I felt good about having the car back.

And Berk wasn't as mad as I'd expected. When I sat down across from him before math got started, he was cool and stiff at first, but he laughed when I told him about a dumb thing that'd happened during homeroom. When class ended, we walked out together, complaining about too much homework. Things felt almost normal.

Also, during the first fifteen minutes of lunch period, Graciana and I got in a quick interview with Mr. Carver, the assistant principal. He'd been close with Coach Colson, and he was a decent guy—fair, reasonable, not too full of himself. Just about every student I knew was hoping he'd be the new principal when Dr. Lombardo retired. He didn't have anything new to tell us, but it felt good to check off our last interview.

As I drove to the cemetery, I felt pretty good. So far, this hadn't been a bad day. Maybe Marie would say something that would let us rule Paul out completely, and then I could go home feeling even better.

I parked in the gravel lot. The cemetery's on the edge of town, a spread-out place with a tall gray stone gate and a wrought iron fence. It's on some registry of historic sites, I guess because it's got a section set aside for graves of Confederate soldiers. Those are toward the front; the farther back you go, the newer the graves get. Some tombstones are large and elaborate, and every so often there's a statue of an angel, or a child hugging a lamb, or a veiled lady weeping over an urn. Tour buses stop here, and some people come for picnics. That seems weird to me, but maybe there's something I'm not getting. The tombstones for the newer graves, toward the back, tend to be smaller and simpler.

I found Marie standing by the newest grave, the one that didn't have a tombstone yet. Her head was bowed—probably, she wasn't praying, just had her head down because she almost always kept it down—but I figured I should play it safe. So I came to stand next to her but didn't say anything, bowed my head, and waited.

After a couple of minutes, she spoke. "Nobody's going to remember her," she said. "She was smart—she always got high grades, even though she ditched classes a lot—and she was funny, and she could act and write poetry. But she didn't have time to do anything. People will forget she was ever even alive."

I didn't know how to argue with that, so I didn't try. "She sounds really special," I said.

Marie didn't seem to mind how lame that sounded. "She was. Nothing scared her. Nothing. Our dad—when he got in one of his moods and came after us, I'd cry and beg, and he'd usually leave me alone. Nina never backed down, even when he started hitting her. She'd keep talking back to him, telling him what a loser he was, saying she wouldn't let him boss her around. Maybe you think that was stupid, but it was really brave."

"It was definitely brave," I said, though I could see the stupid part, too.

Marie nodded. "And when Ted picked on me—he did that lots when we were younger, the first time he lived with us—she'd charge right up to make him leave me alone. They got into awful fights, and she'd get bruised up really bad, but she'd never let anybody hurt me. Not Ted, not Dad, nobody."

"I can see why you miss her so much," I said. "Do you come out here a lot?"

She nodded. "I walk here every day after school, to spend time with her."

"You walked all this way? You should've told me. I would've given you a ride."

She shrugged. "I like to walk. And I'm not allowed to take rides from people. You said you wanted to talk more. About what?"

I had a list of questions in my pocket but thought it'd be crude to take it out. "For one thing, could I see those text messages again? Would I be okay if I copied them down?"

She gave me a sideways look. "Why do you want to?"

"Just to be sure we've got the wording right. Graciana thinks there might be things we're missing, things we might figure out if we looked at the messages more carefully. Would you mind?"

"I guess not," she said, and got out her phone, and found the first message. Balancing my trig notebook against my left arm, I copied it onto a back page: It's official—tomorrow night, Little Becky deflowers Captain America in a doubly shady spot! Take that, Big Brother! That might take some figuring out, all right. "Do you know what she meant by 'a doubly shady spot'?"

"Some place dark, I guess. Does it matter?"

Probably not, but I couldn't help wondering. Marie found the second text message, and I copied that, too. That one didn't seem hard to figure out, but I could see why it felt odd to Marie. It seemed too straightforward, compared to the first message, and it felt too formal. But if Nina had been really depressed, if she'd been as stoned as everybody said she'd been, who knows how that might affect the way she wrote?

I handed the phone back to Marie. "Thanks. On the day it happened, did you see Nina at school much? Did she seem okay?"

Marie lifted her head long enough to give me a sour half-smile. "You mean was she high."

"No," I said, blushing, cursing myself for being so obvious. "At least, not necessarily."

"Of course you think she was high. Everybody thinks that. Nobody at school talks to me much, but I know everybody's always thought she was some big-time addict. She wasn't. She smoked a little weed when she could get it, and sometimes she sneaked a glass of our mom's wine or a shot of our dad's bourbon. But she never did anything harder, and she never did anything at all on school days. She had a 3.94 GPA, and she took three AP exams last spring and got fives on all of them. Could she have done that if she'd been high all the time?"

Maybe, I thought, if she was really smart. I'm not that smart, so I wouldn't know. Anyway, it felt like time to change the subject. "You said when Nina was found, she was wearing a blouse you'd never seen before. I didn't understand that."

Marie shrugged. "She wore a black tee to school that day. But when the police found her, she was wearing a silky light blue sleeveless top, really low cut. That would've got her sent home from school in two minutes. I told the police, but they shrugged it off, said she'd probably had the blue top in her book bag and decided to change after school. So I went to every store in town until I found this lady at a consignment shop. She remembered selling that top to Nina the Saturday before she died."

At this point, I had to agree with the police. "That seems strange to you?"

She lifted her head long enough to give me an exasperated look. "Of *course* it's strange. Nina always showed me the clothes she bought, but she never showed me that top. I bet she never brought it home at all. So what did she do, keep it folded up in her book bag all week? I think she was keeping it at Sherwood Forest, and she put it on that afternoon so she'd look extra-nice when she met Paul Ericson."

"Yeah, I want to ask you about Sherwood Forest," I said, but that was as far as I got.

I heard footsteps behind us, looked over my shoulder, and saw Ted Ramsey. Yesterday, he'd looked suspicious and hostile. Today, he looked furious. Marie gave a little gasp and crouched down to pick up her books.

"What the hell, Marie?" he said, walking up to us. "I told you I don't want you coming here any more. Talking to a corpse—that's sick. And you." He shifted to looking at me, put his hands on his hips. "I told you I don't want you hanging around Marie."

"You said not to come to the apartment. I didn't. Marie and I have to make plans for a social studies project, so we—"

"Yeah, right. I asked around about you. Matt Foley, big-time jock. There's only one reason someone like you comes sniffing around someone like my sister. Well, this ends it. If I see you anywhere near her again, I'll make you damn sorry you ever looked at her. Get in the car, Marie. We're going home. Then we're gonna have a talk."

She was already hurrying toward the car, hunched over as usual. Ted Ramsey took a long moment to stare at me, hacked hard, and spit on Nina's grave. Then he grinned and turned around, walking after his sister.

Two days in a row, I thought. Two days in a row I have to leave her with that guy, not knowing what he'll do to her.

I couldn't stand it. "Wait, Marie," I said, starting after them. "You don't have to go with him. We could—"

He spun around and punched me, landing a hard right hook under my left eye. It hurt a lot—I felt stunned by how much it hurt. I stumbled, and he grabbed my shirt and pulled me forward. The tough-guy grab, I thought. I know how to get out of this. But I was too surprised to remember.

"You're not the one who tells Marie what she can and can't do," he said, shoving his face close to mine. "I am. If you come around again, you'll make things worse for her. And you'll sure as hell make things worse for you."

He pushed me back hard and let me go, sending me sprawling. "Stay away from her," he said, and turned around and left.

I lay on the grass next to Nina's grave, trying to take in what had happened. I touched my cheek. It throbbed, circles of pain pulsing out to my eye, my nose, the whole left side of my face. It made me think of a rock thrown into quiet water, of rings of ripples pushing out even after the stone sank to the bottom. I'd just taken a full-force punch to the face for the first time in my life, and I felt stunned by how much it hurt.

And then he'd gotten me with a tough-guy grab, and I'd blanked. Damn, I thought. I definitely need to practice more.

Twenty-one

Wednesday started bad and kept getting worse.

As usual, I got up early for exercise, practice, laps around the Methodist church parking lot, and a quick shower. When I came downstairs, Mom was cooking again. I bet she and Dad decided hot breakfasts would help us deal with our father being a handyman. It'd take more than eggs and bacon to do that.

"Good morning, Matt." Mom looked up from her frying pans. "Goodness! Your cheek!"

Damn. She'd noticed. I'd made it through dinner last night, because the bruise hadn't set in yet. It'd sure set in now, big and purple and swollen. I tried out the embarrassed laugh I'd practiced. "Yeah, it was dumb. Berk and I were practicing krav moves, and I tripped and pretty much smashed my face into his fist. My fault, not his. Anyway, it doesn't hurt."

Dad frowned as he poured orange juice. "It looks as if it *must* hurt. I hope this class isn't too rough. You never got bruises when you were taking tae kwon do."

"This happened outside class. Aaron makes us wear gloves when we practice this technique. Berk and I didn't have gloves, but we went ahead anyway. Like I said, dumb." Considering I was making stuff up as I went along, it didn't sound bad.

"Well, if anything like this happens again," Mom said, "we should think about whether this class is a good idea."

So now they wanted me to quit krav. Once Aaron started charging us, we probably couldn't afford it anyhow. Maybe I should quit before they had to ask. But I was learning so much, and the things I was learning had never felt more important. It'd hurt like hell to give it up.

Then Cassie came to the kitchen, still in pajamas. "No breakfast," she said, slumping into her chair. "I have a horrible stomachache. I can't go to school."

"Goodness," Mom said. That's as close to cursing as she comes. "How about cinnamon toast? That always makes you feel better. And are you sure you can't go to school? Your English essay's due, and you've worked so hard on that."

"I'll e-mail it to Ms. Andrews. She'll understand." Cassie hesitated. "Maybe *one* slice of cinnamon toast."

Mom put steaming platters of bacon and eggs on the table. Even though I knew they were bribes, they tasted good. I noticed Cassie sneak first one piece of bacon, then another. Not the perfect thing to settle a stomach, maybe, but I was glad she had some appetite.

"I had a good first day yesterday," Dad announced. "I went from house to house, passing out flyers. Lots of people seemed interested. One lady hired me on the spot to fix her garbage disposal." He took a check out of his pocket. "First income for Foley Contracting and Handyman Services. Before I cash it, I'll make a copy and frame it. I've got three more jobs lined up, including one for Berk's mother. She's wanted to put up a kitchen backsplash for years but never gotten around to it. So I'm doing it Saturday."

He paused, like he was expecting applause. Not from me. It's charity, I thought. Berk's mom feels sorry for us, so she came up with something she doesn't need so she can give him money. We're taking charity from my best friend's mother.

"I could use some help on that job, Matt," Dad said. "I could teach you about tile."

Yeah, I'm dying to learn about tile. And going to Berk's house as a handyman sounded like fun. Maybe, at lunchtime, his mom would give us table scraps. "I've got two term papers to work on."

"I still think we should move to a bigger city," Cassie said. "You won't be able to find enough customers in Ridgecrest. In Richmond—"

"In Richmond I'd be competing with lots of other handymen," Dad cut in. "Mom and I are sure we're better off staying here."

"Fine." Cassie pushed her plate away. "Don't listen to me. Don't take me seriously. Nobody in this family *ever* takes me seriously. I'm going back to bed."

She ran upstairs. "Looks like our little girl has hit adolescence," Mom said. "It had to happen, I guess. She couldn't stay sweet and sunny forever."

"Are you sure that's all it is?" I asked. "What if she's really sick?"

"Oh, no reason to worry." Dad started clearing plates. "It's a stage. *You* were plenty grumpy at her age. She'll get past it."

"Nobody in this family ever takes me seriously," Cassie had said. As I drove to school, I thought about that. Mom and Dad didn't take *me* seriously, either. When I said I was worried about Cassie, Dad brushed it off. They both always brush off anything that clouds their happy little view of life. Now they'd decided we'd do fine on whatever odd jobs Dad could scrape together. They were wrong—I felt sure about that. Krav was probably out, college was probably out, and how long could we stay in our house?

In homeroom, another note waited for me: "Go to Dr. Lombardo's office immediately." This couldn't be good.

When I got there, Graciana, Berk, and Joseph already sat stiffly in chairs lined up in front of the big metal desk. I took the last chair, took a deep breath.

Dr. Lombardo's face looked as hard and gray as her desk. "I've had complaints from two people you've interviewed for this so-called memorial issue. They say you asked tactless, disrespectful questions that had nothing to do with paying tribute to Mr. Colson. I'm disappointed in you."

We all looked at each other, stunned. "We've been *very* tactful and respectful," Graciana said, "and all of our questions were relevant. Who made the complaints?"

"That's confidential, and it doesn't matter. Two people described the same problems—I have to conclude their descriptions are accurate. Graciana and Matt, I'm especially disappointed in you. You sat in this office and promised this would be a memorial issue and nothing more. You promised you would make no attempts at investigative journalism and wouldn't stir up unfounded rumors about Mr. Colson's death. You broke those promises, and you drew two other students into your schemes. Until now, I've thought of you as student leaders. I'm sorry to see you use your leadership capabilities in a negative way."

"I don't think any of us did anything wrong," Berk said, "but it's not fair to blame Matt and Graciana most. We all..."

"Loyalty is usually commendable, Berk," she said, "but you're just revealing how strong Matt's influence on you is. I'm calling an end to this project. You are not to pursue it further in any way. You are not to do anything that might create gossip about Mr. Colson's death or damage the school's reputation. And give me all the notes from your interviews. Right now, please."

I started to reach for my book bag, but Graciana stopped me with a glance. "My notes are at home. Probably, we all left our notes home. We can bring them in tomorrow, if you really want us to. But we've finished all the interviews we'd planned to do. We can use the information we already have to put together the memorial issue."

"Out of the question. After the way you've behaved, I am not about to reward you by allowing you to put out a special issue." Dr. Lombardo looked intently at Berk, Joseph, and me. "Is Graciana right? You *all* left your notes home?"

We nodded. My hand had frozen halfway to my book bag. I inched it up and scratched my hip, trying to look innocent.

"All right," Dr. Lombardo said. "Tomorrow morning, on my desk. Graciana, I've already told you you're being considered for Outstanding Senior. Your irresponsibility has put that possibility in jeopardy. Any hint of additional problems will end it. Matt, I'd be sorry to bar you from sports during your senior year. But if you disobey me, I will."

We didn't say anything until we got to the end of the hallway. Then Graciana stopped walking and wheeled around to face us, eyes blazing. "Make copies of everything before you give her even a scrap of paper. Or we could refuse to cooperate. She *can't* have a legal right to make us give her notes we took on our own time. My sister's in law school. I'll call her, and—"

"And Lombardo will kick Matt off the team," Berk said. "Look, I think she's out of line, too. But you're graduating. If you don't get that award, big deal. You've already got your scholarship in your pocket. We're all coming back next year, we'll all be applying to colleges and looking for recommendations, and we all want to play basketball."

"Dr. Lombardo, however, will not come back," Joseph said. "She will retire. Even if she wishes, can she forbid us from the team?"

"Maybe." The fire left Graciana's eyes. "The new principal might not want to overturn her decision. Berk's right. You three stand to lose more than I do. We'd better give her the notes."

"I guess so," I said, relieved. The thought of being barred from basketball hadn't even occurred to me before, and it scared me. Angry as I was at Lombardo, I didn't want to take a stand that'd guarantee it. "I'm sorry about the memorial issue—that would've been a nice thing to do for Coach. Who do you think complained?"

"All the interviews Berk and I conducted were most pleasant," Joseph said. "People seemed glad of the opportunity to convey admiration for Mr. Colson. I cannot think of even one who would complain. Can you, Berk?"

"No," he said, then winced. "Look, this is probably my fault. Yesterday, I was angry about the things you'd said about Paul. So I went to see the lawyer."

"The lawyer?" Graciana said. "You *don't* mean Michael Burns, the lawyer who advised Bobby Davis."

Berk winced again. "Yeah. I called his office and used your idea, said the school newspaper was doing profiles of successful graduates. It worked—he gave me fifteen minutes. I asked some questions about his accomplishments. That went fine. Then I asked about Davis." He paused.

"And that didn't go fine?" I asked.

He shook his head. "As soon as I mentioned Bobby Davis, he clammed up. He wouldn't even say if he knew who Davis was. He started yelling about confidentiality and practically threw me out. You were right, Graciana. Chances are, he's the one who complained to Lombardo, and that's why she shut us down. Sorry, you guys."

I've got to give Graciana credit. She must've been dying to scream, "I told you so!" at Berk. But she let it go. "What's done is done," she said. "Matt, what happened to your eye?"

I gave them a quick explanation, and we broke up to go to class. Two, I thought. Lombardo said two people complained. Maybe she made that up to make her decision seem more reasonable—not that it was reasonable at all if the lawyer complained, since the questions Berk asked him weren't for the memorial issue. But if there *was* a second person, who could it have been? Ms. Quinn, Ms. Nguyen, Mr. Carver—no. Those interviews were fine. And Paul didn't like some of our questions, but I couldn't see him complaining to Lombardo. I could go crazy trying to figure this out, I thought, and gave it up.

The next bad thing happened at lunch. I ran into Graciana as we headed for the cafeteria, and we started whispering about what to do next. Then I felt a soft, firm arm link through mine.

"*There* you are." Suzette kissed me lightly on the cheek. "I've saved us two seats at the table nearest the big window—see? Hi, Graciana."

She took off. Usually, I sit with guys from the basketball team at lunch. But Suzette had saved me a seat. I didn't know how to get out of it without making a big deal. And Graciana was looking at me, not saying anything.

I shrugged. "Guess I'm sitting with Suzette." I loaded things onto my tray without thinking about them. Great. So now the whole school would think Suzette and I were boyfriend and girlfriend, and I wasn't sure I even liked her. And to have her claim me while I was talking to Graciana—I couldn't say why that made everything worse, but it did.

I sat down across from Suzette, and she smiled at me, a bright, flirty smile.

"So, stranger," she said, "it's been *forever* since we've talked."

"I called you."

"You called *Sunday*. It's *Wednesday*. Where've you been hiding since then?"

"I've been here every day." It was a stupid conversation, but it was fun to have a girl going after me, especially such a pretty girl. "And I saw you at krav on Monday."

"Oh, krav." She spat the word out, like it tasted bad. "Krav doesn't count. And oh, my God, I couldn't *believe* how Aaron kept pushing me to demonstrate that technique with him. He *really* wanted an excuse to grab my shirt."

"You would've been playing the tough guy. You would've grabbed *his* shirt."

"He would've gotten off on that, too. But he had to settle for Graciana. *She* really played up to him, didn't she?"

I took a bite of fried chicken. Tough, greasy—not as good as Mom's. "I didn't see that. She did the technique with him, and she had a little fun."

"You *bet* she had fun. All that 'your momma' stuff, trying to look *so* cute. I *hate* it when girls throw themselves at guys like that. But I guess she can't stay away from older men. *Anyway,* how are things going?"

"Fine." I said. Lousy, I thought. I didn't feel like telling her about my dad's job, and I couldn't tell her about Ted Ramsey. I was surprised she hadn't asked about the bruise.

"*I'm* having an *awful* week," she said. "My parents are driving me crazy. My dad keeps snapping at my mom, and she keeps whining and crying and drinking and taking pills. I mean, she always drinks and takes pills, but this week it's worse than usual. It's *pathetic*."

"I'm sorry," I said. "That must be rough."

"It's *terrible*." She gave herself a shake, like she was getting rid of those thoughts. "I sure could use a break. Do you have plans for the weekend?"

So that's why she'd told me those things—so I'd feel sorry for her and ask her out. But I didn't want to make things tense with Berk again, and I didn't want Suzette to think we'd spend every weekend together. "Some plans," I said. "My dad wants me to help him with something. And Berk and I might go bowling." I'd made the last part up on the spot.

"I like bowling," she said. "I'm pretty good. Maybe *we* could go bowling."

"Yeah, with Berk." I stood up. "But I can't make plans till I find out when my dad wants my help. Look, I've got a quiz next period. I should study. See you around."

I picked up my tray and walked away. I'd sounded awkward, and I knew it. I'd told stupid lies, and she probably knew it. Why couldn't I just tell her I wasn't ready for an every-weekend relationship? That probably would've hurt her feelings less.

I went to my social studies classroom and sat brooding. Almost ten minutes to go—for once, I was eager for class to begin. Even listening to Mr. Sinclair drone on about the Great Depression would be better than worrying about everything that'd gone wrong.

Students started drifting in. Gradually, I picked up on an excited, whispered conversation between two girls sitting behind me.

"My uncle works in the ER," one was saying. "He was there when they brought her in, and he says she was a *mess*. Face so swollen and purple it looked like a rotten eggplant, broken jaw, broken collarbone, broken ribs, bruises all over her body, you name it."

"I heard her mother came home from work last night and found her on the floor, unconscious," the other girl said. "And it was a burglar, right? Someone broke into the apartment when she was there alone?"

The first girl snorted. "My uncle says that's what she told the police—some guy she'd never seen before, and she never got a good look at him. Nobody believes her. It was probably her father—he's beat her up before."

"No, her father's in prison," the second girl said. "Probably, it was someone she was sleeping with. She's probably a world-class slut, like her sister."

God, I thought. Please, no. Please don't let it be her. I turned around to face the girl sitting behind me. "Hi," I said.

She broke into a big smile. "Hi, Matt. Oh, my God—where did you get that bruise?"

"It's nothing," I said, feeling almost ashamed it wasn't worse. "Look, I didn't mean to listen in, but I couldn't help overhearing you talk about a girl who got beaten up. Who was it?"

She flipped her hair back over her shoulder and gave me another big smile. "Oh, you know. That weird goth girl. Marie Ramsey."

Twenty-two

After school, we all went to the hospital, but we decided only Graciana and I would try to see Marie. She didn't know Joseph and barely knew Berk, and we didn't want her to feel overwhelmed by too many people. Then we'd all go to Hardee's to figure out what to do next. If we were allowed to see Marie at all.

We weren't. As soon as we mentioned Marie's name, the receptionist shook her head. "She's not allowed visitors yet. But a nurse bought a card so all her friends could send get-well wishes."

She handed us a large card decorated with rainbows and butterflies. So far, there was only one signature—"Angie," written in purple ink, the "i" dotted with a heart.

And no, the receptionist said, she couldn't tell us how Marie was feeling—no information to anyone outside the immediate family. And no, she couldn't say if we could visit tomorrow—we should call before coming.

"But I'll make sure she gets the flowers," the receptionist said, and glanced at the messages we'd written on the card. "Matt? Is that Matt Foley?"

"That's right," I said, surprised. "Why do you ask?"

She hesitated. "Someone mentioned your name. Would you take a seat in the waiting area? I think someone would like to speak to you."

We joined Berk and Joseph in the waiting area, explained what had happened, and traded guesses about who wanted to speak to me—Marie, or her mother? Then the elevator door opened, and we got our answer. Lieutenant Hill.

He stalked over, looking mad. "Outside, Foley," he said.

That didn't sound good. It got worse when we walked to the parking lot, and Hill took a card out of his pocket and read me my rights. I was almost too stunned to feel scared.

He put the card away. "You understand your rights? You want to call a lawyer?"

"I understand." It felt like I was in a television show. "And I don't need a lawyer, because I haven't done anything wrong. What's this about?"

"I'm asking the questions," he said, making it feel even more like television. He took out a notebook. "Have you seen Marie Ramsey recently?"

"Yeah, Graciana Cortez and I talked to her at her apartment on Monday. And yesterday I talked to her again—after school, at the cemetery."

"That's a strange place to meet." He was squinted at me, like he was trying to see past my face and into my brain. "What'd you talk about?"

Damn. He wouldn't like this. "Her sister's death, mostly."

No, he didn't like it. "Her suicide, you mean."

I sighed. "Marie isn't sure it was suicide. You know that."

He lifted just one side of his mouth in a sour, exasperated smile. "You're something else, Foley. You got a murder fixation? First that coach, now Nina Ramsey. How long did you and Marie talk yesterday?"

"Ten, fifteen minutes. Then her brother showed up—her half-brother. Ted Ramsey. He wasn't happy Marie and I were talking, and he made her leave with him."

He wrote that down. "When did you start hitting her?" he asked, not looking up.

I got a sick, hollow feeling in my stomach. "I didn't hit her. I didn't hit anyone."

"No? How'd you get that black eye, then?"

"From Ted Ramsey. Like I said, he didn't like it that I was talking to Marie, and I didn't like the way he was treating her. I tried to tell her she didn't have to go with him, and he punched me."

"Did you hit him back?"

"No. I didn't want to make things worse for Marie."

Hill stopped writing. "I gotta tell you, Foley, this doesn't sound good. You're supposed to be a martial artist, but you can't block a punch from a clumsy lug like Ted Ramsey, and you don't even hit him back. Maybe you didn't get the black eye from him. Maybe you got it from *Marie* Ramsey, when she was trying to defend herself."

"I told you, I never hit her. I wouldn't—"

"All right. Tell me where you were last night, say until 10:30."

Damn, I thought. He's asking for an alibi. How serious is this? Am I going to get arrested? "I was at home. My parents can back that up, and so can my sister."

He jutted his chin out and nodded as he wrote it down, pretending to look impressed. "Alibi confirmed by members of immediate family. *That's* gonna convince a jury. You didn't go out at all? Popular teenage guy, and you spent the whole night sitting in your room? Nobody outside your family came to see you?"

"No. I talked to a few people on the phone."

"Your cell phone, right? So you could've made the calls from anywhere." He did this big sigh, then a pretty good impression of a sympathetic look. "Let's not drag this out. Things will go easier on you if you're upfront with me. You went to Marie's apartment, she was alone, you tried to get romantic, you got into a fight. Those things happen. Who knows? Maybe she hit you first. And you're a minor. If you cooperate, I've got some leeway on the charges."

He sounded almost friendly—that scared me more than anything else. "Lieutenant, nothing like that happened. I swear—"

"All right," he said. "If that's how you want to play it. We've still got forensic stuff to sift through, so I won't take further action yet. Might as well have all the evidence in order first. You're not going anywhere, right? And stop sticking your nose where it doesn't belong. You won't make it easier for the jury to believe you if they think you're some deranged kid obsessed with violence."

He strolled back into the hospital, taking his time, enjoying himself. I braced a hand against the nearest car to steady myself and tried to breathe evenly. God, I thought. How much trouble am I in? I had a quick image of myself in handcuffs, of Hill grinning and putting a hand on top of my head as I got into the backseat of a police car.

Graciana, Berk, and Joseph came running out, practically going crazy with the suspense. I told them about what had happened, trying to be coherent, trying not to sound scared.

Berk looked as terrified as I felt. "Damn, Matt. Why would Hill accuse you? How does he even know you've been talking to Marie?"

"Ted Ramsey." Graciana's face looked grim and tight. "Has to be. We figured he was the one who beat Marie up, and this proves it. I bet the police gave him a hard time, and he tried to deflect suspicion by accusing Matt."

"That is credible," Joseph said. "I am sorry, Matt. You should have a lawyer to advise you. Your parents could help you secure one."

I shook my head. "I don't want to tell them about this, not unless I have to. Sooner or later, that'd mean telling them about everything, including going to Richmond. If they find out about all the things I've been keeping from them, I'll be in big trouble."

"You'll be in bigger trouble if you get arrested," Berk said.

"You won't get arrested," Graciana said. "Hill can't really suspect you. If he did, he would've taken you in for questioning. He mentioned forensic evidence, but he didn't fingerprint you. He didn't even take a picture of your bruise. If he were planning to build a case against you, he'd want a picture, as proof you'd been in a violent clash."

That gave me hope. "Then why did he say those things?"

"Because he doesn't like you," she said, her voice getting harder and angrier. "Because he resents you for questioning his professional opinions, and he wants to bully you into stopping."

"I bet you're right," Berk said, eyes brightening. "Anyway, Matt, if it comes down to your word against Ted Ramsey's, you should be all right. I bet he's got a record—I bet he's done lots of violent things. Who'd believe him over you?"

I shrugged. "It depends on what Marie says. She's scared to death of her brother. If he tells her she has to say I'm the one who hit her, she might."

Graciana shook her head. "She wouldn't send you to prison for something you didn't do. She'll send *him* to prison, so he can't hurt her anymore. You don't have anything to worry about. Let's go to Hardee's. We'll talk everything over, decide what to do next."

"Hold on," Berk said. "I'm not sure I want to do *anything* next. Hill told Matt to stop nosing around. Maybe we should all do that. We haven't gotten any closer to figuring anything out, and look at all the bad stuff's that's happened. We're all in trouble with Lombardo, Matt's in trouble with the police, he got punched, and Marie got beat up—we still don't know how bad. I say that's enough. I'm through."

"I think perhaps we should all be through," Joseph said. "From first beginning, we said we would try to learn all we could. We did so. We did not get the result we hoped, but what can we do more? And now there has been violence. It has become too much."

"I understand why you feel that way," Graciana said, "but I *do* think we've made progress. If we—"

"Look," I said, "maybe we shouldn't make decisions right now. It's been a rough day. We can work off steam at krav tonight, give ourselves a chance to absorb what's happened, talk tomorrow or Friday. What do you think?"

Berk and Joseph nodded right away. "A wise plan," Joseph said. "I concur."

Graciana's shoulders went rigid. So did her face. "Fine. See you guys at krav." She got into her car and drove away.

I looked at Berk and Joseph. "Is she mad?"

"You cut her off," Berk said, "and you made a good suggestion, and we agreed with you. Graciana's supposed to be the one who has good ideas and tells everyone what to do."

Great, I thought as I got in the car. I stepped on Graciana's ego. One more thing to worry about.

Minutes after I got home, Suzette called. "I'm not going to krav. My dad and some of his high-school basketball buddies all of a sudden decided to have some big get-together at that new restaurant in Appomattox—*so* lame, but Dad says I have to go." Her voice got wistful. "It wouldn't be lame if *you* came. Maybe you could skip class, too. Dad wouldn't mind."

"Berk and Joseph are counting on me for rides." I had to be setting some kind of record for using Berk as an excuse. But I didn't feel like listening to Mr. Link and his buddies tell old basketball stories, and I didn't especially feel like being with Suzette. Besides, I *needed* to go to krav, to unload some tension.

Dinner wasn't much fun. Mom must've decided we'd had enough comfort food, so we'd gone back to eggplant hash. Cassie didn't eat much, didn't say much, just whimpered about her stomachache. Dad acted all perky, talking about how many leaflets he'd passed out. Mom fussed about my bruise, trying to talk me into skipping krav. No way. And all the time I was thinking about Hill, wondering what Marie had told him, half-expecting cops to show up at the door any minute and haul me away.

I started feeling better the minute I left the house. Even the slow drizzle beginning to build felt refreshing.

Class was great. I was getting better at physical conditioning—I never had to stand to the side and rest anymore, and I kept passing people when we ran laps. Aaron taught us a cool disarming technique, we got on the floor to practice a new grappling release, and I felt like I was picking things up fast. Toward the end of class, Aaron took me aside.

"Did you go to the police?" he asked.

No, I thought. The police came to me. But I didn't feel up to telling him about that. "Not yet. We may take more time to try to find evidence. We're not sure."

"I hope you decide against it," he said. "I know you want justice for Coach Colson, but the longer you keep this up, the bigger the risk gets. Sometimes, no matter how hard it is, you have to walk away from a situation that's getting too dangerous."

"I know. We don't want to be stupid about this. We know there's a limit to what we can do. We're just not sure we've reached that limit yet."

He winced. "What about that bruise?"

"This guy named Ted Ramsey punched me. I was trying to get some information from his sister, and he didn't like it. It was embarrassing, Aaron. I didn't even try to block. I knew what to do, but I was too surprised to react. I've gotta practice more."

"You've also got to avoid dangerous situations. You've got lots of potential as a martial artist, Matt, at least as much as anyone else in class. And you never hesitate to throw yourself into a new technique, never seem to worry about getting hurt. That's admirable, but it can be risky. It might make you think you can handle situations you should avoid. No matter how many techniques you know, you shouldn't rush into situations where you might have to use them."

"I know. I'll be careful."

"I hope so." He tried to smile, but it was a worried smile. "You're good, Matt, but you're not Chuck Norris. Not yet."

So now I had Aaron thinking I was some arrogant jerk, taking stupid risks, itching to get into fights and show how good I am. How much worse could this day get?

It got worse five minutes later, when I saw Graciana putting her shoes back on. We hadn't said one word to each other during class. Once, when we'd been standing near each other and it would've been natural to pair up to try a technique, she'd turned away and asked someone else to be her partner. I walked over to her, hoping to smooth things out.

"Great class," I said. "What do you think of the new disarming technique?"

"I like it." She focused on tying her shoelaces. "I don't really have it down yet, though. It still feels awkward."

"Yeah, it feels awkward to me, too," I said, though it didn't. "You got lots of homework tonight?"

"Not really." Finally, she stopped fussing with her shoes. "Some reading, and revisions on an essay due Friday. How about you?"

I made a show of shuddering. "Unit test in English tomorrow, on the Harlem Renaissance. Not something I'm looking forward to, since I haven't read half the stuff Ms. Nguyen assigned. My mom's making zucchini cookies for me to snack on while I'm cramming. Mom's zucchini cookies. *Those* will keep me motivated, all right."

Graciana's mouth twisted. "Don't brag about not doing your schoolwork. It's nothing to be proud of. And you shouldn't make fun of your mother's cooking. You should speak of your parents with respect, or not speak of them at all. When you made jokes about your mother's tiramisu, I felt embarrassed for you."

She walked off. I stared after her. She'd felt *embarrassed* for me? Who did she think she was? I'm just being friendly, making a little joke, and she comes back at me with *that*?

By now, it was pouring, sheets of rain crashing down and bouncing off the pavement. Berk, Joseph, and I made a run for the car but still got soaked. For the first part of the drive, I was too upset to say much. So much for Graciana Cortez, I thought. As soon as our pitiful attempt to investigate is over—and it's probably over already—I don't need to have anything more to do with her. Fine.

By the time we dropped Joseph off, I'd calmed down. He lives clear on the other side of town, and I could shave some time off the drive home by taking the interstate. As we pulled onto it, I noticed a silver Toyota following close behind. *Tailgater*, I thought, and sped up to put some distance between us.

He sped up, too, crowding us—really dumb, especially in this rain, in this dark. I pulled into the right-hand lane and slowed down to let him pass, but he didn't. Instead, he kept almost even with us, veering into our lane, crowding us. I peered into the rearview mirror, trying to get a look at the driver. But it was too dark, and the rain was too solid.

Finally, he sped up, but not to pass us. He pulled up exactly even to us in the left lane, flipped on his dome light, turned his face to us, and grinned. Bobby Davis.

Twenty-three

"Holy crap," Berk said.

I agreed. But the exit was only a mile ahead, and then there'd be traffic, there'd be houses. I tried to calm down, telling myself Davis wouldn't try anything once there were people around.

Except that he'd killed Coach Colson in front of hundreds of witnesses.

I put that out of my mind and focused on reaching the exit, speeding up as much as I dared. He sped up, too, still keeping even with us, still grinning. Half a mile short of the exit, he pulled ahead and started turning toward us, into our lane.

"Don't slow down!" Berk shouted.

I had to, though, or I'd hit him. I pulled off the road, hoping I could get around him on the shoulder.

But the shoulder sloped, and I felt the car slide down a small embankment, felt the back tires settle in mud. Twenty feet in front of us, Davis stopped his car.

"If he gets out," I said, "I'll back up and drive around him. We can make it to the exit before he catches up with us."

He got out of his car, opened the trunk, and grabbed something, taking his time.

"Now!" Berk shouted, but I waited until Davis crossed half the distance between us, until he was too far from his car to just jump back in.

As soon as I could see his face, I put the car in reverse and hit the gas. Nothing. The tires spun in the mud. We didn't budge.

Now I saw what Davis had taken out of his trunk. A tire iron. He held it in his right hand, tapping it against his left palm, and headed toward us, moving quickly.

I reached for my phone, but Davis was already standing right outside my car door. He brought his face even with the window and grinned again. The rain had pounded his slicked-back hair down over his ears, making him look like some demented freak. "Don't try calling 911," he said, "or you'll piss me off. That'd be a mistake. And it's too late for that anyhow. Time to get out of the car, boys. All I want to do is talk. Don't make me smash the windshield and drag you out."

I looked at Berk, and he shook his head so hard and fast it almost blurred.

Davis sighed. "I'll put the tire iron on the hood and back off. Then you get out."

He did it and crossed his arms, waiting.

Berk stared at me, his eyes wide. "What do you think?"

I pictured Davis smashing the windshield, dragging us out over shards of broken glass, tire iron still in hand. "We can't fight back sitting in the car. Maybe he *does* just want to talk. Whatever he says, stay cool."

We got out of the car. "We don't want any trouble," I said. I had to almost shout to make myself heard over the rain.

"Really?" This guy couldn't stop grinning. "Could've fooled me. You came to Richmond twice, asking questions about me, and you've been asking people around here questions, too, making them nervous. Why? You think you can squeeze money out of somebody?"

Berk took a step toward him. "You bastard! You killed Coach Colson! You did it on purpose! You—"

"Shut up, Berk," I said. So much for staying cool. I looked at Davis. "Look, we were curious. Our coach got killed, the way it happened seemed weird, we didn't understand, and we wanted to find out."

"So you were curious." He thought it over, or pretended to, and shook his head. "Sorry. I don't buy it. You wouldn't do all that stuff just because you were curious. You're trying to set me up for blackmail, aren't you? Me, or somebody else."

"No. Anyway, we've stopped. We decided it'd gotten too dangerous."

"I'd like to believe that." He took two steps toward me. "But I don't. And I promised somebody I'll make sure you and your friends don't make more trouble. I've already done one thing to help you understand how serious this is. Maybe I should do more. What do you think?"

"We understand," I started to say, but Berk went nuts. Before I knew what was happening, he'd grabbed the tire iron, raised it over his head, and started running toward Davis.

"Murderer!" he screamed.

Davis barely looked at him. He took one hop toward him and brought his leg up for a powerful hook kick to his stomach. Berk dropped the tire iron and slumped to his knees, holding his side, gasping.

Davis chuckled, moved closer, and grabbed the front of my shirt. "Maybe your friend's learned his lesson. How can I make sure you've learned yours?"

Tough-guy grab, I thought, and reached over the top of his hand, grabbed it, and pushed down with my thumb. Twisting my body, I pushed his elbow down with my left hand, getting him in an arm lock, bending him over. Then frantic knee strikes to his face, his stomach—not well aimed, but fear made them quick and hard. He crumbled to his knees, coughing.

I ran for Berk. "Get up," I said. "Get in the car. We'll—"

Already, Davis was back on his feet. Already, he'd caught up with me. He grabbed my wrist and kneed me in the stomach five or six times, knocking the wind out of me. Then, still gripping my wrist, he punched me in the kidney.

The pain stunned me. Barely aware of what had happened, barely able to stand, I started to fall forward. Davis launched a precise front kick, striking me in the stomach, grinning as I collapsed to the ground on my hands and knees. Lazily, not hurrying, he bent over me and wrapped his arm around my neck in a choke hold, pressing hard. I felt myself start to black out. One final burst of pressure against my throat, and he let me go.

"Don't make me finish it," he said softly, and walked to his car.

I stayed there in the mud, on my hands and knees, feeling the rain pound on my back, panting, trying to force air into my body, to stay awake, to stay alive. Berk stumbled over.

"Can you get up?" he said. "We gotta get to the car."

I felt dizzy, only half-aware of the struggle to get to my feet, of the relief of letting myself fall against Berk as he pulled me toward the car. I didn't seem to have any feeling in my arms. For a moment, I think I blacked out. The fear in Berk's voice brought me back.

"How bad did he hurt you?" he asked. "Should we go to the hospital?"

"Your house," I heard myself say. "I need time."

Then I was in the car, collapsing against the seat, only half-listening as Berk gunned the motor again and again, cursing, until at last we were out of the mud and back on the road.

He helped me in through the back door that leads to his basement family room, got me a blanket, got me some water. As soon as I could manage, I called home. Berk and I had decided to study for the English test together, I told Mom. I'd be home in an hour or so. No, she didn't need to bring zucchini cookies over. We'd picked up a pizza. I'd be sure to pack some cookies for lunch tomorrow.

I turned to Berk. "I've gotta wash my clothes. They're covered in mud. If my parents see me like this, they'll want to know why."

He put my clothes in the washer, and I wrapped myself in the blanket and sat on the couch, measuring the pain in places Davis had struck. Stomach, kidney, throat—just soreness, nothing ruptured or broken. And he hadn't marked my face, probably hadn't left bruises that'd prove I'd been beaten up. Had he figured all that out in seconds? How good *was* he?

Berk came back. "God, Matt. I thought he was gonna kill you."

"I thought so, too." I forced a laugh. "Damn, that was pathetic. All the techniques I've learned, all the time I've spent practicing, and I just sat there in the mud, letting him squeeze the life out of me, no clue how to fight back."

"Don't be so rough on yourself. It was my fault. If I hadn't charged him, if you hadn't tried to help me—"

"No, it wasn't your fault, either. He's just too good. He's way, way too good."

"God," Berk said, "what if Suzette had been with us? She usually is when we go down that stretch of road. Do you think he would've hit her, too?"

"He's as low as they come. I wouldn't be surprised if he'd hit a girl."

That was one thing to be grateful for. Bad as it'd been, if she'd been with us, it could've been much worse. Berk threw himself down in an armchair, and we both sat silently. We had lots of things to talk about, but we weren't up to it. At first, I focused on breathing, on thinking about how good it felt to inhale and exhale normally again. I don't think I'd ever realized what a big thing breathing is before.

Berk looked up. "We should warn Graciana and Joseph. Davis might come after them."

That hadn't occurred to me. "Davis might not know about them. We're the ones he saw in Richmond."

"He knows. He knew we'd gone to Richmond twice, and he said he'd promised somebody he'd make 'you and your friends' stop. We've *got* to warn them."

"You're right." But I couldn't stand the thought of calling them. I especially couldn't stand the thought of having Graciana ask smart, sharp questions I was too groggy to answer. "Would you call? Say I feel too lousy to talk."

He made the calls—a short one to Joseph, a much longer one to Graciana. I listened to him try to answer her questions, try to remember exactly what Davis had said, try to tell her, several times, that no, I really couldn't talk. Finally, he signed off.

By then, my clothes were ready, so I got dressed, surprised at how painful something as simple as putting on a shirt could be. When I got home, Dad was sitting at the kitchen table, and Mom was standing at the counter, talking on the phone. I waved and started toward the stairs, hoping I could sneak up to my room before they noticed how stiff I was. The worried edge to Mom's voice made me stop.

"Are you sure?" she said. "I could come right now if—all right. First thing in the morning, then. I'll start an inventory to estimate the damage. I'm so sorry, Sylvia. Please try not to worry."

Sylvia. That was Mom's boss, the owner of Wendy's World. And something was wrong, and I had a sick feeling I already knew more about it than Mom did.

She hung up. "What happened?" I asked.

For maybe ten seconds, Mom stood rubbing her forehead, eyes squeezed shut. Then she gave me a bright little smile. "Oh, there was a small fire at the store tonight. No one was there, thank goodness, so no one got hurt, and the fire department put it out quickly. Sylvia says we lost some merchandise, and the place is a bit of a mess. But I'm sure the insurance company will come through. So! How was your study session?"

"Fine." Don't brush me off, Mom, I thought, half-angry at her. "How did the fire start?"

"Nobody knows yet. People love to speculate when something like this happens, of course, and they say lots of silly things. It'll probably turn out to be something boring, like faulty wiring."

"Is anyone talking about arson?" Dad asked.

Mom gave him a look. What did she think, that I'd have nightmares if he mentioned arson? "I guess some people are. Apparently, a back window was smashed in, and that didn't seem to be caused by the fire. So some people are talking about Molotov cocktails, that sort of nonsense. But that seems *so* unlikely, doesn't it?"

"Maybe not." Dad's face looked grimmer by the second. "Think about what happened to your windshield. We don't get many troublemakers in Ridgecrest, but every once in a while, someone thinks it's fun to destroy things, and sometimes people get hurt. We should all be extra-careful." He turned in his chair to face me. "That means you, too, Matt. Keep your eyes peeled for trouble."

I nodded. *Now he tells me*, I thought.

Twenty-four

I hardly slept that night. I was exhausted, I was hurting, but I couldn't sleep. I'd lie on my bed a while, get up and pace, sit at my desk, lie down again, get up again. Nothing felt comfortable. Nothing felt right.

I felt positive Bobby Davis started the fire at Mom's store. Before Berk charged him, Davis said he'd already done something to make us understand how serious the situation was. Smashing a window at Wendy's World and throwing a Molotov cocktail through it would be a dramatic thing to do. He was threatening my family now, not just me.

And he knew where my mother worked. Had he learned that from the person who hired him to kill Coach? That meant they were still working together, probably meant the person knew me. Davis had said we'd been "asking people questions, making them nervous," and he said he'd promised someone he'd make us stop. So this "someone" knew we were questioning people, and that was making him or her nervous. That had to mean we were getting close.

I ought to feel good about that, but I couldn't. We never should've started this stupid investigation, I thought. We jumped in without thinking about what the consequences might be, for us or anyone else. We've stirred things up, we've upset people, bad things had happened, and who knows what might happen next?

Just this morning, getting kicked off the basketball team had seemed like the biggest catastrophe I could imagine. Now, it was low on the list.

We still didn't know how badly Marie was hurt, or whether she'd recover completely. If she didn't, it'd be partly our fault. If we'd left her alone, her brother wouldn't have beaten her up like that.

And Graciana didn't think Marie would accuse me of beating her up, but I wasn't sure. Yes, Marie would probably love to accuse Ted and get him sent to prison, but what if the charges didn't stick? What if he got a short sentence? She was probably afraid he'd come after her for revenge, and he probably would. I was sure she'd feel bad about accusing me, but if Ted told her to do it, she might be scared not to. Any minute, the doorbell might ring, and I'd get arrested.

Even that might not be my biggest worry. Davis killed Coach, he smashed the windshield, and tonight he started a fire at Wendy's World and ran Berk and me off the road.. And he had said, "Don't make me finish it."

If he decided to come after us again, he *could* finish it. He could kill us both in minutes. That wasn't an opinion. It was a fact.

Or what if he came after the car when I wasn't in it? What if he ran it off the road while Mom was driving Cassie to a viola lesson? What if he did it on an isolated road, took out the tire iron, and—no. I blocked the image before it took shape.

I had to warn my mother. I had to tell my parents everything, right away. They'd panic for sure—no way could they handle this. They'd say no more krav maga, even though krav had nothing to do with it. They might not want me to see Berk anymore, or Graciana or Joseph, since they were involved. They might not want me to leave the house; they might be afraid to leave the house themselves. Maybe Cassie would get her wish, and we'd move to another city, where neither of them would have a real job.

I sat at my desk. And they'll never trust me again, I thought. I'd kept too much from them. I'd told too many lies and half-lies. With everything else I had to worry about, the thought of my parents not trusting me hurt more than I'd ever thought it would.

I'd kept things from them before. For years, I'd told them lots of little lies and never worried about it. It'd felt like a game, to see how much I could get away with.

I'd gotten away with a lot, because they'd always believed me. Lots of times, I'd smirked at them for being gullible. Now, I realized how much I'd miss having them trust me.

Restlessly, I opened my desk drawer and saw Coach Colson's yellow pad—the pad I'd picked up after he was killed, filled with notes about the tournament and doodles of ducks and two flowering trees and lopsided houses. I turned to the page with notes about Berk: "Quick techniques, but keep control. Don't let emotions choose your moves." I started to turn the page, then read the words again. That really sums Berk up, I thought—not just how he spars, but how he makes decisions about everything from what to have for lunch to whether to attack Bobby Davis. I'd read Coach's comment before, but I hadn't realized how perceptive it was. It was like what Ms. Nguyen says about poetry—when you read carefully, you see meanings you miss if you read quickly.

Struck by a thought, I got my trig notebook and turned to the page where I'd copied Nina Ramsey's text messages.

It's official—tomorrow night, Little Becky deflowers Captain America in a doubly shady spot! Take that, Big Brother! Little Becky was Nina's nickname for herself, Marie said, and Captain America was her nickname for Paul. So we'd assumed that if Nina had been killed, the message pointed to Paul.

Or maybe it pointed away from him.

Marie thought Nina and Paul met at the bridge after school that day. They agreed to get together the next night. Nina sent Marie the text message. Then something went wrong, and Paul threw Nina off the bridge.

Now, I realized the sequence didn't make sense. Marie said Nina had been working at seducing Paul for weeks. When she finally succeeded, would she interrupt the moment by saying, "Excuse me—I have to text my little sister"?

No. Nina must've sent the message after Paul left. She sent it when she was standing on the bridge alone.

Paul could've come back, of course, and that could've been when things went wrong. Or maybe someone else had come along.

Take that, Big Brother.

Yesterday, when Marie and I were at the cemetery, Ted Ramsey showed up out of nowhere. He knew Marie went to the cemetery after school, and he was so intent on controlling her that he'd come after her.

Maybe he'd been intent on controlling Nina, too, and he'd known she'd be at the bridge. Maybe he'd shown up there after Paul left and Nina sent her text message.

Now Nina's death was easy to imagine. If Ted had seen Paul, maybe he'd told Nina she had to stay away from him—or she had to go home, or she couldn't wear that top anymore.

And Nina defied him. Marie said Nina had never backed down from either her father or her brother, and she and Ted had gotten into awful fights. Maybe he'd knocked her down and she'd hit her head, and he'd been afraid she was dead or so badly hurt her injuries would send him to prison. So he'd thrown her off the bridge, and later he'd sent Marie a text message to make it look as if Nina committed suicide.

I started pacing. Everything made sense now. I'd never been able to picture Paul killing someone, but Ted—no problem. He'd beaten Marie up, probably while she was crying and begging him to stop. If Nina fought back, if she insulted him, he'd hit her as hard as he could.

The picture of Paul at Nina's grave made sense now, too. He'd liked Nina, or at least been attracted to her, so he felt bad when she died. If he worried she'd had regrets about deciding to have sex with him and that somehow caused her suicide, he'd feel really bad. He didn't go to her funeral, because he wanted to keep their relationship secret, so he found a private moment to put a flower on her grave. Perfectly natural. Mystery solved.

Something else occurred to me, something that made me stop pacing. If Ted went to prison for beating up Marie, he might come back for revenge before long. If he went to prison for murdering Nina, Marie wouldn't have to worry he'd get out any time soon. And I wouldn't have to worry she'd decide to protect herself by accusing me.

I'd still have to worry about Bobby Davis, though. Or would I? Ted kept close tabs on Marie. Maybe he knew she'd talked to Coach about Nina's death, and maybe something made him think Coach suspected him. Ted seemed like someone who'd enjoy watching people pound on each other. Maybe he knew about the fight club and decided to hire Davis. If we could find solid evidence and get Hill to arrest them both, one of them might panic and try to make a deal by testifying against the other. That happens on television; it probably happens in real life, too. Then Ted Ramsey and Bobby Davis would both go to prison for a long time, Marie would be safe, my family would be safe, and both Coach and Nina would get some justice.

I threw myself down on my bed, feeling both excited and frustrated. Finally, I had a theory that made sense, a suspect who seemed capable of murder. But it was too late. Tomorrow, I had to tell my parents the truth, and that'd end everything.

I sat up. *Did* I have to tell them tomorrow?

Maybe tomorrow would be the worst possible time to open up and have my parents overreact. If we pushed to find solid evidence, we might make a breakthrough soon, and my parents might never have to know about all the lies and secrets.

Or maybe I just wanted to believe that.

I spent the next few hours debating, pacing, sitting at my desk, lying wide-eyed on my bed. At some point, I drifted off, and I didn't wake up until Mom knocked on my door, saying I'd be late for school if I didn't hurry. I grabbed a handful of zucchini cookies for breakfast and got going. I felt stiff and had a deep pain in my side, but I wasn't limping, and I didn't have new bruises. Nobody could know what happened last night just by looking at me.

One or two days, I decided. After that, if we haven't figured things out, I'll quit, and I'll tell my parents and face whatever happens. But if we give this one or two more days, or three or four, maybe we can pull this off.

Twenty-five

I didn't forget to leave my notes at Dr. Lombardo's office, or to make copies first. It felt like weeks since we'd sat listening to Dr. Lombardo lecture us, but it'd been one day. Unbelievable.

During the English test, I fell asleep. It didn't make much difference—I would've flunked anyway. But I felt embarrassed when Ms. Nguyen kept stopping by my desk, speaking softly, trying to help me stay awake. She talked to me after class, eyes all sympathetic, asking if I'd been having trouble sleeping since Mr. Colson died. I said no, I was tired from sports, but I don't think she believed me. Too bad. I didn't want to use Coach as an excuse for flunking.

At lunch, Suzette cornered me again, saying she'd saved us seats. I didn't feel like it, but I also didn't have the energy to come up with a way of getting out of it. So I nodded.

As usual, Suzette took charge of the conversation. "Oh, my God. You wouldn't *believe* how awful that reunion last night was! Four of my dad's old basketball buddies and their wives and kids, all squeezed into the back room at Melinda's Grill. It was *so* noisy and stuffy. Then Mr. Quinn said we were going to play games. *Games!* He divided us into teams for a

'Ridgecrest High, Then and Now' version of *Jeopardy!* He'd put all the questions into a PowerPoint presentation."

"Answers." I wound spaghetti around my fork. "With *Jeopardy!* you get answers, not questions."

"Whatever. And he'd recorded bits of songs popular during their senior year for something called 'Name That Tune,' and—oh, it was so *dumb.* I've *never* been so bored."

"Sounds bad," I said. Sounds like Mr. Quinn, I thought. With him, everything has to be elaborate and figured out in advance and under control—preferably, his control.

"Then, right in the middle of a game," Suzette said, "Ms. Quinn stood up and left the room for half an hour, without saying a word to anyone. I bet she went to the bar and had a drink, because she couldn't stand being around him anymore. I don't blame her. Can you imagine what it must be like to be married to Mr. Quinn?"

Fortunately, I couldn't. "Did she seem drunk when she came back?"

"No, just fed up. My mom, though—she never left the room, but she drank way too much. She *always* does. She got too loud, so my dad snapped at her, and she started crying. It was *so* embarrassing."

It did sound bad. "That's rough," I said.

"Yeah, it was. Plus I'm supposed to put posters for the stupid bake sale up around town, but I've got a mandatory dance team meeting, so what do I do about the posters?"

"I'll put them up," I offered.

"Really? You're *sweet!*" Her eyes went moist. "I want to ask you something. Megan's having a birthday party tomorrow. I don't have my license yet, and Dad and Mom can't drive me. But I'd really like to go to that party—I *need* to go, after the awful week I've had."

She probably had girlfriends who could drive her, and I didn't want to get into an every-weekend thing. But her hair was all lit up by light coming through the window. "I'll take you, if you want."

Instantly, her eyes got bright and big. "I'd *love* that! About eight o'clock? I'll get the posters."

When I got out of my last class, Graciana was waiting in the hall, holding her shoulders back stiffly. "I've been worried about you," she said as we walked toward an exit. "How are you? Berk said Davis really worked you over."

"I'm fine," I said, and realized it was almost true. The pain in my side had faded, and I'd gotten used to the general soreness.

"Good. I called the hospital. Marie still can't have visitors. I bet somebody doesn't *want* her to have visitors." She hesitated. "Matt, I apologize for what I said last night. The way you talk about your mother is none of my business."

"I was only joking around," I said.

She lifted an eyebrow. "Well. It's none of my business."

In other words, she still thought I'd been a jerk. I let that slide. We didn't have to be best friends to work together, and I needed to run some things past her. "I had trouble sleeping last night, and I had a bunch of thoughts, mostly about Ted Ramsey. See what you think."

The hall had pretty much emptied out by now, so I gave her a three-minute summary, keeping my voice low. At first, she looked skeptical. By the time I finished, she was nodding.

"That's plausible," she said. "Damn—I should've noticed the message implied Paul had already left. We should—no." She caught herself. "We said we wouldn't do anything more until the four of us talk. We should check with Berk and Joseph."

"They won't mind if we do things that can't possibly be dangerous. I thought I'd go to the library and try to learn more about Nina's death, and about Ted. I'm sure you're better at research than I am. Want to help?"

She grimaced. "I'm babysitting my brother's kids. Ms. Simon can help you. If you find out anything important, call me."

Ms. Simon, our librarian, has been at the school since it opened, so she must be around fifty. She looks younger, maybe because she's built on such a small scale—barely five feet, slim, chin-length hair, little wire-rimmed glasses perched on her head. Even her voice seems small, always hushed, like she was born to work in a library. Her high heels clicked against the floor as we walked to the computers. "What are you research-ing today, Matt?" she asked. "Working on a term paper?"

"No, I'm trying to find anything I can on Nina Ramsey's death. Do I just Google her name?"

"You can start there." She sat at a computer desk. "And other databases can lead you to information you won't find through Google. Take a look."

She spent almost fifteen minutes showing me how to access the databases. It was actually interesting. "Thanks," I said. "I'd never even heard of those databases."

"These are only a start. When you do research in college, you'll use more specialized databases, including some our school doesn't have access to."

"There are *more*? That sounds hard."

She smiled. "Things don't get fun until they get hard. Would you enjoy basketball if the basket were three feet off the ground? And finding information isn't the hardest part of research, or the most fun. The hardest part is interpreting what you find—seeing how things fit together, noticing when they *don't* fit, figuring out why. I think you'll enjoy that."

I winced. "Maybe not. I'm mostly into sports. I'm not the academic type."

"Don't be too quick to decide what 'type' you are. You can be more than one type. Okay. That should get you started. If you get stuck, let me know."

I didn't get stuck. I found lots of information on Nina Ramsey, from her birth announcement to her name on a list of elementary school graduates to reports on her suicide. None of the reports had much solid information, just the same bland sentences from the police, all hedged with "apparently" this and "evidently" that. I'd hoped to find a statement about whether Nina had been drinking or taking drugs before she died, but none of the articles mentioned that.

When I switched to Ted Ramsey, I mostly found arrest reports, mostly for stuff like shoplifting and disorderly conduct. In the earliest ones, he was eighteen. There were two or three a year until he was twenty-two, and then nothing until this fall, when he had an assault arrest at age twenty-seven. I remembered Marie saying Ted used to pick on her "the first time he lived with us." Had he lived with the family when he was younger, gone off on his own, and then come back? I'd look for a way to find out.

Ms. Simon came over to check on me. "How's it going?" she asked, and looked at the computer screen. "Ted Ramsey—I didn't realize you'd be looking for material on him, too."

She didn't ask why, and I decided not to try to explain. "Did you know him when he was a student here?"

She hesitated. "I didn't know him well. He didn't spend much time in the library."

I could believe that. "Did he graduate? I couldn't find his name on any graduation list."

"No, I'm quite sure he dropped out."

She didn't seem eager to talk about him. Probably, teachers have rules about not talking to students about other students.

But he wasn't a student anymore. Maybe I could get her to open up if I gave her a reason. "I've run into him a few times. He seems like an angry guy. In fact, he gave me this." I pointed to my eye. "Maybe I should stay away from him."

She looked alarmed. "You should *definitely* stay away from him. You're right—he's an angry sort. At least, he was when he went here. That was Dr. Lombardo's first year as principal, and he gave her quite a time. He was constantly getting sent to her office."

"That must be rough on a brand-new principal," I said, to keep her talking.

"I'm sure it was, though she handled the situation adroitly." She half-smiled at some memory. "Several students that year were—colorful. One girl thought she was a pagan priestess and decided to put a curse on the school. She performed rituals in the girls' room, ones that involved sacrifices, and when other girls found what she'd left behind, they'd run out screaming. And there was a boy with an odd, the-South-will-rise-again name—Stonewall Jackson Smith, something like that—who was exceptionally talented in track and set two state records as a sophomore. He seemed quiet, even shy, but one day he nearly beat a boy to death. Another student—well. I shouldn't go on and on. The point is, Dr. Lombardo had a challenging first year, but she took a firm stand on discipline. The school has been a saner, more orderly place ever since. Can I help you with anything?"

"No, thanks. I'm just going to check out a few more things."

"Fine." She hesitated. "Matt, I'm serious about staying away from Ted Ramsey. I shouldn't go into detail, but associating with him would be a mistake."

"I bet you're right," I said. "Thanks."

She nodded and walked away, and I got back to work. After fifteen minutes that didn't lead to anything new, I gave up and turned the computer off. Maybe I'd check some old yearbooks and see if I could learn more about Ted Ramsey. As I was stuffing my notebook into my book bag I felt a hand on my shoulder, turned around, and saw Mr. Quinn.

"Working on a term paper?" he said. "Good—I'm always glad to see you in the library. But I was sorry to hear you missed the chemistry review session after school yesterday."

Damn—did Mr. Pavlakis give him daily reports? "I'm sorry, too. It slipped my mind." I almost said I'd gone to see someone in the hospital. It's a good excuse, but he'd want to know who I went to see, and then he'd ask questions about Marie. It could go on forever. It's always dangerous to give Mr. Quinn information. There's no telling where he'll run with it.

He frowned. "You can't let academic obligations 'slip your mind.' Do you make a daily schedule?"

"No, but that's a good idea. Maybe I'll—"

"Come to my office. I've got a packet you can use."

"Thanks, but I should get home. I—"

"Matt." His shoulders stiffened, and all the muscles in his face got tight. "This won't take long. And I've heard enough excuses for one day."

"Yes, sir." Actually, I didn't think I'd given him any excuses, but it's a mistake to argue with Mr. Quinn when his face gets like that. Most of the time, he's pretty easy-going, but if he thinks you're defying him, watch out. I followed him without another word and waited in his inner office while he rummaged through files in the reception area. Bored, I strolled over to take a closer look at a framed photograph on the wall behind his desk.

"Here we go," he said, walking into the office, a thick folder in his hands.

I pointed to the photograph. "Great picture. Is that Mr. Link standing next to you?"

His face brightened. "That's right. That was taken at regionals, right after our final win."

"I can see that," I said, looking at the trophy a young Mr. Quinn was holding over his head, at the triumphant smile that seemed to take up his entire face. "Coach Tomlinson lectures us all the time about how you guys won regionals the first year the school was open, about how we have to work harder if we want to come anywhere close to that."

"And I'm sure he's right." Mr. Quinn's face flushed with pleasure as he gazed at the photograph. "Hard work, Matt— that's what leads to victories you cherish for a lifetime."

I nodded. "I don't think I've seen this picture before. You used to have something else hanging here, right?"

He flushed again. "That's right. After all my years here, I have lots of Ridgecrest High memorabilia. I like to circulate things, so I can enjoy them all. Now, these packets—"

"Your Outstanding Senior award," I cut in. "Didn't you have it in that spot?"

"For a while. Then I decided to put the picture there." He sounded impatient now. "You said you needed to get home, Matt. I'd like to get home, too. Let's focus on the task at hand. I designed this packet myself. Let me show you how it works."

It took him half an hour. He showed me how to list weekly goals and daily objectives, how to fill out the schedule by assigning a task to each hour, how to use codes to link objectives to goals and tasks to objectives. There were spaces for writing summary paragraphs every evening, too, and a page for charting weekly progress every Saturday.

He sat back. "My secretary's making you enough copies to last the rest of the academic year, one for each week. Now, be sure to schedule time for fun, too. It keeps life balanced." He leaned forward over the desk, smiling, and lowered his voice. "So you and Suzette went out last Saturday. She's a lovely girl, and of course she's from a wonderful family. Are you seeing her again this weekend?"

I didn't know how to avoid answering. "I'm driving her to a party tomorrow night."

He chuckled. "'Driving her to a party'—I've heard lots of euphemisms for dating, but that's one of the best. Don't feel embarrassed about being attracted to Suzette. The right girl can help you settle down and find your place at the school. And it doesn't hurt that she's popular. That way, you can count on support from her friends as you build your list of accomplishments for college applications. Have you thought about running for student council?"

"Not really," I said, and felt relieved when someone knocked sharply, then opened the door without waiting.

Dr. Lombardo lifted an eyebrow. "Oh. Matt. I'm surprised to see you here. Is there a problem I should know about?"

"No problem." I gestured toward the papers. "Mr. Quinn's showing me how to keep a daily schedule."

She looked through the papers, as if she didn't believe me. "Fine. Are you almost finished? I need to talk to Mr. Quinn."

"We're *all* finished." He shoved the papers into a folder. "Here. Remember to get the copies from my secretary. And stop by on Monday to show me next week's schedule."

Damn. Now I'd actually have to fill the stupid thing out. As I left, Dr. Lombardo closed the door behind me.

In the reception area, the secretary nodded toward Mr. Quinn's door as she handed me the copies. "Another closed-door meeting with Dr. Lombardo! That makes four today. No wonder. Big changes coming, you know."

"No, I don't know. What changes?"

She looked alarmed. "I'd assumed word had gotten out. If it hasn't, I'd better not say any more. I wouldn't want to get Dr. Lombardo mad at me." She winked. "Or Mr. Quinn, right?"

I had no idea what she meant. In the hallway, I checked a clock on the wall. Four-thirty—I still had time to look at a yearbook or two. I was curious about what Ted Ramsey looked like as a teenager.

Ms. Simon pointed me to the archive shelves, and I found the yearbook from ten years ago. Ted Ramsey would have been a junior then, I figured. I found the pages of junior pictures, and there he was, looking bored and surly, just as I'd expected. Most students had lists of activities next to their pictures—soccer, chorus, French club. The space next to his picture was blank. So he put in his time at school and didn't participate in anything except making trouble, waiting until he got old enough to drop out. We've got some kids like that at Ridgecrest now, and the best thing you can do is to stay away from them.

I started to put the yearbook back on the shelf when I remembered what Ms. Simon had said about the other boy who got into big trouble that year, the track star with what she called a "the-South-will-rise-again type name." I wondered what the name was—Robert E. Lee Rossini? Jeb Stuart Osaka? Curious, I flipped to the picture of the track team. Not a big team—maybe a dozen guys—and I didn't see any flagrantly Confederate names. Probably, that meant I hadn't paid enough attention the last time we had a Civil War unit, and I was forgetting some general.

I took a minute to look at the pictures of the guys standing and kneeling in their black shorts and sleeveless yellow jerseys. My eyes were drawn to a short, skinny guy kneeling in the front row. Something about him looked familiar, though I couldn't have told you what. I matched the picture with a name. Jeff Roberts. Nothing Confederate-sounding about that.

Somehow, I couldn't let it go and turned to the sophomore class pages. These were group pictures of homerooms, so the faces were really small. I found the P-R homeroom, and there was Jeff Roberts, again in the first row because he was short. So his full name was Jefferson Davis Roberts—this must be the guy Ms. Simon had been talking about. I squinted at the picture. Just an ordinary-looking guy, with curly, sandy-colored hair. The way he was holding himself, though, and the way his mouth was twisted in a half-smile, half-smirk—why did he look so familiar?

Jefferson Davis Roberts.

Davis Roberts.

Roberts, Davis.

Bobby Davis. I'd found him.

Twenty-six

"Bobby Davis went to Ridgecrest High," I told Graciana. I'd called her as soon as dinner was over. "It's a small picture, and it's ten years old, but I'm almost positive. His real name's Jefferson Davis Roberts—he called himself Jeff. He didn't graduate, but he went there for his freshman and sophomore years, maybe part of his junior year. The point is, he was there when Ted Ramsey was. They could've met each other."

"And how did he turn into Bobby Davis from Richmond? *Why* did he?"

"I've got a theory about that," I said, and filled her in.

"It's *possible*," she said, sounding skeptical. "I'll go to the public library tonight and see if I can find more information. Want to meet me there?"

"I can't—I have to distribute bake sale posters. But I thought of something else. Didn't Mrs. Dolby say one of her kids went to Ridgecrest High during Dr. Lombardo's first year? Maybe she knows something about Jefferson Davis Roberts."

"And Ted Ramsey," Graciana said. "I wouldn't be surprised. Good idea. I'll call her and ask if we can come over tomorrow. I'll call Berk and Joseph, too, and bring them up to date."

I headed out with the posters. At every store, every

restaurant, people agreed to put up posters, said it was a shame about Coach Colson, and promised to come to the bake sale. We're going to raise a lot of money, I thought.

When I got down to the last poster, I realized I wasn't far from Wendy's World. At dinner, Mom hadn't said much about the fire, only that cleanup was coming along smoothly. The store stays open until eight—I could make it there in time to see the damage for myself and put up my last poster.

But Wendy's World was closed, with a big red-and-white sign out front saying, "Freshening up! Open again soon!" Mom hadn't told us the damage was so bad the store couldn't stay open—but then, when do Mom and Dad ever tell us anything? From the front, the store looked almost okay, except the windows had been covered with brown paper—Mom's boss must not want people looking inside. When I drove around back, I got a jolt. Blackened brick, boarded-up windows, three dumpsters brimming with charred shelving and bags of trash. How much merchandise had they been forced to throw away? How long would it be until the store could be "open again soon"? Would Mom get paid in the meantime? And her boss might've lost so much money she couldn't afford to keep all her employees. If neither Mom nor Dad had regular paychecks coming in, how would we manage?

I sat in the car, brooding, staring at the singed walls of the once-cheerful store. Was this my fault? I'd done what I'd thought was right, and I'd tried to be careful, never imagining anyone in my family could be hurt by anything I did. Now this had happened, and who knew what might happen next? Everything felt beyond my control.

A slow drizzle started, and I thought back to last night, to facing Bobby Davis in the pounding rain. That had been beyond my control, too. When the guy at the fight club tried to punch me, I'd remembered the right technique and used it with no problem. But when Ted Ramsey swung at me, I'd frozen, and when Davis attacked me, I'd fought back for maybe ten seconds before he flattened me. Even when it came to defending myself, the outcome seemed to be up to chance.

Maybe I could at least do something about that. I looked at the last poster, propped up in the passenger seat. Eye of the Tiger Martial Arts was only a few minutes from here. Aaron would let me put up the poster. Maybe he'd give me a few minutes, too, and give me some advice.

When I got there, he was leading some middle-schoolers in a side-kick drill. He spotted me, put Linda in charge, and walked over to the exercise area.

"Are you okay?" he asked. "Did something happen?"

"Yeah, something happened. I'd like to talk. Can I come back when class ends?"

"Linda can handle class. Tell me what happened. I've been worried about you."

"Me, too," I said, and told him about our run-in with Bobby Davis. "It's frustrating, Aaron. This time, I remembered the technique. He was on his knees, out of breath. It stopped him for thirty seconds, tops. You said to avoid dangerous situations, and I'm trying, but we were just driving home. What if he comes after me again?"

He took a moment, biting his lower lip. "Look, what if I went to Lieutenant Hill with you, and you told him about last night? Davis is definitely guilty of assault, and he may be guilty of arson. If we can get him arrested and jailed, you'll be safe."

"For a little while, maybe. But I don't think Hill would listen to me. It'd take too long to tell you about all the other lousy stuff that happened yesterday, but I'm not going to him.

Maybe I should, but I won't. Can you show me some really good technique I can use to defend myself?"

"It's not primarily technique. It's attitude." He paused, then shrugged. "Okay. I'll show you something. I still think you should tell the police, but if you won't, you won't." He went into the office and came back with what looked like half a broomstick. "You said he had a tire iron. This'll do. It's an *escrima* stick—we use these in weapons classes. People usually use two, one in each hand, but one's all we need. Careful—a full-force strike could do serious damage." He raised the stick in the air. "So I'm Bobby Davis, this is a tire iron, and it's a dark and stormy night. Defend yourself."

I took a fighting stance, and he ran forward. I brought my left hand up in a rising block to deflect the stick, fake-punched him in the stomach, and stepped back into my stance.

He charged again, grazing my knees with the stick, then swinging it and tapping it against the side of my neck, so fast and intense I felt confused, unsure of what had happened. Even though he'd barely touched me, I felt literally weak in the knees. I couldn't even try to fight back.

"You're in trouble," he said. "It was a good block, and a full-force punch to the stomach would've winded me. If I'm as tough as Davis, though, I wouldn't stay winded long. So I attacked again. Maybe I broke your kneecap, or maybe your neck hurts so much you're stunned and can't respond. If I want to finish you off, I can. What did you do wrong?"

"I didn't know a technique to counter the strike to the knees, and I didn't know—"

"No. You made your mistake before then." He tossed me the escrima stick. "Now you're Davis. Attack."

I raised the stick. Before I could do anything, Aaron shouted "kadima!" and rushed me, holding both arms forward in a wedge. He pushed his arms between my shoulder and the stick, trapping my right hand in his armpit. Still shouting, he wrapped his right arm around d my neck to control me, fake-kneeing me in the stomach and groin many times, pushing me back. Then he reached underneath my arm to grab the stick, using it to tap my knees and the back of my head, again and again, low and then high, rapid blows, until I fell to the floor.

The middle-schoolers stopped practicing and stood in a cluster, watching. Aaron tossed the escrima stick in the air and caught it.

"So much for Bobby Davis," he said. "If those had been full-force blows, you'd be unconscious, with broken bones. And I didn't use any techniques you don't already know."

I struggled for air, for clarity. "How did you do that?"

"Attitude." He turned to the middle-schoolers. "Did anyone tell you to stop practicing? I didn't think so. Back to work." He helped me up. "The first night you came here, Joseph asked what kadima means. Do you remember?"

I thought back. "Forward."

"Right. In some ways, krav maga isn't actually a martial art. It's a survival system. We emphasize deflecting and disarming, not attacking. You get the bad guy's weapon and make him lie on the ground until help arrives. You escape from the hostage-taker, step back, and let the police take over. In most situations, that works. In some situations, it doesn't. Do you know now what you did wrong when I attacked you?"

I nodded. "I blocked your strike and punched you once. Then I went back into my stance and stood there like an idiot, waiting for you to attack again."

"Don't be too rough on yourself. You're a nice guy—you don't want to hurt anyone. Last night, all you could think about was helping Berk. But when you're up against someone like Davis, with no help in sight, you need a different approach. That's where kadima comes in. You don't wait to be attacked. *You* attack, and you keep pushing forward until he can't fight back."

"So I should've kicked Davis while he was down?"

"Absolutely. He's a killer. You've seen him kill, and you've got every reason to believe he'd kill you. I'm not saying you should kill him. But hurt him so much he can't get up until you've had time to get away."

"You really think I could?"

"I think you'd have a decent chance. You're not good enough yet to kill with one kick, the way he can, but you don't need to be that good. Among other things, as far as he's concerned, you're a kid, you're a green belt, you're a strictly defensive fighter who backs off too soon. If you press forward, you'll take him by surprise."

"And I should shout 'kadima' while I'm doing it?"

"Why not?" Aaron grinned. "I bet he doesn't know what it means. Confuse the hell out of him." He lifted the escrima stick. "Want to try again?"

He didn't make it easy. He countered every move I made, he kept moving forward too, and he shouted as loudly as I did. But it felt different now. This is it, I kept telling myself. *Forward.* No matter what Aaron did, I didn't stop. On the third try, I got the stick away from him, backed him against the wall, and aimed what would've been a skull-crushing blow at his head.

He lifted his hands. "That did it. I'm unconscious now—if I'm lucky, I'm just unconscious. Good work. How did that feel?"

I let my arm drop to my side, let the stick go limp in my hand. "Scary. I'd never want to hurt anybody that much."

"And I hope to God you never have to. Remember, you're not trying to kill him. You're only trying to incapacitate him for two or three minutes so you can get away. Are you sure you won't go to Lieutenant Hill? I'll come with you."

He'd arrest me for beating up Marie, I thought. "No thanks. But thanks for the offer—and for the lesson."

Back in the car, I took a moment to think about what had happened. An hour ago, I'd felt helpless. Everything I did had consequences I'd never intended, consequences I couldn't control. But when Aaron and I were sparring, even when he was winning, things had felt different. They'd felt different because I was fighting back every second, thinking every second, trying to move forward. I wasn't just watching things happen and or leaving them up to chance, and that had made all the difference.

That's the most important part of the lesson, I thought. If I'm up against Bobby Davis again, at other crucial times, all the time, *that's* what I have to remember.

Twenty-seven

In English on Friday, Ms. Nguyen said lots of people had trouble with the test, so she'd give us a new one Monday. I wondered if it was because of me. If she thought I'd messed up because I was missing Coach Colson, would she want to give me another chance? I felt guilty, because that wasn't why I'd messed up. Not studying was why. Maybe I wouldn't feel as guilty if I studied this weekend. I'd think about it. Before lunch, I ducked into an empty classroom and called the hospital. No, Marie Ramsey still couldn't have any visitors. No, the receptionist couldn't say anything about her condition. So much for that.

Berk had a dentist's appointment after school, so he couldn't come along when Graciana, Joseph, and I went to see Mrs. Dolby. She greeted us with butterscotch brownies, happy to talk. She didn't know much about Ted Ramsey, though. She knew the name, and she remembered her youngest son sometimes coming home from school with stories about Ted getting into fights. She also remembered seeing his name in the police reports from time to time after he dropped out. Then, she'd heard, he'd left town. No, she didn't know where he'd gone, but she knew about a year ago, when his father got sent to prison, Ted came back.

"One of my friends told me," Mrs. Dolby said. "He showed up at his stepmother's door one day and simply moved in. She probably wasn't happy about it, but she probably didn't have the courage to throw him out. He's a nasty one, my friend said. She didn't know if he had a job, or if he lived off his stepmother. And I'm sure she was already struggling to make ends meet, trying to support two girls on a short-order cook's salary. Plus people did always say she has a drinking problem—that can't be making things easier, either. That's all I know about Ted Ramsey. Jefferson Davis Roberts, though—I remember lots about him. It was in the newspaper for days, and on television, too. The beating, I mean. That made *quite* a stir."

According to what Mrs. Dolby had heard, Jefferson Davis Roberts—or Jeff, as everyone called him—was a quiet, intense boy. He wasn't much of a student, but he was fiercely dedicated to track and trained all the time. Some people thought he had Olympic potential.

Then, toward the end of his sophomore year, several boys at the school started picking on him. No, Mrs. Dolby didn't think Ted Ramsey was one of them, and she didn't know why they'd decided to target Roberts. Maybe they envied all the attention he was getting, or maybe something else had been going on. Apparently, they kept after him for weeks, and it kept getting worse—knocking his books out of his arms in the hall, jumping him in the boys' room and forcing his head into a toilet, grabbing him when he was out alone running and roughing him up so much he missed the last track meet of the year.

Not that Mrs. Dolby knew about any of that while it was going on. Maybe some people at school knew, but nothing became public knowledge until the next fall, when two of those boys attacked Roberts while he was walking home from school. This time, he fought back. One of the boys ran off after getting a black eye and a broken nose. The other one wasn't as quick, or maybe not as smart, and Roberts nearly finished him off, leaving him bleeding on the sidewalk with multiple injuries. When the police came to Roberts' house to arrest him, he'd disappeared. No one saw him again.

"The boy he'd injured was unconscious for days," Mrs. Dolby said, "and in the hospital for weeks, but eventually he recovered. The police questioned Mr. and Mrs. Roberts many times, suspecting they'd helped their son leave town. But they always said that they hadn't, that their son never came home after the beating. Eventually, they moved away—I don't remember where. Why did you want to know about those two troublemakers?"

No point telling Mrs. Dolby Jefferson Davis Roberts might be the man who killed Coach Colson—it might get her worked up for no reason. "Curiosity, mainly," I said. "I heard stories about them and wondered if you could tell us more. You sure did. Thanks, Mrs. Dolby."

As we walked to the cars, Graciana reached into her purse and took out two folded printouts. "Here," she said, handing us the first one. "A larger picture of Jefferson Davis Roberts— that was in a newspaper I looked at last night at the library. It was taken after he set one of those records. What do you think? Bobby Davis?"

Joseph squinted at it before shaking his head. "I saw him once only, from a distance. I cannot judge. You have seen him several times, Matt. Your opinion weighs more."

I stared at the picture of a skinny, grinning teenager, trying to match it with the sneering man I'd seen in the gym and at the fight club, with the face that had pressed against my car window two nights ago. And the hair was so different, curly instead of slicked back, sandy instead of dark red. Well, the first time I'd seen Bobby Davis, I'd thought his hair was dyed. Now I knew why he might want to change the way he looked. And I still thought I saw something about the mouth, about the way he was standing.

"I can't be sure," I said, "but I think so."

"I think so, too," Graciana said. "And the stories could fit together. Jefferson Davis Roberts runs off to Richmond to avoid arrest, picks a new name based on his old one, changes his appearance, and makes a living as a tough guy, maybe as a collector for a drug dealer or a loan shark. He works on his martial arts skills, too, and gets good enough to star at the fight club. Then an old Ridgecrest High acquaintance, Ted Ramsey, finds out about him—or maybe they've always kept in touch. And Ramsey hires him to kill Coach Colson."

"It's possible," I said. "Can I keep this picture, show it to Berk?"

"Sure," Graciana said. "This may be a crucial discovery, Matt. I'm impressed."

I shrugged. "It was luck. Pure, dumb luck."

"Luck, yes," Joseph said, "but not pure, not dumb. You had luck because you noticed with alertness and pursued curiosities. Without this, there could have been no discovery. My mother says people can earn their luck. You have earned this, by pushing forward."

Forward, I thought. Kadima. So maybe that was a way of controlling chance, and of earning luck. "Bobby Davis has sure been pushing his luck," I said. "He should be playing it safe, staying away from Ridgecrest. Instead he comes back to smash my windshield, comes back again to attack us and start a fire. If the cops had caught him doing any of those things, they might've decided they let him go too quickly last time. He could've found himself charged with murder after all."

"One who is bold enough to kill in front of witnesses," Joseph said, "is not one who plays it safe. As a young man, too, Davis was too bold."

"If we're right in thinking he was once Jefferson Davis Roberts." I shook my head. "And even if he was, it still doesn't get us very far. So we may have learned something about his past. Aside from possibly linking him to Ted Ramsey, how does that help us?"

"It might come in handy," Graciana said, and handed me the second printout. "This is an article about the investigation into the assault on that boy. Look at the name of the detective."

I looked. "What do you know? Our old friend, Lieutenant Hill, only he was Detective Hill back then. I bet he felt frustrated when Roberts got away from him. You think we could interest him in going after Davis so he can finally arrest Roberts?"

"Possibly," Graciana said, "though I doubt he could press charges now. I don't know the statute of limitations for assault, but Roberts was a minor at the time, and witnesses might be hard to find after ten years. But we still might find a way to use the information."

That sounded good. I dropped Joseph off and headed home. Now for a boring dinner, I thought, and probably an equally boring party.

They weren't as boring as I'd expected. Cassie didn't say much while we were eating our quinoa patties and leek *cassoulet*. But when we got to the gluten-free trifle, she drew a sharp breath and looked up.

"I called Grandma Brewster today," she said.

"Did you, dear?" Mom said. "I'm sure my mother was delighted. How is she?"

"Fine. She says I can visit her and Grandpa in Cleveland whenever I want."

"By yourself, you mean?" Already, Mom looked troubled, probably about how much a plane ticket would cost. "That might be fun. Maybe in July, or August."

"I want to go Sunday." Now Cassie talked in a rush. "A flight leaves Richmond at 1:37. I've got enough allowance saved to pay for half. And there's a middle school a few blocks from their house. I bet they could get me registered Monday. I wouldn't miss any school."

"Honey, that doesn't make sense," Dad said. "You can't go to school there for a few days and then—"

"Not for a few days. I'll stay till the school year ends and come home for summer, and next fall I'll go back to Cleveland. The teachers here are stupid. And Grandma and Grandpa are old, and I should spend time with them before they die, and I could help around the house. I really want to, and it'd make them really happy."

Mom and Dad and I all looked at each other. I put down my fork. At least it was an excuse not to eat the trifle.

"Sweetheart," Dad said, "that wouldn't work, and we'd miss you too much. If you're unhappy at school, we'll talk to your teachers."

"No," Cassie said. "They don't know anything. I've thought and thought, and this is the only way. Can I go? Please?"

Mom reached across the table, but Cassie wouldn't take her hand. "Whatever problems you're facing, you need to face them here, with us. We'll help you. Just tell us about it, sweetie. Or you and I can go to your room—"

"No. I told you what I want to do, and you won't let me. Fine. I'll handle it. I don't want your help—your stupid, stupid help."

She ran to her room—she'd been doing that a lot lately. Mom stood up. "I'll go."

Dad and I listened to her walk upstairs, listened to her knock softly and call Cassie's name. "Do *you* know what's going on?" Dad asked.

"How would *I* know? She's seemed weird lately, but I don't know why."

"Me, neither. Maybe she feels unsettled because I've changed jobs. And Mom's putting in extra hours at the store to help with cleanup. We're probably not spending enough time with her."

Mom came back. "She won't open her door. She won't say a word to me. Matt, could *you* try?"

"Me? If she won't talk to you, she sure won't talk to me."

"She might," Dad said. "You're Cassie's hero—the athlete, the popular guy, the one who isn't afraid of anything. She looks up to you."

News to me. I glanced at the clock. Almost an hour before I had to pick Suzette up. "It won't work, but I'll try."

I knocked on her door. "Cassie? Can I come in? If there's anything…"

She opened the door, then sat on the edge of her bed, clasping her hands in her lap and staring down at them, wispy light orange hair half-hiding her face. She looked really small, really sad, but she wasn't crying. I sat in her desk chair.

"So, something's wrong at school," I said. "Teachers or kids?"

She didn't answer right away. Then she looked up. "Kids."

I thought back. "Is that why you dropped Special Chorus?"

Her eyes turned fierce. "That stupid, stupid chorus. I wish Ms. Lambert had never picked me. All the other girls she picked are pretty. I didn't fit in."

"Sure you did. You're pretty, too. You're—"

"I'm not!" She sounded angry, like she thought I was lying

to her. "I'm ugly. My hair's weird—I look like a pumpkin. And my nose is huge, and I'm fat."

"Your hair's fine. So is your nose. And you're nowhere near fat."

"I am! I'm obese. My arms are flabby, and my stomach sticks out. The other girls didn't want me in chorus because I made it look bad. They said nobody would want to listen to us because of me."

She had to be imagining things. "Did anyone actually say that to you, Cassie?"

"They never said anything to me. Not even hello. When I tried to talk to them, they'd stare at me like I was crazy and walk away. But they'd talk to each other, loud enough so I could hear, and they'd say I was ruining chorus, and everybody would think it's a joke because of the way I look. I tried to ignore them, but they kept doing it, so I thought, fine, I'll quit chorus, and they'll stop."

Maybe not, I thought. Not if they'd seen how miserable they could make her, and they were mean enough to enjoy that. "But they didn't stop?"

She shook her head, so hard her hair brushed against her face. "They started saying worse things, spreading them all over school. Even Cindy and Joanne won't eat lunch with me, because they're afraid people will say things about *them*."

Cindy and Joanne had been Cassie's best friends for years. I felt anger building, like a slow weight pressing against the inside of my chest, crowding up into my throat. "What are those girls saying, Cassie?"

"I can't tell you. It's too awful."

"No, tell me. I'll find a way to help."

"No one can help," she said, but I could see she wanted to get it out. "You can't tell Mom and Dad, okay? Promise?"

"If that's what you want, I promise. What are they saying?"

She took a deep breath. "Do you remember Duffy?"

"Sure." Duffy's a custodian at the middle school—he has Down Syndrome or something. "What about him?"

"Well, you know he's sort of different, but he's really nice, and he loves giving people high fives. Most kids, though—when he says hello, they don't answer. They act like they didn't hear him. When he holds up his hand, they won't give him high fives. They keep walking and leave him with his hand in the air. Some kids make fun of him behind his back."

Listening to her made me feel guilty. I'd never made fun of Duffy myself, but sometimes, when other people had, I'd laughed. And I'd walked past him and pretended not to hear him say hello, too, and I'd never given him high fives when other people were around. Back then, I hadn't known better. Or maybe I had, but I'd been more focused on fitting in than on being decent. "Yeah, I've seen that myself. But what's that got to do with you?"

She lifted her shoulders. "I like Duffy. He's so cheerful—no matter how people treat him, he keeps trying. So I always say hello to him and give him high fives. Between classes, I ask him if he's having a good day, like that. And he likes to show people pictures of his dog, but most kids won't look at them. I do."

She's more mature than I was at her age, I thought. And nicer. "That's why those girls are talking about you?"

She nodded, looking straight at me for the first time. "That's why *everybody's* talking about me. They say Duffy's my boyfriend. They say I—well, that I let him touch me. You know. Now they're saying he got me pregnant, and that's why my stomach sticks out."

I stood up and started pacing. I wanted to smash things. "You're sure, Cassie? You're sure people are saying those things?"

"Some say it to my face." She raised her voice in a mocking tone. "'Did you and Duffy have another hot date last night, Cassie?' 'When's the baby due, Cassie? Are you going to name it Duffy?' And they come up to me in the hall, all the time, and they stick their hands in my face and say, 'High five, Cassie! High five!' I hate it, Matt. I hate it so much!"

She started crying, not covering her face, keeping her hands clasped in her lap and staring straight ahead, sobbing in this loud, ragged way that scared the life out of me. I was afraid something inside her would burst. It reminded me of the way Marie Ramsey had cried at the tournament.

I sat down and put my arms around her, and she leaned against my chest, still sobbing in that awful way. "It's okay, Cassie. We'll find a way to make it better."

Dad knocked on the door. "Is Cassie all right?"

That made her stop crying. "I'm fine. Matt and I are talking. Go away."

I waited until I heard Dad go back downstairs. "I'm sorry, Cassie. I knew you were upset, but I thought it was because of something physical. I never guessed it was something like this."

"I didn't *want* you to guess. I hoped they'd get bored and stop. But it keeps getting worse."

"What about going to the principal? Mr. Wheeler's not a bad—"

"No! He's nice, but it's the whole *school*, Matt. He can't punish the whole school without making everyone hate me. And what if he believed it, even part of it? Duffy might lose his job. That'd crush him—he's so proud of his job. What if they sent him to jail?"

"That wouldn't happen," I said, but I understood. Probably, Cassie should go to Mr. Wheeler. Probably, I should go to Lieutenant Hill. Sometimes, though, there are things you can't do, even when you know you should. "Then maybe you should avoid Duffy. If you stopped talking to him and high-fiving him, it might die down."

"I won't." She looked at me straight again, and I could tell she wouldn't give in on this, either. "Especially since this started, I'm almost the only kid at school who ever talks to him. If I could stop going to school there, fine. He'd get used to that. But if I keep going, and I stop talking to him, he'll feel hurt. He hasn't done anything wrong, Matt. I don't want to make him sad. It wouldn't be fair."

I took a good look at her. A gawky, sort of funny-looking kid. Lots of times, I'd felt almost embarrassed she's my sister. Lots of times, I'd thought of her almost as a joke. Right now, I admired her like hell. "You're much braver than I am, Cassie."

She shook her head. "I'm not brave at all. I could never do the things you do, like martial arts. Even watching basketball scares me, the way people keep charging each other."

"You're braver in more important ways," I said. "Are you sure you won't tell Mom and Dad? They might be able to think of something."

"I don't want them to know what's going on. You know how they are. They're so happy—they always think everything's wonderful and perfect. *You* can handle this, but they couldn't. Maybe you can talk them into letting me go to Cleveland, without telling them why."

Now it was my turn to shake my head. "They won't go for it, and it probably wouldn't be a good idea. Let me think it over. We've got until Monday. We'll come up with something."

"Maybe," she said doubtfully, and looked at the dorky Cinderella watch she got for her seventh birthday and still wears every day. "You should get dressed for your date."

"It's not a date, and I'm not dressing up this time." I put my hand on her shoulder. "We'll talk tomorrow, okay?"

"Okay." She picked up a stuffed tiger and plunked it on her lap. She didn't cuddle it, or stroke it, or even look at it. When I left her room, she was still sitting on the edge of her bed, staring straight ahead, the stuffed tiger ignored on her lap.

Twenty-eight

Megan's party turned out like I'd expected—mostly sopho-
mores, mostly girls, Suzette and her friends talking and
laughing extra loud and fast so everyone would see what a good
time they were having. It was boring but okay, and the pizza
tasted good. I never get pepperoni at home, so I was grateful.
Suzette hung onto my arm, and once in a while she'd whisper
some nothing comment into my ear and giggle. I couldn't
walk away without being rude, but I didn't have much to say. I
don't think anyone really wanted me to talk. I think I was just
supposed to stand around so Suzette could hold onto my arm.

So I stood around. Obviously, she was showing me off.
That was sort of ridiculous, but sort of flattering. And she
looked awfully pretty, her hair brushed shiny and full, her
jeans welded to her so snugly it was clear she didn't have even
an ounce where she didn't want it, her top dipping just low
enough to make you think about what you couldn't see. She
could've had almost any guy she wanted, and she'd picked me.
That made me feel good.

Mostly, Suzette and her friends talked about people
who weren't at the party—how weird this girl's new haircut
was, how much weight that girl had gained, how they bet

it wouldn't be long before some couple broke up. Someone mentioned Graciana, and Suzette took off.

"Oh, my God," she said. "Did you *see* the shirt she wore today? I couldn't *believe* it!"

"Well, they like bright colors," another girl said. I wasn't sure what she meant by "they."

"Maybe Mr. Bixby's the one who likes bright colors," a third girl said, and they all laughed.

"Sherry walked by his classroom after school ended yesterday," Suzette said. "His door was closed. She thinks Graciana was there with him."

"No, Graciana talked to me after her last class yesterday," I said. I hadn't spoken in about fifteen minutes, but I couldn't let that pass. "And then she left school."

"Oh." Suzette gave me a sour look, like I'd broken a rule. "Maybe Sherry said Wednesday. But I *know* they spend lots of time there together. Do you think they actually *do* it there?"

"I bet," another girl said. "They can't go to his house, since he's still living with his wife—but *that* won't last much longer."

They laughed again, not that anything was funny. "What'll he do when she goes to college?" the third girl asked. "His poor heart will be broken!"

"She may not make it to college." Suzette paused, looking from one girl to another, like she was warming up to say something major. "Now, I didn't see this myself. But one of my friends saw Graciana in the shower after gym, and she said her stomach was sticking out."

The third girl gasped. "Oh, my God! She's pregnant! You think it's Mr. Bixby's?"

Suzette sighed. "With Graciana, who knows? But probably. Do you think she did it on purpose, to pressure him into leaving his wife? You think she'll have an abortion if he won't marry her?"

That did it. "I'm getting more pizza," I said, and turned away. Suzette called after me, telling me to get her a diet Pepsi, but I pretended not to hear.

I walked out and stood on the front porch. God, the cool felt good. I closed my eyes and let it wash over my face, the music from the party now a dull rumble in the background, the air heavy with something sweet—dogwoods, or something growing in the garden. I liked that rich, fresh smell.

I tried not to think. It didn't work.

She's like those girls talking about Cassie, I thought. And I'd mostly believed it, and I'd let it affect the way I thought about Graciana. What if it was all based on nothing, like the things those middle-school girls were saying? I thought about the last thing Suzette said. She already had her backup story ready. For a few months, she and her friends would talk about Graciana being pregnant. When nothing happened, they'd say she must've had an abortion. They'd talk about Mr. Bixby leaving his wife. When nothing happened, they'd say he must've dumped Graciana. No matter what happened or didn't happen, they'd find garbage to say.

Why did they do it? Did they have some reason to hate Graciana? Those middle-school girls couldn't have a reason to hate Cassie, except she wasn't like them. Was that enough? Did they enjoy hurting people? Were they jealous? Of what? I didn't understand.

And I didn't understand why I'd believed the things Suzette said. None of them fit with anything I knew about Graciana. Nothing she'd ever said or done fit with the idea she'd fool around with a teacher, a married man, a man with children. So why had I believed it?

I'd always assumed girls were nicer than guys. I'd seen guys push weaker kids around, but I'd never seen girls do that. Maybe talking garbage was worse. Maybe it hurt more.

I opened my eyes and stared into the darkness. I couldn't figure it out, not now. I felt like just leaving, like never talking to Suzette again. But I'd brought her here, and I had to bring her home. I went back in the house.

I lingered by the food table, talking to a guy on the JV soccer team who looked as uncomfortable as I felt. Suzette found me, hooked her hand through my arm, and dragged me over to another cluster of her friends. I didn't listen more than I had to, didn't bother trying not to look bored. Finally, people started drifting off. The party was breaking up.

"It's getting late," I said. "I should take you home."

Suzette smiled. "Getting impatient, huh? Okay. I'll say goodnight to Megan."

I watched her walk over to Megan and yet another cluster of friends, watched her point at me and giggle, watched her shake her head prettily as they made jokes. God, I thought. She must be saying I can't wait to be alone with her. Doesn't she ever stop?

When we got in the car, she shot me a flirty glance. "You still want ice cream? We've got lots in the family room fridge. And if you wanna watch a movie, we've got a big-screen TV—and a nice, big couch."

How blatant can you get? Did she want stuff to tell her friends, or did she think if I went pretty far with her, I'd have to keep taking her out? "I'd better get home. Like I said, my father wants me to help him tomorrow, and we're starting early."

"Oh." I couldn't see her face—it was dark, and I was staring straight ahead—but I could hear how surprised she was. "We could watch a movie tomorrow night, then. We wouldn't have to go out first. You could just come over."

Give it up, Suzette, I thought. This is the last night I waste on you. "No, I blew an English test. The whole class did, and Ms. Nguyen's giving us a retest Monday. I better study."

She laughed. This time, it sounded genuine. "Get serious. Nobody studies on Saturday night."

"I do, sometimes." This'd be the first time, but she didn't have to know that. "And the bake sale's Sunday—my mom's baking a bunch of stuff, and she may want help."

"Oh, the stupid bake sale." Suzette laughed again. "*My* mom's baking brownies. Oh, my God. Her brownies always taste like crap, probably because she's too drunk to follow a recipe."

She shouldn't talk about her mother like that, I thought. Then I remembered what Graciana said, about how I shouldn't joke about my mother's cooking. At least, if my mom had a drinking problem, I wouldn't invite people to laugh at her. But maybe making fun of a mother who's always so nice and eager to help is even worse. I saw Suzette's house and felt relieved. I wanted to get away from her, away from these thoughts.

She obviously expected me to walk her to her door and kiss her goodnight again, so I did. She looked as good as she had last Saturday, smelled as good, melted into my arms as sweetly. This time, I felt nothing. What do you know, I thought. The physical part really doesn't count for much, not if you can't stand the person you're being physical with.

"Call me!" Suzette cried as I walked to the car. I lifted a hand, giving her a half-wave without looking back. No need to call. I'd see her at the bake sale Sunday, and I'd spend Saturday thinking up a way to end things without making a big deal.

I'd also spend Saturday helping my father put up a back-splash in Berk's kitchen and studying for the test. I hadn't planned to do those things, but I'd told Suzette I would, so I'd go through with it so it wouldn't be a lie. Lying had never bothered me much before. I'd thought of it as a survival skill. But tonight I'd watched Cassie cry, and I'd spent hours listening to Suzette and her friends talk garbage, and now I hated lies.

I also had to come up with some way of helping Cassie, I thought as I pulled into our driveway. I looked at the second floor and saw her light on. So she was still awake, probably still miserable, probably hoping her big brother could find a way of fixing things.

How could I do that? I sat in the car for five minutes, feeling lost.

Then it came to me. I grabbed my phone and sent a text message: R U still up? Can I come over? It's not about Coach, but it's important.

In thirty seconds, I got an answer: OK. Come to the back door.

Good. I backed out of the driveway and headed off.

Twenty-nine

Graciana opened the door. "Is something wrong?"

"Yeah." Her kitchen reminded me of ours—long and narrow, with big windows over the sink. During the day, it's probably a bustling, sunny place. Now, with the rest of the house dark and hushed, it felt like a bright, cool cave. "It's about my sister," I said.

I'd planned to hint at things, but Graciana kept asking questions, and I ended up telling her everything. I watched her eyes while she listened—sometimes large with sympathy, sometimes hard with anger.

"And her friends aren't standing by her," she said.

"No. It's lousy, but they're afraid those girls will start talking about them, too."

Graciana drummed her fingers on the table. "Maybe we can get her new friends, ones who'll be at school with her but won't care what seventh-graders say. Are you bringing her to the bake sale?"

"I hadn't planned to. She might come when my parents do."

"Why not ask her to come with you and help? When I was that age, I loved it when my big brother included me in things. I've got a cousin who goes to Cassie's school, Anita. She's in eighth grade, and she's pretty popular. I could ask her to help at the sale, and we could introduce them. I could tell her what Cassie's going through—not details, just a general idea."

"I'm not sure. If Anita's popular, she might not take to Cassie. Cassie's—well, dorky."

Graciana smiled. "Anita studies a lot, too. And she hates it when kids are mean to other kids. You know what else you could do? Teach Cassie some martial arts moves."

That sounded like an even worse idea. "Cassie's not into sports or anything physical. She's timid about stuff like that."

"That's why it might help her. Martial arts build self-confidence—I've read articles about that. Lots of anti-bullying programs involve martial arts. Even when the bullying isn't physical, it helps to know you can stand up for yourself. You don't feel like a victim."

Was that why Graciana joined the martial arts club? I'd wondered about that. She didn't seem into sports, any more than Cassie did. Suzette had said Graciana had a crush on Coach Colson, but that was probably garbage, like everything Suzette says. Had Graciana known people were talking about her? I pictured her sitting by herself somewhere, hurting like Cassie's hurting, reading articles about how to build her self-confidence.

"Cassie says those girls keep sticking their hands in her face, asking her to high five," I said. "I could show her some blocks."

"Sounds good," Graciana said, and we talked until I realized it was after midnight. If my parents were waiting up, they'd be worried.

Graciana walked me to the door. "I'm glad you told me about this. I really want to help." She paused. "*Why* did you tell me?"

I hadn't expected her to ask. "Because you're a girl, and I thought you'd understand. Plus I knew you'd keep it to yourself, and you're about the smartest person I know."

"Those are nice reasons." She didn't quite smile. "Was it also because people tell stories about me, too? Is *that* why you thought I'd understand?"

She looked so sad, and so brave, that I felt awful. "So you know about the stories."

"They make sure I know." Her voice had a new bitterness. "It's no fun unless I know. I was hoping *you* didn't know. But when I heard you were going out with Suzette, I figured—well, so much for that."

"I'm never going out with her again. Until Cassie opened up to me, I never realized how much stories like that hurt."

She half-nodded. "Did you believe the stories?"

Two hours ago, I'd decided I'd never lie again. Now, that didn't seem so smart. "Not really. So what if Mr. Bixby closes his door when you're with him? That doesn't mean—"

She laughed, once, harsh and loud. "Do you think he's a fool, Matt? You think he wants to lose his job and maybe go to prison? He *never* closes his door when he's alone with a student. We work late on the newspaper, but it's always a group of us. Once, when it was just Mr. Bixby and Andy Sloan and me, and Andy went to the bathroom, Mr. Bixby practically sprinted out to the hall. I heard him talking to his wife on his cell phone—'Hi, honey, it's 8:37, and Andy stepped out, so I decided to call, check on the kids.' He didn't come back in the room until Andy did. It was almost funny."

"He sounds paranoid."

"No, he's sensible. Think about it. Do you know *any* teacher who stays in a room alone with a student? Maybe Dr. Lombardo warns all the teachers not to. It's dangerous—they might get accused of something they didn't do. Mr. Bixby's marriage is fine, by the way. I babysit their kids sometimes, and everybody's happy. And he doesn't go to church with his family because his wife's raising the kids Catholic, but he's Baptist. They've always gone to different churches."

So she kept up to date on the stories—reporter's instinct, I guess. "This must be hard on you. Knowing about things people are saying, I mean. If it was me, I'd feel like dropping off the newspaper."

"I almost did." Her eyes turned fierce again. "But I couldn't let them drive me away from doing something I love. Then I'd *really* feel like a victim, maybe for the rest of my life. That's the most important reason Cassie shouldn't go to Cleveland, or keep pretending she's sick. We've got to make her feel like a fighter."

"Whether she wins or not," I agreed. I felt so close to Graciana, and so grateful, that I wanted to hug her. I didn't, partly because I was afraid I'd enjoy it in ways I shouldn't after such a serious talk. We could shake hands, but that seemed lame. Graciana's eyes met mine, and she laughed like she understood. She held up her hand.

"High five, Matt," she said, and I gave her a slap and headed home.

———

Saturday morning, I got up early. Dad's eyebrows nearly shot off his face when I said I'd go to Berk's with him. When we got there, Mrs. Widrig said Berk was still asleep, but he'd be glad to see me when he got up. She pointed us to some cinnamon rolls she'd baked and bustled off to work.

Naturally Berk can sleep in, I thought. He may not see his dad much, but at least both his parents have real jobs. Then

I felt ashamed about thinking that, and picked up a sponge and helped wash down the wall area where the backsplash was going.

As we worked, Dad asked questions about Cassie, casual-like. When I'd come downstairs last night and said Cassie didn't want me to tell them anything, Mom and Dad had tried to accept that. Of course, they'd said, a thousand times. If that's what Cassie wants, we respect her wishes. But, they'd said.

That's how it started. But if it's serious, we're sure you'd find a way to tell us. But if we can help, we know you'd say something. But this, but that, but something else.

Now Dad started in again. "It's wonderful you show such respect for things Cassie tells you in confidence," he said, glancing back and forth from a sketch to the tiles he was set-ting out on the counter. "But if she asked for advice, and if you're not sure what to say, we're eager to help."

"I know. But I promised Cassie I wouldn't tell you."

"All right." He sighed, pointing to the counter. "This is the pattern Mrs. Widrig wants. When the wall's dry, we'll put down the adhesive and set the tiles, starting at the center. We'll have to cut some tiles to make everything fit. That takes time. Measure twice, cut once—that's the rule. We'll keep checking to make sure everything's level, and we'll wipe off excess adhesive as we go. Then we let the adhesive dry, and tomorrow I come back and grout."

"It's more complicated than I thought."

"To make everything come out exactly right, yes. But Mrs. Widrig will end up with an attractive backsplash. It'll change the look of the whole kitchen, make her happier every time she fixes a meal here. That's not a small thing. I'm not ashamed of working with my hands, Matt. As long as I'm helping people, I'm satisfied. If that's what Cassie's upset about—"

"It's not." I hesitated. "*I* was surprised by your decision. Maybe you didn't like some policies, but is that worth quitting over?"

"In this case it was." Dad touched the wall tentatively, then leaned against the counter. "The way I see it, my job was to help customers get the best possible result at the lowest possible price. Neil Edson sees things differently. If one company will sell us an inferior product—plumbing fixtures, say—at a price that lets us make a bigger profit, Neil thinks that's the product to push. I tried to go along with him. It's not my job to challenge my boss in public, so I kept my mouth shut when other people were around. Several months back, Neil decided that wasn't good enough. He said I had to show more enthusiasm, speak up when we met with customers and support whatever he said."

"He asked you to lie?"

"Essentially. I can't do that. Keep my opinions to myself sometimes, yes. Lie, no. So I left."

I thought about my talk with Graciana. "Isn't it better to fight back?"

"It's hard to fight back against the person who signs your paycheck. Neil said if I wanted to be on his team, I had to be a team player. I guess he has a right to say that, since he owns the company. So Mom and I decided I couldn't be on Neil's team, not on his terms." He paused. "You think that was a mistake?"

I shrugged. "It sounds like taking the easy way out."

As soon as I'd said it, I felt sorry. Dad winced. "This isn't so easy. At my age, going door to door, asking people if I can please fix their toilets for a few bucks—you think that's easy? And of course I'm worried about money. Mom is, too. But if I'd lied and acted enthusiastic when Neil gave customers bad advice, I'd be sacrificing my integrity. I'd hate going to work every day, and I'd be setting a damn shabby example for you and Cassie. Sometimes, walking away is the best way to stand up for yourself."

He'd been bullied, too, I realized—not the way Cassie and Graciana were, but Neil Edson had tried to push him around. Dad had fought back the only way he could, and it'd taken courage. Lots of people would've given in to save their jobs. "I'm sorry, Dad. I never knew you were going through that."

"Mom and I didn't want to worry you until we'd made a final decision. Maybe that was a mistake. Maybe, if we'd let you know what was happening, it wouldn't have been such a shock when I said I'd quit."

"Maybe." I didn't want to criticize him at such a tough time, but this was important. "And maybe—well, you and Mom always act like you don't have any problems. Sometimes, that makes me feel like if I have problems, something must be wrong with me. It makes me think if I tell you things, it'll burst your bubble, like, and you won't be able to handle it."

"My goodness, Matt." He looked at me like he'd never seen me before. "I'm sorry. We always thought we should protect you and Cassie from worries. We thought if you felt you had a secure base at home, you'd be able to deal with outside problems better. I guess we were wrong." He gave me another super-close look. "Is there something going on now? Some problem you haven't wanted to tell us about?"

I touched the wall. "Feels dry. Should we start the adhesive?"

As we worked, we talked. When I said I was worried about college, he shook his head. "You're going to college. Mom and I have college money set aside for both you and Cassie, and nobody's touching it for any other reason. Plus we'll take out loans. Almost everybody does that these days, and Mom and

I will pay them off, so you won't have to start out burdened by debt. And maybe you'll get a scholarship."

"I wish. But I'm not good enough to play Division Two basketball, let alone Division One, and Division Three colleges don't have athletic scholarships."

"It wouldn't have to be athletic. Colleges have more general scholarships—for academics, leadership, community service. You could try for those."

"With my grades? I don't think so."

"You do fine in math and science. I bet you could pull your other grades up, too. You've still got time to make a difference for this semester. Next fall, if you push, you can show colleges what you're capable of. And you'll probably be captain of the basketball team. That shows leadership, and your work on this memorial issue shows community service."

Except Dr. Lombardo canceled the memorial issue, I thought, and she may not let me play basketball at all. But I couldn't tell Dad that.

Around eleven, Berk came downstairs, still in pajamas, eyes half-closed. When he saw me, his eyes popped wide. He grabbed some cinnamon rolls, mumbled about making phone calls, and ran back upstairs. He's embarrassed, I thought. He feels sorry for me. That's dumb. I felt almost proud I was up and working, while Berk was still lying around.

When half the tiles were up, Dad and I ate the arugula sandwiches Mom had packed. "I've had a decent first week," Dad said. "Slow, but that's how small businesses start. So far, I've only gotten handyman jobs, but if I do good work and keep my prices reasonable, word will get around. Contracting work will come. I hear some out-of-town investors might buy Twin Dogwoods Manor, finally bring it back to life. Maybe I could get that job."

Twin Dogwoods Manor—the burned-out resort on Lake Charlotte, not far from where Nina Ramsey died. Thinking about it made my shoulders go stiff. I felt close to Dad today, closer than I had in years. It'd be a relief to let loose and tell him everything that was going on. But that'd be crazy. Or would it?

He had me set the last tile. "Take a step back," he said. "What do you think?"

I looked it over—an intricate pattern of beige and warm browns and almost-pink, every line straight, every color blending smoothly into the next. "It looks fantastic."

"I think so, too." He put his arm around my shoulders, sort of awkwardly. "Thanks for your help. Without you, this job would've taken much longer and wouldn't have turned out half as well. And I'm glad we had a chance to talk."

"Me, too." He should've told me about his problems at work sooner, I thought. He and Mom should've trusted me to handle those worries. Should I trust them to handle *my* worries? "I want to talk to you some more," I said. "To you and Mom both. I have something to tell you. But not until Cassie goes to bed. I have something to tell her, too, and something to show her."

 Thirty

We stood in the backyard, facing each other, out by the pink-trimmed playhouse Dad built for Cassie years ago. She doesn't play there anymore—she's too old, she says—but she still brings a book out sometimes and sits at the little kitchen table to read, and she still sweeps it out and rearranges things in cupboards. Now, she stood a few feet from the front door, looking at me doubtfully.

"I don't think I can do this," she said. "I don't think it'll help."

"I bet it will. And it's easy. You can definitely do it."

"I don't know. Anyhow, I can't hit people in school. I'd get in trouble."

"You won't hit. You'll block. When people get obnoxious, you'll protect yourself. You won't get in trouble for that. You won't hurt anyone."

"And *I* won't get hurt?"

"Not a chance. Come on. Show me what they do. They come up to you in the hall, and they—what?"

She took a step toward me. "They say, 'High five, Cassie!' And they stick their hands in my face, like—"

She thrust her right hand forward, and I knocked it aside. "Cut it out!" I yelled.

She jumped back about three feet. "I'm sorry!" Her eyes were huge, almost like she was scared of me.

"No," I said. "I wasn't really yelling at you. I was showing you how *you* should yell, when you use the block."

She still looked scared. "We're not supposed to yell in school."

"Speak firmly, then," I said, getting impatient. "Firmly, and sort of loudly. Now, this is called a same-side block. Stand with your feet shoulder-width apart. That's for balance. Good. The trick is you've gotta put your whole body into the block. And you don't shove the arm aside. You slap it."

"We're not supposed to slap—"

"It's not a hard slap. We'll do it in slow motion. Stick your right hand in my face again."

She stuck her hand out cautiously, not getting anywhere near my face.

I had to step forward. "Okay. Now, I'm pivoting slightly on my foot, I'm bringing my left hand up and keeping it open, and I'm making contact with your right arm right below your wrist—see?—and I'm slapping it aside. Meanwhile, I'm bringing my right hand back to my waist in a fist, so I'll be ready with a counter-punch if you—"

"We're not supposed to—"

"You won't really punch. But bring your fist back anyway. It looks cool, like you're ready for anything. And when I slap—when I make contact with your arm, I'll say 'cut it out,' loud and firm. That gets my spirits up, and it intimidates you. Let's try again."

We kept going over it, speeding up each time. She started to get into it—I could see that. "Good," I said. "Now you try. I'll stick my hand in your face, and you block it."

"Don't go too fast."

"I won't. Here it comes." Slowly, I brought my hand forward. "High five, Cassie," I said, making my voice high-pitched and mocking.

She slapped my arm aside, harder than I'd expected. "Please don't," she said.

"Good," I said. "Good pivot, good power, and you put your whole body into it. But don't look away after the block—keep your eyes on me, to let me know you won't back down. And 'please don't' is too polite. Don't ask me to stop—order me. Try again."

She got better and stronger every time, yelling "stop it," speeding up, moving forward, backing me clear across the yard until I nearly stumbled backward into the bushes. Her face got flushed, her eyes shone, and her voice got louder. She kept her eyes right on me, but I don't think she was seeing me anymore. I think she was seeing those girls, feeling the anger she felt every time they picked on her, putting that anger into her blocks. The last time, she slapped my arm aside so hard it stung. "Grow up!" she yelled.

"Great," I said. "You've got it down cold. And 'grow up' is perfect. It's strong, and it lets those girls know what you think of them—it puts you in a superior position. Fantastic!"

"You think so?" She stepped back. Her face still glowed, but she'd started to look doubtful again. "But doing it with you is one thing. Doing it with those girls—I don't know if I can. Whenever they come up to me, I feel so awful. I feel scared. I'll probably forget what I'm supposed to do."

"So we'll keep practicing. Tonight, tomorrow, as long as it takes. Coach Colson always said you have to practice a move a thousand times before it's yours. Then, when you need it, it comes back like instinct. Want to practice more after dinner?"

"Aren't you going out? Don't you have a date with Suzette?"

"I'm never going out with Suzette again. She's not a nice person—I realized that last night. Anyhow, I blew an English test, and I've got a retest Monday. I should study."

Cassie's face turned wistful. "Maybe I could help. If you've got terms and titles and stuff to learn, I could make flashcards and quiz you. But if you don't feel like it, that's okay."

I didn't feel like it. Doing flashcard drills with Cassie isn't my idea of a fun Saturday night. But maybe it'd help her. I'd been acting like the big martial arts expert, telling her what to do. Maybe she'd feel good about taking a turn being the one in charge. "Thanks. Ms. Nguyen gave us a study guide full of terms and titles. I'll give it to you, and you can make cards. When we need a break from studying, we'll practice the block. There's something else. The bake sale's tomorrow. Want to come with me and help?"

I'd expected her to jump at it, but she smiled a quick little smile and looked away. "That's okay. You're already being really nice, by showing me the block and letting me make flashcards. I feel lots better. You don't have to take me to the bake sale, too."

I keep forgetting how smart she is. I felt like putting my arm around her shoulder, but maybe that'd be weird. "I've been a lousy big brother," I said. "Haven't I?"

She shrugged. "Cindy and Joanne have big brothers, too. You're about typical."

"That bad? Sorry." This time, I did put my arm around her. "I'll work on it."

All evening, Cassie and I practiced the block, and she got good at it. She wanted to learn more, so I taught her a front kick. She got pretty good at that, too, and got excited, and said maybe she'd take tae kwon do—great idea, but I worried about how Mom and Dad would pay for it. She made flashcards and drilled me, and I picked things up faster than I'd expected. She said she'd make more flashcards, I promised to read all the assigned poems and stuff, and I started to think I might actually pass this test. Best of all, I showed her the packet Mr. Quinn gave me, and she zipped through it, churning out goals and objectives, finding ways to fill all the slots with tasks, plunking codes into little boxes. It was like a game to her—she enjoyed it. Then she went to bed, and I went to the kitchen to talk to Mom and Dad.

I started by being careful and ended up telling them a lot— nothing about Cassie, since I'd promised, but almost everything about me, even about going to Richmond twice, even about getting punched by Ted Ramsey and beat up by Bobby Davis. Mom said, "Goodness!" a lot, and Dad looked grim.

"When Davis came after you," he said, "why didn't you call 911?"

"I started to, after he'd forced us off the road. But he moved really quickly, and before I knew it, he was standing right next to the car, warning me not to call."

"You should've called *before* Davis forced you off the road. You should've called the second you saw him. If anything like that happens again, will you?"

It wasn't much to promise—he was right. "Definitely."

"You should tell the police Davis attacked you and Berk," Mom said. "That was a crime—you should report it. You should call Lieutenant Hill now."

"He probably isn't in this late."

"Leave him a voice mail message. You *have* to call, Matt."

I made the call. Like I'd predicted, he wasn't in, so I left a message. On impulse, I told him about the fight club in Richmond, too, and said Bobby Davis might've once been

Jefferson Davis Robert. Maybe that'd give Hill something to think about.

As soon as I hung up, Mom and Dad took turns lecturing me, telling me to be more careful, saying some things I'd done were too risky. They said it too many times, but that's okay. If I ever have a son who does half the stupid stuff I'd done, I'll probably lecture him even more. At least they didn't say I had to stop trying to figure out why Coach had been killed or talk about never leaving the house again.

Dad stood up. "It's almost midnight. We should get to bed. Matt, whatever happens, let us know. Even if you think we can't help, tell us what's going on. Okay?"

"I will," I said. Whenever possible, I thought.

Thirty-one

Practically the whole town showed up for the bake sale. That included Lieutenant Hill.

We set our tables up at Northside Shopping Center. It's a good spot, with a Food Lion, a Dollar Store, a Subway, and four other businesses creating foot traffic. We had plenty of stuff to sell, donated by families connected to the school. Most people who donated stuff bought stuff too, hanging around to talk while eating cookies and turnovers their friends had baked. Berk and I sat at the main table, scrambling to make change as people shoved money at us. Between customers, I filled him in on Jefferson Davis Roberts, and about the message I'd left for Hill. At the parking lot entrance, Cassie stood with Graciana's cousin Anita, holding up signs about the sale. Nearby, Derrick, Graciana, and Joseph priced the donations that kept pouring in.

Then I spotted Lieutenant Hill and poked Berk's arm. "Look," I said. "I bet he got my message and wants to talk to me."

But when he got to our table, Hill pointed at Berk. "Widrig, right? Let's see if you can back up his story. Foley, don't go anywhere."

What'd he think, that I'd skip town because I was guilty of reporting a crime? I watched them walk to the far end of the parking lot, watched Berk talking and gesturing while Hill, for once, took notes. Progress, I thought.

Mr. Carver, our assistant principal, came over to pay for some blueberry scones. "Wonderful turnout, Matt. It's quite a tribute to Mr. Colson—and to you, for organizing everything so well." He looked around the parking lot. "It's a tribute to Ridgecrest, too. Not all communities would show so much support for a high-school fundraiser. I'll miss this place."

I looked up, stunned. "You'll miss it? You're leaving?"

"Yes, I've accepted a position at a school in Roanoke. Bigger school, new challenges. Dr. Lombardo decided there's no need for a formal announcement."

"Lots of people will be disappointed," I said. "We were all hoping you'd be the next principal."

He laughed but didn't sound amused. "Not exactly. Take care, Matt."

Damn, I thought. If he's not the new principal, who is?

That's when Lieutenant Hill and Berk came back. "All right," Hill said. "You two have your stories straight. It could all be lies, but at least you're telling the same lies. Why didn't you report this alleged attack sooner?"

"We didn't think you'd listen," I said. "Every time we try to talk to you, you threaten us."

"I've never threatened you. I gave you good advice. It still stands. Mind your own business. This thing with Davis—if it really happened—should've shown you it's not smart to bother people with stupid questions."

"We never asked Davis questions," Berk said. "He said he'd promised someone he'd make us stop. Are you gonna find out who he'd promised?"

Hill shook his head. "Still telling me how to do my job, huh? And what's this business about Jefferson Davis Roberts? How'd you find out about him?"

"I'd heard stories," I said, "and I was looking through old yearbooks. Later, we found this in an old newspaper." I took out my folded-up picture of Roberts. "To me, that looks like Davis."

Hill barely glanced at it. "Not to me. And if Davis *was* Roberts, he'd be afraid to come back here."

"I don't think Davis is afraid of much these days," I said. "And he probably figured no one would recognize him after all this time, especially since he's dyed his hair and built his body up so much. Guess he was right."

"I'm surprised *you* didn't recognize Davis," Berk said. "You spent a long time questioning him, looking him right in the face."

That made Hill flush. "Do I look like someone who goes to track meets? I never met Roberts in person. And by the time I went to his house to arrest him, he'd disappeared. Sneaky bastard." He picked the picture up and stared at it. "Anyhow, I don't think for one minute Davis and Roberts are the same person. You're good at coming up with crazy theories, but you got no proof."

"*You* could probably find proof," I said, "if you questioned Davis. Oh, yeah. I forgot to tell you. When I found the picture of Roberts, I was looking for pictures of Ted Ramsey. He and Roberts were at Ridgecrest High at the same time. Maybe they knew each other."

"More crazy theories," Hill said, and walked off. But he took the picture of Roberts with him.

I turned to Berk. "He asked about what happened with Davis?"

"Yeah, and about the fight club. He made me go over every-thing ten times, probably hoping I'd mess up and contradict something you'd said. I didn't."

I wanted to talk more, but people kept bringing us things they wanted to buy, and we had to focus on making change. Finally, Suzette came over, got a folding chair, set it down close to mine, and kissed my cheek.

"Sorry I'm a little late." She was almost an hour late. She plunked down a plate of brownies. "My mother was too hungover to come today—so what else is new?—but she sent these. Don't eat one by mistake. Hi, Berk."

He nodded but kept his face blank. I hadn't had a chance to talk to him about Suzette, so all he knew was we'd gone out again Friday. And with her kissing me in public, he probably figured we were a couple.

"I can't *believe* how many people showed up," she said. "I guess I did a really good job on publicity, huh? Look—there's Ashley Vaughn. Everybody says she'll be head cheerleader next year. And there's Ken Mulligan, and—oh, look! There's Carolyn Olson! And Paul's with her! Carolyn! Over here!"

Suzette stood up and waved. Carolyn waved back, said something to Paul, and tugged on his arm, pulling him toward us. He didn't look happy, but he came.

Suzette gave Carolyn a big hug. "It's *great* to see you! Oh, my God! I *love* that sweater!"

"Thanks." Carolyn smiled at her, then at me. "Now, why am I not surprised to see you two together? I've been hearing *lots* of talk about you. Quite the hot new couple, aren't you?"

"That's so *silly!*" Suzette said, and giggled, looping her hand around my arm. "We're just friends—right, Matt?" She cast an adoring look at me.

I wouldn't turn my head to look at her. "Yes," I said. God, I hated this.

Carolyn laughed. "A man of few words—just like *my* tough guy." She punched Paul's arm playfully. "Right, tough guy?"

"Whatever you say." Paul smiled at her before turning to me. "I heard you had a shiner the other day."

I shrugged. "Martial arts mishap. No big deal."

"You know who *really* got beat up?" Suzette said. "That witch-girl, Marie Ramsey. Megan says her mother caught her doing a satanic ritual and let her have it."

"*I* heard her brother caught her in bed with one of her mother's boyfriends," Carolyn said, "and did a number on both of them. She's *such* a slut, just like her big sister. Runs in the family, I guess."

Did Paul cringe when Carolyn referred to Nina? I thought so. I hoped so. Carolyn's like Suzette, I realized. Pretty, bubbly, vicious.

They chattered for a few minutes, until Paul sighed. "Come on, Carolyn. Pick out what you want, and let's go."

Carolyn punched his arm again. "*I* don't want anything. All those calories—I *never* eat stuff like this. You two be good, now!"

Neither of them had said a word to Berk. Suzette waved goodbye, then gave me a flirty look. "So, are you're finished helping your father with whatever it was? You could come over tonight, and we can finally have that ice cream."

"I've still got that test to study for." The hell with this, I thought. "I'll have to study every chance I get now, because my father's gonna need my help while he gets his handyman business going."

"Handyman business? Isn't he vice president at Edson?"

"He was never vice president. He used to be a general contractor, but he quit. Now he's doing odd jobs—fixing toilets,
cleaning septic tanks. It's hard making a living that way, so I'll
be helping him on weekends. Lots of afternoons and evenings
during the week, too."

She looked shocked. "What about basketball?"

I let out a sigh. "I hope I can squeeze it in. Plus did you
hear about the huge fire at Wendy's World? That's where my
mom works—or worked. There was major damage—it may
not re-open. She could lose *her* job, too. I hope we don't have
to sell our house and my mom's car. As for college—we'll see."

She stared at the table. I could almost hear the little gears
and wheels in her brain cranking, adjusting to new information. She stood up. "Can you guys handle things? Megan's
here. I should say hi." She sprinted off.

"I'm sorry, Matt," Berk said. He looked stricken—he'd
stopped feeling sorry for himself. "I didn't realize things were
so rough."

"They're not." I tossed two quarters into the cash box and
took one of Mrs. Link's brownies. Suzette had said her mother
baked lousy brownies, so I was determined to eat one, as my
own dumb way of proving I didn't believe anything Suzette
said. "It'll take a while before my dad's business gets going,
but I won't have to help him all the time. And no way am I
giving up basketball, and I should be okay for college."

"You said you might have to sell your house and your
mom's car."

"No, I said I hoped we wouldn't have to. I bet we won't."
I bit into the brownie. Damn. Suzette hadn't lied about this.
"I figured if Suzette knew my dad doesn't have a regular job
and my mom might be out of work, if she thought I couldn't

take her out and spend money on her, she'd take off. Guess I was right."

"I don't get it. I thought she really liked you."

"Berk, she doesn't even know me. We've gone out twice, and we haven't spent one minute talking about anything real. I think the only reason she wanted to go out with me is because Ryan Carter already has a girlfriend."

"Ryan Carter? What's he got to do with it?"

I downed some orange soda to wash away the burned chocolate taste. "He'll probably be captain of the football team next year. He's not available, so Suzette settled for me. I think she wanted to date a senior next year, a team captain. Then she could lord it over her girlfriends, be a big deal at homecoming, go to senior prom, all that. After prom, she'd probably dump me, go after a junior who looked like a good bet for team captain, get to be a big deal all over again. I decided to speed things up."

"So you don't like her at all?"

"No. If you want to try for her again, be my guest, but I think it's a bad idea. All she ever thinks about is herself. And she's a gossip and a liar. Those things she said about Graciana and Mr. Bixby? They're all crap."

A young mom with two little boys trailing behind her walked up, carrying a plate of wheat-germ muffins. She spotted the brownies and picked those up, too. Maybe I should warn her, I thought. But it's for a good cause. And those kids don't need chocolate. They'll be better off throwing out the brownies and sticking to wheat germ. I took the money and smiled.

Berk sat there, letting things sink in. "Wait a minute. Do you like Graciana?"

I shrugged. "She's leaving for college soon. And she's too smart for me."

"You *do* like her." He broke into this big, dumb grin. "That's great. And maybe you're right about Suzette, but I'm gonna find out for myself. If I can." He stood up. "I'm tired of sitting. I'll find somebody else to help you."

He headed for Graciana. Again, I watched him talking and gesturing. Graciana started toward my table. I struck up a conversation with an old lady deciding between banana bread and crescent rolls, watching out of the corner of my eye as Berk stuck his hands in his pockets and sauntered off in Suzette's direction.

Graciana slid into Berk's chair. "We're getting *so* many donations. I bet we'll bring in over five hundred dollars."

"I bet we will." I looked toward the entrance to the parking lot. Cassie and Anita were handing their signs over to Berk and Suzette. Berk was talking and smiling like crazy. Suzette looked bored. Not far from them, Dr. Lombardo greeted people as they arrived, shaking hands with parents and smiling at students. Mr. Quinn stood a few yards away from her, doing pretty much the same thing.

I picked up a paper plate next to the cash box and handed it to Graciana. "I set these aside for you. They're called truffles. My mom made them. They're great."

She blushed. "Matt, I said I was sorry."

"No, you were right. I was being a jerk. Have a truffle."

She bit into one. "Wow. Delicious."

"I know. But if you hadn't yelled at me, I wouldn't have tried one, just because the name sounds weird."

"I didn't *yell* at you. I was out of line, but I didn't *yell*."

"Close enough." I smiled at her before making change for a middle-school kid. It felt as if something had changed between us.

I wanted to tell her about Lieutenant Hill, but a big clump of people surged up to our table, all with baked stuff in one hand and money in the other, and for several minutes we couldn't do anything but make change. Finally the crowd dwindled down to one tall, thin girl with frizzy blond hair, wearing a short leather skirt, a denim jacket, and sunglasses. She was holding a plate of cupcakes and a five-dollar bill.

"Nice party," she said. "Are you having another one of these next weekend, to raise money for an award named after Nina?"

Graciana made change for her. "Thanks for coming, Angie. And I'm sorry about Nina."

Angie shrugged. "You probably are. You came to the funeral, anyway. And Mrs. Ramsey told me you brought Marie flowers, and I saw your name on that card. Except for me, you're the only one who signed it. Plus someone called Matt." She peered at me over her sunglasses. "Are you Matt?"

I nodded. "Matt Foley. Are you Angie Kovach, the one who was doing one of the assembly *Scenes from Shakespeare* with Nina?"

"Yeah, I was the pure and virtuous Desdemona." She grinned. "Typecast again! So, I saw you talking to Hedda Hopper a while ago. How can you be friends both with Marie and with the uber-bitch?"

Here we go again, I thought. I looked to Graciana. "Hedda Hopper?"

"Gossip columnist," Graciana said. "Very big in the 40s and 50s, I think. Known for her nastiness."

Sounds like Carolyn, I thought. "Was that Nina's nickname for Carolyn Olson?" I asked Angie. "Did she spread gossip about Nina? Is that why Nina hated her so much? And was Captain America Nina's nickname for Paul Ericson? Did Nina plan to get back at Carolyn by sleeping with Paul?"

Angie's eyebrows shot up. "Marie told you all that?"

"She also told us Nina had a special place." Might as well go for broke, I decided. "Sherwood Forest. Do you know where it was?"

"Nobody knew." Angie looked me over, like she was trying to figure me out. "There are lots of boarded-up stores near her apartment—I figured she'd found a way to get into one of those. Why do you want to know?"

"Marie thinks Nina left a book there," Graciana said, "a book that was special to both of them. It'd be nice if she could find it."

"Good luck with that. Last year, when Nina was gone for several days and I got worried about her, I looked all over for Sherwood Forest. Nothing. Did you know Marie's getting discharged tomorrow?"

"No," Graciana said. "I called the hospital this morning, but the receptionist wouldn't tell me anything. As usual. She's feeling better?"

"Yeah. No permanent damage, her mom says. Better not try to see her, though. Ted's not allowing any visitors at the apartment, either. When I asked him, he just about slugged me. Anyway, I'm glad Marie has some friends." She gave Graciana a sympathetic smile. "I hope Hedda doesn't go after *you* twice as hard now, since she doesn't have Nina to abuse anymore."

We watched her walk away. "So Carolyn's one of the people spreading gossip about you?" I said.

"As you say, one of the people. She has many helpers."

I nodded glumly. "That was quick thinking about the book. Look, we should talk about what Angie said, and I've got other stuff to tell you, too. Want to get a Coke afterward?"

"Fine," she said, and switched to customer service mode as a young couple approached, arms loaded with coffee cakes and loaves of bread.

I took a moment to look around. Cassie and Anita had strolled off to sit in a grassy area near the parking lot and were talking nonstop. Mrs. Dolby kept walking from table to table, urging people to buy more, flashing us a thumbs-up with every sale. Ms. Nguyen was chatting with some students, and Ms. Quinn stood at a table with her daughters, talking to a bald man, very tall and thin. I touched Graciana's arm.

"Look," I said. "Talking to Ms. Quinn. Isn't that the lawyer who advised Bobby Davis? Michael Burns?"

Graciana craned her neck. "I think so. That makes sense. If he's the lawyer Dr. Lombardo was talking about the first time we went to her office—and I bet he is—then he's an alumnus and a big-time school supporter. Naturally he'd come to something like this. And Ms. Quinn's been here a long time. Maybe she was his social studies teacher."

I watched as Ms. Quinn and Burns shook hands, as he moved on to another table. Maybe five minutes later, it was Graciana's turn to touch my arm. "Look who just arrived," she said. "Getting out of that dented Mustang. Ted Ramsey. I didn't expect *him* to show up."

I watched as he headed straight for Dr. Lombardo and started talking. He looked angry, and he gestured a lot. He pointed at Mr. Quinn, came close to jabbing Dr. Lombardo in the chest with his index finger. Mr. Quinn went rigid, smile frozen on his face. Dr. Lombardo said something curt and turned away, but Ramsey wouldn't leave her alone. He stood inches from her, still talking, looking angrier by the moment.

We weren't the only ones who'd noticed. We watched as Ms. Quinn left her daughters and hurried over to talk to the lawyer, pointing at Ted Ramsey. Burns set off for the entrance to the parking lot.

I stood up. "I've got to hear this," I said.

"Careful," Graciana whispered. "If Lombardo catches you eavesdropping, you'll get in trouble."

"I'm already in trouble," I said, and made my way toward them carefully. With so many people standing around, it wasn't hard to stay in the background, to dart from one chattering cluster to another. In about a minute, I got close enough to hear Ted Ramsey's voice rising above the rest. It sounded slurred. I guess some people drink on Sunday afternoons; I guess that might have something to do with why he was so worked up. I stood behind a group of men munching on macaroons, keeping my head down.

"Fine," Ramsey was saying. "Ignore me. I know what I know. They drove her to it, and you let them. You knew they were bullying her, and she *told* Quinn she was going to kill herself, and neither of you did a damn thing to help her. Schools have to pay when these things happen. Settle with me now, or you'll hear from my lawyer tomorrow. Then it'll be a front-page story, and you can kiss your fancy new job goodbye."

Burns, too, had made his way to the parking lot entrance. I couldn't hear what he said, but I saw him give Ramsey a card, saw him say something to Dr. Lombardo, saw her nod. Burns turned back to Ramsey and spoke again.

"The hell with that," Ramsey said. "Nobody's taking me aside. If you wanna talk, we'll talk right here. My sister's dead, the school's responsible, and someone's gotta pay. My lawyer—"

"I don't believe you have a lawyer, Mr. Ramsey," Burns said, too loudly. I guess Ramsey had gotten to him. "I know you approached several Friday, and they all turned you down. They could see this was a shakedown, pure and simple." Too late, he caught himself and lowered his voice. I watched as he talked to Ramsey, softly, intensely. I saw Ramsey's eyes glaze over, saw his shoulders droop as the words overwhelmed him. He stared at Burns, at Dr. Lombardo, at Mr. Quinn. Then he cursed and walked off.

Burns and Dr. Lombardo exchanged a few words and shook hands. Mr. Quinn joined them, and he shook hands, too. They watched as Ted Ramsey got in his car and drove away.

Quite a show, I thought, and turned around to find myself facing Ms. Quinn.

"Hello, Matt," she said quietly. "How much of that did you hear?"

"Not much. I wasn't really paying attention. I—"

"Of course you were paying attention. You walked over here so you could pay attention. Well. Graciana probably needs your help. Let's go."

It felt like I was walking with a police escort. When we got to the cashier's table, Graciana had a smile in place, but for once even she looked awkward.

"Everything's going well, Ms. Quinn," she said. "I just did a quick count, and—"

"You can give me a report later. Or had you forgotten I'm your advisor for this sale?"

"Of course not. We'd—"

"That's good to hear," Ms. Quinn said dryly, "since apparently you forgot I'm also your advisor for the memorial issue. Or was. You didn't even tell me when Dr. Lombardo said you couldn't go forward with it. That's all right. *She* told me. She said you were using the memorial issue as an excuse for investigating Coach Colson's death. She said you'd become obsessed with it. I had to admit that was a possibility. And now, it seems, you've become obsessed with Nina Ramsey's death, too."

"Not obsessed," Graciana said. "But we've wondered—"

"Stop wondering. Her suicide was sad and terrible, but no one could have prevented it. Nina was one of the brightest students I've had in years, but she was very emotional. Big highs, big lows. My husband thought she was bipolar, and he'd noticed she seemed especially unstable lately. That's why he asked her to come see him on the day she died—but you already knew about that, didn't you?"

No, we didn't, but admitting that felt like a bad idea. A shrug seemed like the safest response.

Ms. Quinn nodded. "Of course you did. And now her brother's trying to blame John for what happened. It's not fair. Nina never told John she was going to kill herself. And he's not a psychiatrist, only a guidance counselor. He *was* deeply concerned after he talked to her. Later that afternoon, he called a psychologist at the university to ask for advice. Even the psychologist didn't think there was any immediate cause for alarm. Of course, it was probably too late by then—she was probably already dead. The point is, how could John have foreseen what she'd do? How can anyone blame him?"

"I see what you mean," Graciana said—and I was glad she said it, because it would've taken me a year to come up with a neutral response.

"I hope so." Ms. Quinn let out a short, joyless laugh. "He has his faults, but not being concerned enough about students isn't one of them. If anything, he's *too* concerned. And this should be a happy time for him. Leave him alone, Graciana. A muckraking article about Nina's death won't do her any good, won't do the school any good, won't do anyone any good. So keep what happened today to yourself. That was just a greedy drunk trying to profit from his sister's death—there's no substance to anything he said. I won't ask you to make promises. I'll leave it to your good sense, and to your conscience."

We waited until she was a safe distance away. "Wow," I said. "What do you think?"

"I think we've got a lot to talk about later," she said.

The bake sale went on for another hour. Toward the end, Aaron showed up with a woman and two little boys—his wife and sons, I found out—and looked over the dwindling displays of baked goods, trying to get the boys to agree on something. Right about then, Cassie ran up to our table, eyes bright. Anita had asked her to come over after the bake sale, she said. Could I pick her up in a few hours?

"Sure," I said. "So, you and Anita hit it off?"

"She's awesome." Cassie turned to Graciana and smiled. "Thanks for telling her to be nice to me." She ran off.

"Your sister's pretty smart," Graciana said.

"Yeah, she is. And you were right about teaching her some blocks. She loved it so much she's talking about taking tae kwon do. Speaking of which." I nodded toward Aaron, who was headed our way, carrying lemon bars and raisin cookies.

"How are things going, Matt?" he asked. "Any more trouble?"

"From Bobby Davis, you mean? No. I haven't seen him again." And maybe I won't, I thought, not if Lieutenant Hill decides it's finally time to go after Jefferson Davis Roberts.

Thirty-two

As I went through my workout routine Monday morning, I felt good. Cassie had come home from Anita's house in a great mood. She and Anita had a plan, she said. She wouldn't tell me about it yet, but she said it was amazing. After dinner, she helped me study again, and I'll admit the flashcards worked. The idea of pulling my grades up and trying for a college scholarship seemed less crazy now.

Both Dad and Mom had come home with good news, too. Mrs. Widrig had loved the backsplash and given Dad the name of a friend who wanted her entire kitchen renovated; he was talking to her tomorrow. Mom, after putting in a long, exhausting day at Wendy's World, said they'd turned a corner on cleanup. One more day of washing walls and restocking shelves, she said, and then the staff would meet to decide when the store could reopen. And her boss had promised no one would be laid off.

And the time with Graciana had been good—just Cokes and fries at McDonald's, but it felt right. We'd talked about the bake sale, analyzing what people said, speculating about why they'd acted the way they did. I liked listening to the way Graciana's mind worked. Mostly to see how she'd react, I told her my father quit his job. Her first question was, "Why?" I told her, and she got upset, saying it was wrong an honest man had to quit a job he loved because he wouldn't lie to customers. She said Dad should go to the newspaper and expose Edson Construction. I couldn't see him doing that, but when I thought about how Suzette reacted, the contrast felt huge.

I finished my situps and headed out for my run. The Methodist church parking lot's perfect for laps. It's big, and it's always empty this early in the morning, so I could focus on building speed, not on zigzagging around cars. It's quiet, too, far back from the street, on the edge of a wooded area.

I did my first few laps, enjoying the rush of cold air against my face, feeling good I hadn't gotten tired yet. When I'd started this routine, even one lap was rough.

Then a silver Toyota pulled into the lot, and I froze. Even before the door opened, I knew. Bobby Davis.

He got out, slammed the door, and stood leaning against his car, hands in pockets, grinning. It was a cool morning, but he wasn't wearing a jacket, just jeans and a sleeveless black tee-shirt. Maybe he thought his biceps would intimidate me. He was right.

Damn. No one was around to hear if I yelled for help, and I'd left my phone at home. If I tried to run, he could get back in his car and could plow me down before I made it to safety.

He was still grinning, still standing with hands in pockets. "Good morning, Matt," he said. "Nice day for a run. You had your Wheaties yet?"

I focused on making my breathing regular. Don't panic, I told myself. Whatever he's planning, you'll make it worse if you panic. And you've trained for this. "What do you want?"

"I don't want to hurt you, if that's what you're worried about."

Sure you don't, I thought, but didn't say anything. No point in making him angry and getting his adrenaline up—it'd just make him that much more enthusiastic about beating me up. So I kept quiet. He waited for a moment, then shook his head.

"If you tell me what I want to know," he said, "I'll go away. You told Hill about me, didn't you?"

My parents made me, I almost said, but stopped the words in time. "So what?" I said—not much, but I hoped it sounded tough.

"So Hill and a Richmond cop came to see me yesterday. So they asked me questions about you and your friend—and about the fight club, and about some guys named Ted Ramsey and Jefferson Davis Roberts. Around midnight, there were more cops, giving me a hard time. It didn't go very far—nobody had anything solid—but I didn't enjoy it much."

Good, I thought, but didn't say anything. It was hard. He'd killed Coach Colson, and he was standing a few feet away from me. I wanted to throw insults at him, call him every bad name I knew. But that'd be stupid. So I focused on my breathing, knowing he might attack any second, trying to be ready, trying not to feel too scared.

"I've got good news," he said. "I'm thinking of moving on. I'm sick of Richmond, and I've got a good opportunity some-where else. You'd like it if I left, wouldn't you? You wouldn't have to worry about me showing up anymore. But I've got a debt I haven't quite settled, so I've got a question you need to answer. Why did the cops ask me about Ted Ramsey?"

If I'd been thinking straight, I would've said, "Ted who?" It probably wouldn't have fooled him, but at least it would've made sense. Instead, I said the dumbest thing possible. "I was looking at old yearbooks, I saw he went to Ridgecrest High the same time you did, and—"

"So did hundreds of other people. Tell me the truth. Don't make me beat it out of you. You wouldn't enjoy it, believe me."

I did believe him—about that, if not about anything else. But I still didn't understand what was going on, and I didn't want to sic him on Marie. "I told Lieutenant Hill everything I know about you," I said, "so you've got nothing to gain from beating me up. I don't know anything else that could hurt you."

He took another step forward. "But maybe you know something that could hurt someone else. Maybe you're holding something back for blackmail. Tell me about Ramsey. Then I'll leave, and you'll never see me again."

I let myself think about it. I'd give him some version of the truth, he'd drive away, and I'd be safe. Then I'd call the police. I'd call Marie and warn her.

But Davis had to know I'd do that. If I told him anything, he couldn't just leave. He'd have to kill me.

So whether I told him about Marie or not, I was dead. The only question was whether he'd kill her, too.

I shook my head. "I've told you everything I know."

He lunged forward, grabbing my jacket with both hands. Tough-guy grab, I thought desperately. But Aaron had shown us what to do when someone grabs your shirt with one hand. I didn't know a defense against a two-handed grab.

"Tell me how you found out about Ramsey," he said, and kneed me hard in the stomach.

It hurt like hell. I doubled over, struggling for breath.

"Not so tough, are you?" He grinned, still holding onto my jacket. "Look at you—I hit you once, and you're ready to fall over. Just like that sissy coach. I thought it'd be fun to kill him, but it was too easy."

So he'd admitted it. I'd known he'd done it on purpose, I'd known since the day of the tournament, but now he'd said it.

That made it more real. No matter what happened, I had to hurt him. As I straightened up, I lifted my right fist and got him with a solid roundhouse punch to his face.

I heard him grunt, probably with surprise more than pain. He let go of my jacket and jumped back.

"You bastard," he said, pressing his hand against his face. "You stupid little bastard."

He went into a boxing stance and came at me, jabbing twice with his left fist and then punching with his right. But the blocks came to me automatically, maybe because of all the practice with Cassie. I didn't let anything land. He aimed a kick at my thigh, at a pressure point, and I stopped it with a low block.

He jumped in close, grabbing my shoulders. I saw what was coming and lowered my head. He butted it, and it hurt plenty, but at least he'd caught the top of my head, not my forehead. That would've been worse.

He backed off a few steps. "You're bleeding, kid. Had enough?"

I touched the top of my head, then brought my hand down. Yeah, I was bleeding. And I'd blocked the punches and the kick, but my arms hurt from absorbing all that force. I can't keep this up, I thought. If I stick to defense, he'll wear me down. Kadima, I remembered. I have to attack, and I can't stop, not till it's over.

He stepped toward me, grinning, sure he'd won.

"Kadima!" I shouted, and charged at him with a right front kick.

He blocked it, but I came at him again with a left elbow strike. Then I grabbed him around the neck with both hands, pulling his head down. Payback, I thought, and kneed his stomach as hard as I could, again and again, still pressing forward. He backed up, doubling over, gasping for air. I'd taken him by surprise—I could feel that.

I had to catch my own breath. I let go of him, shoving him back, and he stumbled, nearly losing his balance. I came forward again, and he backed up, throwing punches at my face. I blocked them, and now the blocks didn't hurt as much. He's getting weaker, I realized.

Energy surged through me. I shouted "kadima" again and hopped toward him, shoving off my back leg and turning to the side. I snapped my right arm forward, catching him with a fast backfist to his nose. He cried out, and I saw blood spurting.

Don't stop, don't stop, don't stop. I stepped forward, aiming a low side kick at his left knee. I felt my heel connect, heard something crack. I'd broken his kneecap.

He collapsed to the pavement. It took two seconds. I stood watching, still in a fighting stance, hardly believing it. It was like someone had stuck a pin into a balloon. One moment he was standing, and the next he was on the ground, cursing, groaning, blood still pouring from his nose. He leaned his head back, trying to breathe through his mouth, exposing his throat.

I could do it now, I thought. I could kick him in the throat, just like he kicked Coach. I could finish him.

But that wasn't what this was about. You're not trying to kill him, Aaron had said. You're just giving yourself time to get away. I'd done that. It was over.

He struggled to get up. When he tried to put weight on his left leg, he cried out in pain, collapsing to the pavement again. He looked up at me, and I saw fear in his eyes.

I forced in air and found my voice. "I could kill you while you're down," I said. "That's what you'd do. But I'm not like you. Thank God."

I turned my back on him and ran.

Thirty-three

"We can't let Cassie know," I told my parents. "She's got something planned for today. I don't know what it is, but it's important to her. We can't ruin it by getting her worried about me."

So when the police car arrived, Mom went upstairs to distract her, and Dad came outside with me to talk to the two uniformed cops. They'd been to the church, they said. No sign of Bobby Davis, except a little blood on the concrete. Was I sure it was really this guy from Richmond? Maybe I'd got in a fight with someone from school, and made up a story to explain the cut on my head to my parents.

"It was Davis," I said. "Lieutenant Hill and some Richmond cops questioned him yesterday. So you should let Hill and the Richmond police know about this right away, and you should put out a bulletin or whatever about Davis' car. It's a silver Toyota. I didn't get the license number, but Hill probably has it. Davis must've dragged himself to his car. Maybe he's left town—he said he wanted to 'move on'—but he might make more trouble here first."

One cop shrugged. "I'll tell the lieutenant when he gets in. Anyway, if you really broke this guy's kneecap, he's in no shape for making trouble. Or did you forget what you'd said about the kneecap?"

"I didn't forget," I said, getting angry. "It's true. But Davis isn't an ordinary guy. Even with a broken kneecap, he could be dangerous."

"Yeah, he's a professional karate killer," the cop said. "You told us. But somehow a high-school kid outfought him. Great story. Get a doctor to look at that cut. And don't get in more fights."

I heard them laughing as they got in their car. Frustrated, I turned to my father. "*You* believe me, don't you?"

"I always do," he said. "I'll call the station, try to make sure Hill gets the message right away. But first I'm taking you to the emergency room."

"I'm okay. I just need to shower. And we've got to think of what to tell Cassie. She'll expect me to drive her to school."

We negotiated, finally agreeing Mom would tell Cassie I'd overslept and offer to take her out for pancakes on the way to school. Dad and I would sneak off to the hospital, and he'd call the station and then take me home for a shower.

While Dad drove us to the hospital, I texted Graciana, Berk, and Joseph, telling them what happened, warning them to watch out for Davis. But I bet he's left town, I thought. I bet he won't go back to Richmond, either. He's already in trouble with the police in both places, and he told me things he shouldn't have. Plus he's injured, and he said he had "a good opportunity somewhere else." I bet that's where he's gone, to heal up and start over. Someday he might come back for revenge, but it probably won't be soon. Maybe he'll never bother.

Dad reached Hill, and he showed up at the hospital right after the doctor finished my stitches. Hill listened to my story soberly, not making cracks, taking notes.

"He admitted to killing Colson intentionally," I said. "He said he'd thought killing him would be fun, but it was too easy."

Hill nodded. "And he admitted he was Jefferson Davis Roberts?"

"Practically. When I said he and Ted Ramsey went to Ridgecrest High at the same time, he said, 'So did hundreds of other people.' He wouldn't have said that unless—"

"—unless he was Roberts. Good enough for me." Hill wrote it down. "Damn! When I talked to him yesterday, he smirked at me. He knew I couldn't press charges for what he did back then. Roberts skipped town before we even got his fingerprints."

"But can't you press charges about Coach Colson's murder?"

"Based on one thing he said to you? Too shaky. But you and Widrig can testify to the assault Wednesday night, and you can testify to the assault today. That's what Roberts would've been charged with if he hadn't run off—assault." He snapped his notebook shut. "You got a concussion?"

"The doctor doesn't think so. Will you put out a bulletin about Davis' car?"

"Already done. That scumbag's not getting away from me again, not after two more assaults."

"And what about the person Davis was working for? He was obviously working for somebody when he killed Coach Colson. He said—"

"Davis said he thought killing Colson would be fun. Probably, that's why he did it—not that we can prove even that. Don't get caught up in crazy theories about hired killers."

I shook my head in frustration. "Why did Davis keep asking me about Ted Ramsey, then?"

"How do I know? Maybe he was just surprised I mentioned him. I got no proof of a connection between those two. I talked to all Roberts' friends back then, and Ramsey wasn't one of them. I don't think they even knew each other."

"There *has* to be a connection," I said, and thought for a minute. "Marie Ramsey talked to you after her sister died, right?"

"Yeah." Hill chuckled. "She's even better at coming up with crazy stuff than you are. She made some wild accusations."

"Maybe she wasn't right about everything. But remember the text messages Nina sent? The first one ended, 'Take that, Big Brother.' Doesn't it sound like she was defying Ted about something? And if he was at the bridge, and she defied him in person—well, you saw what he did to Marie."

Hill's face stiffened. "I don't know if he did anything to her. She's still saying an intruder beat her up. Maybe that's true. Or maybe *you* did it."

"You know I didn't." I said, relieved Marie hadn't accused me. "You know it was Ted. He's got a history of assault, and he's hit Marie before. It probably won't be long before he hits her again."

"Look, I gave her every opportunity to tell me about him. She wouldn't. Maybe she figures if she told the truth this time, he'd hurt her worse next time. Maybe she's right. That's how it is in these domestic cases. Sometimes, if we push too hard, we make things worse."

I understood what he was saying, but it wasn't right. "Will you talk to Marie one more time? She's getting discharged today—you could go upstairs, talk to her before she leaves the hospital. Even if you think there's no chance Ted killed Nina, will you run the possibility past Marie, mention the last line in the text message? If she thinks he might've killed Nina, maybe that'll make her tell you the truth about who beat her up. Then you could at least put him in jail for a while, right?"

Hill chewed on the inside of his cheek. "I don't know if that'd do her any good long-term, but I'll think about it. Anyway, as far as you're concerned, this thing's over."

He walked away. I didn't know if I'd done the right thing or not, but getting Ted Ramsey locked up while we tried to figure things out seemed like a good idea. And maybe we'd think of some other way to help Marie.

Dad tried to talk me into resting at home all day, but I didn't want to miss the test. And I had a million thoughts going through my head and needed to talk them over with Graciana. I grabbed a quick shower, grabbed my book bag. Before I left my room, I opened my desk drawer, took out the yellow pad Coach had left on the bench the day of the tournament, and turned to the comments about me. There they were, surrounded by doodles of squirrels and fish and two flowering trees. "Really quick backfist," Coach had written. "Wow."

I'd broken Bobby Davis' nose with a quick backfist. It helped save my life. Coach had taught me the backfist, had made me practice till it was focused and powerful. I owed Aaron a lot. Without his help, I never could've stood up to Davis. But Coach had been part of this morning's victory, too. I'd used what he'd taught me to defeat the man who'd killed him.

I stuffed the yellow pad into my book bag. Somehow, I wanted it with me today.

Dr. Lombardo was in the office when I went there to sign in. When she saw me, she frowned.

"You're almost two hours late, Matt," she said. "That's automatic detention."

I held up the note the doctor had given me. "Emergency room excuse."

"Emergency room? I hope it was nothing serious."

Of course not, I thought. Who goes to the emergency room for something serious? "Not too bad," I said. My hair mostly covered the stitches, and I'd worn a long-sleeved shirt to hide the bruises.

"Good. Ms. Quinn gave me the final figures for the bake sale. Over eight hundred dollars, including cash donations. That's impressive. You and your friends did a fine job."

"Thanks. Everybody worked hard." Except Suzette, I thought, but kept that to myself.

"I'm glad to hear it." She hesitated. "You took some missteps with the memorial issue, but that's in the past. You've redeemed yourself with this bake sale. It was a highly positive experience, for the school and the entire community, and it was a lovely tribute to Mr. Colson. It's a fitting way to end your efforts on his behalf. Do you understand what I'm saying, Matt?"

You're saying I better not try to do anything more, I thought, like find out who hired Bobby Davis to kill him. "I understand," I said. "Before I go to class, may I stop by Mr. Quinn's office? I want to drop something off."

Instantly, she looked alarmed. "What is it? Let me see it."

Talk about paranoid. I handed her the packet Cassie and I had worked on. "It's that time management packet he gave me last week. Remember?"

As she leafed through it, her face cleared. "Fine. He's not in his office now—I'll put this on his desk. I won't be here next year, Matt, but I'll follow Ridgecrest High basketball online. I'm sure you'll be a fine captain."

"Thanks." So that's my reward if I keep my mouth shut, I thought. She doesn't want any more trouble to cloud her last weeks at Ridgecrest High or jeopardize her new job.

I made it to English just as the period began. The test went fine. Answers for definitions and identifications came smoothly, and I had plenty I wanted to say for the essay questions. It was hard to stop writing when Ms. Nguyen called time.

When class ended, Graciana was waiting in the hall. "I couldn't believe it. Are you okay?"

I came close to kissing her. Right there in the hall in front of everyone, even though I didn't have any right to do it, I came close. It just felt so damn good to see her. But I caught myself in time. "Fine. I could use a ride home, though. I've got things to tell you."

"Of course." She touched my shoulder. "Thank God, Matt," she said softly. "Thank God."

Then Mr. Quinn was standing next to us. I didn't see him walking toward us, didn't hear him. He was just there. "I'd like to talk to you, Matt," he said. "Graciana, shouldn't you get to class?"

"On my way," she said. "See you later, Matt."

"I'll walk you to your next class." Mr. Quinn fell into step beside me. "I saw the schedule you left on my desk. Impressive. Everything was detailed and specific, and you worded your goals and objectives well. Frankly, I hadn't expected you to do such a thorough job."

That's because you don't know Cassie, I thought. "Thanks."

"I hope it's a sign that things are settling down for you," he said, "that you're putting everything in perspective. You've seemed—distracted lately. Troubled."

He probably knew about Dad quitting his job, and about the fire at Wendy's World. Hell, he might even know about Cassie's problems. Mr. Quinn always seemed to have radar about stuff going on in kids' personal lives. "It's been rough," I admitted, "but things might come together tonight." If Cassie's plan with Anita works, I thought, and Dad gets the kitchen renovation job, and Mom's staff meeting goes well, lots of things could get better.

Mr. Quinn gave me a look. "That sounds encouraging. If you'd like to discuss it with me, I'm always ready to listen."

"Thanks." We'd reached my social studies classroom. "But we should be able to straighten things out."

"Good." He managed a smile. "So, how was that party you and Suzette went to Friday?"

I shrugged. "Okay."

"Just okay?" Another smile, but a faint one. "I expected more enthusiasm. Remember what I said. The right kind of girl can help you succeed, at Ridgecrest High and afterward. The wrong kind of girl, though, can hold you back. She can be a bad influence on you and damage your reputation. Any time you want advice about something like that, come see me. I may not be able to monitor your progress as closely next year, but I'll always be eager to help."

I watched him walk away. "The wrong kind of girl"—was he talking about Graciana? Had he overheard what we'd said in the hall, and realized we were getting close? If he thought I'd avoid Graciana and stick to Suzette just because he said so, he had a disappointment coming.

At lunch, I practically bumped into Suzette. She mumbled something about deciding to drop krav before rushing off to sit with girlfriends. Good. I headed for the basketball table and took the chair next to Joseph. Right as I was starting to relax, Paul Ericson came over.

"I heard you went to the emergency room this morning, Matt," he said. "Feeling better?"

"Yes." I tried to act natural but couldn't. I couldn't even make myself look at him. And how the hell did he know about the emergency room?

"Good," he said. "Carolyn and I are watching a video tonight at my house, maybe getting a pizza later. Maybe you and Suzette could come."

Two weeks ago, I would've jumped at that invitation. It'd be the next best thing to having Paul nominate me for captain. "No thanks. I've got krav maga, and after that I have something else I need to do. Something really important." Until now, I hadn't considered studying for the trig test with Berk "really important." Now, I was glad to have an excuse.

"Are you sure?" Paul gave me a big smile. "Carolyn's looking forward to it."

Don't say anything more, I told myself. Don't be stupid. But my anger and suspicions had been growing all morning, and I couldn't hold back. "Guess you'll have to find a way to make it up to her, then. Maybe you could take her to a doubly shady spot."

Paul's forehead creased. "A doubly—what's that supposed to mean?"

I shrugged. "You tell me."

He stared back at me, then shook his head. "I don't know what the hell you're talking about, Foley. Carolyn's not that kind of girl. You should know that."

Joseph waited until he'd left. "'A doubly shady spot,'" he said quietly. "It is from the text message you showed us, yes? From Nina? Why did you say it now?"

"If somebody else sent the second message—the one that's probably fake—maybe that person read the first message. I wanted to see how Paul would react."

Joseph winced. "Was that wise?"

"No. But I had to see if he recognized it."

"And did he?"

"I couldn't tell." I picked up my tuna sandwich. "He didn't like it. That's for sure."

The day seemed to drag until finally I could be with Graciana. As she drove me home, I told her about Bobby Davis, and she got emotional several times. When I described everything that'd happened since then, she asked a lot of sharp, smart questions, as usual.

"I have some other things to tell you, too," I said. "First, I think Mr. Quinn's the new principal. We know it's not Mr. Carver—like I told you, he's leaving."

"And Ms. Quinn said 'this should be a happy time' for her husband," Graciana said. "That fits."

"So does what Mr. Quinn said about not being able to monitor me as closely next year," I said. "I guess he's a logical choice. He's been a guidance counselor here forever, and making a Ridgecrest High graduate the principal might seem like a good way to celebrate the school's anniversary. No wonder everybody wants to avoid controversy this spring."

"Makes sense," she agreed. "There's something else?"

"Yeah." I took a deep breath. "I've been thinking. Bobby Davis knew where to find me. Every morning, I run laps in a church parking lot. Davis didn't follow me there. When he showed up, I'd already been there several minutes. And he knew where to find my car when I took Suzette to the movie, and how to find Berk and me when we were driving home from krav. Someone's been telling him about my schedule."

"You're right," she said. "That's scary. Do you know who it was?"

"Probably not Ted Ramsey. How would he know any of that? I think it had to be somebody at school. Almost everybody knew about my date with Suzette, and lots of people must've known we all go to krav Mondays and Wednesdays."

I paused. "One person knew I've been running laps at the church. Paul Ericson. Last Sunday, when we went to see him, he asked if I was keeping in shape, and I told him."

"He could've told someone else."

"Sure, but why? When would that come up in conversation? I don't know, Graciana. I'd almost convinced myself it couldn't be Paul. But this makes me wonder."

"We'll keep thinking about it," she said. "Maybe there's another explanation."

I hoped so. But it was getting harder to believe.

Thirty-four

When I got home, Cassie ran to the door, pulled me up to her room, and started in.

"It worked *exactly* the way you said it would," she said. "After homeroom, Nancy Dixon came up to me, smirking, with two of her friends, and she stuck her hand in my face and said, 'High five, Cassie,' the way she always does. And I blocked it—I did it *exactly* right, the first time—and I said, 'Grow up!' I didn't shout, but I was loud. You should've *seen* the look on her face! She didn't know *what* to say. It was like that all morning. Whenever anyone tried anything, I blocked it and said 'Grow up!' really loud. Then, at lunch, Whitney Miles tried, and she's *so* popular. And I blocked it, and I shouted, 'Get a life!' And people laughed! They laughed at *her*, not at me! And when she passed me in the hall later, she didn't even look at me. I think she was embarrassed. I think *Whitney Miles* was embarrassed! All afternoon, nobody even *tried* anything."

"Amazing, Cassie," I said. "You did great. Congratulations."

"That's not even the best part. See, yesterday Anita called lots of her friends and hinted at stuff, and she said she thinks it's too bad people aren't nicer to Duffy. So all day, whenever Anita and her friends passed Duffy, they'd give him high fives.

It caught on, and soon lots of people were doing it. Even *boys* did it. Duffy looked so happy! All day, he kept smiling and *smiling*. That made me feel *so* good, Matt."

"You gotta keep it up," I said. "If anyone tries anything tomorrow, keep pushing forward. I hope Anita and her friends keep it up, too. It could make a real difference in Duffy's life."

"I know. Wouldn't that be *wonderful?*" Her eyes got shiny. "It's all because of you, Matt. You taught me how to block, and you got me together with Anita."

"No, it's all because of Graciana. Showing you the block was her idea, and so was introducing you to Anita. I don't deserve any credit."

"You deserve *some*." Cassie's voice sounded teasing now. "But I don't mind giving Graciana credit, too. She's really nice. And she's pretty. Don't you think she's pretty?"

I started to get uncomfortable. "Sure."

"I think she's *really* pretty. Do you like her?"

I shrugged. "Sure. She's nice, and she's smart. And her side kick's improving."

"I don't mean stuff like that." Cassie grinned. "Anyway, I *hope* you like her, because Anita thinks she likes you. A *lot*."

"That's nice." I stood up. "See you later."

Mom and Dad didn't want me to go to krav. I'd had enough rough stuff for one day, they said. Besides, Bobby Davis might be watching for me, or even Ted Ramsey. Then Lieutenant Hill called. A Delaware cop spotted Davis' car a few hours ago but decided to wait for backup. While he was waiting, Davis slipped away.

"And you were right about Marie Ramsey," Hill said. "As soon as I suggested her half-brother might've had something to do with her sister's death, she started talking. She said he'd beaten her up because he wanted to know what she was talking to you about. She didn't want to tell him the truth, so she made up some story about thinking the school was responsible for her sister's suicide."

"He was yelling about that at the bake sale," I said. "He seemed drunk."

"Yeah, he was drunk when we picked him up, too, decided to put up a fight. So now we've also got him on resisting arrest and assaulting an officer. The judge said no bail. That should give your friend some breathing room." He hung up.

"Bobby Davis left the state, and Ted Ramsey's in jail," I told my parents. "So I don't have to hide at home tonight. Plus Berk and I need to study after class."

"All right," Mom said. "You may go. Only to watch, though. Don't risk getting injured again. Give yourself time to heal."

So now I sat on a folding chair, book bag at my feet, watching students practice a new grappling technique. It felt frustrating. At least I'd gotten a chance to tell Aaron about what happened with Davis this morning, to have him shake my hand and get choked up when I thanked him. That'd felt good. And at least I had plenty to keep my mind busy.

I kept going over things. Yesterday, I'd felt almost sure Ted Ramsey killed Nina and hired Davis. Not anymore. No way could he have told Davis where I run laps. And could he have written the second text message? I reached into my book bag, took out my trig notebook, and looked at the words I'd copied. I need rest—I need peace. Never blame yourself. No, that didn't sound like him. It sounded too smooth, too smart. Too nice.

It didn't sound like Paul, either, but if he'd been trying to sound like a girl who read a lot, he might've come up with something like that. He definitely knew where I ran laps. Angie had confirmed that Nina called him Captain America and planned to seduce him. If he'd realized Nina planned to humiliate him, that could've given him a motive for striking out at her. And if he'd killed her more or less by accident, he'd have lots of motives for covering it up. So he sent the fake text message and planted a library copy of *The Bell Jar* in her locker to make it look like she'd committed suicide.

I frowned. Marie's theory about how Paul could've gotten Nina's locker combination still seemed lame. But Marie knew Nina well; I hadn't known her at all. Or maybe Marie was wrong about the book, and Nina put it in her locker herself. After all, would Paul know *The Bell Jar* was about suicide? Maybe, but I sure hadn't.

Then what? Marie told Coach Colson her suspicions, and he said he'd look into it. Would he go straight to Paul? He might—he was a direct kind of guy. And if Paul panicked, he might've decided killing Coach was the only way to save himself. That's when he turned to Bobby Davis. Later, when Davis told him Hill asked about Ted Ramsey, the name "Ramsey" made Paul panic again. He was afraid I was closing in on the truth, so he decided Davis should kill me, too. When that didn't work, Paul tried to bribe me with an invitation instead, to make me think I'd gain so much from being friends with him that I'd stop asking questions.

I guessed that made sense. Marie's evidence didn't seem like enough to make someone panic—the police had shrugged it off, and Graciana and I had come up with innocent explanations for it—but maybe Coach had found more evidence, too. I didn't know what he might've found, and I didn't know why he would've told Paul about it, instead of going to the police. And how did Paul know about Bobby Davis, and where did he get money to pay him? Two more things to figure out.

We still didn't know where Nina's special place was, either. For some reason, that felt important. Angie thought it might be near the Ramsey apartment, but who'd call a boarded-up store in the oldest part of town Sherwood Forest? And Marie thought Nina went there to change into a new top on the day she died. Would she have had time to go to the other side of town before meeting Paul at the bridge and sending a text message at 3:52?

I looked down at my copies of the text messages. Something still didn't feel right.

Aaron clapped his hands twice. "Back to the center. Let's discuss a core principle of krav maga. 'Simplicity, simplicity, simplicity.' Who said that?"

Graciana's hand shot up. "Henry David Thoreau. *Walden, or Life in the Woods*, 1854."

Aaron grinned. "I'll have to take your word about the date, but yes, it's Thoreau. In krav, we repeat 'simplicity' as often as Thoreau does. Joseph, will you give me a hand?"

Joseph sprang to his feet, and Aaron picked up a rubber knife.

"So we're in a dark alley," Aaron said, "and I'm coming at you with a knife. Defend yourself."

As Aaron advanced, Joseph lifted his right leg, his body spinning as he aimed a roundhouse kick at Aaron's head. It was an incredibly high kick, precise and graceful.

Aaron didn't bother blocking it. Instead, he ducked his head and stepped forward, shoving Joseph in the chest. Joseph fell over backward, and Aaron moved in with the knife, pretending to stab him.

"Great roundhouse kick," Aaron said, helping Joseph up. "I wish I could still kick that high. But it was too complex, too indirect. You didn't deal with the knife. You hoped the kick would take care of it, but I knocked you down before the kick could land. I like the roundhouse kick—I teach it in tae kwon do. But it can make you vulnerable. In krav, we don't have fancy kicks, and we aim low. We go for the stomach, the groin, the knee. That's more efficient, and doesn't expose you to counterattacks as much. Now you attack."

Joseph took the knife and moved forward. Aaron lunged at him, hooking his left arm under Joseph's right arm, trapping it. At the same moment, with his right hand, Aaron grabbed Joseph around the back of his neck and kneed him gently in the stomach, shouting "kadima" and driving him back. Joseph couldn't use the knife because his arm was trapped. Finally the knife fell from his hand, and Aaron let him go.

"Good job," he said, shaking Joseph's hand. "Thanks. So, that's the defense. Not elegant, but it works. Notice I trapped his knife hand and kneed him simultaneously. Simultaneous defense and attack—that's another core principle of krav. And I kept moving forward. That's kadima. For tonight, the main point is simplicity. The more you complicate things, the more you increase your chances of making mistakes. Okay. Pair up and practice knife defenses. Remember—simplicity, simplicity, simplicity."

Good lesson, I thought. Probably, it's one of those lessons you can apply to other stuff besides martial arts. "The more you complicate things, the more you increase your chances of making mistakes." But some people always have to make things complicated.

I frowned. Something was nudging at me, some connection I should be making. Most of the things I'd thought about Paul seemed to make sense, but I felt like there was another way of putting things together, a way that'd leave fewer unanswered questions. I looked at the copy of the first text message, the one Nina herself sent. Take that, Big Brother! If she wasn't talking about Ted, who *was* she talking about?

Confused, I shook the questions off and looked up. Rubber knife in hand, roaring, Derrick was charging Joseph. Joseph countered, using the moves Aaron had demonstrated. Nice job, I thought, but I bet it was tough for Joseph not to use his roundhouse kick, with Derrick's head such a tempting target. Joseph's proud of his roundhouse, and I can see why. Even Coach had been impressed. Hadn't he mentioned it, in his notes on the tournament?

I opened my book bag again, pulled out the yellow pad, and found the page bordered with doodles of dogs, of two flowering trees, of pizzas and cars and bikes. "Joseph—nice, high roundhouse kick," Coach had written.

Then, for the first time, I focused on the doodles, not the words. Bikes—on that first night after the tournament, Joseph said something about Coach bicycling for hours on weekends, exploring areas outside town. Mrs. Dolby mentioned that, too. And two flowering trees. Coach had drawn those on every page, more often than he'd drawn anything else.

Two flowering trees.

A doubly shady spot.

Sherwood Forest.

"Great work, everybody," Aaron said. "Give yourself a round of applause."

They all stood clapping, smiling, trading jokes.

I shoved the pad back in my book bag. It'd be a stupid thing to do, I thought, especially at night. But if I wait till tomorrow, I might be too late. If I can figure it out, so can the killer. And I can't trust Lieutenant Hill, and if I tell my parents, they'll say no.

Berk ran over, face flushed from exercise. "Ready to hit the trig book?"

"I can't," I said. "Sorry. Can you and Joseph get a ride with Derrick or Graciana? I have to check something out."

Berk looked confused. "Want me to come?"

"No. It's probably nothing. And you should study." Trig comes easily to me, but it's tougher for Berk. "There's Graciana. Ask her for a ride, okay?"

He didn't look happy, but he did it. I saw him speak to Graciana, saw her stare at me, saw her shake her head and say something quick. Then she headed for me. Damn.

She put her hands on her hips. "They'll get a ride with Derrick. Berk says you're checking something out. What?"

"Just a dumb theory. I'm probably wrong. I'll check it out for two minutes and leave. If it turns out to be anything, I'll text you." I started to turn away.

Her hand clamped down on my shoulder. "You're going to do something stupid and dangerous, aren't you? Tell me what it is. What's your theory?"

I shrugged, trying to act casual. "Just a theory about where Sherwood Forest might be, and about the doubly shady spot. I think they might be the same place. And I should check it out now. I said some stupid things today, to two different people—I might've tipped the killer off. If there's any evidence there, I don't want it destroyed before I can get to it, so—"

"You shouldn't go," she said. "It's dangerous. You should at least wait until morning. But if you won't change your mind, I'm coming, too. Where are you going?"

Time to take a stand. "I won't tell you. It probably isn't dangerous, but it's definitely stupid. Go home, Graciana. I'll text you."

She gave me a look. "I've got my own car. You can't stop me from following you."

Thirty-five

She followed me to the far shore of Lake Charlotte. While I was driving, I tried to sort out my thoughts. Sending that second text message was stupid. Why work so hard to make Nina's death look like suicide? Most people would've assumed it was suicide anyway. Marie might've thought it was an accident. But she knew Nina wasn't suicidal, knew she couldn't have written that message. That's what made her turn to Coach for help, made him start looking into things. And planting the book in the locker, doing other things to cover up—way too complicated. This killer couldn't keep things simple.

"The more you complicate things, the more you increase your chances of making mistakes." I was counting on that.

But I'd made mistakes, too. Just today, I'd made two big ones. Twice, without realizing it, I'd made it sound like I was close to figuring everything out, like I was planning to tie things up tonight. And I'd called attention to that phrase from Nina's text message. With the way talk got around at school, anyone might've heard all that by now. I might not be the only one out searching for the doubly shady spot tonight, looking for evidence that would point straight to the killer.

I might've even made someone decide to follow me, to see

if I was up to something. I checked the rearview mirror again. Graciana's car, practically tailgating me. I didn't spot any other cars that seemed to be sticking close. But I wasn't exactly an expert at this. When Bobby Davis had followed Berk and me last week, I didn't notice his car until he was almost on top of us. So I shouldn't let myself relax too much.

I parked in the main lot of what was left of Twin Dogwoods Manor. Twin Dogwoods—two flowering trees. If this was the place, if Coach figured that out, it would've been on his mind. It'd explain the drawings.

I got out of the car, switched on the plastic flashlight, and saw two tall, slender dogwood trees, their branches reaching out wide, thick with small pink blossoms. The hotel named after them died decades ago, but the trees still come back to life every spring. I couldn't see the lake from here, not in the dark, but I could smell it, could feel the heavy moistness of the air. I heard frogs and crickets going at it loud and steady, with some bird—a loon, maybe—chiming in. Not a boarded-up store, I thought. *This* is Sherwood Forest.

Graciana pulled into the lot and walked over to me. "Twin Dogwoods Manor—a doubly shady spot. That works."

"Sherwood Forest works, too. This'd be a good place to hide out from a violent father or brother. Most of the building's probably a mess, but Nina might've found a room in decent shape where she could more or less camp out."

I turned my flashlight on the hotel. The multicolored stone walls still stood, singed but intact, and the peaked slate roof seemed to be in decent shape. Sheets of plywood covered doors and windows, and the sloping lawns were overgrown, but otherwise the place didn't look bad. We circled the building slowly. As far as I could tell from the exterior, the worst damage seemed to be in the central section and the west wing.

"The east wing looks okay," I said, pointing. "I'll check it out."

"You're going in? At night? Matt, it's an abandoned building. A floor could collapse. Wild animals could be living in there. And the property must belong to somebody. You'd be trespassing."

"I won't stay long. One quick look, and I'm out. You should go home, but if you won't, wait here. If I'm not out in half an hour—"

"Half an hour! I will *not* stand here for half an hour, wondering if you've fallen through a floor or gotten eaten alive by coyotes. Wait." She ran to her car and came back with a battery-operated lantern. "My brother uses this when he's camping. If we're going in, we should have real light."

"*You're* not going in. Go home, or wait here."

It was too dark to see the look she gave me. I felt it, though. "Don't tell me what to do. This is incredibly stupid, but if you're going in, so am I. Let's get this over with." And when you got right down to it, there was no way I could stop her.

She led the way. We yanked on plywood sheets, hoping to find a loose one. A large sheet over a side entrance came away easily. "Maybe this is where Coach got in," I said, realizing we might be retracing his steps. My spine tightened. "I still think you—"

"No." She stepped through the doorway, holding up her lantern. A long corridor with faded, musty carpet and peeling wallpaper, elaborate chandeliers with ancient, lightless bulbs. Only a few spider webs, though, and no animal droppings, no trash anywhere in sight.

"Not as bad as I'd expected," Graciana said. "It looks as if somebody's been keeping this place clean. And nothing looks singed. The fire must've been put out before it reached this part of the building. You want to keep going?"

"For a few minutes. Let's open some room doors."

I tried the knob on the first one. Not locked—no reason it should be, when you thought about it. I opened the door to what had obviously once been a large suite. More musty carpet, more peeling wallpaper, a rusted bed frame, some odds and ends heaped in a corner, lots of dust. We opened several more doors and saw pretty much the same thing.

"So you think Nina planned to bring Paul here for their big night together?" Graciana said as we neared a corner. "I guess that makes sense. This isn't exactly my idea of a romantic getaway, but it wouldn't be safe for them to go to his home, or to hers. And he was probably afraid someone might see them at a motel. She'd kept this place strictly secret for years, but she thought she'd be graduating and leaving town soon. She might've figured she wouldn't need Sherwood Forest anymore. Do you think she told him where they'd be going?"

"I don't think she'd reveal her secret until she was sure he'd show up. She probably just said she'd found a safe place and told him to meet her on the bridge again Friday night."

"Then they got into an argument," Graciana said, "or he changed his mind and didn't want anyone to know he'd considered sleeping with Nina. Carolyn would drop him, and people at school would laugh at him. Mr. Perfect Ericson wouldn't want to be the subject of gossip. So he killed her. Is that how you think it happened?"

"Maybe. Or maybe Paul didn't kill her after all. Maybe the killer is someone else, someone who wanted to avoid a scandal as much as he did."

"Someone else who—you mean Dr. Lombardo?"

We turned the corner. "I mean Big Brother," I said, and opened the door to the first room.

No musty carpet this time, no peeling wallpaper. The carpet had been pulled up and the hardwood floor beneath it buffed until it gleamed; the walls had been scraped clean and painted a soft, cool gray. A double bed with a dark blue spread and white throw pillows, and several pieces of furniture, all painted white—a small bureau, a narrow table pushed against the wall, a wooden chair. Nina might've salvaged these things from various places in the hotel, or found them at garage sales over the years. Either way, she'd created a simple, orderly refuge in the middle of all this ruin. I took a hard breath. How awful must Nina's life have been, if she'd worked this hard to make a real home for herself?

I walked over to the table and switched on the electric lantern Nina had left there. She must've used the table as a desk. She'd left her book bag leaning against it, her purse tossed on top. I saw a notebook and several pens, along with a neat row of books propped against the wall. I peered at titles. "Look," I said. "*The Bell Jar*. So maybe Marie's right. Maybe somebody planted the other copy in Nina's locker. Somebody who'd have access to a list of students' combinations and could unlock the school library after hours."

"That could be Dr. Lombardo," Graciana said. She was holding up her lantern, looking at framed drawings on the walls—they looked like ones Marie had done. She pointed to something Nina had hung directly above the bed. "Or not. In fact, I think you're right. I think it was Big Brother."

I came over to see. A framed certificate with an elaborate border and fancy lettering—John E. Quinn, Outstanding Senior, Ridgecrest Senior High School. "What do you know," I said. "He always had that on the wall behind his desk. When I was in his office last week, he had an old basketball picture there instead. I bet Nina stole the award on that last day. Remember? Ms. Quinn said her husband asked Nina to come to his office that afternoon."

Graciana nodded slowly. "Supposedly because he'd noticed she seemed especially unstable. You think it was really for a different reason?"

"Yes," I said, and turned to face her. "I think he might've been telling her to stay away from Paul."

I could tell Graciana was thinking it over, trying to fit the things we knew into this new possibility. "Maybe," she said, "Mr. Quinn had seen her flirting with Paul. Maybe he'd been spying on them, the way he was spying on us in the hall today."

"The way he spies on everyone," I said, "especially athletes. He keeps a close watch on us, always giving us advice, trying to make sure we do the right thing. Hell, he knows my weekly quiz scores, knows when I sneak out of a chemistry review session a few minutes early. I'll bet he watches Paul even more closely."

"I'm sure he does," Graciana said. "After all, Paul's his biggest success story. Basketball team captain, a sure bet for Outstanding Senior—he's giving Mr. Quinn a way to relive his own glory days at Ridgecrest High. Quinn wouldn't like it if he saw Paul hanging around with Nina."

Just as he didn't like it when he saw me hanging around with you, I thought, but didn't say it. Graciana didn't need to know Mr. Quinn considered her "the wrong kind of girl.'"He probably thought that any scandal involving Paul would reflect on him," I said, "just as he was about to become principal."

Graciana smiled grimly. "I guess you were right when you said Big Brother was a reference to *1984*. Anyway, if he told Nina to stay away from Paul, I bet she defied him. She defied everyone. And Mr. Quinn doesn't like it when people defy him."

"No, he doesn't." I remembered how his temper had flared whenever I'd put up even a little resistance about anything. "And then—I don't know. Maybe he stepped out of the office for a minute, and she grabbed the certificate and put it into her book bag. She'd told Marie she planned to take a picture of Paul in her bed and post it on the Internet. Maybe she decided it'd be fun to get the certificate into the picture. That sounds like her sense of humor."

Graciana gazed at the certificate again, scrunching up her forehead. "So what did he do when he noticed his certificate was missing? How did he end up at the bridge an hour or so later? What happened when he got there?"

"I don't know," I said.

But I could picture some possibilities. Nina heading for Sherwood Forest, changing her top, grinning to herself as she hung the certificate on the wall before going to the bridge to meet Paul. Mr. Quinn pacing around his office, cursing, wondering what Nina had in store for the certificate, desperate to get things under control. Paul smiling as he left school, feeling excited and a little nervous, getting into his car and heading for the nature preserve. And then—then it got murkier. Maybe Mr. Quinn followed Paul to the bridge. Maybe he stayed out of sight and listened to Paul and Nina make plans, or maybe he didn't get to the bridge until Paul was gone, until Nina was sending that first, triumphant text message. Maybe. As I'd told Graciana, I didn't know.

"We'll probably never know—not for sure." Graciana said.

I nodded. "One way or another, they must have all ended up at the bridge, or near it. Paul must have left first. Then Mr. Quinn confronted Nina, and they probably got into an argument. Then—well." I paused. "Then I guess he killed her."

I could picture this part, too. The two of them standing on the bridge, Mr. Quinn red-faced and earnest, ranting at her, trying to reason with her, demanding his certificate back, insisting that she stay away from Paul. Then Nina smirked. Or she laughed in his face or said something outrageous. Maybe he struck out blindly, hitting her harder than he meant to. Maybe she fell and hit her head, and he threw her over the bridge to hide what he'd done. Or he grabbed her without thinking, throwing her over just to shut her up.

Or something like that. I could imagine other possibilities, too. All bad.

Graciana put her hand on my arm. "I know. It hardly seems possible. He doesn't seem like a violent person. I bet he didn't plan it. I bet it happened in a moment, before he realized what he was doing. When he *did* realize it, I'm sure he was horrified."

"And scared." I pulled back from the images that had grown so strong in my mind. There's more, I reminded myself. Try to figure out the rest of it. "So he tried to cover up. Nina must've dropped her cell phone. He picked it up and went back to school to give himself an alibi. He went to the *Scenes from Shakespeare* rehearsal to make sure people saw him. He called a psychologist to ask for advice about Nina, to make it look like he thought she was still alive."

"And I'm sure he said plenty to bolster the suicide theory," Graciana said. "Then, at some point, after people had seen him, he sent the second text message. That message sounds like something an adult would write, more than anything either Nina or Paul would."

"Or Ted Ramsey," I agreed. "And after school closed, Mr. Quinn got a copy of *The Bell Jar* from the library and put it in Nina's locker. That sounds like him. It's a complicated cover-up, and he complicates everything." I thought of his attempt to talk about the grieving process, the games he'd made up for the basketball reunion, the schedule he'd made me fill out. Talk about someone who couldn't keep something simple.

"It all fits," Graciana said. "But can we prove it? And do we have anything to link Mr. Quinn to Bobby Davis?"

"Well, Paul must've told Mr. Quinn where I run laps, and Quinn must've told Davis. That's a link."

Graciana frowned. "An awfully indirect one. And it seems to implicate Paul more than Quinn."

"Then how about this? Mr. Quinn was a guidance counselor when Jefferson Davis Roberts went to Ridgecrest High, and Roberts was an athlete with Olympic potential. The Mr. Quinn we know would've taken a huge interest in him. During his sophomore year, Roberts was an easy target for bullies. The next fall, he beat one of those bullies almost to death. I'm betting that over the summer, someone taught him how to defend himself."

"And Quinn has a black belt." Graciana's eyes widened. "God, Matt. I bet you're right. Quinn taught him martial arts, and that changed his life. Didn't Davis say something about paying off a debt when he attacked you this morning?"

I nodded. "Mr. Quinn might've also helped him avoid the police and get to Richmond, might've given him money. It'd be hard for a kid to disappear like that without help. I've had some thoughts about Coach, too, but let's get out of here. We can go to our cars and call 911."

"Good idea." Graciana hunched her shoulders together. "This place gives me the creeps." She opened the door and started down the darkened hall.

I took a moment to glance into the bathroom. Camp toilet, large jugs of water, towels, soap—she'd made this place into a refuge, all right, gotten everything all set up. Poor Nina, I thought, and stepped into the hallway.

That's when I heard Graciana cry out. I pointed my flash-light ahead to see Mr. Quinn grab Graciana's arm and yank her in front of him, hooking his left arm around her neck. The lantern fell from her hand and landed with its beam aimed straight at them. For a long moment, he stood there holding onto her, his eyes darting. Then he took a gun out of his jacket pocket and pointed it at me.

I'd practiced gun defenses, lots of times. But this was a real gun. I drew my breath in, staring at it. Still, the practice with fake guns made a difference. A few weeks ago, I would've felt helpless.

"Stay calm," Mr. Quinn said. "Matt, Graciana, I want you both to stay calm." He was holding a gun on me, but he still sounded like a guidance counselor. It was like he was telling us not to freak out about SATs.

Slowly, Graciana raised her hands. She caught my eye, and I raised my hands, too. The ready position, I thought. She remembers. She's not panicking, and she knows how to get out of this. I have to be ready.

"We'll stay calm," I said. He's a black belt, I reminded myself. He's probably rusty, but he knows more than I do. Plus he's strong, and he's fast. I've seen him play basketball.

"That's good," he said. "Matt, put your flashlight on the floor. Slowly."

He had a gun, and he was worried about my plastic flash-light? But I did it.

"Point it toward yourself," he said, "so I can see you. Now put your hands back up. Good. I don't want to hurt you kids. I don't. But we've got a situation here. I have to figure out how to handle it."

Move in, I thought. If Graciana can't get the gun away from him, I'll have to, and I can't unless I'm closer.

"We didn't come here to make trouble, Mr. Quinn," I said, without much hope he'd fall for it. "We heard Nina Ramsey had a special place, we thought it might be here, and we were curious. We just wanted to have a look. We'll go home now." I took one step forward.

"Stop!" Mr. Quinn raised the gun another inch. "Stay where you are. Let me think this through. And don't lie to me. I've been standing in the hall for ten minutes, listening to you. I know why you're here. I know what you think."

Yeah, I thought. I think you're a murderer. I think you killed Nina Ramsey because she pissed you off, and then you had Bobby Davis murder Coach because he was figuring things out. I tried another step. "I don't know what you mean. We don't—"

"Shut up!" he said. "And stay where you are! Maybe there's still a way out of this."

Graciana kept her eyes locked on mine. I didn't dare move. I should keep him talking, I thought. I should distract him, so she can take him by surprise. "Did Coach Colson come talk to you?" I asked. "Marie told him she thought Paul killed her sister, and you're so close with Paul—it'd be natural for Coach to ask you if Paul was involved with Nina."

"Yes, he asked me," Mr. Quinn said. "I said I'd talk to Paul. And I did."

I bet you did, I thought. You told him Coach was suspicious, and that's why Paul acted weird every time Coach's name was mentioned. And Paul felt more indebted to you than ever, because you knew he'd been with Nina that afternoon but promised to keep quiet. He never dreamed you'd killed her—he thought *you* were protecting *him*. "So you told Coach there was nothing between Paul and Nina," I said. "But he wouldn't believe you?"

Mr. Quinn shook his head. "He said he'd found some evidence—but it'd created more questions in his mind. I was afraid he'd start having questions about *me*. I said I'd talk to Paul again, and Randy agreed to wait a few days before going to the police."

So you decided to have him killed before he got the chance, I thought. I strained to keep the disgust out of my voice, to try to sound sympathetic. "That put you under a lot of pressure," I said.

"It did. I had to do something. If he kept poking around, who knows what he might've found? And it was all over nothing. *She* was nothing. Paul had a moment of weakness, I lost my temper, and she never would've amounted to anything anyway. If Randy had just let it go, it would've all been over. But he wouldn't. He—"

Graciana made her move. She twisted her body to the side, grabbing the barrel of the gun with her left hand, forcing it down. Then she swung her right fist up, striking Mr. Quinn's wrist, and wrenched the gun away from him, twisting her body again to get away from his arm. But when she tried to shove him off, he punched her in the face, really hard. The gun went flying into the darkness, and Graciana fell, hitting her head on the floor. She lay there, not moving, her hair covering her face.

Mr. Quinn jumped back. "Check on her, Matt. Make sure she's okay."

I wanted to. More than anything, I wanted to. I couldn't let myself. If I crouched down to check on Graciana, he'd knock me out, and then he could kill us both. He could drag our bodies to the basement, and it might be decades before anyone found what was left of us. Or he could set the place on fire, and people would think we'd come here to make out and knocked over a candle or something. He'd get away with it.

Keeping my hands up, I took one more step forward. "Let's figure this out together, Mr. Quinn." If I could get close enough to kick him—

"Stay back!" he shouted, and lifted his right leg, leaning his body back for a spin. Roundhouse kick, I thought.

Before he could finish his spin, I got him with a quick front kick to the stomach. He doubled over, gasping, and I came at him again, trying to grab his shoulders so I could pull him down and knee him in the face. But he straightened up, landing a solid punch to my eye.

The pain nearly knocked me out. I staggered back, leaning against the wall, holding my eye, trying to shake off the dizziness. Already, he was moving toward me. This time, he got me with a side kick to the stomach, knocking the air out of me.

As I struggled for breath, I saw Graciana on her hands and knees, feeling around on the floor in the darkness. The gun, I thought. She's searching for the gun.

It gave me hope, and my strength surged back. He was coming for me again.

"Kadima!" I shouted, and twisted my body around, bringing my right hand up. Just as he reached for me, I rammed my open palm against his chin as hard as I could. One grunt of surprise, and he dropped to the floor, unconscious.

Graciana was standing now, holding the gun in both hands, pointing it at him. "You okay?"

"Yes. Let's go."

We didn't look back at him. We got outside as fast as we could, stumbling, helping each other. Then I slammed the piece of plywood back in place and stood with my back braced against it, both arms outstretched, breathing hard, while Graciana called 911.

Thirty-six

Graciana didn't get the Outstanding Senior award. Paul Ericson didn't, either. For a while, people thought he might face charges, since he'd lied to the police when, weeks ago, Lieutenant Hill reluctantly followed up on Marie's questions and asked Paul if he'd been with Nina on the day she died. But Paul's parents got that smoothed out, and Paul never had any legal problems. He didn't lose his scholarship, either, and Carolyn fussed a while but forgave him after he gave her a sapphire promise ring.

But his reputation was tarnished. So at graduation, Dr. Lombardo called up Don Webster, the student council president, and gave him the award. Don's a nice enough guy, but he doesn't compare to Graciana. Of course, in my opinion, nobody does.

The members of the martial arts club came up on stage next, to hand out the first Randolph Colson Memorial Award for Excellence in the Study of History. Somebody had taken the tired yellow-and-black banner that'd hung in the gym all year and strung it across the stage, and we all stood in front of it—Derrick, Joseph, Berk, and I in the suits our parents made us wear; Graciana in her cap and gown, with the gold honor society cord draped around her shoulders; Suzette in a frilly spring dress, smiling and waving like she'd done all the work singlehandedly. I hear she's been dating Rick Jenson. Some people say he might be captain of the golf team next year.

I looked out into the audience and saw Mrs. Dolby dabbing at her eyes with a big pink handkerchief, saw Ms. Nguyen sitting next to her, grim-faced, keeping a hand on her arm. Aaron sat in a back row, looking straight at me, eyes steady and, I thought, proud. Ms. Quinn was in the audience, too, but she wasn't looking at anyone. Her jaw was set, her face expressionless. Lots of people thought she wouldn't show up for graduation, but I wasn't surprised to see her. After her husband was arrested, after he'd confessed to killing Nina and asking Bobby Davis to kill Coach, Ms. Quinn stayed out of school for exactly one week. Then she came back, looking exhausted, looking older, but acting as if nothing had happened. As far as I know, she never talked to anyone about it. When I pass her in the hall, she still says hello to me. She never makes eye contact, though, and I don't blame her. I hope she'll be okay.

I made a three-sentence speech, announced the name of the senior who'd won the award, gave her an envelope, and shook her hand. Graciana went back to her chair on stage, and I went back into the audience to sit with my parents. They'd been mad about me going to Twin Dogwoods Manor without telling them, but eventually they'd gotten over it, and I'd made fresh promises about being more open. So far, I've kept them.

Cassie had decided to sit with Anita, not us. Those two are both taking tae kwon do at Aaron's school now, and they've gotten close. I looked over at them, their faces intent as Dr. Lombardo came to the podium. That's all it took to stop the gossip, I thought. Cassie just needed somebody at her school to stand up for her. If someone at Ridgecrest High had stood up for Nina Ramsey years ago, would any of this have happened?

Dr. Lombardo began her speech. As always, she was dressed extra-formal, from pearl earrings to slim black suit to three-inch heels; as usual, her speech was confident and smooth, full of references to the school's accomplishments and of hints she was personally responsible for them. She kept it short, though, and she looked tired. The last few weeks couldn't have been easy for her—the man she'd supported as her successor arrested for two murders, front-page stories about his crimes in the newspaper every day, editorials saying the next principal should work harder to crack down on gossip. One editorial even brought up the incident from ten years ago, saying it wouldn't have happened if Lombardo hadn't looked the other way when Jefferson Davis Roberts was bullied. She hadn't lost her new job as superintendant, but she wouldn't be starting it with a glowing, spotless record, and this somber graduation couldn't be the sendoff she'd imagined. It felt like she just wanted to get it over with and go home.

She finished her speech, and Mr. Carver brought up the box of diplomas. When Graciana's name was called, I clapped and cheered and stamped my feet. Mom frowned, and Dad shook his head. They always do that at graduation. In their day, they've said a million times, graduations were more dignified. People waited until all the graduates had their diplomas and then gave everyone a polite round of applause. Maybe that *had* been more dignified. But today, I didn't feel like holding back.

We all stood to sing the school song, the minister from the Methodist Church gave a benediction, and it was over. People started pushing programs into purses and collecting their kids. I turned to my parents. "I gotta find Graciana. See you back at the house?"

"Fine," Mom said. "Tell her I'm making profiteroles for her party tonight."

God. What are those? But I'd try one. These days, I always try one. I nodded and took off.

I found Graciana as she was walking out into the parking lot. She had her graduation gown draped over her arm, her cap clutched in her hand. She was wearing a new sleeveless white dress, her dark hair shining down over her shoulders. God, I thought. She's beautiful.

I handed her a small blue box. "Happy graduation," I said.

"I *told* you not to get me a present." She opened the box, lifting out the ivory and gold bracelet. "Oh, Matt! It's so lovely, so delicate! White roses—like the ones in the corsage you gave me for prom. But it looks expensive."

We've had this discussion before. She always fusses when I spend money on her—or on anything, actually. I've started a savings account for college, and she thinks every penny I get should go straight there. "It wasn't much," I said. "And you know my dad's business is picking up. He can use me almost full time this summer, and he pays pretty well. Plus Aaron spoke to me before graduation. He's starting a Self-Defense for Teens class, and he wants me to help teach it. He pays pretty well, too."

She looked skeptical. "He could hire a black belt for that."

"He says he'd rather have someone with real-life self-defense experience." I grinned. "He says I've got more of that than almost anyone else he knows."

"I can believe it." She smiled at me wistfully. "Don't line up *too* many jobs, Matt. Leave some summer for me. Fall will be here so soon."

"Charlottesville's not far away. We play Charlottesville. So I'll be coming up for games. And for other reasons." I took her hand. "And you'll come home some weekends, right?"

"So many my parents will get sick of seeing me." She gave my hand a squeeze. "They're waiting out front. My dad's taking pictures, and I want you in them."

"I'll come in a minute. I should say hi to Berk."

She squeezed my hand again and ran off. I looked for Berk but couldn't spot him. No wonder. The parking lot was clogged with people—families hugging, parents chasing after little kids, seniors giving each other high fives. Glancing at the far side of the lot, I caught a glimpse of a man's back as he walked toward a car. Not tall, but a muscular build. And he was limping.

My body went tense. Bobby Davis, I thought.

Someone called, "Dad!" He turned around, and my shoulders sagged. Forties, glasses, big smile. Somebody's father. Not Bobby Davis.

Damn, I thought. I've got to get over this. I've got to stop watching for him.

I hate being so paranoid. The day he disappeared, that one cop had spotted him in Delaware. Since then, nothing. Lieutenant Hill says the police are still looking, but I don't know how hard. I can't get past thinking Davis will come back to finish things.

Shake it off, I told myself, and scanned the parking lot again. The girl who'd won the Randolph Colson Award was showing her check to her parents, so happy she was grinning, bouncing in place. That's one thing we did for you, Coach, I thought, and turned away.

I finally caught sight of Berk, but he and Derrick were already getting into Joseph's car. When I called out, they didn't hear me. Joseph backed out of his parking space too fast, at an angle, nearly grazing a girl wearing a black skirt and a gray hooded jacket. She jumped out of his path, and her hood fell back. Marie Ramsey.

I walked over to her. When she'd first come back to school, her face had still been bruised, and she'd walked like every step hurt. She'd seemed much better lately. "Hi," I said. "I didn't expect to see you here."

She looked up at me. I'd noticed that she doesn't stare at the floor as much as she used to, and she pushes her hair back more, so it doesn't hide her face all the time. "Nina would've graduated today," she said. "I didn't go inside, but I felt like I should be here. And I was hoping I'd see you. We're leaving town next week. My mom and I are moving to Buffalo. We'll live with her sister until Mom finds a job."

"That sounds great," I said. Maybe Marie would be happier at a big-city school; maybe she'd fit in better. "Will your father join you there—well, eventually?"

"I hope not." She smiled—I think it was the first time I'd ever seen her smile. "He hates cold weather. So does Ted. That's why we're going to Mom's sister in Buffalo, instead of her sister in Atlanta. And the counselor Mr. Carver sent us to is pretty good. Mom's joined AA."

"That's fantastic, Marie. I'm really glad."

She shrugged. "She's joined before, three times. It never lasts more than a few months. As long as it gets us to Buffalo, that's good enough. Anyway, I wanted to say goodbye, and to give you this." She reached into her purse, took out a small, flat package wrapped in white paper, and pressed it into my hand. "Thank you," she said, and hurried away.

I unwrapped the package. It was a framed drawing of Coach Colson in his tae kwon do uniform, grinning, both arms lifted in the air. He looked like he did at the tournament, like he couldn't wait to get started.

I looked at the drawing more closely. No, I thought. Not like he couldn't wait to get started. Like he'd just won his match.

I stood there another minute, looking at it, then rewrapped it carefully and walked off to find Graciana.

Acknowledgments

In *Fighting Chance*, Matt Foley gains important insights into many things, including friendship and courage. This book is dedicated to the memory of my friend Eloise Gershone, the most courageous person I've ever known. Even when locked in a long, painful battle with cancer, she stayed cheerful and determined, fighting as hard as she could against an opponent she knew she couldn't defeat. Her generosity of spirit never faltered. Always, she thought first of others, not of herself; always, she focused on trying to make things easier for the rest of us. She was a gifted and dedicated teacher, a loving wife, mother, grandmother, and friend. Eloise left this world better than she found it. Her memory is a blessing to everyone whose life she touched.

So many people have contributed to this novel, either directly or indirectly. I can't possibly list them all, but I'll mention a few.

I'm grateful to many people at Poisoned Pen Press /The Poisoned Pencil, including Jacqueline Cooper, Beth Deveny, Diane DiBiase, Ellen Larson, Robert Rosenwald, Tiffany White, and Pete Zrioka. I appreciate every effort they've devoted to this book, every perceptive comment and piece of good advice they've offered me. It's an honor to have *Fighting Chance* published by such a distinguished and exciting press.

Alfred Hitchcock's Mystery Magazine gave me my start as a mystery writer and continues to provide a home for the short stories that mean so much to me. Editor Linda Landrigan always treats writers with respect, and her insights and high standards spur me to do my best. I also owe an enduring debt to my first editor at *Hitchcock's*, the late Cathleen Jordan.

Many people in the mystery community have helped by reading and critiquing drafts, by encouraging me through every disappointment, and by joyfully applauding even the smallest success. I especially want to thank the infallibly supportive Sisters in Crime Guppies, my good friends at the Mid-Atlantic chapter of Mystery Writers of America, and the enthusiastic, inspiring Malice Domestic family.

Two writers who are not part of the mystery community, Miriam Greystone and Julia Palmer, read and commented on early drafts of *Fighting Chance*. Their perspectives and suggestions were tremendously helpful.

I'm not a martial artist, but I've learned a lot about martial arts from the people who have taught and studied with my husband and our daughters. My husband began his study of krav maga at FEKS Martial Arts in Lynchburg, Virginia, where he was taught by David and Bruce Rubinberg. Their school was the inspiration for the Eye of the Tiger School in *Fighting Chance*, and their knowledge of krav maga informs all the lessons Matt learns there. And of course I have to mention the martial artists who were such an important part of our family's life for so many years back in Sioux Falls, South Dakota: Charlie Azzara (always first and foremost, and not just alphabetically), Doug Blomker, Chuck and Shelly Johnson, Master Al Pepin, Steve Sinning, and Laurie Soldake.

I'm focusing on writing now, but I'm still a teacher at heart, and chances are I'll return to the classroom some day. I owe more than I can say to the teachers who helped me learn to love reading and writing, to the co-workers who shared frustrations and triumphs, and to the students whose energy and creativity challenged me to keep thinking and growing. The Talmud says it best: "I have learned much from my teachers, more from my colleagues, most of all from my students."

Finally, there's my family. My parents, of blessed memory, were both teachers, and they set me on a path I've loved. When I was in the second grade, my mother gave me a diary and told me to write something every day. It's a good habit, and it's made a difference. My father loved to write—stories, novels, humorous verse. I remember sitting on the floor of his study, waiting impatiently until a fresh page unrolled from his typewriter, talking with him endlessly about character, plot, and theme. I wish they could have seen *Fighting Chance*. I hope they would have liked it.

Ever since I decided they were old enough to start reading stories about murder and other nefarious acts, my daughters, Sarah and Rachel, have been two of my most enthusiastic, valuable supporters and advisers. With *Fighting Chance*, as with so many other projects, they've helped me with everything from fixing plot problems to keeping my slang reasonably up to date. This time, I have to give special thanks to Rachel, who read two complete (and very different) drafts of the novel from the first page to the last and helped me make significant improvements in both. She's also a demon proofreader who has saved me from many embarrassing mistakes.

I met my husband, Dennis Stevens, when we were eighteen years old, on my first day of classes at Kenyon College (he was already a sophomore). Within a week, we knew we'd be spending the rest of our lives together. If anyone has been wondering why I think young love can be deep and real, there's the answer. Dennis has guided and encouraged me in everything I've done since then, including my writing. A fifth-degree black belt in sogo ryu bujutsu, he choreographed all the martial arts scenes in *Fighting Chance*—but he's done so much more than that. He reads everything I write and always finds ways to make it better. When I could have papered all the walls in our house with rejection letters, he told me to keep trying. When I was itching to make the transition from short stories to novels, he insisted on taking all the responsibility for supporting our family so I could write full time. And every day, with everything he does and everything he is, he reminds me that life is unspeakably precious, and that truth is always worth fighting for.

About the Author

For many years, B.K. Stevens (Bonnie K. Stevens) taught English, both in high school and at colleges and universities. She's published almost fifty short stories, most of them in *Alfred Hitchcock's Mystery Magazine*. One of her stories was nominated for Agatha and Macavity awards and also made the list of "Other Distinguished Mystery Stories" in *Best American Mystery Stories 2013*. Another story won a Derringer from the Short Mystery Fiction Society, and another appeared in *Family Circle* after winning a suspense-writing contest judged by Mary Higgins Clark. B.K. has also published a mystery novel, *Interpretation of Murder*, and a mystery e-novella, *One Shot*. In addition, she's the author of three nonfiction books (Holt, Harcourt, and Behrman House), as well as of articles that have appeared in *The Writer* and other publications. For more information, please visit her website at http://www.bkstevensmysteries.com.

To receive a free catalog of Poisoned Pen Press titles, please provide your name and address in one of the following ways:

Phone: 1-800-421-3976
Facsimile: 1-480-949-1707
Email: info@poisonedpenpress.com
Website: www.poisonedpenpress.com

Poisoned Pen Press
6962 E. First Ave. Ste 103
Scottsdale, AZ 85251

2 1982 02876 4912

CPSIA information can be obtained at www.ICGtesting.com
Printed in the USA
BVOW11s0632180915

418372BV00002B/2/P